More Than Just A Life

Steve Little

authorHOUSE®

AuthorHouse™ UK Ltd.
500 Avebury Boulevard
Central Milton Keynes, MK9 2BE
www.authorhouse.co.uk
Phone: 08001974150

First published by AuthorHouse 3/5/2010

ISBN: 978-1-4490-7089-2 (sc)

This book is printed on acid-free paper.

In memory of great-uncle George, aged 18, who was there but disappeared and was presumed dead. Also to my two granddads who were there and came back.

PART ONE -
CALAIS, NORTHERN FRANCE
1918

CHAPTER 1

The young Frenchwoman was pulling a brush through her long wavy hair sitting at the dressing table. She looked into the mirror to check each side of her head and put both hands above her ears and pushed up her hair to remove the flatness.

Satisfied, she got up to change into her walking-out clothes. As she put the brush down onto the dressing table she glanced out of the front bedroom window and along the street. There were very few people about as it was just after lunch on an autumnal Sunday afternoon, so it was strange to see a single soldier at the corner of her street just as it turns left and back towards the town. He seemed more than a little pre-occupied and suddenly waved frantically as if beckoning someone further down the street to come and join him.

Suddenly, he was joined by a group of soldiers and they moved purposefully towards her end of the street led by the one in the Officer's hat. It seemed he was trying to follow the somewhat erratic numbering of the close-knit houses.

The young woman ran to the top of the stairs and shouted down in English.

"Soldiers, Eddie! There are some soldiers outside in the road."

Eddie Wilson thought he had heard some voices outside just before Marie shouted down to him and was already out of his chair. He put down his half-eaten apple and then thought better of it and shoved it into his pocket. He picked up his light jacket from the table and moved quickly towards the door but as he opened it and went through he hit his shoulder on the doorjamb. He cursed as he went into the kitchen and he rubbed it instinctively.

He paused for a moment trying to think what to do for the best. He glanced back towards the door to the living room and Marie appeared, her face a picture of concern. He started to move back towards her but a loud shout from outside in the street stopped him. This noise was followed by the knocking on the front door at the house opposite and then by another shout. She half turned towards the noise and then looked back at him. Her eyes filled with tears yet she half smiled and mouthed, "Go!"– He hesitated but gave a resigned shrug as he turned and moved towards the back door and the garden beyond.

He passed Marie's father sitting, half asleep, at the kitchen table where they had not long before been eating their Sunday lunch. The old man was supposed to clear the dishes whilst his daughter got herself ready to leave for a walk with the Englishman but he had decided to leave that for now, have a doze and sleep off his lunch. As Wilson passed the old man, he squeezed his arm and the old man half opened his eyes. Wilson smiled and the old man smiled back a toothless grin, looking a little bemused as Wilson moved away.

As Wilson went out of the door, the autumn sunlight caused him to blink as he emerged from the relative darkness of the kitchen. He thought for a moment that the soldiers might be protecting the back here but then doubted if they would have come right up to the house. As it seemed they were actually over the other side of the road, there was a good chance they were not out the back of the house at all but, if they were, they would probably wait at the end of the house's long thin garden or at the far end of the street to his right where a series of gardens stretched behind the line of tightly terraced houses.

He had planned this moment in his mind over the past few months. He had always known that the time would come when he might be found and he had carefully thought out a way of getting clean away but the first few seconds outside the door would be important because if the soldiers were there he was doomed but, if not, maybe he had a chance.

Having turned to his left from under the porch outside the back door he stepped over the small rows of vegetables he had lovingly cultivated throughout the summer. Even now he stepped over them gingerly to avoid damaging them. He easily leapt over the low fence and his plan was to go along the gardens and emerge further up the street and make for the woodland beyond the town. Most of the neighbours' fences were in varying degrees of disrepair through neglect over the War years and many of them were entangled with brambles and other tall weeds. He could hear raised voices out in the street, a shouted order to the men and a loud thumping on a door on his side of the street. He guessed they were now at Marie's house. He hesitated for a moment but then moved on. He guessed that Marie would try to delay them as much as possible as he and Marie had often talked about this moment and how they would deal with it.

The soldiers had wasted no time once Marie had opened the door on their third knock. Some of the men brushed past her but one stopped – it was the Officer she had seen earlier from the bedroom window.

"Pardonnez-moi, madamoiselle," he asked gently somewhat taken back by the attractive young woman in a robe standing before him. "Ou est Private Wilson?" he eventually managed. She shrugged.

With a brief apology he pushed past her followed by one of his men. She tried to complain but they were gone and already in the hallway. The Officer went up the stairs while the other man went through to the kitchen. The old man stood up from his chair and remonstrated with the soldier who pushed him to one side. The old man let off a fierce mouthful at that soldier but lost balance and fell back into his chair.

4

The soldier looked out from the kitchen door. He shouted back to the Officer:

"Sir, he's run off down the gardens to the left."

The Officer leapt down the stairs two steps at a time and joined the Private by the backdoor. The Private spoke first:

"The men who've gone round the back have started after him but as they've had to go right to the end of the terrace to find a path along the bottom of the gardens, they're already some way behind him and he's out of sight already."

"Well you and the others follow him and I'll get Collins and make sure he takes this young lady into custody but I want to put some quick questions to her first then I'll catch you up. Tell the others to put a few shots above his head if they have to, yet remember we want him alive. Alright?"

With that the man was off out of the back door to join the others at the bottom of the garden.

The Officer went back into the living room followed by the old man who continued to rant at him but the young man just ignored him. Private Collins had followed the other two soldiers into the house from the street and had got the young woman to sit in the armchair that Wilson had been sitting in moments before.

The Officer crouched down beside her and took hold of her arms and looked into her eyes. . She recoiled from him, pushing him away at the same time – he could see tears rolling down each cheek. He tried to get hold of her arms but she turned half round and was side on to him.

"Do ...... you.... speak ...... English?" he asked. She shrugged again "Parlez-vous anglais?" he tried again. She stared at him blankly. He turned to his Private and said:

"Collins, stay here and check upstairs and see if you can find any evidence of Wilson having been here as we might need it but don't let her out of your sight. When you have finished, take with you whatever you find and can carry, then escort this lady down to the local police station that we saw earlier and tell the gendarme in charge to put her in a cell for now. I'll join up with the others and I'll see you a bit later. Just make sure she does not escape but go easy on her, do you understand?"

"Yes sir," said the Private who then led the woman towards the stairs so she could accompany him on his search of the upstairs' rooms. Her father stood in the hallway even more bemused now at what was happening. The young woman touched the old man's arm and spoke to him in French. He returned to his chair as she went up the stairs, muttering to himself as he went.

5

The Officer stepped outside and went to the end of the garden just as his men returned along the path to his left. "Sir, we've lost sight of him but he definitely went that way," one of them said pointing down the line of houses.

"Hawley, take two and get into the neighbours' houses and look for him there, just in case he's doubled back. Corporal Shipley, get into all the gardens down here to the left with Andrews and search them then sweep out to the edge of town and we'll meet near the bridge across the river, you know the one we looked at earlier on the map. McDougall, you and Lawson come with me.

Captain Watkinson guessed Wilson would be smart enough to have planned his escape route. After all, he had been on the run for long enough. Having deployed his men he felt confident that this time he would have his man. Wilson had already defied them once – he wouldn't get away this time. He guessed Wilson would aim for the woodland in from the sea, as it was likely that the cover provided would be his best chance.

CHAPTER 2

Wilson, despite not having had any particular athletic exercise for months, had still been agile enough to clear the old fences with ease. His decision to turn left down the gardens had proved a good one as he had correctly guessed the soldiers would come from the opposite end of the row of houses and he had to be mindful that they might have left someone covering the rear at the bottom of the garden. Having leapt at least three of the garden fences dividing the properties and with two to go before the open land, he knew he had got some advantage as he was sure there were shouts still coming from back at the house. He half turned for a look back but could see no one following him. As he turned back to look forward he suddenly saw this head right in front of him.

A sickening feeling welled up in him as his nose cracked as it met the back of a thinly covered head. Wilson reeled away with the impact and clasped his nose. The two men fell to the ground and Wilson immediately put his hand to his nose and pulled it away and looked at the warm blood smeared across his palm. He looked at the body beneath him and recognised the old man as Du Feu who had been thrown forward across the bed of flowers, now crushed under his weight. He was winded as Wilson's full weight fell on top of him. Wilson's head cleared in an instant despite the blow and he half pulled the old man to his feet, thought better of it and was over the next fence and all Du Feu could do was mouth a stream of abuse and wave his arms at the fleeing figure.

Two more leaps over the last fences and Wilson could see the wood across the meadow. He crouched momentarily gasping for air and felt his nose for a second time. It was now very tender and his eyes were watering with the pain; he could feel the blood running into his mouth and he spat some out onto the ground. He could feel his heart was pounding against his chest not just from the exertion but also from the excitement. He wiped his face with his other palm and then wiped the blood on his trousers. Not only was his nose throbbing but also his shoulder was sore from the bang on the doorframe back at the house and it had taken another blow when he had fallen on Du Feu.

He could see the heads of some of the soldiers as they walked along the back gardens looking into each garden in turn. He could make out their insignia even from this distance and recognised them as Military Police.

Towards the end of the row of gardens the houses curved to the left and he disappeared from any view the soldiers might have had. Just beyond the last garden there was a track leading to the left and back towards the street. Away to the right the track went towards the wood across a small field used as a play area by the local children. There were hedges each side and this afforded him cover. He dropped down onto the track from the bank skirting the last garden. He ran to the right and towards the wood. There was soon a junction with a left turn that would have taken him towards the bridge that he thought the soldiers might cover. Another option was to stay on the track and go straight ahead and this would take him directly to the large opening into the wood. Instead he turned right along an old path, which was now largely overgrown with tall grass and weeds. He knew that this would take him to the denser area of the wood. This old track ran along the side of another hedgerow and afforded yet more cover, so there was no chance of the soldiers seeing him from where they were.

Eventually, he had to cut across the field to the wood and there were about thirty-five yards in all to cover so he sprinted towards it but keeping his head down so that it remained below the level of the hedgerow. However, he was still keen to get to the protection of the wood as quickly as possible as he might be a sitting duck if they spotted him.

As he anticipated, the soldiers had not put anyone at this end of the terrace of houses so the advantage was still his. Within seconds he reached a small gap in a long line of hawthorn bushes. He had particularly chosen this gap when he looked along here a few months earlier as it was not easy to spot and he knew the soldiers, if they were following him, would waste time trying to find a way into the wood which did not mean running through thick, prickly bushes. He guessed they would probably head towards the large opening along the main track that he had left.

Almost immediately two shots rang out, he instinctively dived to the ground but the whistling bullets were way to his left and random or perhaps deliberate warning shots into the air. He had been through these dense woods countless times and had carefully worked out his path. The trees extended for nearly half a mile. About half way to the southern side he took a right turn, which meant he would come out well to the right of the bridge. Once clear of the wood he would be near the Boulogne road.

Part of his plan was to pick up a change of clothes and, to this end, he had previously secreted a shirt, jacket, boots, some trousers and a hat in the garden shed at the house of Madame Perlier, one of Marie's aunts, who lived in Escalles which was along the coast from Calais towards Boulogne. This had been some months ago but he had checked they were still there one evening the previous week, when he and Marie had visited the old lady for supper. If he could get to Boulogne it should be easy to find somewhere to hide. There certainly would be no going back to Calais now.

He made good progress to the Boulogne road but kept low along the hedgerows to keep out of sight of his pursuers. Down on the road, there were two locals walking with a pushcart about three hundred yards in front however they were already past where he would cut across the fields towards Escalles. There was no way he wanted to meet people who may know him so that he would waste time having to pass the time of day with them and giving them the possible opportunity of telling his pursuers the direction he had taken.

The sun was bright and in his eyes as it lowered to the horizon, another twenty minutes or so and it will have gone and dusk would be here. He felt confident. Everything was, so far, going just the way he thought it might and in the short term at least he just might avoid being captured. If he could get to Boulogne he might have another opportunity to get a boat back across the Channel. It would be difficult, as the Army would be more than doubling their efforts to look out for him. He would have to find somewhere to hide away for a while, while he searched through the boatyards. He had decided that he would prevail upon Madame Perlier for a few days until, hopefully, his pursuers might give up their search in that area.

Wilson knew that if he could avoid capture for just a couple of months more, then the Army might just lessen their desire to chase after him, and the many like him, because throughout all of 1918 the locals had been talking of peace happening some time before the end of the year– the war had been going nowhere for a while particularly after the German push in Belgium during the Spring had come to a halt. Wilson had heard that the troops from all sides had remained stuck in their trenches in that sector; he had thought both Armies must have become all played out after the huge campaign of the Ypres salient in 1917 and surely it was not possible to sustain the effort for much longer. He had also heard that tanks were now successfully being used against the Germans and were sapping further the enemy's already shattered morale.

Then came rumours that the Germans, by all accounts, were making yet another huge push, with perhaps one last throw of the dice to end the stalemate. Surely though, everyone thought, the strength, and maybe the will of the troops had long gone. Then came rumours that both sides had started talking to each other about a peace settlement of some kind.

In the past month or so the artillery had continued to thunder its daily bursts. The locals had told Marie that the German push in the French sector had put them forty miles from Paris in early June but the Allies had now pushed them back and the Americans were making all the difference. Wilson had seen the Americans arriving through Calais, they all seemed so young, so happy, so naïve, they just did not know what confronted them. Fleetingly in his mind's eye, he could see the mud, the bodies, the filth, recall the stench, feel the wet and he shuddered and felt a little sick inside just to remember what it had been like and what these new troops had to look forward to. Not in their wildest dreams could they possibly imagine what lay ahead.

CHAPTER 3

Captain Watkinson led the unit of military policemen based in Calais and the most senior of his men was Corporal Frank Shipley. Watkinson found Shipley an engaging and friendly young man who he felt had potential to rise through the ranks and was definitely senior NCO material. The other men respected him and Watkinson had already recommended his promotion to Sergeant and ratification from higher level was expected at any time.

Frank Shipley was a Londoner by birth but his parents had moved to Somerset when he was four and they lived on a smallholding in Wedmore, not far from Cheddar Gorge and at the base of the Mendip Hills.

His mother had died of pneumonia in 1911 and his father had continued to carry on his business as a painter and decorator with Frank's help. However, as a sideline they had a cider press and after the apple harvest the old man bottled as much as he could and sold it to Tucker, the landlord of the George Inn in Wedmore. It was strong stuff and unfortunately the old man had spent far too much time sampling his own produce. Frank felt that the alcohol had taken over, as his father was permanently in some drunken haze and his health had worryingly started to deteriorate. So, it had left Frank with the responsibility for the running of the business, into which he had thrown himself with his customary zeal. It had done well in the years immediately after his Mother's death but the events of 1914 had changed all that as life, as people had known it, had been turned on its head.

Frank had wanted to join up straightaway but his father and the villagers told him he was needed too much at home. Once into 1916 and with the huge losses on the Somme, the call eventually came. Despite his craftsman's skills he was put into the Rifle Brigade but then was eventually transferred to the Royal Engineers and was sent to France. Whilst he heard the action somewhere off in the distance, he hardly saw any of it and had been kept well behind the frontlines. He had spent an inordinate amount of time working inside very smart houses. His skills had been put to great use in converting many a chateaux into a headquarters to be used by the senior commanders and their staff. His greatest moment to date had come when he helped build a temporary toilet specifically for the visit of some high ranking official from the British Government – the rumour was that it was the Prime Minister but some had said it was the King!

However, on his very occasional visits to the areas not far behind the Front he had been horrified at what he had seen. The number of ill and injured men that filled the field hospitals, many of which he had helped build in his early days in France, was beyond belief. Some were in an awful state and he was only too pleased that he was out of the frontline fighting. The rumours about the number of deaths and those missing had been difficult to believe with some saying that nearly 20,000 fellow Tommies had died on the Somme in one day alone in 1916. Frank often thanked God that his old man had put a paintbrush in his hand and that the Army wanted to put his skills to good use well behind the action!

Before he joined up, the work in the village had dribbled down to almost nothing. The whole of Somerset had already mourned the loss of so many of their young men and many of the locals had begun to feel that perhaps Frank should now be out there supporting the cause. Whilst he was well liked by all, there had been some pointed remarks made and finally he decided to join up, although technically he had a reserved occupation and might have been able to avoid being conscripted.

Whilst his father had taught him the finer points of painting and decorating he had always been a good shot. The old man had kept a shotgun in the house and many a summer's evening had been spent with his son picking off the rabbits and anything else that appeared in the fields particularly around harvest gathering time when the cornfields were cleared.

Whilst his first jobs in the Rifle Brigade and the Engineers were using his attributes of his chosen trade, Frank had heard that volunteers were requested for a special unit, within the Military Police, with the proviso of being a very good shot, so he had put his name forward. He thought it might be for a sniper job, which he would have relished, but then he had questioned if he was that good a shot. However, it turned out the unit was mainly set up to track down deserters. Not so much those who ran off and were either captured or gave themselves up within a day or so, but the seemingly clever, or lucky, ones who stayed at large and evaded capture for months on end.

The unit under Captain Watkinson had had a lot of success. They were based around the channel ports because the deserters, almost to a man, would try to find a boat and make for Dover or one of the other English south coast ports. The deserters would lie low for months, sometimes being given sanctuary by the locals before persuading some local boatman to get them to England or even having a go themselves. Some had even tried to secure a permit from the British Consul, posing as Frenchmen trying to secure work such as firemen on the Channel boats travelling to and from those English ports. Some had even been successful in getting back to England and then apparently just disappeared.

To date, Watkinson's men had been successful in rounding up three men who had all found it too difficult to cope with life at the Front and had simply ran away. Watkinson's men had heard that all three had subsequently been tried, found guilty and executed. The rumour was that they had been taken back to their own regiments to be tried and the execution squad was made up of men from the same regiments and apparently, in some cases, men actually known to them. This they had been told was supposedly all part of the Army's strict disciplinary principles to show those still fighting that there was no easy way out.

Frank Shipley enjoyed the work and at an early stage had been promoted to Corporal, something that his father had been so proud of and something for him to boast to his mates in the George back home.

Despite being a crack shot, he had never shot at anyone whilst he had been in the Army, unless just a warning volley, and it had already seemed to him that there was an irony in all of this in that they were not allowed to shoot at the prisoners unless in exceptional circumstances. Then all that happened was that the prisoner was eventually likely to face a firing squad anyway. However, this is the Army and that is what the Army does, he thought.

They had been looking for Private Edward Wilson for about four months. Apparently, Wilson had been on the run since November 1917 when he had deserted his post during the Third Ypres battle whilst with the East Lancs Regiment. Rumour has it that Wilson had been on the verge of becoming a professional footballer in 1914 as he had been on the books of Burnley who had won the FA Cup in 1914.

This had not been the first time Wilson had been in trouble as he had previously been disciplined in the field for disobeying an order and the punishment had been carried out at the Front.

It was generally thought that Wilson had somehow got back to England but exhaustive searches in his native Lancashire and calls on any family he might have visited, had turned up nothing. So, Watkinson had been given his orders to concentrate searches in the Pas de Calais and extend this if he felt it necessary. He had been given the dossier on Wilson and shared it with his men.

Shipley had often felt a degree of sympathy towards these young men who had given up and run away – he felt he would have probably felt like doing the same thing after what he had seen on the occasions when he had got near the frontline. He was interested in this Wilson; the fact that he might be a professional footballer intrigued him. Shipley had himself had trials in Bristol and it had appeared quite promising for a while but the travelling was difficult and then his mother died and, as the old man went on the slide, he had concentrated on the business side of things. He turned out for Bath City a few times but then the War came and football virtually packed up as so many of the young men left for France, Belgium and elsewhere.

They had started their search for Wilson just after the German offensive in the Spring. It was fun in a way during those summer months. The distant sound of the guns was a constant comfort that they would rather be here than where the guns were. The weather had been good and it was hard to think at times that the wanton waste of life was a mere handful of miles away and apart from the noise of the guns the only thing that destroyed the serenity of Summer was the constant flow of troops, artillery and other machinery to the Front, not to mention the constant transport of supplies be that by mechanised transport or by horse.

Watkinson had originally split up his men to mix in with the locals to find out if anyone knew of the whereabouts of any British soldier, hiding from the Army. It had been difficult as none of the soldiers spoke French apart from the usual smattering that soldiers used to get by with. Also, the French they met seemed to have an in-built reticence when it came to dealing with Army authority.

Shipley had been given a photograph purporting to be Wilson but he knew from past experience that there was a good chance the photograph could possibly not be of Wilson and, in any case, surely he would have changed his appearance during his time on the run, so it would probably be of little use anyway. However, Frank would often stare at the unsmiling face with its curly hair and what seemed like very pale eyes staring dispassionately at the camera. It seemed like life had been drained out of the face. The photograph must have been taken since the War started as Wilson was in uniform. He looked much older than he probably was as he was supposed to be under twenty.

Shipley had noticed this was a familiar feature with most of the men he had seen on their way to, or back from, the Front. Often they seemed to look much older on their way back but by then of course they were normally in a completely dishevelled state. Even behind the lines when they were trying to relax and recover, he saw men of his own age seemingly years older and as time went on they appeared more bitter, constantly moaning about everyone and everything; the lowering of morale had, over time, been very clear to see. Even back in Wedmore when he had been on leave, boys that he had known from his schooldays had become old men almost overnight – the Somersets had taken an almighty mauling and a few friends from the village had been killed, severely injured or were simply missing.

He had felt a little awkward at times given that he was not in frontline action and felt that some of the local boys and their families were more than a little resentful of that fact, thinking he had a cushy number. Nothing had been said to his face but his father had heard some talk and on one occasion had taken one of the mothers to task when she had made some comment about Frank having it easy.

After three weeks of no success in mixing with the locals, Watkinson had decided on a different strategy. The only way Wilson could really get to England was by boat. Despite the latest German push it was inevitable that the War could not last much longer and, not for the first time, he expected to be back home with his family and return to college at Oxford by the time Christmas came around. However, he had heard that before! So, Watkinson briefed his men by telling them to concentrate on the shoreline from just north east of Calais itself down the coast to Boulogne. If Wilson looked for a passage in this sector then the men would be ready. Watkinson suspected that Wilson would have to make a move because he would be aware that the War would end soon and it would be more difficult to hide amongst the locals once the confusion the hostilities brought also came to an end.

He knew other units would be working on other parts of the coast. He had told his men to be patient. To question anyone who owned a boat. To build up a relationship with the fishermen, enjoy some wine with them, chat with them as best they could. Even get to know their wives, their sisters and their children. In Watkinson's experience most deserters, who have evaded capture for any length of time, would have formed some sort of relationship with a local French family. He had known some to live with a Frenchwoman as man and wife – as there had been no shortage of young widows or young women who had lost their boyfriends. A whole family, who had perhaps lost a son, would take in these deserters and nurse and protect them as if they were their own.

Corporal Shipley had been paired with Reg Andrews for the task of getting to know the fishermen of Calais. Quite a task but Watkinson had told them to take their time and be thorough. They were billeted with a French family whose house had been used by the Army since the very early days of the war. Henri Masson was a quiet man who rarely spoke. He ran the local bakery and, since the shock of losing his two sons at Mons in 1914, had quietly gone about his work, lost in his own world. Madame Masson was English by birth having been bought up in Margate. She met her husband Henri when he visited her hometown in the early 90s. They had married in 1892 and had two sons, one born in 1893 and the other in 1894. Rita Masson, too, had been devastated when her sons were lost in the very early stages of the War within days of one another.

Nearly four years on she was now not alone in her grief, she had done her best to try to get on with her life but she constantly worried about the depressed state of her husband: there was hardly a mother in France, who had not lost a husband or a son or seen one return a broken man either physically or mentally. She was an ox of a woman who still spoke very good English but now with a peculiar accent that often made Shipley smile.

She was a great help in their search, as they did not have to try out their poor French when they had her to help them deal with the locals. Watkinson, despite his relative inexperience in dealing with people, had been clever enough to spot this when he had visited the bakery during a period of leave over Easter.

Mme Masson had introduced Shipley and Andrews to most of the local boatmen during the summer evenings in the bars in the Calais area. In early September one of the older men had told her of an unusual occurrence when he had caught someone hanging around his tethered motor boat. He had shouted at the young man who had run off without a word – it was unusual in that there were hardly any young, fit Frenchmen around the town as they were either in the army or carried some form of injury. The fact that the young man had appeared physically strong and well had seemed odd, especially when he just ran off.

Shipley had reported this to Watkinson who had then briefed his men to maintain a close watch on this area for at least the next week. Shipley had asked Mme Masson to obtain a better description of the young man from the old boatman. He was not much help but Shipley felt this could be Wilson, or at least someone else on the run. He and Andrews decided to operate a shift basis at night with three hours at a time spent watching the same area.

Shipley had almost given up following night after night of tedium. However, he comforted himself by listening to the distant burst of shellfire, which told him there were lots of other places he could be that were worse than this!

It was the third week of September and the autumnal evenings meant that he had to wrap up against the chill of the north easterly coming off the Channel. At about two in the morning he had positioned himself in the doorway of one of the shops. He had a good view across the little harbour with its array of ramshackle boats of all shapes and sizes, most of them, seemingly, in advanced states of decay. He saw a dark figure moving along the line of boats to the eastern side of the harbour. Even in the darkness he could see the figure moving purposefully and athletically from boat to boat, obviously looking for something. He waited until the figure had his back to him and then he set off towards the small wall above the harbour – he crouched down and peered over the top. With the moon hidden behind the clouds it was difficult to see very clearly but Shipley felt that this was no local boatman as they were all much older and, anyway, they were never about at this time of night.

He carefully looked over the wall again and for a moment there was no sign of the figure – he caught his breath but then was relieved to see movement at the far end of the line of boats to his left. The figure was moving away. He felt a surge of excitement, what he had seen had looked suspicious and he was sure this could be the man they had been looking for. He edged along the wall and peered over yet again. Shit! He thought - he's going away. Shipley took a moment to reflect on what Watkinson had said which was to use your own judgement but approach with caution – you have a gun and he probably won't have one, yet still be careful.

There was no way he could see the face in this light and, as he thought back to Wilson's photo, it was not likely that he could recognise someone from an old photograph at this distance especially if he has, as expected, changed his appearance.

Shipley knew he had to make his approach before the man disappeared into the streets. He quietly slipped the safety catch on his rifle more to give him confidence than anything else because he knew that he would follow Watkinson's orders and only shoot if he had to.

He decided to act before it was too late. He ran in a crouched way along the remaining length of wall and when he got to the end he jumped up and shouted in English – "Stop or I'll shoot" was the best he could come up with, the figure stopped in his tracks and looked in the direction of the voice. In a second the man was off and running, slightly zigzagging along the pavement. Shipley tighten his grip on the rifle and ran after him. This was no local man he thought to himself. The man turned down Rue de Normandie, which headed towards the little market square; the man was about fifty yards ahead of Shipley whose mind raced as he thought of what he should do. He could chance a shot but again he remembered the orders.

Before he could decide on what to do the figure disappeared from sight on the right hand side of the market place. He looked around and listened; there was hardly a sound, no footsteps, nothing. He moved towards the end of the line of small shops. To his annoyance there was a small alleyway leading off to the right and he slowly edged to the corner of the shop at the beginning of the gap. He put the rifle round the corner first and then he swung out and crouched looking down the alley. There was nothing. He walked down to its end but he knew the man had got away. The alley exited onto the harbour road but there was nothing there.

Shipley jogged back to the Masson's to speak with Andrews. They decided to go and see Watkinson at his billet in the centre of the town.

Like Shipley, Watkinson was convinced that this was their man. If it was not him it was certainly someone with something to hide

The following day Watkinson called his men together and briefed them on what he had decided to do next. He had decided to use Le Fevre, the local liaison officer, to help. Jean Le Fevre had lived locally before the War but had spent some years working in the docks at Dover before the call to arms and he spoke pretty good English. He had been badly injured in 1914, not by the forces of the Kaiser but by a broken leg sustained in a football match during some leave. The leg had turned septic where the compound fracture had split the skin. It had been touch and go for a while but he pulled through but not before gangrene had set in. The leg had been amputated below the knee and he now got around on some old crutches. When the hostilities were over he had been promised an artificial leg replacement.

Despite his problem he was a pleasant chap and had made friends easily with the young Tommies.

Watkinson had used him in the early days when they set up in Calais and he had helped in forging the relationship with Mme Masson.

He had now been asked to help his British friends to search the houses down near the market square. He was to ask the locals to see if they had seen or heard of a young man living in the area, who was not a local.

The whole of the Saturday had been spent moving from one house to another. Some of the locals were keen to help but many were indifferent. They were tired of the War; many had lost loved ones and were not too disposed to help the army, especially the British. Old man Rive lived towards the end of the terraced row of houses that had frontages opening straight into the road. Rather shabby looking places with small back gardens often piled high with all sorts of rubbish but Rive's was different. He grew what he could and had tended the plants with loving care.

Le Fevre had known Rive as the younger Frenchman's grandmother had lived opposite and she had been a friend of Rive's wife.

The two spoke at some length. The soldiers stood and waited; they had no idea what was being said. Shipley and Andrews had spent the past six hours or so only half listening to these conversations. They could not understand anything that was being said and both were by now pretty fed up and beginning to think that Watkinson's idea was something of a long shot. Shipley started to move towards the door and to move to the next house but suddenly Rive's voice became more animated. He was gesticulating and waving his arms, the old man kept repeating over and over "Oui! Oui! Oui!" nodding his head furiously.

Le Fevre turned to Shipley and quietly reflected on what he had just heard before saying, "Monsieur Rive is suspicious of a young man living along the next street but he's not sure at which house. The man is supposed to be the brother of a young widow but the old man says he has seen them out together and they act more like husband and wife than brother and sister. Apparently, the so-called brother has been suffering from some sort of mental illness brought on by shellfire and cannot, or will not, speak. He has been there for most of this year. He had asked about them only last night in the bar down the road and was told that they might have left today to visit a relative but are expected back tonight or tomorrow morning."

"Tell the Monsieur "Merci" and to keep this to himself. We had better see Captain Watkinson and tell him about this." Shipley then indicated to Andrews with a jerk of his head to follow him.

Le Fevre duly thanked the old man and joined the soldiers in the street. "Promising?" he said, looking at Shipley. "Sounds like it but we aren't going to be too hasty, let's go and see Captain Watkinson."

The Captain looked up from the pile of papers on his desk in the small room at the back of the church, which served as his office. He jumped up as soon as he saw the look on Shipley's face. "What is it?" he asked his Corporal.

"I think we have something, sir. Right, Le Fevre, tell him what the old man said." Le Fevre recounted the story.

Watkinson slowly sat back into his chair and ran his hand through his thick mane of wavy hair. "You're right, Corporal. From what you've said and from what you saw last night, this could be Wilson or failing that one of the other missing chaps."

He said nothing for a nearly a minute but Shipley could see he was thinking of the next move as he stared blankly in front of him. Shipley looked at him waiting for some change in his expression. Le Fevre and Andrews exchanged glances and then both looked at the ground waiting for the Captain to speak.

"I am referring this to Major Brown," he finally said, "however, as far as I'm concerned, we'll assume it's Wilson and go in tomorrow."

Watkinson eventually got hold of Brown at about nine o'clock that evening. Brown took no time in giving the go-ahead and they agreed that the soldiers would go in the early Sunday afternoon. It was more likely that the suspect would be there at that time maybe sleeping off his lunch.

Watkinson briefed his men just after ten on the Sunday morning having walked down to the market square area to have a look at the area for himself. They had been to the bar where Le Fevre had heard of the couple and Watkinson had been given an idea of which house they lived in. He decided that he would put some of the men at the end of the street and would have liked some insurance by covering the surrounding countryside where he thought Wilson might head for. However, he opted to concentrate on the immediate area of the house as he only had nine men plus himself. He would put two at the end of the street and two at the end of the garden and would go into the house himself. Once in he could deploy his men as circumstances dictated.

At just after two they were ready. He looked at Shipley, Andrews, McDougall and Lawson and they stared straight back into his eyes. He raised his eyebrows and mouthed, "Go," they nodded back in unison and he moved off on the run, the men sprinting after him. They rapped on the door of the address they had been given and when the door opened had stormed in only to find the sole inhabitant a very old woman. She had shooed them away in no uncertain terms. He looked across the road and saw a young woman's face at the window and she moved away very quickly when she saw the Officer looking towards her. Watkinson called to his men, "Let's try that one over there!"

CHAPTER 4

Having left the main road, Wilson cut across the fields in the general direction of the coastal town of Sangatte, which itself was on the road to Escalles. In a direct line it would take very little time being about five miles away but he decided that the hedgerows provided the only real cover in this flat area just inland from the sea. He had not planned this part of his escape but knew that he could rely on his sense of direction sufficiently to get him to the coast. There were very few villages or hamlets in this area and by heading directly to the coast he could then go southwest to Escalles. Once at Madame Perlier's he would lie low for the night and then move on as he guessed it would not take long for his pursuers to check Marie's family to see if they were protecting him as the young woman had done.

The sun had now almost disappeared and the western sky was mostly dark clouds with just a tinge of red, so it would be completely dark within half an hour. This would allow him to slip into Escalles and into the old shed at the back of the Perlier house to pick up the change of clothes.

He thought back to Marie and hoped that the soldiers had not treated her badly. It was likely that she would have to face some sort of charges but he knew the Army often passed these matters back to the local police and from what Marie had told him the usual French bureaucracy would mean the matter would likely take so long to be dealt with that the War would be over well before any proceedings took place.

He suddenly felt the urge to relieve himself and stood facing some bushes by the side of the track to his right. Casually he looked back towards the road and Calais in the distance. On top of the small hill above the town was the woodland he had run into to escape his pursuers. The road meandered down into the small valley where he had turned off the road. In the far distance there was still the occasional smattering of artillery fire, the constant reminder.

Just as he shook off the last drips he could see what looked like a horse and cart coming down the road from the woodland. He immediately crouched down letting the hedgerow hide him from any view from the road. The gathering darkness made it difficult to make out its occupants but there was definitely more than one and it was the speed that caught his attention. Farm workers on their way home would never move that quickly. Suddenly a filter of late sun lit up the hill and the valley before it. He could see that there were at least three heads bobbing up and down as the horse headed almost directly towards him at something between a trot and a gallop. They were about a mile away and he had to decide whether to wait and let them pass or head off along the same path continuing to use the hedgerow as cover.

The sun disappeared again and the gathering gloominess was all the more noticeable but just at that moment he saw that two of the men in the front of the cart were wearing the unmistakable British Army khaki. The driver was in a much darker, almost black, colour and Wilson assumed he was a local.

For the first time, he felt ill at ease; he had hoped by now that he had got well enough away to feel confident that he would not be caught. Now he was less sure.

CHAPTER 5

Shipley and Andrews had lost sight of their man as they had stumbled down the gardens, stepping over some old local as he sat there, in his garden, cursing away. He stood up as they went past almost knocking Andrews to the ground. Andrews swore at the old man and for a moment turned his rifle at him in his frustration but he turned it skywards and fired two shots in the general direction away from the houses towards some woodland.

He had been immediately admonished by Shipley who was some twenty yards or so ahead. Shipley reminded him that they were only to shoot if threatened and the last thing they wanted would be to endanger the locals.

Shipley was first to clear the gardens and there was nothing but some open space in front of him and the wood a little distance away to his right. He was sweating despite the fact that he was only wearing his lightest army clothing but he felt excited that the chase was on and that this must at last be when this Wilson chap would be hunted down.

Andrews caught him up. He was so breathless that he had trouble speaking but was still swearing about the old man from the gardens.

Shipley was gathering his thoughts whilst Andrews got his breath back. Watkinson had told him to meet at the bridge, which was slightly over to their left. If he were Wilson what would he do? The wood was the obvious choice as it provided cover so he set off telling Andrews to follow him.

"But what about the Captain?" called out Andrews, "He said meet at the bridge on the edge of town?"

"Yeah, I know what he said but Wilson ain't going that way is he? So come on, I'm heading for the wood, we'll search for him there." At which point Shipley sprinted off and Andrews lumbered after him, now having someone else to swear about.

Shipley had wasted some time deciding where to enter the wood but in the end took the option of continuing on the track towards the large opening; he saw that a lot of the edge of the wood was impenetrable hedge, so he did not wish to waste time by searching for a way in. He had to wait for Andrews to catch him up.

"Come on Reg, keep up or we're going to lose him."

Reg Andrews had quite frankly had enough. He was now wheezing and very warm and, although he would not admit it to his mate, could not care a stuff if the bloke got away or not. He had long since lost all interest in what he was doing and simply longed for this whole war saga to be over. Just the previous Christmas his wife had written to say that she had found solace with a badly injured Corporal she had helped nurse at their local hospital. Apparently, the man had only one leg and had also a lot of facial injuries from a shell during the Ypres offensive in the early part of the war – it made Reg feel so annoyed to think his Ellie would prefer something like that.

Momentarily his mind was filled with thoughts of home and when he looked around he wondered where Shipley had gone until he heard the Corporal's shout of, "Reg, move your arse!"

It took them almost half an hour to search through the wood and eventually they were back at the point where they had entered.

"If he's here, then he's bloody well hidden, that's all I can say, Frank." At which point Andrews began to slope away in the general direction of the bridge.

"Where the bloody hell are you going?" said the Corporal.

"Look, Frank, this bloke's probably well away from here. Let's go back and find Watkinson and the others. It will be dark in a little while and then we won't find him, anyway."

"We're not going back that way – this bloke is Wilson, I'm sure of it and I'm not wasting months of work to let him get away from us. If I were he I would head back towards the sea then double back into Calais or head off down towards Boulogne, as he won't want to go back to that woman. I would go to Boulogne, so we're going that way. Watkinson would understand, he doesn't want to lose him either. He's lost Wilson once already last January, remember?

Andrews shrugged, "But we ought to tell him what we're doing, he'll be bloody annoyed if he doesn't know where we are and what we're doing."

Frank thought for a moment, "Yeah, it's a good point, let's run down to the bridge and see if he's there, we can always pick up the trail soon enough."

Within five minutes, they were with Watkinson, who agreed with his Corporal that Wilson, assuming it was him, would probably head along the coast. Watkinson and the other men had commandeered a horse and cart from one of the local farm lads, who knew the young Private, McDougall. Being a Sunday, the French lad, Juste, had little work to do apart from take the milk churns from his father's farm down to the dairy in Calais. He was on his way back when he saw the soldiers running along the street. He recognised McDougall who had been billeted with his family at the farm for a while in the summer and they had become friendly both being of similar age. McDougall, showing enterprise that had impressed Watkinson, had called for his new friend to stop. The soldiers had jumped on the cart and asked Juste to drop them off at the bridge on his back to the farm.

When they got to the bridge Juste had stayed with them, offering further help – he decided this was far more exciting than sitting at home with his family.

Watkinson told the French lad to head off to the West whilst he gathered his thoughts. The cart slowed as they climbed the small hill towards the wood where Andrews and Shipley had just come from. As soon as they started downhill the sun shone almost its last for the day and they all had to shield their eyes. The horse seemed surprised by the sudden flash and his trot became more of a gallop. Juste pulled on the reins to slow the animal down. The cart was not in the best condition and he was keen not to put too much pressure on it, especially as it was carrying these extra passengers.

No sooner had the sun come out then it went in again and the darker light returned. The horse slowed and the French lad relaxed and looked down as if to check the wheels were still there.

Shipley was not sure that they stood any chance of finding Wilson. Andrews was right, once it was dark they probably had no chance.

Suddenly, a sliver of light panned across the fields to his right from a break in those clouds away to the West. There was a momentary flash as the light caught something about half a mile or so up the hedgerows along side the vast fields. Shipley was sure the object was moving. The sunlight quickly disappeared.

"Sir," shouted Shipley, "I think I saw something over there, by the side of the field, it was moving."

"Are you sure, Corporal? It's a funny old light."

"I dunno… but it was something."

"Fine, I suggest you get off here and have a look but then make your way to the next town. It's called Escalles, I think – we were there last week, remember? It had that funny statue near the sea front, some Greek looking thing. We'll meet you there in about an hour. Be careful. First though, I want to go back and question that Frenchwoman Wilson was living with and see if we can get some idea where he might go to along this part of the coast. We'll catch up with you later at the statue and if you are not there we'll double back across country and look out for you."

"But, Sir, shouldn't someone come with me?"

"Wilson is not armed, as far as we know, and I need to cover all the other possibilities and, after all, we are not sure that you are chasing anything and you are probably not going to find anything or anyone in this light!"

Watkinson grabbed the reins indicating for the lad to pull over. Shipley jumped down by the side of the road and gave a quick wave to the faces a few feet above him. Watkinson gave a half-salute/half-wave and the others nodded back as the lad shook the reins and the horse moved away back towards Calais.

Shipley headed off in the direction of where he had seen the flash.

Wilson had stood as if transfixed when the light came across him but it had gone as soon as it had come and he moved off. He looked back towards the road and saw the cart slowing. It appeared that one of the people on the cart was getting off. Shit! He thought to himself. It's bound to be one of the soldiers; they must have seen something. He told himself not to panic, as there was still more than half a mile between them. The light was almost going by the second and he should be able to use this to his advantage.

Nevertheless, he quickened his stride as he took off up the field, mentally double-checking that he was heading the right way.

Within minutes the darkness had closed in and he had to feel his way. His lightweight boots did not grip like his old army issue but of course he had had no time back at Marie's to change into something more suitable. He was at least pleased with himself that he had decided to always keep something decent on his feet in case he had to make a quick getaway!

The clouds had built up and there was no moon, which was lucky for him. For half an hour he pressed on often stumbling on the uneven ground. He was aware that the ground was now rising in front of him. He had been able to keep to the hedgerows almost in a straight line and he guessed the coast could not be far away. As he came to the top of the incline he could see the horizon and also could just make out the line where it met the sea.

To his left was a town with its twinkling lights seemingly winking at him as if they were welcoming an old friend. To his right was the coast road weaving its way down from Calais, there seemed to be some movement on the road but he was not sure. He thought back to the soldiers left on the cart, could it be them down there, where were they going when they dropped their man off?

He tried to pick out some landmark that would tell him this was Escalles and that Madame Perlier's was down there among the lights. He thought back to his visit here with Marie before but could not really remember much about the place apart from some odd statue of a Greek or Roman god, which looked out of place in a northern French town. That was someway into the town he recalled.

The September dew had made the ground slippery and he continued to stumble and slither down the slope towards the road. He was really pleased with this darkness. It had enabled him to get down almost to the edge of the road without having to think about anyone seeing him. However, he was still having difficulty finding this road, which had seemed easier to make out from up the hill.

Suddenly, as he pushed through a thick bush laterally in front of him, there, suddenly, was the road. The one from Calais. There was no one about but he did not want to take any chances so he stayed the field side of the hedge rather than show himself on the road itself. He had almost forgotten about his pursuer but suddenly stopped as he remembered. He looked round and again became a bit panicky but told himself that the chances of this soldier finding his way to here was unlikely given the darkness and his probable lack of knowledge of the area.

Almost at once Wilson's shin hit a large wooden sign and he fell headlong over the top of it, his head hitting his knee. Suddenly there was a sharp stab of pain and his eyes watered. He had completely forgotten his accident with Du Feu when he had unwittingly head-butted the old man when in the gardens back in Calais. He felt the nose, which had become somewhat bulbous as a result of the two blows. Almost certainly broken he thought. Not for the first time as he recalled some of the more violent football matches back in the Lancashire Leagues especially against teams from Blackburn!

He could feel some dried blood on his face and spat on the palm of his hand so he could wipe it away. As he moved the sign away he could make out some of the faded lettering. It appeared to come from a shop and he could make out what looked to be the owner's name and what he was sure was the words "… d'Escalles".

At last he came to the houses. Now was the time to walk out onto the edge of the road. He pulled up the collar of his jacket, hunched his shoulders and shoved his hands into the pockets. He kept his eyes on the ground. Again, there was hardly anyone around. He still could not recognise any of the town and was annoyed with himself that he had not attended to this detail during his previous visits.

In his pockets he had found the half-eaten apple he had shoved there when the soldiers had arrived at the house. He walked briskly munching on the remains of the apple. One or two strollers passed and offered the odd greeting to which he managed a gruff reply.

Just when he was beginning to think this might not be Escalles after all he saw the somewhat grotesque statue he had seen in the town previously. He knew exactly where he was now and it was only about 100 yards to Madame Perlier's.

Some fifty yards from the statue he noticed a rather familiar horse and cart pull up and at least three British soldiers jumped down and stood right next to the statue. One, who was clearly the Officer, spoke to the local who still sat on the cart with the reins and with a wave he was off. Wilson stopped momentarily not sure of what to do. He turned and made as if to look into a shop. He could make out some unattractive looking fruit and vegetables set out on display. His mind raced and he glanced again to his left towards the soldiers. They now seemed to be milling around and it dawned on him that maybe they were waiting for his pursuer. He now looked quickly to his right to check that their friend had not caught up with him.

He decided he had better move back a little way from where he had come from and then turn down the next side street to avoid the statue and work round the back of it to the Perlier house. Again checking that there was no pursuer, he quickly made his way down the small road, cut through the churchyard and came out onto the road, which ran parallel to the main street. From here it was only a short distance to the house. Once there, he made for the substantial garden and the small shed where the clothes had been left. Whilst Marie had told the old lady about him he did not want to involve her now, maybe tomorrow though. He scaled the small fence, all the time looking around him to check he had not been watched. He easily slipped the lock to the shed and he was in. In the small box in the corner and under some sacks were the clothes. He had forgotten that he had also left some apples, a small amount of chocolate, an old bayonet and a small bag to carry everything in. He looked around, there were some old sheets and some clothes in the corner so he flattened them out and sat down.

He sat for a good five minutes gathering his thoughts. He decided he would stay here for the night and try to get some sleep, as he now felt distinctly tired. Eventually he stretched out and made a pillow with an old greatcoat he found in the other corner and soon dropped off to sleep.

After about two hours he suddenly woke with a start. He thought he had heard a noise outside. Or was it? He gingerly opened the door, having picked up his bayonet grasping it tightly. He gently opened the door and moved outside. Crouching, he listened hard and peered into the darkness. Nothing.

Next to his leg was a small oil drum about knee high at the end of the shed. He slowly sat down and peered up the garden to try to see if anything moved. He began to relax again. Again, the tiredness began to overwhelm him. Suddenly, he heard the familiar sound of the catch of a gun and felt cold metal against his left temple. He froze.

"Are you Wilson?" came the voice from the darkness behind him.

CHAPTER 6

Wilson slowly stood up and looked into the face of the young British soldier. He could see a trace of fear in the soldier's wide-eyed face as he stared along the barrel of the rifle. Instinctively, he raised his arms into the air but said nothing. "Are you Wilson?" repeated the soldier, his breathing heavy and forming a mist as he spoke. Wilson half thought about running for it but the eyes of the young soldier narrowed as his look became more determined than fearful.

Shipley felt he was shaking inside as he looked at his quarry and he gripped the rifle tightly to stop his hand trembling. He searched his mind and went back to that photograph of Wilson he had seen some months before. There appeared to be no great resemblance but it was dark here in the garden and of course he had never been sure whether or not the photo had definitely been Wilson. The face in front of him was young and lean and there was no moustache. It could still be Wilson. "Right, then let's move that way," and he moved the gun, pointing towards the gate at the side of the house that would take them out into the main street. Shipley kept the butt of his rifle pressed against his shoulder and pointing it at the head of his prisoner. They started off up the long, narrow garden.

Within a minute they were in the street and heading towards the group idly standing by the statue. At the sound of the footsteps all the soldiers stood up immediately and raised their rifles. Watkinson drew his revolver from its holster. "Corporal Shipley, is that you?"

"Yes sir, with a prisoner... I think it is Wilson."

Watkinson walked towards them holding his gun in front of him pointing in the general direction of the prisoner. As he reached him he put the gun down by his waist but it was still cocked and ready.

"Right, stop there, you men fan out across the road and cover any escape."

The soldiers behind him shuffled across the full width of the street. Suddenly a door opened and a shaft of light shot across the road. Everyone turned towards the brightness and saw a woman in a nightgown silhouetted in the doorway. Wilson moved as if to turn and run for the alley to his left but Shipley had anticipated this and Wilson was caught by the Corporal's left leg and crashed to the ground. Two of the soldiers ran forward and stood over him but Watkinson was crouching by his side with the revolver pushed into Wilson's face. "Get up," shouted the Officer. The woman in the doorway moved inside and slammed the door shut. The darkness returned to the street. Wilson stood up but looked away from the Captain's gun as if it was a torch shining in his face. "Look at me, will you?" Slowly Wilson turned his head and looked disdainfully at the fresh-faced Officer. He said nothing.

"Well?" the Officer continued. Wilson did not move a muscle. Watkinson's eyes narrowed and he walked round with the gun now gripped tightly at his waist and pointing at the prisoner. "Fine, play it your way… Andrews go and find the local police station; we'll take him there for now. Lawson, you and the Corporal cover the prisoner and stand him against the statue."

Andrews moved off, a little confused as to exactly where they should go. "Move it" shouted the Officer. "Look around the square, it's bound to be there somewhere."

"I think it's back in the far right corner," said Shipley, " I saw it when I came in."

Andrews looked around trying to work out exactly where he meant. "Try over there, next to the grocer's." Watkinson pointed over to the right. Andrews moved quickly in that direction and gave a thumbs-up when he saw the small building that appeared to be what they were looking for.

Within the hour, Watkinson had his prisoner secured in the small cell at the back of the building. It had taken all his powers of Grammar School French to explain to the rather old gendarme that they would be taking over his station for the night. The Frenchman had started to complain but in the end could not be bothered so gave the cell keys to the British Officer.

Wilson was pushed into the cell. He had said nothing to his captors and had decided to keep quiet for as long as possible. The Officer had opted to leave the Corporal, who had caught him, and Andrews on guard outside the cell.

CHAPTER 7

There were no lights at all in the cell and once the door had been locked it was difficult for Wilson to make out anything until his eyes became accustomed to the change of light. Not that there had been much light in the station at all. The old gendarme had a candle on his desk and had used a paraffin lamp to show them the way through the corridor to the back of the building.

Wilson had noticed that the Corporal was stationed outside the cell with the man Andrews and clearly they were there for the night – he could hear Andrews bemoaning his luck that he could not return to their billet and a more comfortable bed. Typical soldier! Always complaining, some things never seem to change he thought to himself and allowed himself a smile!

It had been odd for Wilson. Once the Corporal had held the rifle to his head hardly a word had passed between them. Even when they had joined the group in front of the statue no one, apart from the Officer, had particularly taken any notice of him, except from making sure any escape was covered. The young Captain had been efficient in deciding what to do but had not even attempted to question him further or to seek any sort of confession as to who he was. The Officer seemed to accept that they had their man and that they could wait until the morning to sort out what their next move would be. Maybe he had to speak with someone in higher authority.

Wilson sat on the rickety chair in the corner and put his elbows on his knees and his chin rested into his cupped palms. He thought for a moment, looking back over the events of the day. How did they know he would be at the old woman's house? Had they got this from Marie and, if so, did they force it out of her? He frowned at the thought and shivered a little. He hugged himself to warm up.

As he sat there staring and thinking, he made up his mind that it was fairly useless trying to pretend he was someone else. They would have other photographs and descriptions from people that knew him and his attempts to look different would not get past a closer examination. It was unlikely these soldiers had just stumbled upon him and they were clearly some sort of special unit set up to track down the runaways like him.

He stood up and flapped his arms against his body to make himself feel warmer. Just at that moment a shaft of moonlight suddenly lit up the cell and it was easier to make out what was there, not that it was much. There was a bucket in the corner with what looked like a piece of muslin over the top of it but, on closer inspection, it was a very old and worn towel. From the smell, it seemed the contents left there by the previous occupant had not been emptied. The smell mixed offensively with the dampness of the cell walls, which appeared

31

to have a slimy green mould covering most of what Wilson could see. There was no bed as such but just a pile of thin blankets and a small piece of soiled mattress. He shivered again as the evening cold further penetrated beneath his jacket. He was glad now that he'd put it on before he had left Marie's. He felt in the pocket and found an apple he had stuffed there earlier from his small store at Madame Perlier's. He took it out and rubbed it on his thigh and took a bite. He then realised how hungry he was.

The mattress provided hardly any real protection and he could feel the uneven, solid stone floor beneath him. He pulled the smelly covers over him to give some warmth and he tried to settle down but realised that, whilst he felt tired, sleep might not come that easily. The apple had helped with his hunger but he was thirsty. There was a small table in one corner with a jug on it. He stood up and went over keeping the covers wrapped round him. He picked up the jug and smelt its contents, there was a trace of staleness but he decided it must be water and having sipped at first took a couple of large swigs.

He settled back down on the floor. He could hear the two men chatting outside the cell but could not make out what they were saying. The Officer and the other men not on guard had left and he had heard their footsteps down the street for some time. A few minutes later the gendarme also left but not before he had appeared to lock the front door, leaving the British soldiers to look after the station and the only prisoner in the cells for the night. The old man felt it had been a far more exciting Sunday evening than he had anticipated but the warmth of his home was much more attractive. It seemed that there would be no more developments tonight and he decided that he would return at about seven in the morning to see what had happened, if anything, overnight.

The moon continued to appear and then disappear, as the clouds moved across the sky. The two remaining soldiers had become quiet now. It must be well after eleven, Wilson thought.

Gradually the cell became dark again as the clouds took over the sky. Wilson could hear the rain falling outside and it became harder by the minute. It had never ceased to amaze him how much rain fell here. His beloved Lancashire had its fair share of horizontal winter rain, and the summers were often not that good either, but this place was at times even worse than that. For a moment his mind went back to last winter spent over the border in Belgium and those terrible days of the rain and then the thick, slimy mud, which the soldiers from both sides had had to cope with and to this could be added the constant threat of death either from a bullet or a shell or just from drowning in the water filled shell holes. He recalled the hours on end of sitting over his Lewis gun with his small team shivering from the cold, the wet and the fear.

He thought back to the men he had known all too briefly. They had enjoyed drinking and laughing together in the bars before they went up the line. He doubted many of these were alive now – he had seen many die in front of him, often blown apart or just disappearing completely.

He shivered at the images of what he had seen and he knew it was something he would never forget.

CHAPTER 8

Wilson turned his thoughts back to Marie. He wondered how she had coped after he had run off. The soldiers here with him seemed a decent bunch and they were Military Police after all and would be expected to maintain a high level of discipline. They would always want to treat the local population as well as possible as these locals would be a source of valuable information, which, he presumed, was how the MPs got onto him anyway.

He doubted if Marie would get into too much trouble for harbouring him. She may get a bit of a difficult time at first but the military had no jurisdiction over her and it would be most unlikely for the French to take the matter much further, especially as he was a British soldier; had he been German it might have been different.

Marie had told him that locals had all had enough of this war. There had been rumours of mutinies in the French army and even trouble for the British as well in this respect. The French people just wanted their country back. The Americans had now arrived to provide support and it was assumed this would accelerate some form of peace. Everyone was exhausted. The Germans had rallied a little in recent months but had fought to a standstill and it was thought old men and young boys were now being used to replenish them at the Front; such had been their losses.

He thought how marvellous Marie had been towards him. Perhaps, he also thought, she had used him in some way to make up for the absence of her husband

She had shown a great kindness to him over those months since he stumbled into her life. It had been a strange coming together. Closeness had developed between them from a very early stage. She a young widow and only twenty-two. She and her husband had only been married a matter of weeks before he had been called up. To this day she did not know exactly what had happened to him. The letter had said "Missing in action" but it was pointless trying to find out where he may have fallen, there was some hope that he may be alive and a prisoner or perhaps badly injured with no one knowing who he was. There had been so many losses that the Army just could not tell for sure and, if he had been captured, the Germans were not that quick to provide names. She had received a letter from her husband's Commanding Officer but it read like it was written as if to be copied and issued to the thousands of wives and families in a similar position. She had learnt that once the War was over every effort would be made to find out where every Frenchman had fallen and some form of memorial set up to honour the dead, even where there was no known grave. That was scant consolation to her, she thought. She lived in hope that he might still be alive and some day would return to her. As time went on that hope was nearly extinguished and she sought solace in helping this young Englishman who had arrived on her doorstep almost as a manifestation of her returning husband. She had doted on this stranger like an older sister or even a mother. She also had her father to care for and this all helped her cope with her grief.

Wilson thought back to that day when he, totally exhausted wet and cold, had sought shelter from the relentless November rain and cold in the outhouse of this small farmhouse near Gravelines, a town between Dunkirk and Calais and near the Channel coast. It had taken him over a week to get somewhere near the coast from the front line.

His instinct at that time had been to head to the coast there but this had meant only moving under cover of darkness to avoid the constant stream of troops and the never-ending vehicles taking supplies to the Front.

The awful weather and the appalling casualties had halted the action around Ypres and reserves were being rushed up from the coast to reinforce the line. Old "Wipers" had been a familiar area for the soldiers in view of the action there over the years but now the action was centred on a place called Passchendaele. To Wilson it had been a hellhole like all the rest.

Having collapsed when he arrived at this farmhouse, he had slept for what seemed hours and it was light when he had woken. He now recalled that he had started to panic and had just re-orientated himself when this young woman appeared in front of him. He would have run off but, surprisingly, she spoke to him in English, which startled him somewhat. There was hardly a trace of an accent but there was no doubt she was French, or possibly Belgian. He was pretty sure he had crossed the border into France but was not certain where he was exactly but he knew he had made sure he had headed towards the West and away from the Front.

When she found him, he was still wearing his uniform so there was no point in him trying to pretend he was anything but a British soldier. Although he had been somewhat oblivious to what she was saying her voice was gentle. She had helped him to his feet and supported him into the kitchen of this small farmhouse. She had placed him in an old armchair in front of a small fire barely burning in the grate. There was a man in the scullery; he was much older. He busied himself but did not speak to the soldier. Wilson noticed that Marie had had some sharp words with the old man and he took him to be her father. She gave Wilson some bread and a cup of a warm drink, which turned out to be soup of some kind.

She did not ask him for days where he had come from or where he was going. He at first lied about his name; unimaginatively telling her it was Tom Brown. She had provided him with some fresh clothes that had obviously belonged to an older man by their age and cut. He had seen her throwing his uniform on a bonfire at that back of the house. At first he wanted to stop her but realised there was no point – he would not want it again and, in fact, was pleased she made the decision for him.

He had discovered she was a teacher at the local primary school but had spent some years in England when her mother was alive. Her father had worked for the French Government in London but only a menial clerical job. It never became clear how she came to be back living in this somewhat desolate farmhouse and she did not say what had happened to her mother. Her father now lived with her but despite being of working age did not do anything more than potter around the house and grow a few things in the garden and occasionally rear some sheep or pigs and sell them on.

He made no attempt to speak English although Wilson thought he must have been able to do so if he had lived with his family in England and worked there too. He also seemed continually in a state of fear; his hands often shook as if he suffered with his nerves and he had some kind of tick which meant he kept nodding forward all the time. Marie had changed the subject when Wilson asked her about her mother and father, so he had decided to leave the matter alone.

Over the next few days, Wilson poured out his story to the young woman. She in turn told of her struggle to come to terms with the apparent loss of her husband so early in their married life.

Wilson had been happy to spend as much time as he could with her and her father and they seemed in no hurry to get him to leave. It appeared the farmhouse was a long way from any other houses although in the distance they could frequently see a stream of men and materials heading inland along the road about a mile and a half away. There seemed hardly a time when there was nothing on this road – this was a constant reminder to them of the War but it was as though they were cocooned in a different world and another life was just passing them by.

Marie often went into Gravelines to obtain what food she could. She had even managed to get hold of some clothes that fitted him better. With so many local men having been killed there was no shortage of second hand clothes available and she had picked up what she wanted from the school. There was a hut that the school janitor had used to store his equipment and inside was a pile of his clothes. He, like so many others, had perished and someone had dumped his unwanted belongings in the hut.

There had been no visitors to the house apart from an elderly aunt who had stayed for two days at Christmas. This had been the first time that the old man had come out of himself and, helped by a fair amount of wine, had even spoken to Wilson in very accented English. The old aunt had joined in with

36

Marie translating for her. For them all it was not quite the Christmas of the old days before the War but they were making the most of it. On Christmas Eve Marie had told Wilson that she had some news. When the new school term began she was going to teach in Calais. The developments on the battlefields had meant that many of her children had been moved away and the class was down to just two, so the authorities were moving her to a larger school in Calais.

She thought Wilson should go with her although she would leave her father behind for now. Apparently, Marie's uncle was coming over to stay with his brother for a while but in the longer term he would also move to Calais. Marie had been matter of fact ever since Wilson had got there – just as if she took in fleeing soldiers every day! She had often said that if she could just save one life it would somehow help her cope with the loss of her husband. She also suggested that the move to Calais would help Wilson's search for a way back to England. There were too many army people in this area and whilst Calais had its fair share of soldiers it was a much bigger place and finding a boat or something to get across the Channel may well be easier.

Whilst on the farm it was easy to hide her guest from prying questions as they remained isolated from the local village but Calais was a different proposition. Wilson felt he could not learn to speak French well enough to fool anyone. Marie came up with the idea of passing Wilson off as her cousin from the South who had been so severely injured in the neck from shrapnel that his vocal chords had been damaged rendering speech almost impossible and also that he was suffering from shock. He felt this was a bit flimsy but perhaps the locals would accept it or, perhaps, just not bother to get involved. Injured and maimed soldiers were two a penny anyway and another one would make little difference to them.

As the winter months gave way to the spring the young couple's relationship became closer, at no time did Marie pry into his background and go into any reasoning as to why he had run away. They talked for hours of their life prior to the conflict but very little of the past four years or so.

Marie rarely spoke of her husband and Wilson very little of his family but there was a bond between them, at first it was more brother and sister but as time went by there was more tenderness, more closeness, but it never went beyond that. Of course they had talked of Wilson's return to England. Whilst the War was on it was fairly easy to blend into the community but Wilson knew the army would be looking for him and they were unlikely to give up.

Through the summer he spent his time planning his return - he planned the escape route from the town as best he could but how to get across that strip of water back to England was always going to prove difficult. Stealing a boat seemed the only option as there was no way he could negotiate any form of hiring as he could not risk the likelihood of betrayal. How to actually get the boat across the Channel was something that concerned him greatly but he would just have to give it a go.

They planned to meet up in England once the War had ended. Marie felt she would be able to teach in the English schools as she had done before the War and maybe they could rebuild their lives together.

CHAPTER 9

For a moment Wilson was not sure where he was, he had somehow dropped off to sleep after lying awake for hours. The soft light from the September sun filtered through the small window of his cell. At first he could hardly move his legs, as they were so stiff from the hardness of the mattress and the floor but gradually the feeling returned as he stretched the tight muscles, moving about the cell as best he could.

Although his stomach felt very empty, waves of nausea made him retch. Twice he tried to be sick into the bucket but nothing came up either time. All it did was make him breathless and his stomach ached even more with the effort.

He suddenly remembered the soldiers. Were they still outside the cell? He listened for any noise with his ear against the door but could hear nothing. A somewhat pitiful and inquisitive "Hello" had gained no response so he sat back down on the floor. Within a few minutes he heard a voice, moving to the door he could just make out it was French and the man was talking, or more like muttering, to himself.

He recalled the policeman from the night before and called out, "Monsieur?" but there was no response so he tried again. Eventually the Frenchman shuffled to the cell door. "Oui?" he said gruffly and Wilson tried his best with "Ou est les soldats?" There was no reply and Wilson was sure the man had walked away. Within a minute or so he could make out two sets of footsteps one the unmistakable sound of the military boot.

The door opened inwards and Wilson had to step back to avoid being knocked over. The Frenchman held the key and then retreated locking the soldier inside the cell. Wilson recognised him as his captor from the garden. He appeared unarmed and looked somewhat dishevelled and unshaven so he must be one of those who had stayed the night in the police station.

He smiled at Wilson and walked towards the window and peered outside as if he was looking for someone. He turned and said, "Look, stop messing me about I want to hear you say you are Wilson so we can move on and get out of here. Well?"

Wilson hesitated for moment but felt there was little point in keeping up any sort of pretence. "Yeah, I am," he eventually muttered. He turned away as the nausea returned and he retched again into the bucket but as before, nothing came up.

The soldier stepped back slightly startled. "You alright?" Wilson nodded. "You probably need some food, I'll try and get you something." He moved to the door and called out for his mate, Andrews, who after a minute or so returned with the key and opened up letting his Corporal out of the cell.

After about ten minutes Shipley returned with some bread and what looked like raspberry jam plus a cup of something that was steaming hot and clearly not ready yet to be drank. Wilson quickly ate the slightly stale bread having spread on the jam using his finger. The jam tasted unusual and was certainly not raspberry but some form of mixed fruit, he guessed. The drink tasted a bit like tea but also had the distinct taste of the soup from the night before and it did seem to be the same cup that was being used.

Before he could finish the rather odd tasting mix the Captain marched briskly into the room accompanied by another Private. Watkinson was clearly bristling with impatience and apparent annoyance. He pushed out at Wilson with his fingers and Wilson rocked back against the wall.

"Right," said the Officer, "stand to attention Private, I am only going to say this once – I could waste a lot of my time and get one of your old Company over here, taking them away from valuable work at the Front, just so I can confirm that you really are Private Wilson of the East Lancs – or you can continue to mess me about and get me really annoyed…"

"Excuse me Captain," butted in Shipley, "I have established that this is Wilson – he admitted it to me just before you came in."

The Captain removed his hand, which was holding Wilson against the wall, "Oh…right…good." Wilson relaxed and flashed a look at Shipley and saw the resigned smile from the Corporal.

"Now Wilson," the Captain continued, "we have to get you back to some of your people over the border in Belgium and there you will almost certainly face a Court Martial as soon as possible. You do realise that there is every likelihood that you will be shot. You are aware of that, aren't you?" Without waiting for a reaction the Captain continued, " I have got to go back to a village near Calais to deal with another runaway, so, Corporal Shipley, I want you and Private Andrews to take Wilson back to Belgium. It is not going to be easy as the German push has caused a lot of disruption but I have managed to commandeer a lorry for you so we can handcuff Wilson and you will have to make your way as best you can. If you come into the outer office here, Corporal, I will provide you with a map and some directions but there is no certainty that you will be able to take that route due to all the disruption. Is that alright?"

"Yes sir," replied Shipley who glanced at Andrews; the Private looked decidedly miffed that he would have to spend more time on the road and away from the relative comfort of his normal billet.

Wilson was somewhat surprised by the news that he had to return to Belgium he had always thought for some reason that he would be returned to

England for the Court Martial. There had been rumours amongst the troops that justice was meted out fairly swiftly and often by your own Company but it was thought this was just a myth. Apparently not.

The Captain continued, "Right, I want you all outside and Wilson left here to stew for a couple of hours so I can brief you men on the route and we can get some breakfast. The lorry is not here yet and I have to tell you that we have been very lucky to get this as everything is in short supply and it might be taken from us at the last minute if it is thought that the war effort needs it more than we do!"

"What happens if we have to give it up then, sir?" asked Andrews fearing what the answer might be.

"You'll just have to walk, Andrews, or at best get a cart and hope that there is a horse with it!"

Andrews's face was a picture and even Wilson smiled and glanced again at Shipley who smiled back.

"Sir?" asked Andrews, "What sort of distance are we talking of here?"

"Oh, it's about 50 miles as the crow flies so it should take you about a day, provided there are no hold ups or you have to give up the lorry," answered the Officer.

"Right – thanks sir," responded the less than enthusiastic Private.

"Right," continued the Captain, "let's go." He went up to Wilson and looked at him squarely "Private, as I said before I have no time for people like you who run away, letting down your comrades, your King and your Country but what I will say is that what awaits you is likely to be a firing squad – you do realise that don't you?" Before Wilson could respond the Officer continued, "I realise the hell you might have been through at the Front but if we all did what you did the Kaiser and his boys would be in Paris and even London by now. There is one bit of advice I can give you and that is make sure you get someone to represent you, maybe an Officer you know or even someone intelligent from the ranks – it might be your only chance to dodge the firing squad. God help you."

With that he turned on his heal and was gone, the others followed except Shipley who had the key – he, almost sympathetically, half smiled at Wilson and told him he would be back in an hour or so and they would set off.

Wilson returned to his mattress and stretched out on his back staring at the damp ceiling. Slowly but surely he started to shake uncontrollably. First his arms and then his legs. He felt really cold but he was sweating profusely, his hands were all clammy. He felt giddy and nauseous and his stomach seemed to drop. There was this awful feeling in his guts that he was about to soil himself. This went on for over ten minutes and eventually he removed the cover from the foul smelling bucket and took his trousers and pants down and stood above it. The hot, brown, watery liquid poured out of him. Some went in the bucket the rest on the floor.

This shaking and trembling with the subsequent reaction had been a regular occurrence – he would often wake at night like this – it started in the trenches and had continued on and off the whole time he was at Marie's. Sometimes it would just be a sweat but often he would wake up screaming. It always followed the same recurring nightmare. There was these visions of the horror he had witnessed in what had been his brief period in the frontline trenches. He had heard that a lot of the men had suffered from this – he had seen some of them at home following the battles of 1915 and 1916. Some even had been locked away in an old hospital out towards Colne. The stories that came out of there defied belief, if they were true.

Gradually the symptoms began to fade and another wave of tiredness came over him but sleep was still difficult for him and all he could think about were those awful days from a year ago when his life had changed forever.

PART TWO –
FRANCE AND BELGIUM,
OCTOBER 1917

CHAPTER 10

For the umpteenth time Wilson had been sick over the side of the ship or over himself. The old troop carrier had lurched across the water from England for what seemed like hours; jammed full of soldiers most of whom had never been in a boat of this size before and certainly never on a sea as rough as this one. Of Eddie Wilson's unit only Billy Penrose had not succumbed to the seasickness. He just sat in the corner smoking and grinning from ear to ear over the plight of his mates.

For Wilson he imagined this was just the beginning of a nightmare that had been waiting to happen for some months. When the War started he had just signed forms with Burnley Football Club aged 16 and it was his chance at last to live his dream as a professional footballer for his hometown club. He had been with them for a little while and such was their appreciation of his promise that Burnley had taken him with them down to London for the Cup Final at Crystal Palace in 1914. For a lad who had never been any further than Blackpool in his short life this was quite something. To see the match, celebrate the one nil win and spend two nights in a proper hotel and follow this with a charabanc ride through the streets of Burnley at the end of the following week, was something that dreams were made of.

That all seemed a far cry from this nightmare on this pitching ship in the middle of the North Sea, he felt so ill that he thought he might well accept a German bullet there and then just to relieve the misery. Even what he expected in the trenches seemed a more attractive proposition.

In the early part of the war years he had been too young to join up which just suited him fine. He worked anyway on a farm off the Todmorden Road and it was unlikely farm workers were going to be called up, or so he thought. The football in the area as with anywhere else pretty well came to a halt. Many of the players went into the army. Apart from a few friendly matches, he played very little.

As time went on the news from the Front became grimmer and grimmer. So many men Wilson had known from his schooldays, from his football and from his neighbourhood had just not returned or, if they had, it was in a box. Many that had returned had one or more limbs missing or, worse still, blinded by the gas. Some had become different people. Noisy outward-going young men had become withdrawn and some had ended up at the hospital near Colne, their nerves shattered by their experiences.

Eventually the pressure grew to call up all the remaining young men so in early 1917 Wilson went off to Blackburn and signed up for the East Lancs. He spent a reasonably easy few months endlessly sticking his bayonet into pretend

Germans hanging like scarecrows from posts. This was supposed to make him proficient at killing the foe at close quarters but, from what he had heard, most of the regiment had been blasted into pieces by shells in their trenches or buried alive there or drowned in some water-filled shell hole.

It would only be a question of time before his Company went off to join the mayhem and sure enough as the autumn set in there were rumours of a big effort to relieve the pressure around Ypres and push out further across Belgium. Apparent stalemate had existed for so long. Sure enough the call came. Eddie had said goodbye to his family in what turned out to be a very emotional moment for all concerned. Everyone believing that they, in all probability, would not see each other again.

He had made good friends within his Company and, as was the Army's practice, many of those from the same locality had been put together into one Section. Particularly, there was more than a little hero worship for Wilson in view of his having signed for Burnley except, of course, from any of the lads from Blackburn– the archrival – or even from Preston!

With twenty or so in the Section it was difficult to get to know them all but for whatever reason little groups of diverse characters inevitably gravitated together.

There was Alf Penrose who himself had become a bit of hero on account of him being able to take anything the Army threw at him including this diabolical sea trip! There was also Jim Simpson a somewhat timid lad from Nelson who had been picked on by any number of the non-commissioned Officers and, in particular, Sergeant Goddard a very unpleasant person who had made everyone's life an utter misery during training and who had, for some reason, bullied the unfortunate Simpson to something resembling a shambling wreck at times.

Simpson had said, with a hint of the macabre but perhaps with some foresight, that as soon as he got in the trenches he would make himself available for a German sniper just to get away from Goddard's taunting and bullying.

Roly Johnson was a good mate of Wilson's and the Army had spotted his ability by making him the Lance Corporal of the Section. He was such a powerful man with huge forearms and the sort of bloke you would want by your side when the going got tough. Whether that would help in a muddy trench under fire remained to be seen.

Then there was Don Taylor. He knew it all, had been there and done it – or so he said, but no one could quite understand why he had not apparently done anything from 1914 to date despite being one of the eldest at thirty-two, whilst the rest were mostly in their late teens. There was a rumour that he had done time in prison for killing someone in a pub fight – it had apparently been something of an accident but no one felt able to find out from him. He did seem, however, another you would want by your side if the Germans turned up in your trench!

The rest were a mixed bag. Some were youngsters, most too young to fight when the War started. Then there were the older men who had managed to dodge the action until now, probably due to some physical problem or protected occupation. As time went on and the losses continued they, like Wilson, had also received the call.

Well, they all now looked literally "green" thought Wilson to himself, except Penrose of course, as the North Sea continued to take its toll.

Suddenly the pitching eased and through the rain and spray they could make out land and a jetty. So this is France, or is it Belgium, thought Wilson, not that it really mattered. Figures appeared on the jetty ready to secure the boat but such was the swell and the strength of the wind that it was very difficult to steady everything to tie up. Another hour of suffering and then at last they were off and onto dry land – except that it wasn't. The rain continued to lash down and, whilst most were past caring, the inexperienced soldiers were soaked through to their underclothes, with their kit bags equally soaked through so the chance of changing into dry clothes was unlikely.

It was now completely dark and about ten in the evening. The debilitating seasickness had left nearly all of them exceedingly weak and now craving for something to put back into their stomachs.

Sergeant Goddard got them all lined up and loosely standing to attention. "You look a right shower and now you know what being in the Army is really like after spending the last few months sitting around like a group of girls on a Sunday school trip – this lot will sort you out," he said generally pointing in the direction of what was presumably "The Front".

This didn't do much to improve the morale and what he said next was to make it even worse.

"Right boys we have the small matter of a four mile hike to our quarters for the night and when we get there we can have a bite to eat and get some sleep."

There was a collective groan from his men, which made him smile.

What would normally have been a relatively quick march turned into something of a nightmare as what passed as roads were in fact slimy mud tracks and there was no light to guide the column. It seemed a lot more than four miles and took over two hours to reach their billet.

The billet, which most expected or hoped would be a pleasant inn with soft beds and local girls to serve hot food and beers, actually turned out to be a leaky barn in the middle of nowhere with straw for bedding, no proper toilet facility and a pervading smell of cow dung to go with it. As it turned out they were about six miles now from the Front and as Goddard said this was like the Ritz compared with the trenches further on so make the most of it.

As they settled down and tried to dry themselves off and lay their clothes out so they might be dry by the morning, it became clear that it was unlikely there would be any hot drinks and they would have to make do with Scotch Mutton straight out of the tin. Once the food was opened the rats appeared. There had been some scurrying overhead in the lofts and across the rafters for some time and now they put in an appearance. They were bigger than any Wilson had seen before. There had been all sorts of tales coming back home from the Front that the rats there were the size of cats gorging themselves on the flesh of the dead, as they lay rotting in the open.

"Can we shoot them Sarge?" Roly Johnson had asked.

"No you bloody can't," replied Goddard, "You'll need as much ammo as you can carry when you get to the Front so don't go wasting it on a lousy mouse."

"Right, Sarge…. but actually they're rats," someone piped up.

Eventually fitful sleep came to most but Wilson tossed and turned. His head and neck were itching and the snoring from his companions didn't help either. He just could not get out of his mind what lay ahead. He thought there was a good chance he might not live much longer and this was not the sort of place he would choose for his final hours in this world.

Whilst it was still very dark he had woken with a start and realised how cold he was. The rain still poured down outside beating on the roof. He looked around for some added warmth and scooped up as much straw as he could from the floor and the pile in the corner and stuffed it under his tunic and wrapped his cape tighter. From a few feet he could hear some whimpering. It was Jimmy Simpson. As his eyes became attuned to the light Wilson could just make out the youngster's body – it was shaking almost uncontrollably.

"What's up Jimmy – Cold?"

There was silence from the young man.

"Jimmy, what is it?"

"I dunno," and the crying became worse.

"Come on mate, try to look on the bright side."

"What's the point," Jimmy sobbed out, "We're all going to die – this whole thing's just a nightmare and we ain't going to make it home – and I don't want to end up in some shell hole filled with water and drown or get blown to bits or shot in the head."

48

"Jimmy, you're be alright, we'll stick together, you and me, we'll look after each other, come on, cheer up."

"But I'm so cold and I can't stop shaking, my legs are numb and I can't take much more of this cold, I'm freezing." Wilson looked round to make sure the rest were asleep and moved across to Simpson. "Come on let me rub your legs to get the circulation going and warm you up a bit – I am just as cold as you, you know." So the two of them laid there almost in an embrace trying to get some sort of warmth around their bodies. Eventually they both drifted off to sleep.

It was still pretty dark despite it apparently being the morning as Goddard was shouting for them all to get up. "Officer coming – get up and look lively you lot," he boomed.

"Attention!"

"Thank you Sergeant – at ease men." It was Lieutenant Harcross. He was a young man from Chorley only about twenty-two himself. He had been away at University in London when War broke out and immediately joined up. He had been twice wounded in 1916, the second time quite seriously and he had taken some time to recover and he had been sent to help train these new recruits in Blackburn as the final part of his recuperation.

The men respected him and to them he seemed a nice chap. Any Officer who had survived 1916 was quite a hero and there was a rumour that he had picked up a medal during the Somme campaign but he neither wore it nor mentioned it.

"Look men, I'm going to be very frank with you. You all know there has been this big action in Belgium. Now we were to go to a place called Etaples near Dieppe so we could complete your training and get you fully ready for action. However, we are needed here now so we shall have to rely on the training you had back in England. Later today we will move up to the rear of our line and be ready to be moved forward to relieve those in the front line when required – probably in two to three days time. This weather is playing havoc with the movement of all those new troops who arrived yesterday and you must prepare yourselves for the very wet conditions underfoot and keep as dry as you can. Make sure you tie your boots and puttees tight. There is always the chance of getting trench fever or trench foot and all sorts of colds and so on, which are just as likely to inconvenience you as much as the enemy will. So have another hour's rest and then we'll move off – hopefully this bloody rain will have stopped by them. Get some food inside you and make some tea. I'll see you soon."

As he left Simpson turned to Wilson, "Well, that's cheered me up no end" he said very sarcastically "Dead in a couple of days then!"

"Oh shut up Jimmy for Christ's sake."

"He's right you know," said Alf Penrose, "this is not good news – the fact that we are desperately needed at the Front looks like we're being thrown at the Germans like lambs to the slaughter. I hope I'm wrong but this looks like 1916 all over again!"

Whilst Wilson thought Simpson a bit of a weakling and worrying perhaps unnecessarily, he respected Alf Penrose's opinion on most things and perhaps he was right about this current situation.

After a somewhat unusual breakfast of meat and more meat plus some ghastly lukewarm liquid passing itself off as tea, they set off on their next hike to "behind the lines" wherever that might be. The rain had at least relented during a five-hour march but the last part was helped when they were able to get a lift from a truck commandeered by the Lieutenant for his Section for which he got some cheers from the men.

The new billet was much the same as the one from the previous night except that this one had most of its roof missing. Alright if it doesn't rain but the past couple of days had suggested that this was unlikely. True enough at about nine in the evening it started again.

Normally the men would be told to bed down by this time but Sergeant Goddard had at least relented and told them they had until midnight before they had to settle down to sleep – fat chance of any of that though was the general view!

The small group sat in the driest corner of the barn and they had put all their capes across the beams as best they could and this at least offered some extra protection from the elements. Penrose had found some wood and had managed to light a fire and Wilson had taken over the food and drink duties and had at last come up with a better tea brew, which they all now sat quietly drinking. Sergeant Goddard hovered around them yet not feeling comfortable in joining them.

Lance Corporal Roly Johnson was the first to break the silence, "Well this place is a bit far removed from the barracks back home, I must say – and I thought we only stayed in hotels when we were abroad!"

All managed a chuckle except young Jimmy who had really retreated into himself. Wilson had been watching him all-day and noticed the tremor was still there but this appeared to go unnoticed by the others.

Don Taylor had spent the last 10 minutes scratching himself, "Am I the only one who itches all over?" he asked.

"Probably – you manky old sod," responded Penrose.

"Like most people from Preston, you've got fleas!" said Wilson.

Taylor playfully grabbed Wilson round the neck, "Of course footballers from the town of the holders of the Cup are so clean they don't attract fleas," he mocked.

"Lice actually," chipped in Penrose, "not fleas but lice and once you have them it's difficult to get rid of them. The best thing to do is to get a candle, light it and then run the flame up and down the creases of your clothes – it takes hours but it will get rid of them. The alternative is to have the Germans put you out of your misery!"

"Probably the best thing for us," said Jimmy Simpson, "why worry about lice when in a couple of days we'll all be dead anyway."

"Bloody hell Jim – cheer us up why don't you!" Roly added sarcastically.

"Simpson – none of that nonsense," the Sergeant interrupted, "anymore of that talk and you'll be on a charge. Penrose is right using the candle is the best way to get rid of them until we have some repellent. The trouble is we don't have any candles here so you'll just have to scratch away."

By this time, whether they had lice or not, they were all scratching away until Simpson, having rummaged in his bag, came up with a candle. "Here, my Dad sent me this and said it might come in handy one day."

Taylor grabbed it and lit it. For the next hour or so they passed it round working at their seams. The atmosphere warmed up as the fire continued to burn away – those that smoked all pulled out their cigarettes and sat chatting with the two non-smokers in Wilson and Simpson.

Jimmy Simpson had not said a word since he found the candle. He was ashen white, he had hardly eaten all day, he had been outside countless times to the makeshift latrine and the ever present slight shaking remained.

Wilson was by now more than concerned and mentioned it to Sergeant Goddard who for once was more sympathetic than usual but his view was that Simpson would get over it and that it was quite common for many soldiers to be like this ahead of any action. However, Wilson was not so sure, he knew how he felt but there was no way he was likely to act like Jim.

"Right lads," said the Sergeant, "turn in now." Just at that moment there was a kafuffle outside the barn door. The door flew open and in came a medical orderly.

"Hey – come here you lot – I need some help." The poor man was drenched and covered in brown, slimy mud, "I've got to get some badly wounded men out of our lorry and into the dry."

The entire group rushed outside. They felt the cold rain hit them as the wind whipped around the barn entrance. A lorry at a weird angle was stuck

51

firmly in the mud. They could just make out the red cross on the white circle on the side of it. The rear doors were open and some of the Section were already unloading stretchers.

Apparently, as the orderly explained to the Sergeant, the lorry had developed some fault with its gears and it was only able to move in the one low gear at a snail's pace – seeing the billet ahead the driver had pulled over but the wheels had become stuck in a particularly deep area of previously churned mud and the more he tried to move away the deeper the lorry sank into the mire.

Seeing he could not help much, Wilson went back inside the barn to clear some of the mess made by the Section and create some room for the injured men from the lorry. Jimmy Simpson still sat on the floor with his kit – he had not moved. His face was still pale and wan and his eyes were slightly fixed and staring at the floor. "Come on Jimmy, for God's sake give us a bloody hand here," shouted Wilson. Simpson did not move and at this Wilson went over and pulled him to his feet. He put his nose almost to the tip of his friend's. "Look mate there are some blokes here who need your help – we need to make them comfortable and it's time for you to stop feeling sorry for yourself – Right!"

Jimmy nodded, "Sorry Eddie – of course – what shall I do?"

"Get some of those stoves lit so we can give the men a hot drink and then help me prepare some makeshift beds for them, for a start."

It took about fifteen minutes to bring all the stretchers in and settle the men down. The three orderlies busied themselves over their charges watched by a doctor.

As Wilson's Section started to dry off they began to take in the dozen or so patients they had offloaded. One by one the soldiers stopped chattering and turned to look at the sights on the stretchers.

Apparently, these men had been moved down from the front line earlier in the day, some had been rescued from No Man's Land during a lull. Before they got to the dressing station, it had been hit by shells with most of the doctors, nurses and orderlies being killed or wounded. These men were the most seriously injured and needed to be taken a few miles to a station that had better facilities than those at the Front. The torturous journey had begun a couple of hours ago during which time the wounded had endured increasing pain and distress in the appalling conditions.

Two of the injured were clearly dead and the orderlies closed their eyes and covered their faces with the blankets. The rest were swathed in bandages, which were wet and streaked with red where they had bled more recently and black where the blood had dried. Two had their right legs strapped but the telltale green of gangrene had seeped through and another three had their whole faces wrapped in bandages so they had no way of seeing anything. Another had what must have been a gaping stomach wound that seemed to be spurting blood all over the orderly who attended him. Within minutes the orderly slumped back the spouting blood ceased and the blanket was pulled over the soldier's head.

The rest of the injured were in no better shape and the scene was so horrific that Wilson and the rest of the Section just stood there in stunned silence.

For Jimmy Simpson this was all too much, he staggered back to his kit and slumped to the ground his arms trembling and his body shaking. One or two were physically ill near the latrine at the back of the barn and even the solid Penrose was taken aback.

Sergeant Goddard had been called over by the doctor who had asked that the dead be placed outside and put in shallow graves for now and he would make sure they were moved, eventually, for a proper burial. He asked that they just be marked with a cross with their name and number carved on it. He explained to Goddard that each had a nametag attached to their clothing and he could get what he needed to know from there but if he needed more help he should speak with the orderly.

The Sergeant called over towards his men, "Penrose, Wilson and Simpson - Burial party – the three here with their faces covered with blankets need to be buried in a temporary grave out the back." He explained how the graves were to be marked. The orderly came over to Goddard and offered his help and Goddard introduced him to Penrose, who had been told to make sure the men carried out the task properly.

Simpson did not move at first until lifted to his feet again by Wilson. In almost total silence the three youngsters carried out their task, fortunately the rain had stopped and, with the ground being so wet, it was easy to dig down about two feet and slip the bodies in, cover and place the makeshift cross with their names, rank and the date.

When they returned everyone has settled down but the remaining injured soldiers were in some distress – they moaned, groaned and even whimpered as the orderlies flitted between them.

Wilson and Alf Penrose grabbed themselves a cup of tea that Roly Johnson had thoughtfully made. Wilson looked round for Jimmy but he was no longer with them and not sitting with his kit as before. Perhaps he's in the latrine Wilson thought but five minutes later he was still not back. Wilson was now thinking the worst – he excused himself from Roly and Alf saying he needed a pee and went out the back and past the three graves.

As his eyes adjusted to the darkness, he walked round the barn along the path back to the muddy road where the truck still remained. The driver and his mate plus Don Taylor had their heads in the engine trying to effect a repair. Wilson asked Taylor if he had seen Jimmy. "No – why?" had been the reply.

"Oh – it doesn't matter," said Wilson as he walked off down the road. Taylor looked at him for a moment and then returned to his task.

Wilson had gone about fifty yards when he saw his friend leaning against a tree smoking, seemingly casual as you like. "Bloody hell, Jimmy, I was worried about you," he said with relief.

But before he had got the words out Jimmy's expression had changed, the cigarette had dropped to the wet ground and he had his rifle raised. Wilson instinctively ducked and cowered back a few paces. "Christ, Jim what the hell are you doing," he said.

"You saw them back there – no bloody chance, have they? – And they're the ones that are alive – I'm not going to where they've come from – if I'm going to die I'm going to do it right here." With this he lifted the rifle to his head but Wilson moved quickly towards him anticipating what his friend was about to do as Jimmy shouted, "Mum – please forgive me, I ..." but with this Wilson pushed him at the same time as the rifle went off, both fell to the ground. Wilson was up in an instant but Jimmy had rolled face down into the wet grass under the tree. Wilson turned him over and baulked at what he saw; a small part of the right side of Jimmy's head appeared to have gone and there were pieces of hair, flesh and bone hanging down from the gaping wound. But, somehow Jimmy was still alive with bubbly blood coming from his mouth.

Having heard the shot Taylor and the other two who had been working on the engine arrived, closely followed by Sergeant Goddard who quickly took charge, "Bloody hell, Wilson, what in God's name has happened here?"

"He's shot himself, Sarge, I tried to stop him but the gun went off – it's caught him a glancing blow but he's still alive – let's get him to the doctor." Goddard grabbed a handkerchief from his top pocket and held it against the wound holding back what had been hanging down.

An hour later, with the lorry now back in action and pulled from the mud, the remaining patients were loaded up and gone. Wilson had remained with the doctor for a while as he attended Simpson but eventually he had gone to sleep almost on his feet. He slept through the departure of the wounded and the medical staff. On waking he enquired of Simpson; Goddard told him that Jimmy had gone off in the lorry. No one saw him again.

PART 3 –
BEHIND THE FRONT LINE AT
PASSCHENDAELE, BELGIUM
OCTOBER 1917

CHAPTER 11

Following the Jimmy Simpson incident, the Section had moved on the next morning, joining up with the rest of the Platoon and then into the Company before marching into what was mostly a tented encampment someway behind the trenches.

Simpson's apparent attempt to end it all, and maybe by now he had been successful for all the men knew, had severely affected his friends and none more so than Wilson. So much so that Roly Johnson had spent the whole time on the march to this camp trying to talk Wilson round. Even Sergeant Goddard had surprisingly shown sympathy with some words of encouragement.

Wilson had felt fairly miserable all day and could not but help thinking that he could have done more to save his friend and even began believing that maybe if he had not gone for him he might not have pulled the trigger and had only been bluffing. Perhaps his grab for him had actually made it worse and, if he had left Simpson alone, he would still be alright.

He had shared his concern with Johnson who laughed it off and told him he was a hero for trying to prevent it. He should not worry about what he might or should have done.

Although Johnson's support and that of the others comforted Wilson, he felt really depressed. He also recalled the sight of the injured soldiers that they had comforted the night before in the barn. He felt that Jimmy was right in that he'd rather have a bullet or shell to end it all than suffer like those poor souls who, even if they survived, would probably have no life when they got home.

His mood was not helped by the sounds they could now pick up from the Front away to the East. When they arrived at the camp the wind had been light but now it had grown stronger and had changed its direction and the explosions and sporadic gunfire could be more clearly heard. There was also this peculiar smell – it was like the bonfires from home but yet there was something else –sort of sweet and sickly. The old lag Don Taylor had said it was the smell of the dead wafting out of the trenches and from No Man's Land because no one had time to bury the dead and they were just left rotting where they had died.

All sorts of stories were rife in the camp about the conditions a few miles up the line to the Front. Each story struck poor Wilson another depressing blow. He couldn't bring himself to eat very much because, when he did, it went straight through him.

He also noticed that his hands were a bit shaky, just like Jimmy's had been.

Later in the day he had made a big effort to get himself out of his mood when the lads from the Platoon organised an impromptu football match behind the mess tent. Some knew he had been at Burnley and were keen to see what he was like. The group split into two teams – North v South although there were hardly any who came from further South than Birmingham and they seemed, in the end, to split into North and South of Manchester!

Even this failed to lift Wilson's mood although for a while he felt more like his old self as he showed his undoubted footballing skills in the match. The relief to the men was short-lived as Lieutenant Harcross had arrived with Captain Strudwick and wanted to see the whole Company immediately.

"Right fall in you lot – Attention!" roared Sergeant Goddard. The men obediently gathered in front of him as the two Officers moved alongside.

"At-ease men," said the Captain who looked even younger than the Lieutenant. No one knew much about the Captain but it was thought that he had less experience than the more junior Officer, which had seemed odd to the men. However, perhaps this was due to the Lieutenant's serious wound at the Somme and then being away from the action for such a long time.

The Captain continued, "Lieutenant Harcross has told you of the plan to move us up to the front line to support the push and I can now give you some more information and some orders I want you to follow."

He went on to explain that they would be part of the 197th Brigade and be moved up the day after tomorrow when there would be a sustained attack with the Brigade made up from a mixture of the East Lancs and West Riding regiments. It was intended that it would all start at about five a.m. when it was still dark and he would give final instructions the night before.

However, in the mean time there were some general points he wished them to bear in mind. The terrain from here to the Front is swampy and covered with water filled shell holes. Duckboards have been laid for most of the way up but some have been washed away and the ground everywhere is extremely slippery. Under no circumstances was the movement up to the Front to stop. Should anyone fall into the shell holes, do not stop to help the man in the hole, just move on. If anyone does fall in, God help them was the only advice he could give; so be careful was his message and he suggested that they try to get as much of their kit off as possible in the event of them being in water. He advised that they should do everything possible to get out as fast as they could, reminding them that no one was going to stop and help, so they were wasting their time and energy by shouting. He went on to explain how he had seen men use their bayonets to lever themselves out by pushing the bayonet into the side of the hole.

Once clear they should retrieve their kit as best they could and catch up with the rest.

He warned that if anyone gets injured they were to stay where they were, use their own field dressing and wait for help. Under no circumstances were the others to stop and help their mate because they must keep going. If they get split up then join another Section or any group.

"Not any from Yorkshire though," some wag had muttered, at which even the Captain had smiled.

He advised them all to write letters home, as it might be some time before they get another chance, "Or we might be dead," whispered Don Taylor.

The Captain told everyone to get some rest for the next twenty-four hours and then be ready early tomorrow afternoon for the move up to the starting off point for the planned attack.

Wilson's mood became even worse and his visits to the latrine continued but less often. Many of the others were now suffering the same problems. Roly Johnson and Alf Penrose tried to get him to eat and Alf even offered him some of his tasty birthday cake that he had been saving but Wilson refused. He could not even bring himself to write home. He had sent a letter to his parents and younger sister just a week ago and did not feel like making them happy to receive another only to get the dreaded telegram a few days later. He thought of his mate, Jimmy Simpson, and wondered if the lad's Mother had yet received that telegram or maybe Jimmy was on his way home to her, but somehow he doubted it.

He tried to lighten his mood by thinking of the good times he had had in his teenage years. Football had been great for him and he smiled as he thought of the girls he had known during those few years. He remembered how they had indulged in all sorts of fumblings in the park or down by the river but he had never actually "done it".

He thought he might get a chance to change that when he got over to France, or wherever, as stories were rife back at training camp about the availability of some local women who, it was said, were of easy virtue. However, the lecture from the MO back at barracks in England had rather put him off the whole idea. The MO had pointed out that more soldiers had died this year from some disease caused by having sex with the local girls than from a German bayonet! He was not sure if that was true but it was a bit of a sobering thought.

Roly Johnson was becoming concerned about his friend's change of character. He tried to get him to organise another football match - perhaps we could get a Burnley side up to play a mixture of Blackburn and Preston, he had suggested. For a moment Wilson was interested as he remembered the rivalry between these clubs so close together down the Ribble valley but in the end, he just could not be bothered.

He returned to his tent and tried to sleep. Every time he closed his eyes he could see Jimmy Simpson's head wound with flesh and bone hanging from it or the faces of the terribly injured soldiers' at the barn. He could not begin to believe the hell those soldiers must have seen and his mind wandered as he tried to imagine what it was all likely to look like as they moved forward. Would he ever see a German or would he just drown in a shell hole or would a shell blow him apart? He shivered. He felt like some air so he opened the tent flap – the rain had started again and he slumped into the tent and onto his back. He shivered again and felt cold right through his body – he felt so miserable that he just curled up and tried to blank out the world outside.

CHAPTER 12

Penrose, Taylor, Johnson and Wilson were all in the one tent – Roly Johnson choosing to be with them although, as a Lance Corporal, he could have been sharing with other NCOs. Two lads from Colne, both just 18, who had barely completed the most basic of training back in England, joined them. The first was Gerry Mitchell who was a little backward and had spent some years away at a Home, as he was one of eleven children and, when his father died, the three eldest had to been placed in this Home to try to help their struggling mother. Without proper schooling for a period of time and having left school at twelve he was hardly able to read or write and was far from being wise to the world. His friend Jack Horsfield was a much brighter lad who had worked, like Gerry, in the mills around Nelson and Colne. Jack, as it turned out, was an adept pilferer who, it is rumoured, was an expert pickpocket. He apparently had never experienced the long arm of the Law and had proudly owned up to being a modern day Robin Hood by only stealing from those who he thought could afford it but never from anyone he knew.

The two lads did lift the mood as the rest brooded over Simpson and the past few days but they all remained worried by what lay ahead. Gerry and Jack could not give a damn – this to them was an adventure – they had rarely been outside their own town with a visit to the coast near Southport just about the best they had had. This tent was almost an improvement on where they lived and even the latrines were better than the buckets they had to use at home. They had never eaten so well in their lives and the fact that they might be blown to kingdom come in the next day or so did not appear to worry them one little bit.

All except these two youngsters slept fitfully and, taking the Captain's advice, did little the next day. Wilson remained in the tent on his own just laying there staring at the roof. The rain continued to fall outside but it was reasonably mild. Despite this, Wilson's body still shook and he felt cold. He had put on his jacket and added his greatcoat for extra warmth but the shaking didn't go away. The lice had returned and were a constant irritation.

Roly Johnson had organised the digging of a narrow trench about six inches deep round the tent to stop any chance of flooding as a nearby ditch was threatening to come over its small bank and flood the area where they had pitched the tent. He had excused Wilson explaining to the others that Wilson was feeling like he had a chill. Don Taylor in his inimitable way remarked that Wilson might as well come out in this rain and catch his death of cold, as he'll probably die tomorrow anyway. Taylor had laughed uproariously at his own joke but none of his mates joined in and Johnson felt it necessary to rebuke Taylor on this occasion threatening him with being reported to the Officers and being put on a charge if he continued with such stupid comments.

Just before it got dark Captain Strudwick and the Lieutenant arrived to give them some final instructions before they all turned in for the night. As it happened, it was little more than a pep talk providing some encouragement, wishing them good luck and reminding them of the discipline expected from them.

The Captain explained that despite the appalling weather we had managed to push the Germans back in this sector creating a bulge in the Front to the north of Ypres and the Generals wanted the line straightened out along about ten miles of the Front. Apparently the Germans had brought up a fresh force near Passchendaele in the past few days and the four British brigades would push towards them – the going would be tough and, with the Germans holding the ridge near Passchendaele, they had the advantage in that this gave them a full view of their attackers below and a clear field of fire.

The Captain reminded the men that the Chaplain would be here for about an hour from seven that evening and if anyone wanted a chat with him they could see him then. They would probably now move off at about eight when it was fully dark to avoid any artillery attack. They would then be in position for the jumping-off point at the scheduled five o'clock in the morning. He added that this should give them the chance to get about four hour's rest before hand and he reminded them of the importance to try and sleep as there would be little chance of this in the next day or so.

Wilson toyed with the idea of seeing the Chaplain but really could not be bothered to raise the effort so he remained huddled under his greatcoat. The two lads from Colne also decided their sleep was more important than the minister but the other three had a brief chat with him before they, too, turned in to get some rest.

After about three hours of fitful sleep, the men got up and opened some cans of food, mostly meat. They were nearly all still suffering from the after effects of their seasickness on the boat. However, all but Wilson managed to get some food inside them. All Wilson had was a cup of tea along with the rest of the men. Penrose gave him a snifter from a little bottle he always had with him. Wilson coughed and gasped as the strong spirit went down his throat. He had no idea what sort it was but it did warm him up a little and he felt better for it.

Lieutenant Harcross was to lead them up to the Front supported by Roly Johnson at the head of their column with Sergeant Goddard at the rear to encourage any stragglers. Before Harcross briefed Goddard and Johnson more fully he kindly dished out some chocolate his mother had sent and he had saved for just this moment. Alf Penrose gave them all a sip of his spirit.

Just after eight they set off. They joined the stream of men from the East Lancs and West Riding regiments who were to form two of the prongs of the four-pronged attack up the ridge.

Whilst it was a sensible idea to move under cover of darkness under normal conditions, in order to avoid being shelled or even picked off by a sniper, the terrain they were about to encounter was treacherous in daylight let alone in the middle of the night! At first the going was quite easy, the rain relenting a little but still drizzling enough to make it feel unpleasant, until suddenly the whole of the ground underfoot became deeply rutted, thick mud, which at times came right up to the men's knees. Many became stuck and had to be heaved out by their mates – it was decided the lightest should share the task of carrying the Lewis Gun on the basis that if he became stuck or fell in a shell hole it might be easier to get him and the vital gun out! The Officers had long championed the importance of the Lewis Gun during their training and the men all thought it might be more useful to them than a rifle and bayonet. So, Gerry Mitchell at about nine and a half stone was given the 25lb gun to carry at the start. Despite the theory of the lightest being best suited to the task, the decision was soon changed, as Mitchell had no strength to carry this as well as his own kit. The much more robust Alf Penrose took over.

Occasionally flares went up from both sides at the Front ahead of them and even this far back the landscape became clearly visible for a few seconds at least. The first time this happened the men stopped in their tracks and stared open mouthed at the sight before them. There were trees but all that was left were the trunks and oddly shaped shattered branches decimated by shells and gunfire. Beneath them were a series of muddy mounds interspersed with foul looking water with all sorts of debris floating in it. There was still that sweet sickly smell again even though the rain fell and there was no wind. Penrose reckoned it was the lingering smell of gas and perhaps they should put their masks on. He mentioned this to the Lance Corporal who went up close to the Lieutenant and asked what he thought.

"No, Corporal, it's not gas it's the smell of war and you'll all get used to it in time."

Johnson shrugged and went back and told the men as they walked forward.

Wilson had hardly spoken to anyone to start with – he felt so shaky that his legs would hardly move for him and the mud didn't help. His stomach churned constantly. He was soaked to the skin; not so much from the rain, which had eased, but from the sweat under the several layers of clothing and the exertion of carrying his pack, with the ammunition for the Lewis adding to his load.

He had developed an irritating cough, which added to his woes and the wretched lice were starting to make his body itch all over, making him feel even more uncomfortable. There was tightness across his chest from the tension of it all, as he struggled through the slimy mud slipping from one side of the narrow track to the other.

He tried to take his mind off all this by again thinking back to before the War started. He thought of that wonderful time when he had travelled down to London with the Burnley team for the 1914 Cup Final against Liverpool at Crystal Palace. He was never going to be in the team but he was invited to be there, the ride down was exciting with thousands of Burnley fans cheering them on. They stayed in a posh hotel – he had never been into a big, proper hotel before just the Sparrow Hawk in Burnley from time to time to have a drink. Following the one-nil win they had a most wonderful evening in London. The end of it, though, had all become a bit of a blur for him at the time as they drank themselves to a standstill. However, he could recall the procession around Burnley parading the cup when the whole of the town seemed to have turned out to salute their heroes.

For a while these thoughts cheered him up a bit but just at that moment a randomly fired artillery shell fell about fifty yards to their right. They all instinctively ducked down but young Mitchell in front of him slipped back and knocked Wilson over into the mud. Wilson swore at him but realised that Horsfield, who was further in front, had in fact, slipped badly himself and in turn knocked down the lad and Alf Penrose with the main section of the Lewis Gun.

As Wilson picked himself up he realised that Mitchell had disappeared, initially he thought he might have done a Simpson and run away but suddenly there was a gargled shout in the darkness to his right – it was Mitchell, he had slipped into the water filled shell hole and was desperately shouting for help. Wilson called to the rest of the Section and Horsfield and Roly Johnson came back, "Can he swim?" Johnson asked. "I bloody hope so!" was Horsfield's reply.

Almost at once the Lieutenant arrived and knelt down next to the men who were leaning into the shell hole. Seeing what had happened the Officer said, "You know what the orders are – we're to leave him here – if he can swim like you say then he'll get himself out."

"Sorry sir but not with that pack on him he won't he's only a slight lad and he's got no strength really," answered back Johnson somewhat angrily.

"I'm sorry Johnson but we must move on we are already a long way behind schedule and this will make it worse plus that artillery shell came from the German lines and if they send out another it might be closer."

Wilson looked at Johnson who shrugged as if to say what more can I do. Horsfield, already removing his pack and putting down his rifle, screamed out to his friend, "Hang on Gerry, I'm coming in after you." He disappeared into the hole and the men heard the splash as he went in. Mitchell was still flapping around calling for help but it was difficult to see them in the murk.

"Bloody fool," said the Lieutenant as he squinted in an attempt to see exactly what was happening.

"We can't leave them both now sir, surely?" said Penrose who had now arrived still holding the other part of the Lewis Gun.

"Right," said the Officer, "let's see if we can pull them out!"

They all lay in the mud calling out for the two youngsters to grab their hands. There was a lot of spluttering from the water and at last Wilson got hold of a slippery hand. He managed to grab the wrist with his other hand and gradually started to pull. He thought this was easier than he imagined it was going to be and suddenly the body came out of the water with a rush. There was an arm, a shoulder, a head, another shoulder, another arm and that was it! Wilson looked down in total shock for what he had grabbed was what was left of a body. The shoulder markings had an Anzac insignia and that was about all that was left of the uniform.

He recoiled and dropped the remains back into the water. He retched several times and was leaning over the side of the shell hole. Penrose pulled him clear and told him to pull himself together and to wait behind them, out of their way.

There was still shouting from the left and someone was being pulled from the water – he stood up and could just make out Mitchell – he was coughing up the brown water and could hardly stand. He shouted, "Where's Jack, he pushed me up out of there so I could grab Roly?"

Johnson and Penrose looked at each other as if trying to decide what to do. The Lieutenant pushed past them and Wilson followed. They both got on their stomachs and leant over the side of the hole. The other two immediately got hold of their ankles to make sure they did not slither in.

Soldiers passed by them on their way up to the line as if they weren't there. It became eerily quiet; there had been no further shelling just the occasional flare lighting up the sky but some way from them.

Lieutenant Harcross swished around in the water for some few minutes and Wilson and Penrose moved further round the hole so Wilson could try a different part of the water. Penrose held his legs again. Wilson felt something and told Penrose to hold his legs tighter and higher up so he could reach further down into the hole. He leaned over a little more and pulled at the hand. With some effort and with the Lieutenant joining in they pulled the body onto the mud above the hole. It was, indeed, Horsfield and his eyes were gazing upward but totally lifeless. Mitchell stood there in total shock with his hands almost covering his face, his uniform dripping wet from his time in the water. "Oh my God, Oh my God! Is he dead?"

No one answered and the Lieutenant turned over the limp body but put the head to one side. He pumped the body's back. He had been shown how to do this during training, the idea being to get the water out of the lungs and get Horsfield breathing again. He kept this up for at least two minutes.

"It's not working, let me have a go, like this," shouted Wilson. He turned the body over and opened the mouth and put his over the top of it and pumped air in. Then he turned the body onto its front and pumped the back. Still nothing happened. He kept it up for at least five minutes. The rest of the men had all stood up except for Wilson and Horsfield's limp body. Eventually the Lieutenant got hold of Wilson's shoulder and pulled him away. "Come on Wilson, there's nothing more we can do, we've done all we can, let him rest in peace."

Wilson was on his knees and came back a yard or so. Horsfield was on his back, his eyes still staring as if watching the stars. The Lieutenant leant over and shut the eyes. He tapped Wilson on the shoulder as if to say well done. Penrose lifted him to his feet and patted him on the back.

They all stood there for a brief moment and then the Lieutenant said, "I'm sorry men but I have no choice but to do this, we can't take the body with us and we can't leave him lying here so people trip over him." With that he let go of the body and it slithered back into the watery grave. "We must move on, I'm sorry."

With that they all moved off except young Mitchell he just stood there with his hands still covering most of his face, as if in a state of shock. Someone had lent him another greatcoat to keep him warm. Johnson went back, put his arm on his shoulder, pushed the young man's rifle into his hand and eased the lad forward towards the others as they moved along the duckboards. He had to keep his hand firmly in the lad's back as he stumbled forward. Every yard or so Mitchell half turned, looking back. A tear fell down his face and made odd rivulets through the mud that was caked on there.

Eventually he stopped completely but Johnson urged him forward with a push and said, "Come on son, you'll be alright." The young man looked at him and pushed the older man's hands away. He looked over Johnson's shoulder and back down the track to the shell hole. All he could make out in the darkness were men coming towards him. They pushed past him, moaning at him for blocking the way.

He gave them a foul-mouthed volley and then trudged off with Johnson to catch up with the other men of the Section.

The Lieutenant and the other men eventually pulled over to one side and waited for Johnson and Mitchell to catch up.

They all moved off, slipping and slithering along, now more mindful than ever before of the dangers of slipping off the duckboards and into the shell holes. Wilson now felt that his legs were like jelly, his arms really ached and he was shaking with the cold. He looked at his uniform; it was caked in mud, as were the other men's where they had earlier laid in the slimy mud around the hole.

He thought of Simpson. Now it's young Jack that's gone. He had known both for such a short time but in that time he had really got on well with them both. Two gone already and they're not even at the Front yet. Better get used to this he thought to himself, this is just the beginning of the nightmare. How many more of these men around him would perish in the days to come? What about himself, how long would he last? He remained miles away with his thoughts when suddenly Captain Strudwick was by his side.

"Wilson, what do you know about Private Horsfield? I shall have to write a letter to his mother and father when I get time and I didn't want to bother Mitchell as he seems in a state of shock at present."

"Well, I don't know him very well, sir, he was from Colne and I think his father was dead and he lived at home with his mother but you really should ask Mitchell as he and Jack grew up together, I'm sorry I can't help more."

"Never mind – thanks. Well done, by the way, back there, I've heard about it from Lieutenant Harcross – you did a good job. How did you know about this mouth to mouth to try to get him to breathe?"

"Oh, I saw it once on the beach at Blackpool. A youngster got into difficulties and someone did it to him and got him breathing. Sir, just before you go – how are we getting on - will we soon be there? You know, where we stop before we finally move up into action."

"Unfortunately, we are way behind our schedule – the set off point is a long way off and this mud has slowed us more than anyone had allowed for –

at this rate we will miss the push off along with hundreds of others. If only the rain would stop but it actually seems to be getting worse plus the Germans are going to suspect something is happening and before long we will be well within range of their shells and that's going to slow our progress even more. Anyway, chin up Wilson – I've got to get up ahead now so I'll speak to you later."

What a bloody farce Wilson thought – don't we ever learn! Almost on cue there was an explosion not more that twenty five yards to Wilson's right, it threw him off balance and down again into the mud to the side of the boards. The flash of the exploding shell lit up all around and Wilson could see hundreds of half-crouching men scurrying around a mass of water filled shell holes. Bits of mud and the odd piece of shrapnel had dropped all around him but he was fine. He stood up and decided to move away as quickly as possible in case there was a similar burst. Another flash went up further still to his right and he got another glimpse of the men moving off, silhouetted against the horizon. Many, however, remained face down in the mud, motionless. Some medical people, who just happened to be in that part of the column, were already bending over some of them and moving from one body to another trying to see if there were any signs of life. It appeared there was none. Wilson saw the medics move off as the darkness returned.

Of his own group, no one had moved at first. Suddenly, he could hear Lieutenant Harcross's voice urging everyone to move up to join him. Shells now dropped ahead of them and to both sides, each time there was an explosion all the men dived onto their stomachs apart from the Lieutenant and the Captain. Suddenly there was a huge explosion in front of the Officers, there was a scream from the Lieutenant and he fell and rolled onto his back – again the scene was lit up by other shells exploding above their heads throwing shrapnel in all directions.

Wilson was first to the man's side and could see the painful grimace on his face.

"Are you hit sir, what is it?"

"It's my shoulder – bloody hell – right on the end!"

Wilson felt down and could feel something warm against his cold hand – it must be blood he thought and he tried to make out where it was coming from. "Shit!" he said and jumped up taking a few steps back.

"Get down you silly arse," yelled Sergeant Goddard behind him. Wilson turned with a look of horror on his face but fell to his knees over the Officer. He put his hand down on to the Lieutenant again – there was no arm on the right side – there were just bits of torn uniform, some shredded bone, the oozing blood and a little stump of the collarbone.

"Sergeant, come up here the Lieutenant's badly hurt." With this the Sergeant was at his side and Wilson pointed to the shoulder. "Christ," said Goddard, "Where's the Captain?"

"He's gone," answered Wilson.

"What do you mean gone?"

"Well he was in front of Lieutenant Harcross and there was this explosion and I dived down and when I looked up the Lieutenant was injured and shouting and Captain Strudwick had disappeared."

With this the Sergeant shouted to Lance Corporal Johnson to get some medical help adding that there was a medical orderly somewhere just behind them and perhaps he could help the Officer. With this Johnson disappeared back along the muddy track. He returned about ten minutes later with two orderlies. In the mean time the group had tried to help the Lieutenant but he had now slipped into unconsciousness. Wilson, Taylor and Johnson were trying to stem the flow of blood and Goddard was trying to cover the Officer to keep him dry.

At least the shelling had stopped but the rain had started to come down heavily again and this was not going to be much help. Goddard had sent Penrose and Mitchell ahead to see if they could find the Captain.

Whilst they were stopped there, men continued to squeeze past them, all stopped momentarily and glanced down and then moved on. Wilson noticed that none of them was from the East Lancs and most seemed to be Aussies or New Zealanders. "What a mess," he thought.

Without the shelling to light up everything, the whole area was in darkness again; there was a lot of shouting all around and clearly not only the Lieutenant had been hit.

After about fifteen minutes Penrose and Mitchell returned – the young lad who had lost his friend earlier looked just like a zombie – his eyes were staring blankly and he was as white as a sheet. "Where's the Sarge?" shouted Penrose.

"Over here," shouted back Goddard, "did you find him?"

Penrose dropped to his side and whispered, "No Sarge – but I found this." He produced a holster with a gun in it. "This was the Captain's, Sarge," he added, "because the holster had this distinctive mark on it," he said pointing to some kind of emblem near the buckle. "There's worse, Sarge – there was blood and bits of body everywhere around this but no sign of the Captain."

"Bloody hell," was all the Sergeant could muster. The whole group sat looking at each other. Eventually, Goddard spoke to the orderlies, "You'll have to take the Lieutenant down the line as quickly as possible and we'll have to move on and find another Officer to tell us where the hell we're going."

"Don't you mean the hell we are going to Sarge?" moaned Wilson. No one smiled and they moved off and rejoined the duckboards, or what remained of them, with the orderlies going off in the opposite direction with the Lieutenant on a stretcher. The rain was now absolutely lashing down and straight into their faces. The wind had also become very strong and they all leant forward bracing themselves as they moved ahead.

Wilson was at Goddard's side and turned to him, "Sarge, the Captain told me that we were already behind schedule and were running late for the push off time in the morning."

"Might not be a bad thing – the whole thing's another cock up already as far as I can see!"

Roly Johnson caught them up, "Sarge, look over there, it's a group of what looks like West Riding and there's an Officer with them, as well."

"You're right," and with that Goddard moved round the back of the shell hole to his right and the men followed.

True enough they were a small group from the West Riding's. The Officer introduced himself as Captain Kennedy and Goddard explained what had happened to the unit and that they had lost contact with the other Sections and had only seen ANZACS for the last half an hour or so.

"Well," said the Captain, "I did get information that a large stream ahead has burst its banks and we cannot get across it in this sector – it is too dangerous to move over to another sector as the last bout of shelling has made so many shell holes that there are no duckboards and no proper paths. So, we shall have to wait for some light in the morning so we can make our way forward. For now we are going to have to stay here and dig ourselves in just in case there is more shelling."

"Won't we miss the jump off though sir?" said Sergeant Goddard, "our Officer told us it was likely to be touch and go whether we got there and so now there is no chance; weren't we supposed to go about five in the morning?"

"Yes, Sergeant, that was the plan but there is no point going on in this," he said with a wave of his arm. "We have had a lot of casualties already – so let's dig in for the night – have a word with my Sergeant here and get the men to dig a short trench to protect themselves and tell them to try to get some sleep but I would have thought the chances of that are a bit slim, Sergeant."

"Right sir," and with that Goddard explained the plan to his group and introduced himself to Kennedy's Sergeant.

For the next half an hour or so the rain got even heavier and as the men were digging the trench so it was fast filling up with water. There was so little room to extend the trench too far to the right or left because of the shell holes. In the end they had enough of a slit in the ground to get into and they dug into the side so they might get something over their heads to protect themselves from the heavy rain.

The men took the opportunity to have something to eat from their ration cans but the rain made the meat and pieces of cake so runny that it was like lumpy soup. There was no chance of a hot drink and those men that could not dig into the side of the trench had to crouch with their helmeted heads tucked well into their capes as the rain ran down them into the bottom of the trench.

After about two hours the water was almost up to their knees – they had given up trying to bale out the water as a lost cause that was far too tiring anyway. None of them could feel anything in their feet and legs with the cold water and as the dawn approached the temperature had dropped and the water around them had a thin covering of ice. One or two were coughing and sneezing and all were shivering with the cold. The rain had relented a little to a drizzle but the cold wind remained strong and cut right into their already freezing bodies.

At what must have been about four, Wilson had nodded off and he suddenly woke with a start, as there was shouting to his left. Young Mitchell had been at the left end of the trench. Lance Corporal Johnson had made a routine check on the men and he had come across Mitchell apparently asleep but with his cape partly over his face, presumably to protect himself from the rain. As Johnson had moved the cape down, the young man slithered down the bank of the trench on which he was leaning and fell face down into the water at his feet. Roly Johnson pulled him up and was about to admonish him but realised the lad was dead and had been for sometime by the look of him. He then noticed the rifle seemingly stuck to Mitchell's chest. He pulled it away and recoiled. The bayonet was attached and was stuck deep into the chest. As it came out he saw it was covered in blood.

When Johnson had shouted over to the Captain, the group including Wilson had woken up. They all stared in disbelief at Gerry Mitchell. What could have happened they thought to themselves; had he just collapsed or gone to sleep and accidentally fallen onto the bayonet or had it been deliberate?

Captain Kennedy knew there was no time to really find out and dwell on the matter. Wilson and Penrose were told by him to go and place Mitchell over to the right at the other end of the trench and stick his rifle upside down next to him so the burial detail coming up from behind would sort it out. Wilson found a piece of wood from a fallen branch and carved Mitchell's name using his bayonet and placed the wood as a marker next to the rifle.

The Captain made a note of Mitchell's name in the little green book he carried with him. It was difficult as the pages were wet and he only had a pencil. He thought to himself that let's hope he lives to be able to pass the information on!

Once they had completed their task, Wilson helped Alf Penrose clean the Lewis Gun. They had been told during training that it was such an important

71

weapon that it was important to keep it clean, as it did have tendency to jam in damp and muddy conditions with the occasional feed blockage. This passed through Wilson's mind as they tried to clean it up – the conditions here would certainly put it to the test!

There was a lightening of the sky as dawn approached but it still remained fairly dark with full cloud cover with the drizzle now a little heavier than before.

Wilson kept lifting his feet and stamping them to try to get some circulation going but it was really a waste of time. He and the others were all shivering and shaking with the cold and not a little from the anxiety as a result of what they had already been through and the thought of what lie ahead. He did manage to eat some more rations and thought that this was the first time he had fancied something for quite a while. The resourceful Don Taylor had managed to get one of the little fires going and was attempting to brew some tea. He thought back again to the injured Simpson – was he dead or not – if he was alive what sort of life was he going to get if he survived – not much of one probably. Then there was the drowning Horsfield and those eyes, followed by the limp body of the young Mitchell – his slight frame seemingly frozen stiff. How was the Lieutenant he wondered –would he bleed to death or would the medical people manage to save him? How do you cope without an arm? Then the Captain – blown to kingdom come it seems – what a waste, he thought to himself.

He could now see across the wasteland around him and as far as the eye could see there were men in makeshift shallow trenches or on the sides of the drier shell holes. Further to the left and right where the so called stream had cut off the advancing troops there were lines of men able to move forward. As he watched there were explosions further in the direction that they were going. He could hear the shells passing overhead from his own artillery and someway in front he could hear the explosions as they reached the German lines.

Taylor produced his tea, which looked more like the water they were standing in but didn't taste that bad. Wilson's abdominal pains had eased a little with the food and the tea but he now felt like he needed to empty his bowels. He looked around and all he could see were the men in the small trenches or holes. There were no trees or bushes for cover and he would be in full view of everyone if he went. He decided that he would just have to hold on for now and if the worst happened he would just have to dirty himself and be done with it.

The tea did warm him inside but with the rain still falling and the trench water still rising, his legs and feet were still so cold. However, he had noticed a slight tingling in his right foot, which felt strange, as the foot seemed frozen solid. He thought it might be cramp, as his calves did feel a little tight, so he flexed the foot as best he could up and down and stamped even harder to get the circulation going again. He guessed he was wasting his time and thought to himself how nice it would be to get away from here and out of this damned misery.

Captain Kennedy came over and spoke with Sergeant Goddard and they then called over Roly Johnson. Something was about to happen Wilson thought. Kennedy left and the Sergeant and Lance Corporal called the men together. There was about sixteen of them left from the original Section that had landed a few days before. Goddard told his men that they would now be moving forward but that they would miss the push off time in view of the delays. Apparently, the push would start as soon as the present artillery barrage came to an end. The Section would have to move a couple of hundred yards to the right to get round the flooding caused by the stream. They would stay with the West Ridings and then try and link up with the East Lancs in the trenches behind the frontline and they would join the second or third wave of attack. It was likely the Germans would start shelling in the next few minutes once they suspected an imminent attack and they tended to concentrate on the areas behind the front line to prevent the support troops and supplies moving forward. Goddard went on to explain that they would move forward in single file with him leading and Johnson would be at the rear. It was imperative that they push forward and under no circumstances were they to stop to help anyone in difficulties or injured and that included anyone who slips into a shell hole.

Wilson was told to help Penrose with the Lewis Gun. Alf Penrose looked grim and turned to Wilson, "Well this is it mate, it ain't going to be any fun from now on not that it's been that great up to now anyway!"

Wilson felt more than a little uneasy and was not comforted by the fact that a man not fazed by anything was too, just as apprehensive as him. Wilson asked, "What do you think our chances are of getting out of this alive?"

"Well – less than 50/50 I'd say but at least we have avoided the first wave and if our blokes do their stuff we might be alright and the German lines may be destroyed before we get there."

Wilson thought for a moment and then added sarcastically, "Yeah that's what they said about the first day at the Somme and that didn't work out, did it?"

Alf shrugged and moved off following Taylor who was behind the Sergeant. Wilson followed but had only moved a pace when the cramp started in his left leg and he collapsed down on to the mud. Ronnie Noakes, another Burnley lad, was right behind him and lifted him up, Wilson stamped his leg into the ground and brought his toes up towards his ankle keeping his leg straight, the usual way footballers tried to get the cramp out of their legs. The tingling in his foot got worse but at least the cramp eased and he was able to move off. He had been tempted for just a moment to stay right where he was and claim he couldn't go on – it would be a good way of getting out of here in one piece, he thought to himself.

Noakes pushed him forward saying, "Eddie, you know what you've got? It's probably trench foot. Have you got a tingling in your feet?"

"Yeah, I have," said Wilson.

"Bound to be it then," replied Ronnie.

"Should I stay here and get some help?"

"No, it'd be a waste of time. They'll tell you to carry on and get it treated when the push is over but by then you might be dead and it'll save them the bother!" he laughed out loud.

"Great!" said Wilson ironically.

Just as the Sergeant had said, the shelling started from the German side but the explosions were some way to the left at the moment and the whiz of the shells from the British side continued for about another ten minutes and then suddenly stopped. The Germans seemed to respond immediately and also stopped. There followed about five minutes of eerie silence with only the rain making any sort of noise.

Wilson and his group all stopped and waited to see what happened next until Captain Kennedy crept towards their position shouting at them to move. He pointed out that the rest of their Brigade was just to their right and that they will be able to support the Brigade in the second wave. He looked around at the faces of his men expecting them to be buoyed with excitement but all he saw was fear and concern etched into their features.

Suddenly, there were whistles some way in front, one following the other. "The men in the front line are moving forward," Alf Penrose informed them all, "come on!"

Almost as soon as the whistles sounded, the gunfire also started. Not that he considered himself an expert but Wilson was certain they were machine guns. From his crouching position he peered into the distance and could just make out what looked like pillboxes over where the German lines were. God, he thought to himself, they must be picking off our blokes just like shooting rabbits in a field.

The German shells seemed to be creeping towards Wilson's group. Roly Johnson called forward to the Sergeant that perhaps they should dig in to protect them from the fire and wait until it passes but the Sergeant was having none of it.

Almost immediately shells were falling all around them. Screams came from in front as a shell exploded and Wilson and the others were covered with pieces of shrapnel and mud. It all went quiet for a moment and then the screams started again as the injured called out for help.

"Get moving," shouted the Sergeant. They all moved forward at pace with Penrose and Wilson trying to run, keep their balance and carry the Lewis plus their rifles and kit all at the same time.

They slipped into a newly created and dry shell hole and tried to catch their breath. They had only been there a few seconds when two bloodstained Tommies slid down beside them. They were in a terrible way and had clearly been hit by that previous shell.

One had his stomach ripped open and he was holding his innards inside his bloodstained jacket, blood was belching out of the wound and his eyes appealed for help as he was clearly in too much shock to speak. His mate had no left leg or left arm and his left ear and some of that side of his head had also gone. He was screaming out for them to shoot him. Wilson recoiled back in shock and for a moment cocked his rifle as if to fire a shot at the badly injured man but Penrose pushed the gun down and added, "Steady, Eddie lad."

"What we going to do, Alf?" he mouthed.

"Sod off out of here, that's what! There's nothing we can do for them," was his only reply and he started to climb out of the hole.

"We can't do that, these blokes need some help," said Wilson appealing to his mate with a spread of his arms.

"Look Eddie, you know what the orders are we have got to move on and the blokes up there need this bloody gun, so shift your bloody arse!"

Wilson felt uneasy inside and looked down at the screaming soldier still demanding to be put out of his misery. He was tempted to put a bullet in the youngster but instead turned to the other man "Sorry mate – help's behind us – good luck!" and with this he followed Penrose out of the hole. As he moved forward he could still hear the two men shouting out. Just to his right as he moved along the path he saw a dead man with a rifle next to him. Wilson picked it up as he passed and threw it behind him and into the shell hole he had just left. A few strides further on he heard a shot from there and it all went quiet.

The two of them caught up with the rest of their group, who had stopped fifty yards ahead for a brief rest. Captain Kennedy told them that they were now in what's called the "reserve" trenches and that they were about a mile from what had been the front line. Apparently, he told them, the men had got out of those trenches at just after five and had made good ground but were now pinned down by machine gun fire from some pillboxes (the ones he had seen thought Wilson to himself) on the higher ground to the North West. The Captain explained that they would now be joining up with the 198th Brigade of the East Lancs. The Captain explained that he had been ordered to support the East Lancs attack and that they would have the task of attacking and putting out of action these pillboxes later in the morning. He warned them to be on the look out for possible gas attacks and to have their masks at the ready.

Having told them all that, he moved off down the line to brief the other Sections.

Following a brief lull that coincided with this briefing, the shelling started up again. The group quickly dug themselves a makeshift shallow trench for protection. Explosions, followed by the usual screams and shouts, continued for over an hour. The noise was awful as much from the injured men as the shells themselves. Wilson actually crouched, for most of the time that followed, with his hands over his ears and head. He had taken off his helmet until the Sergeant had told him not to be so bloody stupid and put it back on.

Wilson's cramp had returned and now both feet were tingling. In the move up from the previous stop his feet had really began to hurt as if they were rubbing on his boots – it seemed like he now had blisters. It was difficult to tell for sure as his feet were quite numb and it felt like he had pins and needles.

Suddenly the shelling stopped and Penrose leapt up and peered above the top of the makeshift slit trench. At that very moment a shell exploded not four yards in front of him; all the soldiers ducked but Wilson was first to look up and as he did so he saw a ball coming towards him and instinctively caught it in front of his chest almost like a goalkeeper. He looked down… it was not a ball but it was a human head with eyes wide open and what seemed like a broad smile, there was some matted hair but most of it had been singed off – Wilson recognised the face immediately … it was Alf Penrose.

Wilson stepped back with a scream, then turned around and started to move away but went straight into the arms of Don Taylor who was just behind him. The head dropped into the mud at their feet as Taylor looked straight at Wilson. "Steady, lad, steady, easy," Wilson tried to push past him but Taylor continued to hold him firmly for at least twenty seconds. Wilson slowly calmed down and his body relaxed and so finally Taylor released his grip.

While all this was happening, the Sergeant had knelt and picked up the head and tossed it as far as he could in front of the trench.

The Sergeant, Taylor, Wilson, young Noakes and, behind them, the rest of the Section, sat slumped and motionless with their backs against the side of the narrow trench. Wilson pulled his handkerchief from his pocket and covered most of his face with it, mainly to hide the fact that he was lightly crying and he then blew his nose. Taylor leant over and took the handkerchief. Wilson resisted at first and looked at Taylor angrily. Taylor, however, used it to wipe the side of Wilson's ear and then without speaking showed Wilson the blood that he had wiped from there. It had come from Penrose's head.

Sergeant Goddard for once was at a loss for words. Not only had they all lost a good mate but also the way it had happened was about as bad as it could be.

It all remained quiet for a few more minutes. Other groups pushed past them. Nearly all of them swearing at the men as they sat there motionless, partly blocking the pathway.

Eventually Goddard told the group to get up and move on. Wilson now struggled with the Lewis Gun on his own until Noakes offered to help. The shell that did for Penrose had appeared to be something of a stray and was not followed by anymore. As Wilson moved forward he suddenly stopped and dropped his end of the gun causing Noakes to fall over as he took its whole weight. Wilson looked behind him to where they had come from and then he looked forward. He suddenly realised that the shell that did for Penrose had come from behind them and not from the German lines at all. He apologised to Noakes and picked him up. They both took hold of the gun and moved off.

Suddenly, as the weather began to clear, they could see they were now moving along a well-constructed trench. They were told it was the "support" trench and this had been about twenty-five yards behind the "front" trench when the attack had begun earlier on. They were told by their Sergeant that, apparently, the West Riding lads to the left were now not only pinned down by the pillboxes but also by a concealed machine gun along with sniper fire from dry shell holes on the slightly higher ground, which had not been affected so much by the wet weather. Also, it seemed that the British had come up against more than forty yards of wire in front of the German lines in that western sector. The British shells had simply buried themselves in the mud and had failed to explode and remove the wire, as had been the original intention. All the troops that had attacked in this area were now almost up to their waists in water in the lower lying holes and small trenches created by the soil being churned up by the shelling and where the troops that had dug themselves in earlier. Apparently the rest of the West Riding brigade to the East had been prevented moving forward by a lake that had been created by the river bursting its banks and had made the area impassable.

Wilson's group were now to move forward to what had earlier been the front trench and follow and support their comrades from the 198th Brigade whose progress was hampered by the mud in what had previously been "no man's land" and the water-filled old German trenches beyond. They had been able to successfully move forward quite quickly but were now pinned down by the pillbox positioned on the higher ground, which strafed their positions with bursts of machine gun fire. This was also made worse by the sniper fire picking them off if they ventured out of their protective holes.

Once Wilson's group and the others with them were in position in the reinforced line, the intention was that the men would rise out of their holes and carry out a massive assault on the pillbox, at the same time drawing the sniper fire. There would be inevitable losses but the sheer weight of numbers would hopefully bring about the breakthrough and destroy the pillbox and secure the high ground by clearing out resistance from the holes and trenches stretched along the ridge.

CHAPTER 13

The order came that they were to rest here for a while and take on some food and drink before moving any further.

Since the incident with the head, Wilson had completely withdrawn within himself despite the fact that Roly Johnson had tried to lift his spirits with a brief chat. His legs seemed as if they had warmed up a bit and the cramps had gone but there was still the tingling sensation. The numbness had worn off a little and his feet seemed to have regained some of their feeling but that meant that he could feel the blisters chaffing against his boots more than he could before.

Roly pointed out that he also thought it was the onset of trench foot. He told Wilson that he should mention it to the Sergeant should it not get any better or particularly if it actually gets worse but he'd have to wait until the attack on the pillbox was over.

As well as the discomfort in his feet, Wilson felt tightness in his chest and he was breathing far more quickly than normal and seemed permanently short of breath. Don Taylor had made some tea and they all took the chance to eat what was left of their rations. Most had tins of processed meat and supplemented this with biscuits. It was all tasteless stuff but welcome to them nonetheless. Some lit up their cigarettes. Hardly anyone spoke.

Wilson finished his snack and sat a little away from the others with his knees up to his chin. He hugged his legs tightly. He was still breathing far too quickly and he also felt himself shaking. Roly Johnson came towards him on his hands and knees and tapped him on his shoulder but left him alone.

The order soon came to carry out the planned manoeuvre to draw the fire as intended and move up towards the pillbox. There was now no shelling in their vicinity from either side but the strafing of gunfire was relentless up ahead and this was pinning down the rest of the198th scattered about in front of them. They were readied and they waited for the order to move forward. They all nervously checked their equipment and fastened their bayonets. Wilson leant against the side of the trench; he felt extremely nervous about this first taste of real battle and could feel his hands shaking. He tightened the grip on the Lewis gun. Noakes was next to him ready to help with the equipment, as before.

Captain Kennedy had been called away for an intelligence briefing and had been temporarily replaced by an even younger Officer from the East Lancs.

Wilson recognised him as Lieutenant Winstanly-Booth who could not have been more than 19. He had been at their initial training camp back at Preston. The young Officer moved up and down the trench and reiterated to the group what the plan was. He told them they were to run hell for leather to the old German trenches and beyond. He reiterated the usual order that they were not to stop unless shot and were also not to stop and help fallen comrades or the German snipers would pick them off. Their target was still the pillbox, which just had to be put out of action. Once that went it was felt the Germans would fall back and a new British Front line would be established on the high ground around the pillbox, from which it would be possible for them to control about a mile or so to the East and so forcing the Germans back to positions vacated by them a couple of years before.

Wilson felt that this was likely to be the last thing he would do on this earth and what he had really been dreading ever since he joined up. He felt sure that as soon as he jumped out of this trench and ran straight into the hail of bullets, there would be one with his name on it.

Suddenly, as he stood there, he felt he urgently needed the latrine. He asked the Lieutenant who at first was not very sympathetic, knowing that if he allowed one to go they would all want to do so. He eventually relented when he saw Wilson's pained expression.

There was an old latrine that had been hastily constructed by the trench's previous occupants who had left that morning. It was truly awful – there was filth all over the floor with some even smeared on the wooden support struts and the door. The piece of wood that served as a seat was covered in brown slime, mixed with blood and vomit and he removed this with the sleeve of his jacket. The smell was truly awful and Wilson retched as he went in and then held his breath.

Despite the pains in his stomach, which had been with him for so long, he found it difficult to shift anything from his bowels. Whilst he was in there he thought he might take his boots and socks off and have a look at his feet but thought better of it. His breathing was now more even and the pain in his chest had gone away but he looked at his hands and they were still shaking uncontrollably.

He pulled his trousers up and adjusted the rest of his dress. He stood still for a moment. Suddenly he had this urge to get away and his mind raced. Could he just go the other way down the trench away from his mates? If he could look purposeful and as if on an errand where could he get to? It would not be easy whilst it was light but he could perhaps hide somewhere and wait until dark. There was so much confusion around he might get away with it or, if challenged, he could say he had been sent back by an Officer to get treatment for his trench foot? Then, as he shook his head dismissing the idea, he opened the small door in order to go back into the trench to re-join Noakes. Suddenly, there was this huge explosion and the whole of the latrine walls and door were blown away and he was thrown forward and ended up at the base of the trench. He lay there unconscious.

When he came round, his ears were absolutely ringing and he could not hear a thing apart from a peculiar muffling sound. His eyes were full of dust and he could barely open them due to the grit in them. He rubbed them and blinked as much as he could and gradually they cleared and the irritation stopped. His ears and now his head were painful. He felt his right ear and there was blood but it did not seem too bad.

He stumbled along the trench heading back towards where his mates had been, just around a slight bend. He was about to shout for help when he realised that there was no one there. All that remained was a black, scorched area with two rifles, some odds and ends of clothing, the odd mug and that was it! There were no men though but then he saw the blood smeared along the wall of the trench and there were large lumps of bone and flesh, just above this was a leg dangling back into the trench. He reached up to pull it down towards him mindful of possible further explosions and the sniper's fire. One further pull and the body rolled down into the trench – it was Roly Johnson and he was barely alive. Wilson laid him on the driest part of the trench, which was exactly where the shell had landed, the water, for the time being at least, had been dispersed by the explosion there. Wilson looked at his friend but could not see any obvious injury but Johnson's eyes said it all and slowly they closed and his body relaxed.

Wilson looked for help from further down the trench and ran back along it towards the old latrine. He went round the bend in the trench but the soldiers who had been there had apparently moved off. He then ran for about twenty-five yards back past where Johnson was but the men had gone from there as well. The shell had clearly made them all move forward and out of the trench earlier than planned. What of Noakes and Taylor and the young Lieutenant - they had all been with Johnson when Wilson had gone to the latrine? What was left in the trench suggested that the remains were more than just those of one man and only Johnson's body was mainly intact. Wilson realised that the rest must have been blown up whilst he had luckily chosen that moment to relieve himself. He sat down on the fire step on the side of the trench next to Johnson's body and took off his helmet and put it on the ground. He brought his knees up to his chest and put his head into his hands and looked at his friend's still body next to him.

Shells continued to fall all around the area in front of the enemy side of the trench and small pieces of slimy mud fell on him. Suddenly three British soldiers came running round the bend in the trench towards him and he stood up. Two ran past hardly taking any notice but the third stopped briefly and asked Wilson if he was alright. Before he could reply the young man was gone.

A shell exploded about five yards from him and just over the parapet of the trench and he dived onto his stomach and into the bottom of the trench. It had started raining again and water had begun to fill the trench once more. He immediately felt the wet through his tunic, which had been badly scorched by the explosion.

More shells exploded a little further away. He sat up and moved his hands to his ears, holding both sides of his head and bent his head over his knees.

After several minutes the shelling seemed to slacken off a little and moved away further down the line. Wilson eventually took his hands from his ears and wiped the tears from his face. He searched around and found a rifle. It was not his but it would do. Surprisingly, he found his pack tucked into a small alcove to the right of the fire step and he put it over his head so it hung down by his left side. God knows where the Lewis Gun had gone to, he thought. Gone with the other men, he assumed.

He began to consider his next move. His inclination was to go back towards the rear lines. It had all gone quiet both in front and behind him. Apart from the three soldiers he had encountered a little earlier, there appeared to be no one else in that part of the trench network. He didn't want to be seen as deserting the front line but, in the circumstances, felt he had very little choice but to retreat back to where he assumed he would find the reserve troops.

Just as he tried to make up his mind on what to do, he heard voices along the trench and they were coming his way. He cocked his rifle and pushed it out in front of him. The bayonet was in place. He crouched and aimed the point towards the voices coming towards the bend of the trench just in front of him. He relaxed a little as he heard them speaking English but decided to still be on his guard. Suddenly four soldiers appeared. They stopped when they saw him and dropped to their knees and pointed their guns at him but they, like him, relaxed when they each recognised the other's uniform.

The soldier at the front of the group had a pistol and was wearing an Officer's uniform.

"Who are you and what are you still doing here?" he asked Wilson.

Wilson came to attention and saluted, "Private Wilson, East Lancs and I've been left behind, sir"

"What do you mean, left behind?"

"Well, sir, my group had received a direct hit from a shell and they appear to have all been killed or perhaps some might have run off. I'm still here because I was in the latrine over there," he said pointing to the scattered remains of the wooden convenience. "I don't know how long since we were hit and I must have been knocked out and, when I came to, I had tried to help my friend here," he said pointing at the lifeless body of Roly Johnson, "but he died and I was a bit stunned and I was just trying to decide what to do next but I thought I should go back and …"

The Officer waved him to stop. "Steady, at ease Wilson, I'm Major Slattery from the Canadian Army and this is Captain Sholto and Captain Mackenzie with Private Hamilton. We have been sent towards the front line to observe so we can make an assessment of the area as we were due to reinforce the line in the next few days, but the Germans have overrun the area to the West and most of the line has been vacated and most of the troops, or what's left of them, have withdrawn back about a hundred yards along this part of the line but the Germans haven't reached this area just yet. Have you seen anyone from our side along here?"

"Three blokes came through here a few minutes ago but didn't stop. They weren't East Lancs as far as I could tell and they just kept on going."

"Right – fine– well you had better go back from here as the Germans might turn up at any moment. Try and find some of your pals back in the new reserve lines. Do you feel alright now?"

"My ears are still ringing and my hearing is not what it should be and I feel a bit queasy. My feet are sore and I can hardly walk without a lot of discomfort – someone said I might have trench foot, sir."

The Major thought for a moment and spoke to the Captains but Wilson could not hear what was being said. The Private came over and produced a piece of cake wrapped in a dirty handkerchief from his pocket and offered it to him. He also offered a drink from his water bottle. Wilson smiled and thanked him but the Canadian said nothing. As he took a swig from the bottle but spluttered and gasped a little. It was not water but some strong spirit. The Canadian smiled broadly. "Alright?" was he all he said. All Wilson could do was nod as the spirit burnt his throat.

Finally the Major turned to Wilson, "Look, Wilson, we have more work to do here so we'll have to go but you can't come with us, so I want you to follow this trench and if you turn left each time you come to the first two junctions, you should be able to find your way back to our own lines but be on the look out for Germans and make sure you identify yourself clearly when you get near our line as someone might mistake you for the enemy!" With this the four Canadians moved off but not before the Private had shaken Wilson's hand and patted him on his back.

With this Wilson saluted as they moved off, picked up his pack and was gone. He did what he had been told and kept left and after two turns was at what he recognised as the Reserve Trench but there was no one in this part of the trench either. He leaned against the trench walls, which had been fortified here with strong wood using what looked like railway sleepers with the odd one jutting out thus forming a bench, so he sat down. No sooner had he done this than a large group of British soldiers slid over the side of the trench from the direction of the Front. They were in a terrible state with most seemingly injured and covered in a mixture of mud and dried blood. Most had no helmets nor weapons and they were all out of breath and lay collapsed in the trench gasping for air.

One was a Corporal who looked up at Eddie who was trying to help what appeared to be the most seriously injured. "Who the bloody hell are you?"

"Private Wilson, East Lancs, Corporal."

"You sure?"

"Yes Corp."

"So what are you doing here, deserted have you?" By now the Corporal was up on his feet and staring right into Wilson's eyes from about three inches.

"No sir, I was told to come here by a Canadian Major."

"What! There are no Canadians up here Private, only British."

"He told me he was and he was with two Captains and a Private. They definitely spoke with a funny accent."

"So why, if they did exist, did they send you back here then?"

Wilson recounted his story but the Corporal still seemed suspicious. The Corporal turned to the men most of whom had all remarkably recovered and were listening in. "Smith go and get the Captain. I saw him down there when we came over the side of the trench – ask him to come here as soon as he can."

Smith followed where the Corporal was pointing and headed off.

The Corporal turned to Wilson, "Quite frankly I don't believe you but I'll get Captain Harris to sort you out - he'll be here in a minute so I suggest you come clean if you know what's good for you."

"Excuse me Corporal but who are you with?"

"East Lancs like you – the 197th – we are a machine gun unit – well we were but we ain't got no machine guns anymore – we had to leave them behind when the Germans started to overrun us – we got out but all those who attacked the German line seemed to have either been killed, injured or captured, I guess. I've lost six men that I know of.

Wilson nodded as he visualised what it must have been like for them. He thought now that he must have been unconscious for longer than he thought which is why the trench had emptied. Perhaps they had left him for dead.

Within a couple of minutes Smith returned with Captain Harris who was briefed by the Corporal. Wilson stood to attention as the Captain came over and what he said gave Wilson quite a shock, "Are you Eddie Wilson who plays for Burnley?"

"Well - yes sir I am," he replied.

"Private Smith thought you were - he saw you play a few times for the reserves. I support Burnley too but prefer rugby really. So what's this all about – tell me?"

Wilson recounted his story again and the Captain seemed a little more convinced about the Canadians than the Corporal had been. "I'll give you the benefit of the doubt. You will join us now - there's no point going up there," he said pointing towards the Front because everyone is still coming back – those that can anyway. I've got some medics on their way to tend these men and I'll get them to look at your feet whilst they are here. Is that alright?"

"Yes, sir – thank you sir," replied Eddie.

"Oh, Wilson you might be handy at football but what are you like at making tea? Get some will you for the men – from what I remember when we were here before there is a small area in the back wooden wall just along here which acted as a sort of kitchen."

With that the Officer was gone and all the men sat down. Some attended their own slight wounds but some helped their more badly injured comrades. Only Private Smith remained standing and he introduced himself as George Smith from Brierfield. He spent some minutes asking Wilson all about Burnley Football Club and the Cup Final win in particular. Their conversation came to an abrupt end when the Corporal, called Renton, told Wilson to "get the bloody tea!"

Having served the tea, Wilson settled down and heard from the men of their horrific day up near the German lines – they had set up a series of machine gun posts but had come under such penetrating fire from the pillbox and the machine guns that they could hardly get any rounds away at all. They were all of the opinion that they had maybe lost up to 6,000 men one way or another during the morning assault, the Germans had simply mown down so many as they moved forward. There must have been so many men killed or badly injured. Whole sections of their line had then been overrun and a lot more men killed or taken prisoner.

As the afternoon wore on they all settled down but there was no sign of the medics and some of the men who had been badly injured died and were buried in the banks of the trench in very shallow graves. Whilst not ideal it did at least prevent them getting eaten by the rats and the smell of rotting corpses would be kept to a minimum.

The Captain had said this would be temporary until a proper burial could be organised but he had made a note of their names and if anything happened to him could someone pick up the list and notes – he told them there were also notes about those from their platoon who had died or gone missing earlier in the action.

As darkness began to fall, the rain that had eased as Wilson had arrived in the Reserve Trench now began to fall heavily. The Boche true to form had started an artillery barrage almost simultaneously with the opening of the heavens.

Once again a similar pattern began to emerge – the trench began to fill with water all too quickly and the soldiers would be kept awake by the shelling, if not the rain, plus they had to ready for a possible attack. However, night time attacks had never really been a tactic for either side so they would now use the time to busy themselves with digging in and making life as comfortable as possible in these appalling conditions. There might be the occasional shell and some flares but both sides would take time to rest from the battles of the day.

The Captain had sent a small group out back towards the German line to pick up any of the injured that they could find. All night there were cries from the land between these new front lines, mostly from the British but there was also the occasional shout from a German. Gradually they subsided as the men were recovered and brought back or they simply died where they were.

As soon as his legs and feet got cold the extreme numbness returned and he dreaded taking off his puttees and boots. Smith had told him it would help if he could find some dry socks, especially if the medics are not going to show up to treat him now that it was night time. Wilson did not think there was much chance of finding any new socks. Smith suggested he should take a pair from one of the dead men but Wilson said he was not able to quite bring himself to do that.

At about eight in the evening the shelling became more intense and very close to them – the well-constructed trench did afford more protection than most they had seen before but they all knew that a direct hit would see the end for them. Suddenly a shell burst in front of Smith and Wilson. It had landed on the top of the trench right where their dead mates had been buried not long before. The bodies were thrown into the air and various body parts and mud fell onto the soldiers pinned against the trench side. Another group, apparently sappers had been hit about 40 yards down the trench and were apparently all dead.

The noise was all too much for Wilson. He threw off his helmet and took up the same position as before with his knees up to his chin and his hands over his ears. His eyes were tight shut and he was shaking uncontrollably once again.

Another shell landed just in front of the trench a yard or so ahead of the previous one. This time Wilson screamed out but fortunately the next shell bursting a few yards to the right drowned the sound out. George Smith was shocked at the plight of his new friend and shook Wilson to try to get him to come to his senses but Wilson just stared ahead. Smith thought he had better do something before the shelling came to an end so he hit Wilson hard across the face with the back of his hand. Wilson slumped face down in the water but immediately jumped up, mainly from the shock of the cold water, and grabbed Smith by the throat. They rolled through the water, which was now about a foot deep. Wilson was raining punches onto Smith's back and crying at the same time – the punches were of no substance but almost an hysterical lashing out and he ended up beating Smith's back with his clenched fists.

Corporal Renton had seen this develop and was there in a flash and pulled Wilson away and pinned him to the trench side firmly holding both shoulders. "Wilson, calm down and stay there" but still holding the Private the Corporal asked Smith if he was alright to which he replied he was.

Wilson had his eyes shut but his body had relaxed so the Corporal let him go. The barrage continued but not as near to them as before.

"Right, " said the Corporal, "Wilson you do that again and you'll be on a charge, now sit down there with Smith and make your peace and keep your heads down - this ain't over yet."

Wilson stood with Smith up against the wall of the trench once more – both of them were soaking wet and Smith put his arm on the other's shoulder, "It's fine, forget it."

Wilson half smiled and gave him a playful little punch on his upper arm but said nothing; Smith noticed the hand was trembling so much that Wilson could hardly keep still. They both then sat on the trench wall seat together.

CHAPTER 14

The evening wore on and the shelling ceased, as did the rain to little more than a drizzle. The Captain had told them all that the medics would not be arriving tonight as they were so busy at the dressing stations with the injured and dying being dropped in there almost non-stop.

He did have some good news in that some men had got through with some supplies and at least they could all now have something to eat and drink. The men had been able to take the few remaining seriously injured men back with them on stretchers but they had also left some stretchers behind. The Captain went on to say that within the next thirty minutes the NCOs would be organising small parties to go out under the cover of darkness to seek out and bring in any injured men that could be moved as the Army did not want these men falling into the hands of the Germans and possibly giving up vital information.

The men in the trench had heard distant moans and shouting from some way off after the last round of shelling but had tried to put them out of their mind because the job of going into what was now effectively the new "no man's land" was not something anyone really wanted to do!

Following some more of the inevitable tinned meat and a mug of tea, Wilson felt much better, especially now that the shelling appeared to have stopped for the night. He still kept getting images of the dead and dying flashing before his eyes and he still felt this tremble within him. The water in the trench was still rising and had covered his ankles and yet again his feet were numb. The chatty George Smith who, it appeared, preferred to be called "Smithy" had helped him get over his worries by quizzing Wilson endlessly about the 1914 Cup Final. What was it like to be there he asked and what about the bus ride with the Cup around the town – what was Bert Freeman's goal like because on the newsreels it had not been captured? And so he went on and on.

"Clearly, Smithy, you are quite a fan!"

"You're right there mate – do you know in the two seasons up to the Cup Final I did not miss a single home first team or reserve match and I can tell you all about every game – I can even recite the 1914 Final team – Sewell Bamford Taylor Halley Boyle – Watson Nesbit Lindley Freeman Hodgson. What about Mr Haworth as a manager, what's your view of him?"

"He was good to me and has encouraged me a lot and he put together a team to win the Cup for the first time, didn't he?"

Smith went on, "I wonder if the blokes from that team are still alive? I wonder if any of them are out here somewhere, dead or alive?"

"Just before we left home there was an article in the local paper saying that up to that point none of them had been killed and it was hoped they could pick up where they left off when the War comes to end, as long as that is fairly soon and before they get too old!"

They continued chatting until at about ten thirty when Corporal Renton called the fifteen or so at his end of the trench together.

"You know what the Captain said earlier," he started, "whilst we are a machine gun unit we have been told we must try to bring in any survivors that are out there beyond the trench here whilst it is still dark. We don't want any moon coming up so the Boche can see us. So, I want the fittest twelve of you to split into two groups of six and take three stretchers each and bring in those that are alive and look as though they might survive but, and I know this might sound hard, leave those who are not likely to make it. It's tough but we've no way of saving them here so let's pick up those that we can."

"Excuse me Corp, "asked Wilson, "what about me?"

"Wilson, you're a bloody footballer so you should be fit and it'll be a bit of experience for you, so you're one of the twelve."

Wilson looked disappointed, "But I've had no training for this sort of thing and I can hardly walk with these feet. I've been told it might be trench foot."

The Corporal came up to him and almost put his nose against the Private's, "Look Wilson, you are going and if you don't then that's disobeying an order or even cowardice, if I wanted to stretch a point, and do you know what that means? Either you get some sort of field punishment or even shot, "So what's it going to be then?" The last few words were shouted and Wilson felt the spittle splash into his face – he turned away, picked up his rifle and stood waiting.

Smith moved towards his new friend saying to the Corporal, "I'll go with him, Corp, and make sure he keeps his head down and I can show him what to do, alright?"

"That'll do me Smithy and I'll come with you in your group," and with that the Corporal split the men into the two groups leaving the more seriously injured men out of the party and telling them to get some rest.

They set off just after eleven with a confidence which surprised Wilson bearing in mind what the men had been through just that morning and goodness knows what else in the recent past. As soon as he was out of the trench, Wilson found he was able to move freely but could not feel his feet at all except from this tingling feeling yet again from about half way down his shin to his toes and his boot seemed very tight.

89

It was impossible for Wilson's group to move anything else but at a snail's pace across the mud which was still knee deep again in places and there were shell holes all round, some inevitably full of water and some of the more recently made ones filling up all the time as the water seeped into them.

Of course they could not use any light for fear of being picked off by the enemy snipers and the sky was absolutely black with little chance that night of the moon breaking through the cloud. Wilson, Smith and the Corporal made up half their group with three more making up the party. Wilson kept close to Smith who offered plenty of words of encouragement and guidance.

To start with there was very little sign of any noise coming from the men who were still alive so the Corporal told his men to call out as softly as they could yet still able to be heard within a range that was not likely to be picked up in the enemy trenches. Still nothing. The Corporal had just told Smith and Wilson to fan out to the right when a flare suddenly went up and the whole of the immediate landscape around them was lit up. Wilson then saw a sight that was beyond belief – as far as he could see there were bodies in all manner of positions. He looked at the shell holes close by and there was at least three bodies floating in each. Rats bigger than he had ever seen scurried over and round the bodies pulling the flesh from the bodies. Most of the bodies had no eyes as these appeared to have been plucked out presumably by birds. Some of the bodies had no heads on them and were missing various limbs. All had the brown British uniforms and most were smeared with the peculiar reddish black colour of dried blood.

Wilson stood there taking all this in but was pulled to the ground by the Corporal telling him to get his head down. Just as well as it turned out because machine gun fire opened up from in front and they could hear the whine of the bullets above their heads and the earth splattered up around them. The flare died away and the darkness returned.

"Quick, move!" shouted the Corporal, "so they don't know where we are."

The six moved to a slightly raised area above a shell hole to the right and they crouched for cover behind the rise in the ground with their feet dangling over the side of the hole. No sooner had they done that than another flare went up but this time there was no gunfire but mortar shells were flung up in their general direction with many of them exploding nearby.

For Wilson this was becoming impossible again; his whole body started to tremble and his mind began to race and suddenly he stood up and shouted towards where the firing was coming from.

"Shut up – bloody shut up…!" He gesticulated towards the Germans with the end of his bayonet.

Smith jumped up and pulled him back down. Wilson struggled swearing and cursing and, totally out of control, pushed his friend out of the way and he was off, running as fast as his numb legs would allow. He stumbled over the bodies and slipped and slithered in the mud.

"Come back you idiot," shouted Smith who made an attempt to follow until Corporal Renton pulled him back down.

Wilson was silhouetted against the landscape by the flare and the gunfire tracked him as he ran away. The bullets following him but they were a few feet behind, kicking up the soil in a neat row. He was panting and crying at the same time. As soon as the flare's effect had gone away again, he slowed down. The gunfire had stopped and the Germans had no doubt decided that they could not see clearly enough so there was no point continuing.

For one who had always been so fit, Wilson was struggling with his breath again and the pain across his chest was more acute than ever so he had to stop. He found a shell hole with only a little water in it and crouched down. He was sucking in air in great gulps and was now panicking as he thought he would die from a heart attack or something similar as opposed to a bullet or a shell. Gradually, his breathing returned to something like normal and the pain eased from his chest. No sooner had this happened and, for the first time in a while, he could feel the pain in his feet – they felt raw as if the whole of the skin had been sliced off. He decided he must get his boots off and have a look as soon as he could.

However, he had no choice at the moment but to stand in the few inches of water. So, removing the boots, puttees and socks was not an option. What to do now, which way to go? Wilson pondered over his options and decided that even though it was dark again and he couldn't really see where to go, he would have to move on.

He knew he could not go to his left, as that was where he had come from and with the enemy up ahead the only option was to go back behind him. He had thrown down his rifle when he had run from the others and had nothing else with him. To pick a way through the morass behind him was bound to be difficult and then he had to find a way round the rear of the British trenches because he felt joining another group was not an option and he would probably not be able to explain how he came to be where he was in any case.

He started to push himself out of the hole when he heard voices about twenty yards away. Listening carefully, he realised that they were not speaking English and although he had never heard a German speak he assumed that was the language they were using. They appeared to be stopping and searching amongst the bodies; perhaps they too are looking for survivors to take prisoner and question. There was nothing else for him but to play dead as they were now too close for him to get up out of the hole without them seeing him. He chose to lie face down in the water. As it was not that deep he was able to keep his head out enough to breathe until he heard the voices almost on top of him.

He stretched out his arms and legs and put his face into the water so that he floated like all the other corpses he had seen. He held his breath for what seemed like an hour but was really about three minutes. He then slowly moved his head to the left so that he could breathe out of the corner of his mouth and hear what might be going on above. He guessed that the Germans would not be able to pick up any slight movement in the darkness but he was taking no chances. After about five minutes there was no sound at all but the rain had started up again so it was difficult to pick up much but he decided to take a chance.

He slowly moved his face forward to the slope of the hole and hauled himself upwards desperately trying to get hold of something substantial or, at least, dry. Finally he had enough grip to haul himself out but just at that moment someone grabbed his arm and pulled him up. His heart sank, disappointed that the Germans had not in fact moved on. However, he was surprised to hear a familiar voice: –

"Come on you silly sod let's get out of here!" It was Smithy.

He was with the Corporal who whispered, "Wilson, you are in big trouble but we'll have to sort this out when we have finished the job we came out here to do." With that he led them away telling Smith and Wilson to take the stretcher with them and see if they can find some of the injured and take them back. Corporal Renton went with one of the others but kept only a few paces behind Smith and Wilson.

For about an hour they scoured the area frequently having to fall face down to avoid being seen when the occasional flare went up. These flares became very sporadic and the British men could hear Germans moving around some fifty yards or so in front of them presumably looking for some of their comrades or adding to the number of prisoners they could interrogate.

In all they bought back nineteen injured men. It was very tiring but for Wilson it meant that for the moment at least he could forget about his problems and at no point did he again experience the shortness of breath or chest pains. However, his feet were now much more sore than before and he longed to get his boots off and have a look. He tried to put to the back of his mind what fate might befall him when the Corporal puts in his report.

Not much had been said by any of them as they had carried on with their work.

Eventually, they were ordered to remain in the trench to where they had delivered the injured. Some further supplies had arrived with some of the slightly injured having returned from the rear dressing stations with two of the medics. Somehow they had managed to work their way back and returned to the front line despite the shelling, gunfire and the difficult wet conditions.

Corporal Renton had pulled Wilson to one side as they drank their welcome mug of tea and ate some of the hot stew prepared by those who had remained behind.

"Look here Wilson, you are in deep trouble if I report that you deserted your post. I've heard of men being shot for that or serving a prison sentence for a long time. Now, you might think being in prison would be a better option than being here but believe you me they are horrible places and it'll be the end of any football job you might get after this is over. Private Smith has pleaded with me to go soft on you and after a lot of thought I am going to report to Captain Harris that you disobeyed my order and whilst you will still get disciplined it will not be the same as cowardice or desertion."

"Thanks Corporal, I appreciate that, so what happens now?"

"I'll speak with Captain Harris as soon as possible but for now get the medic to look at your feet and then get some sleep, the Captain will probably see you in the morning. I'll just say to Mr Harris that you refused to move forward and I won't mention that you actually ran away. The others will back that up but I doubt whether they'll get asked but I've told them just in case."

With that he left and Wilson looked round for the medic. He was busy looking at the wounded that had been brought in so Wilson decided to take off his boots and socks and have a look at his feet for himself.

The sight he was left with was quite frightening with most of each foot just red raw. It was clear that blisters had formed and then been rubbed away. His socks were soaking wet and smelt quite revolting. Just at that moment Smith arrived at his side.

"Bloody hell, they look awful," he said, pointing at the feet. "These might help," he added giving Wilson two pairs of dry socks.

"Where did you get these?" asked Wilson.

"Don't ask!" responded his friend.

Wilson almost threw them down into the water at the bottom of the trench guessing Smith had taken them from the bodies they had seen earlier. Having then thought differently about it, he thanked his friend and tucked them inside his tunic whilst he waited for the medic to finish with the other casualties.

Wilson relaxed as best he could and had dozed off for a while until he was shaken by one of the medics who had already seen the state of his feet.

The medic, who appeared to be completely done in himself, told Wilson that he did indeed have trench foot and all that could be done for now was to wash the feet thoroughly to get the sore parts clean and then let them dry. If at all possible Wilson should try and wear dry socks and he asked Wilson if he had any. Wilson told him of Smith's "gift" and mentioned his reservations about where they had come from. They both laughed but as the medic said, "Needs must!"

He went on to tell Wilson that he should bathe his feet for about five minutes at a time in very warm water as often as possible with a gap of about ten minutes between each wash. The medic appreciated that this was difficult here but encouraged Wilson to at least try. The secret was to stop any infection getting into the foot because if that were to happen a man might lose both feet if gangrene were to set in. He added that it seemed as though the skin had been chafed so much that any infected areas might have been inadvertently cleaned. He thought that Wilson should really be moved down from the line and he would mention this to an Officer but he thought it unlikely to happen whilst the situation remained as it is. He added that further orders were awaited from GHQ before any move should be made anywhere on this new Front.

Wilson sat down on an old ammunition box and thought to himself that there was not a lot of chance in getting much warm water here and anyway the NCOs and Officers are not going to be as sympathetic as the medic, especially as he will be facing some sort of charge. If this involved being moved to a makeshift secure area away from the Front he might however be able to get some more treatment.

With that thought Wilson rejoined Smith and the others and found a suitable cranny in which to get some sleep and it was only now that he realised just how tired he was.

CHAPTER 15

When Wilson awoke the sun was shining for the first time in days and the sky was the most beautiful blue. However, the October sun did not have a lot of warmth at this time of the day and in fact there had been an early morning frost and even the water in the bottom of their trench had a thin layer of ice on top. Wilson had managed to keep his feet out of the water once he had put on his new dry socks, drier boots and puttees. The men had rigged a series of footrests sticking up above the water made out of ration tins and any other piece of metal they could find and, so, they were able to move about without getting their feet wet.

Smith had got himself and Wilson some warm tea and the men around had managed to cook a decent breakfast. The talk was of their withdrawal from these forward trenches for some respite and the rumour was that they would be relieved by the Canadians, who would be used for the next attempt to secure the higher land that they had been told was called Passchendaele Ridge, so called after the nearby village of the same name. Wilson had confirmed to the others that the likelihood of the Canadians arriving was strong in view of his recent meeting in the trenches with the Canadian Officers.

Despite all their recent trials and tribulations of the past few days their humour was good and their spirits higher that one would imagine they could be.

Wilson even began to brighten up and occasionally joined in the laughter with the others. This relatively comfortable trench seemed far away from the death and mayhem he had experienced only hours before. Even the Boche seemed to be taking a day off and enjoying the warm, sunny weather or perhaps just spending time recovering, like the British, from the intensity of the previous days' fighting. Wilson sat on a raised ledge below the top of the trench and cleaned his rifle, whilst the men around him laughed and joked with one another and enjoying their smokes. He even wondered if the Corporal had taken pity on him and not reported the previous night's incident to the Captain as nothing had been said to him so far this morning.

However, at about ten he was approached by Renton and told to report to Captain Harris in the Officer's quarters. He followed Renton along the trench, this time splashing through the water as he went. They turned left and headed towards the rear trenches. Renton stopped at an opening in a hastily prepared wooden construction pushed into the banked mud. It was about six feet square and the walls were assorted pieces of wood gathered from all around where the trees had been blown apart by the shelling.

Squashed into this small area were three men. Harris introduced two other Officers, one of whom was a Captain and the other a Second Lieutenant. Corporal Renton remained with Wilson just outside the makeshift quarters along with another NCO, who appeared to be a Sergeant Major, who had tagged along behind them from the forward trench.

Wilson had hurriedly smartened himself up whilst Renton had marched him to the Officers and now stood at attention in front of them. Captain Harris spoke: -

"Private Wilson, we have heard from Corporal Renton that whilst out in No Man's Land you wilfully disobeyed his order to move forward and retrieve some of our fallen comrades. Normally you would be taken before a Court Martial and a full hearing of your case would take place but we cannot facilitate that in view of the current circumstances and so we have convened this special gathering, which has the same jurisdiction. We will apply appropriate disciplinary action under the Army Act and the Field Service Regulations. Do you understand that?"

"Yes sir," replied the Private.

The Officer continued, "As I said, we have received a full account from Corporal Renton, who also told us that eventually you helped bring in the injured and acted in a manner we would expect from a British soldier. We have also taken into account that this is apparently the first time you have seen any direct action since your arrival here a few days ago. Now before we consider a sentence is there anything you might wish to say or add?"

"No sir," he replied.

"Right then Wilson, go with the two NCOs and wait along the trench outside whilst we consider what to do – I'll call you back as soon as I can."

"Thank you sir," Wilson said as the Corporal marched him out of the Officer's room following a salute.

The Sergeant Major left them alone and returned to his other duties promising to return later. The Corporal lit himself a cigarette and said to Wilson, "You don't realise how lucky you are that this is being treated lightly!"

"Yes I know, thanks, but what do you reckon will happen to me?"

"I'm not sure because it is still a serious charge and you could get Field Punishment Number One or, if you're lucky, Number Two."

"What happens with those?"

"You'll find out," said the NCO.

After about fifteen minutes they were called back in. The Officers looked a lot more serious than before, Wilson thought to himself. The other Captain spoke this time introducing himself as Captain Franks from C Company.

"Private Edward Wilson, after careful consideration of the facts put before us, we have found you guilty of disobeying a lawful command by a superior, in this case Corporal Renton. We have the authority to impose, or arrange to have carried out, an appropriate sentence at the Front in order to maintain the discipline within the ranks. The decision will be added to your service record in due course but in the mean time the decision of this hearing is that you will receive Field Punishment Number One to be carried out immediately."

With this Wilson faltered a little, being taken aback and the Corporal moved forward as he fully expected the Private to keel over. However, Wilson steadied himself and the Captain continued.

"At noon each day for the next seven days the punishment will be carried out here at the Front as far as possible. It is not expected that we will be moving from here for at least a week with our current orders being to hold where we are, get some rest and wait for some reinforcements before the next push. The punishment will take the form that you will be shackled and fixed to a suitable object, in your case probably a stake in the ground, for two hours for each of those seven days. You will not be afforded the protection of the front of the trenches or any other cover but will be placed at the back of the trench where you will be exposed to the effects of a shell attack but not to gunfire from their machine gunners or snipers. You will remain shackled for all of those seven days by your feet and hands. Do you understand or do you have any questions?"

"No sir, I do not have any questions, thank you sir," he answered straightening his back and saluting as he came to attention.

With that he was marched out by the Corporal and they were met by the Sergeant Major. He was briefed by the Corporal and confirmed that he would take over the disciplinary task. He introduced himself as RSM Banks. It was now just before eleven and Wilson was told to sit and wait near the latrines for the next hour when the first two hour punishment would take place. The RSM immediately arranged for two Privates to shackle Wilson's hands and ankles with irons and to leave him in a small alcove in the trench wall. For the best part of an hour Wilson just sat there miserable and downcast. He had heard that these punishments were terrible if the enemy started shelling as there was little protection and you just hoped that the shells landed far enough away. Should the enemy overrun the position you would be bayoneted, shot or, at best, taken prisoner. Wilson felt as bad as at any time since that dreadful crossing from England. He now regretted his foolishness in trying to run away but consoled himself with the fact that the Corporal seemed to have decided to treat him leniently. It was sobering to think that the Corporal could have had him shot. However, the more he thought of what might happen to him as he was about to be exposed in the line the more he felt, at that moment, like it could be a fate worse than death!

As noon approached and with the sun now making it feel really hot, Captain Harris and RSM Banks arrived with the two Privates who had shackled him earlier. One of them was pushing a spoked wooden wheel similar to that seen on supply carriages. These wheels were not hard to come by with many stuck in the muddy paths or floating in the watery holes, their carriages either having been hit by the shelling or simply having slithered into the shell holes. It had been a common sight on the way up to the trenches with, too often, their horses lying dead beside them or floating in the water.

Wilson stood up and stretched his legs and arms. As he did so, one of the Privates placed the wheel against the back wall of the trench at its widest point and the other undid the irons on Wilson's hands and ankles.

Captain Harris instructed the men to shackle Wilson to the wheel with his arms and legs outstretched; his legs at five and seven o'clock and his hands at ten and two, which meant that he was no longer in contact with the ground.

Wilson's face was grim and with a pained expression. The two Privates went about their task without ever looking at him but glances between them and a little pat on his arm from one suggested that they were not enjoying this task one little bit.

Most of the enlisted men there had heard that this sort of "crucifixion style" punishment was commonplace but it was not something they had seen before. Even the RSM's demeanour was less rigid than usual and it appeared that he found it difficult to deal with this sort of thing. He shuffled his feet and kept looking along the trench trying to find something happening that could mean he could absent himself from the situation and leave the others to carry on without him.

Eventually Captain Harris spoke, "Wilson, we are adopting this punishment in this way not only to make an example of you but also to show this as an example to the rest of the men here. We will not tolerate insubordination and ill discipline to a more senior rank, be it to a Corporal or to an Officer. We shall leave you here for two hours and this will occur on every day for a week. It is likely that the machine gun unit will be moved back from the line but you will stay until the end of your punishment period. Once you have been removed from the wheel you will remain shackled by your feet for the whole time, which will allow you to at least move about but will prevent you from running away. Do you understand?"

Wilson opened his mouth to speak but it is clear the Officer was not expecting an answer. The Captain instead stared out towards No Man's Land and continued, "At least you have a nice day for it – some warmth in the sun and the Germans seem to be having a day off from shelling us. God help you if they start up because you will stay exactly where you are now at the back of this trench and under no circumstances will you be moved from here. I'm leaving the RSM in charge until he goes back down the line and he will then let you know you who will take over from him."

With this he turned and left. One of the Privates remained with the keys and the other followed the Captain. The RSM hovered nearby checking on his other charges as they relaxed in the trench. Not one of the men along the trench had seemed at all interested in Wilson's plight – it was just like they were treating this as if it were some common occurrence. Wilson guessed, though, that deep down the men were taking it all in and talking about it amongst themselves when away from the watchful eye of the RSM.

After a few minutes the RSM came over and told the Private that under no circumstances was he to speak with Wilson and he was to ensure no one else did and at two o'clock precisely he could release his man but replace the foot irons as the Captain had ordered. The poor Private looked embarrassed and had to admit that he did not have a watch so could not tell when it would be two o'clock. The RSM huffed and swore under his breath but said he would come along and tell him when the time was up.

Through all this Wilson tried to appear that he was taking all this in his stride. He felt nervous and his mouth was dry and he asked the RSM for some water. The RSM told him that he'd have to wait until the end of the punishment period. With that the RSM left the two men alone and went off along the trench.

The Private looked at Wilson and winked and tapped his water bottle and winked again as if to say, "I'll see you're alright." Later he gave Wilson a sip when there was no one around and said his name was Cyril Armitage.

The sun did feel warm on Wilson's face and his soggy clothing actually began to steam a little and, with this, to dry out – perhaps that was one good thing that would come out of this, he thought and he even ventured a smile to himself.

As his feet had remained dry during the night the soreness was nowhere near as bad as it had been. He did ask Cyril if he would mind taking off his boots and socks for him but the Private shook his head and shrugged as if to say he was sorry he could not help.

Wilson was mightily pleased that there was no shelling. As he laid back there against the trench parapet facing the enemy he contemplated exactly how he would cope with that, if it were to happen. He knew his nerves were pretty well shattered anyway and, recently, when any shelling had started he would shake uncontrollably and however hard he tried he could not stop it. This even occurred when his own side put up fire and the shells whined overhead from behind the forward lines.

Wilson knew it was sure to be a long two hours and, whilst all was quiet and the warmth of the sun was most pleasant, there was plenty of time to think and worry about all the aches and pains brought on by the conditions and the activities he and his fellow men had undertaken. There was also the tiredness he now felt due to the lack of sleep over what seemed such a long period of time. Then of course was the problem with the infernal lice that had got into everyone's clothing. He and the rest of the men had spent as much time as they could delicing one another during times when they were resting. However, it was impossible to free themselves from these creatures despite using candles when available to run down the seams of a uniform, which is where the little creatures seemed to like to congregate. However hard the men tried, they were never able to get rid of the wretched things it seemed.

Just thinking of this whilst tethered and with nothing else to take his mind off it, Wilson began to notice the irritation around his neck and in his hair. He thought to himself that when you cannot move your arms and legs the itching seems to be worse and gets even worse the longer you couldn't do anything about it.

As if the lice were not bad enough the pleasant sunshine had created yet another discomfort. With so many bodies still out in No Man's Land the rotting process becomes faster as the sun gets warmer. The horrible sweet smell of rotting flesh permeated everywhere and nowhere more so than in the nostrils. Many of the men were wearing their gas masks to keep out the smell, despite this being against Regulations. The NCOs tended to turn a blind eye but not the Officers so as soon as one of them appeared the masks were whipped off.

To Wilson the smell was equally nauseating and what made things worse was the appearance of swarms of flies. If a shell or gun went off they would all rise as one from the bodies of the men and horses still out there between the respective front lines, it was quite an exciting sight if it was not so revolting. During the two hours, the flies occasionally landed on Wilson's face and not being possible to swot them he had to develop a way of blowing at various angles from his mouth to ward them off. Occasionally when they were alone Cyril would come over and brush them away.

With the drying out of the bottom of the trenches the rats were able to scurry about at will. The men set traps and killed as many as they could, normally by wringing their necks or cutting off their heads once caught. Bayonet practice was used on them but rarely worked and it proved so difficult to catch them with a single thrust of the sharp point as they moved so quickly. Everyone was worried that they might be carrying all sorts of diseases and would easily pass these on. They were enormous in size and some men said they had seen some as big as cats. Today the odd bloated one scurried past Wilson. On two occasions they stopped and nibbled at his legs and seemed annoyed when they received a small kick for their trouble from Cyril.

For Wilson there was not much he could do but watch all this going on, try and get some sleep and keep the flies off as best he could. Cyril furtively came over three times and gave him a drink. Everything remained so quiet.

As the time wore on there was much more activity along the trench as more replacements arrived and some of his fellow soldiers from the past few days were taken down the line. Those that replaced them were a hotpotch of men from various brigades and battalions. Such had been the losses in the past week that the Front had to be bolstered by any fit men that could be found and put together. The rumour remained that a major Canadian force would arrive shortly and that the Commander in Chief had decided to use them for one last and vast push to secure the Passchendaele Ridge as this was key to the original plan of reaching and relieving the Belgian Channel ports. It was beginning to look, however, that this part of the plan would not be completed in view of the onset of winter and the fact that the British had become bogged down around Ypres with penetration of the higher ground, still held by the enemy, proving almost impossible.

As the new troops arrived they were intrigued and even upset as they passed along the trench by the sight of one of their own tied to a wheel and exposed in this way. Like the rest of the men who had been in the trench before them they, too, had heard of this form of punishment but not many had actually seen it in practice – whilst the Officers and the Generals had thought it a good idea and there to discourage poor discipline most of the men thought it had the opposite effect with the general morale now lower than at anytime in the past three years of the War.

The other Private returned and joined Cyril. Between them, they had hurried the curious new men on their way and the RSM arrived with some fifteen minutes of the two hours remaining and he threatened to put anyone of the new men who lingered on a charge. When these men settled down they became even more intrigued when they found out who the prisoner was. Some either recognised Wilson or one of the Privates on guard told them. Whilst the story started that Wilson was a mere reserve at a big football club, by the end of the day he was a full England international!

At last for Wilson the two hours were up and apart from the itching from the lice and the biting flies it had not been too bad, well at least for today he decided!

The next two punishment days passed off much the same as the first. The sun shone from time to time and the rain stayed away and for the time of year it was mild. The most important thing was the fact that there was no shelling – it seemed both sides were licking their wounds and taking the opportunity to have some time to recover after the devastating recent fighting. As often happened at times like these both sides turned a blind eye to each recovering as many bodies of their own men as possible from all around – the Germans appeared to have moved back into their old trenches as the British had retreated from the area. As a consequence, the Germans would, no doubt, have found bodies heaped in their old trenches and removing and disposing of these was a lengthy and difficult task. This probably explained why all had remained quiet for these past few days.

The British whenever possible would spend time in No Man's Land picking up or burying as many as possible often putting up a large flag with a red cross on a white background to indicate what they were doing. The Germans would not turn a blind eye for long and eventually the common practice was to fire off some shots over the heads of the soldiers to indicate that any truce was over and to warn that hostilities could recommence at any time.

This happened on the morning of Wilson's fourth day of punishment but the firing lasted for a few minutes along the line and had ceased when he started his punishment at noon.

As these shots started all the men who had been out retrieving what they could scurried back to their own trenches. As they dropped down near Wilson he noted how haunted their faces appeared and the sights they must have seen would have defied belief, he thought to himself. He heard stories that they had had to bury the bodies in shallow graves and had even resorted to throwing any German dead into shell holes filled with water. In some instances even body parts of their own men were disposed of in this way.

When Wilson was tethered all was quiet but before five minutes had gone by the Germans decided to flex their artillery muscles and the concentrated barrage began in earnest again. At first the explosions were some way to the West but gradually they started to creep towards Wilson's position. Cyril and his mate were the only soldiers within sight of Wilson at this time. Most of the other groups did not really wish to witness Wilson's plight so, as far as possible, they kept well away unless ordered to do otherwise.

He was already beginning to feel extremely frightened. He could actually see the shells flying towards their trenches, some exploding nearby and showering the area below with shrapnel or landing and throwing up mud in all directions.

Suddenly and to avoid the worst of the shelling a lot more men had moved position and joined the two Privates in front of him. They were huddled into the front of the trench with most of them facing him. They all looked at him sympathetically and with a degree of concern. Many of them showed their disgust at this sort of treatment, swearing about the Officers and the Army in general. They all wanted to know what Wilson had done to deserve this and Cyril had answered for him. Cyril took delight in telling any of the men new to this area that this was the famous Eddie Wilson but most of the men were simply not interested now that they were well and truly in the firing line. To Wilson the whole thing about his footballing past was totally embarrassing and he told Cyril to keep his mouth shut. The shelling continued but had now moved away to the East and was no longer threatening their part of the line.

Wilson had been heartened when Smith and Corporal Renton had turned up and found him. They had been told to remain with their newly acquired Lewis Gun and provide specialist support to the new troops in the trenches. Smith now crouched a few yards away from Wilson and, when he could, would engage him in conversation.

Suddenly, the shelling started again and once again the shells were passing overhead and landing towards the rear of the line of trenches. Smith turned his head towards his friend and noticed how pale he had become. Although his legs were tied to the wheel they were visibly shaking. Smith started to move to help his friend but Cyril put a strong right hand on his shoulder and told him to get back. Shrapnel fell harmlessly a few yards from their part of the trench but the explosions were now creeping very close indeed as the Germans adjusted their range. Wilson now had his eyes firmly shut and his whole body began to shake as it had done in the past. A shell landed about fifteen yards away causing a lot of damage to the trench with a few casualties – Wilson could hear the screams of the men through the din of the shells exploding overhead. The noise was at first deafening but after a while all Wilson could hear was a ringing in his head and a throbbing caused by the blast effect from the shells.

Smith again looked over at Wilson. Whilst being frightened himself he couldn't begin to understand how his friend might be feeling but there was little he could do right then. Suddenly, Smith noticed that Wilson's trousers were soaked down the front where he had wet himself. He also saw the tears rolling down his friend's contorted and frightened face. There was still this awful shaking. Most of the other men around him just could not bear to watch but Smith just could not bring himself to look away.

A shell exploded on the back of the trench so close to Wilson that the wheel rolled away two or three yards down the length of the trench and fell forward so he was face down in the mud at the base of the trench. At first he could not breathe and he could not move his mouth out of the inch or so of wet slimy mud that still remained at this lower part of the trench. Had it rained at all in the past few days and a few more inches of water had remained in the trench, as it normally did, he would probably have drowned if he had been alone. This time Cyril and his friend pulled Wilson up and stood him back up against the back of the trench.

Like Wilson all the men around him were dazed and confused by this latest explosion. Shrapnel had hit some but none seemed too badly injured and the men around them were caring for them. Although Wilson could not see behind him, he was aware that the men were all looking aghast at the point where the shell had thrown soil up into the air.

He was able to pick up from their shouts and animated talking that bodies, buried from action in previous days or months, had been thrown up and out of, or lie scattered in, the trench. There were limbs, skulls with decomposing flesh on them and other body parts plus pieces of uniform, helmets and other personal effects. Even dead and rotting rats had been blown out of their makeshift graves.

For some of the new men in the trench this sight was just too much and many just sat there as if paralysed, shocked by these most dreadful sights.

Smith recovered his composure quicker than most as all this was nothing new to him he having seen it all before. Despite the ringing in his ears he went over to Wilson and with some help from one of the others they slowly manoeuvred the wheel and they placed Wilson with his back leaning against the front of the trench thus providing a bit more shelter than he had previously. The two Privates had started to object but the look from Smith made them back away.

Smith came over and wiped the mud from Wilson's eyes and face and he stared into his friend's eyes but there seemed there was nothing there. The eyes just stared out looking at nothing in particular, the shaking had stopped and the whole body was limp. It was as if he was dead but spittle and regurgitated food was seeping from the mouth on each breath in a sort of bubbling froth.

"Eddie, Eddie, wake up mate," said Smith grasping Wilson's shoulders and trying to support him but the body did not respond. Smith lifted up Wilson's chin and looked into his friend's eyes again – still nothing.

"Sorry mate but I've got to do this," Smith slapped the face has hard as he reasonably could on both cheeks, using his palm on one side and the back of his hand on the other. Wilson's eyes focussed with a start and inadvertently the remaining contents of Wilson's mouth and throat shot out over Smith's shoulder. Wilson coughed again and seemed to come round completely; it was as if he had been unconscious with his eyes open. He did not say anything at first but then looked at his mate saying:

"Smithy I can't cope with this any more you might just as well shoot me now and get it over with – look at me I'm puking up, I've got the shakes, I'm pissing myself and probably crapped myself as well. We are not going to get out of this because some bloody stupid General will send us over the top before we're much older and that will definitely be the end – so bloody shoot me if you really are a mate and let me get out of this hell into another one – it's got to be better than this."

"Come on Eddie you've got to be more positive than this – think of your family and friends, think of Burnley and getting back there and another Cup Final! This can't go on forever the Canadians will be here soon and we'll get moved out and we might even get some leave. You've only three more days of this punishment and then you can move on. I bet we miss any push and we can leave it to the Canadian boys to finally sort out the bloody Germans."

Before they could do anything else the RSM had arrived, "Put that bloody prisoner back where he was – now!"

This Smith did and he moved away.

"You alright, Wilson?" asked the RSM, not really waiting for an answer and he, too, left making sure Cyril was there to keep an eye on Wilson.

For the rest of the time up to two o'clock everything quietened down with the enemy no doubt feeling that was enough for the day, especially as the British artillery had started up and was raining down on their positions.

Wilson's arms and legs were released with, as before, only the chains left on his feet. He slumped down in one of the small alcoves cut into the trench wall and retreated into his own world. His strange staring eyes just looked down at the floor of trench. His face remained so pale and he was now muttering to himself with his head shaking and his body rhythmically pumping against the back wall behind him. The force of this was such that it was almost as if he were trying to injure himself.

This continued for a while until Smith came over and sat down next to him. He and his fellow soldiers had all agreed they were supportive of army discipline, especially in the front line, but to a man they agreed that this type of punishment was too barbaric and they had all shared Smith's concern over Wilson's physical and mental state.

Many of them encouraged Smith to at least try to get someone to arrange for a Doctor to see Wilson. Fearing disciplinary action might be taken against him if he made too much fuss, he had been loath to push the matter too far. However, seeing what state Wilson appeared to be in now, he decided he would speak to the Corporal, especially as it was he who had instigated the disciplinary proceedings. Smith hoped the Corporal would take up the matter with those in higher authority on Wilson's behalf and indeed that of the men as well.

Renton appeared just as Smith had told his mates that he had decided to do something. Smith called Renton to one side.

"Look Corp, have you seen Wilson, he's in a terrible state?"

"Yeah – I saw him on my way through he looks like he's lost it – was he like that all through the shelling?"

"I couldn't see him all the time but he appeared to suddenly lose it halfway through – can we get a Doctor to look at him, do you think?"

Renton shook his head, "I doubt it mate the bloody RSM seems to be enjoying the whole thing and had little sympathy when I told him the men were concerned at the type of punishment being dished out – in fact I wished I'd never bloody reported it. I am now beginning to think we're all now close to doing what Wilson did. Like the rest of us, he's had virtually no experience of the front line until just recently and there's always got to be a first person to want to get away from all this crap. I've been told that Wilson and his first Section apparently didn't even complete the training like we had at Etaples. That was helpful in a way to get us to cope with all these bloody situations."

"Could you try though – if he has to go through all this again in the next few days I don't know what might happen?"

The Corporal thought for a moment and then slapped Smith on the back and smiled. "I'll speak with the RSM and try to get him to speak with an Officer but I don't hold out much hope. I'll see you later." With that he went off to find the RSM who he had seen, earlier, resting in the shade 25 yards along the trench. Just at that moment the Germans put up another barrage with explosions all around and Renton had to move slowly, crouched against the front side of the trench to protect himself. He had to pass Wilson who he could see sitting and leaning against the wall and clasping his knees to his chest and slowly rocking.

By the time he got to the RSM the barrage had moved away to the East once more. Unbelievably, despite the noise, the RSM was fast asleep. Renton shook him and he awoke with a start.

"Oh, it's you, what do you want now?"

"Sarge, I'm worried about Wilson, he's lost it in a big way."

"Tough – he should have thought of that when he didn't do what he was told – you were there so don't you agree?"

"I didn't think it would end up like this; the bloke's having some sort of breakdown, shouldn't you speak with one of the Officers?"

"Bloody hell, Corporal, you should have bloody shot him for running away and we could've been saved this – as if we haven't got enough problems." He thought for a moment and then looked up at Renton, "Alright, I'll see Harris or whoever's left." With that the RSM stood up, smartened himself up and marched off.

Renton sat and waited and the RSM returned in about five minutes. "Not really interested," he said, "they say that Wilson's got to serve out the punishment and they've got no time to find a Doctor or spare anyone to go fetch one from further back but they did say that when one comes up, they'll get him to look at Wilson. That's the best I can do so bugger off and let me get back to sleep."

Renton left muttering under his breath, "Bloody idiots these people, I hope the same sort of thing happens to them sometime."

He found Smith waiting with a small group. "Sorry blokes, no go. The RSM had a word but the Officers won't do anything apart from getting a Doc to look at him if and when one turns up here."

"That's stupid Corp what's the point of reducing a perfectly good bloke to a bloody wreck?" said Smith looking for support from the group, which he got as they all nodded and muttered their approval.

"Well, he'll just have to see out the next few days and then you'll have to give him some support – he's gonna need it but let's hope a Doc turns up and I'll make sure the Sarge keeps on at the Officers at least."

With that they all sat down and remained quiet for a couple of minutes and then once one started they all started and spent the next half an hour moaning and cursing everything and everyone connected with the British Army – some spoke of mutiny, some spoke of releasing Wilson and telling him to get away from here. In the end they ran out of ideas and settled back down to their routine of rat catching, rifle cleaning, bayonet sharpening, writing home or just dozing.

CHAPTER 16

During the evening Smith had managed to bribe the two Privates, who were by now back guarding Wilson, using a small supply of cigarettes that he had. They turned a blind eye to Smith moving in close to Wilson. He found Wilson in much the same state as he had been earlier in the day. He was sitting down with his knees clutched with his arms up to just below his chin. The rocking motion had stopped but he simply stared into space. He aroused slightly when Smith arrived and started talking but it was very much a one-way conversation. Eventually he said:

"Come on Eddie I'm trying to help you here, you've got to pull yourself together and get through the next few days, it'll soon be over."

Wilson stopped staring ahead and suddenly leapt to his feet pushing his face right into Smith's shouting:

"Why the hell don't you just sod off and leave me alone."

Taking a step back Smith pleaded: "For God's sake Eddie I'm on your side here!"

Wilson shouted back, "Well I don't need your help or anyone else's just go back, pick up your gun and wait for some stupid, bloody General to make sure you're bloody killed before you're more than a few days older. You don't think we're going to get out of this do you? I'll give you a week and then you'll be going over the top and then end up floating dead in a shell hole before you know it." With that he slumped down and returned to his knees up position.

Somewhat taken aback Smith started to move away, "If that's your attitude well sod you too mate – you can kiss goodbye to anymore help from me." And with that he was off.

Later Smith found Corporal Renton and told him what had happened. Despite what he had said to Wilson he was still concerned about him and would try to help when Wilson's punishment came to an end. Renton repeated what he had said earlier and promised he would have another word with the RSM and hopefully the Officers but didn't hold out much hope: he did, however, promise to help Smith when Wilson was released.

For Wilson the next two days passed off without too much incident but word got around about his outburst to Smith and many of the men felt even more strongly that this type of punishment was likely to break the will of any of them were they placed in the same situation. With very little to do in the trenches and with the enemy taking some time out from their shelling and any other action, this somewhat mutinous talk was to them an interesting way to while away the hours.

On the final day of Wilson's punishment, he was again placed in his usual position at the back of the trench. Once again the Germans had been quiet during the morning and many of those who had been in the trench alongside Wilson were now taken back to the rear lines as the Canadians finally arrived. With them, however, came the rain as if to baptise their presence and to provide them with a welcome to their new hell.

The guarding Privates had provided Wilson with a cape and his helmet to help protect him from the rain, although they guessed the RSM might not approve. This rain was about as bad as it had been at any time, the other soldiers huddled for whatever shelter they could find. About halfway through the two hours, a Second Lieutenant, one of the remaining East Lancs left behind following the withdrawal, came along and immediately ordered the Privates to remove the helmet and the cape. The two of them looked at each other and were on the point of arguing for some sympathy for the prisoner when the Lieutenant said, "That's an order and if you don't want to be put on a charge and end up like Wilson, then do it – and do it now!"

The Privates quickly moved in and took off the items. The rain immediately drenched Wilson's hair and previously dry uniform. The rain got even harder and as the two hours came to an end Wilson was shaking with cold and even appeared to be unconscious. One of the Privates released the shackles and shook him. His eyes opened but stared ahead fixed on the trench wall opposite. Once again he seemed to have dropped into a trance and did not respond to the Private's questions but he stood up and offered his arm as if asking to be led away.

By the time Wilson was moved from his open position there was water up to the soldiers' ankles in the trench. The Canadians were bemoaning their lot even though many of them were veterans of the Somme in 1916 and were used to the rigours of the trench but even they found the amount of water and the appalling conditions somewhat different from the summer action in 1916.

Smith and Renton had not been taken down from the line but had stayed behind, much to their disgust. They remained with a squad to support the Canadians who, it seemed, were light on experienced machine gunners so the Officers had decided to leave some of the experienced men with them to help out.

The Privates had moved Wilson back to the alcove he had been in previously and made sure he now had a helmet and cape. It was only some relief because underneath these he remained soaked through.

With the rain still pouring down, Wilson had been completely freed but not before the Second Lieutenant had given him a real talking to and warned him that if he got into trouble again by disobeying orders or even running away he stood a good chance of being shot.

Wilson at first just sat in his alcove with his guards remaining close by until one of them went to get Smith and Renton. These two eventually escorted Wilson back to where they had set up their equipment. They had dug into the side of the trench and rigged up their capes to form a small roof to get some relief from the rain. This time Wilson made no outburst but refused to say anything very much and spent the rest of the day sleeping fitfully out of the rain.

At first light the next morning a Captain Morrison called the machine gun squad together and told them they were now going down the line as someone at HQ had realised, at last, how long they had been right up the Front. They would be able to spend a few days further back but would be moved back to here when the next attack on the ridge ahead of them was to take place. This time to support the Canadians.

They made their way back down the trench system and eventually out into the more open areas not so exposed to the German gunfire. Smith had remained with Wilson who had at last started to come out of his stupor and actually had struck up more conversation with the men than in the previous few weeks. Smith had urged his friend to seek some sort of help from a Doctor and Renton had agreed to put in a word. Now that the RSM had gone down the line and was actually no longer in direct control of the squad since the Canadians had taken over, Renton felt more comfortable going direct to one of the Officers who was aware of Wilson's situation.

The journey back down the line was as hazardous as it had ever been. The rain that had continued on and off for what seemed like weeks had returned the whole area to one of the water filled holes. The duckboards, where they still remained, providing only slight relief from the muddy conditions with the mud, at some points, up to the shins. Coming the other way was a constant stream of troops moving up to the forward trenches. Most of them were the Canadians. Whereas in 1916 they had been cheerful and hopeful as they went to the Front, they were now grimfaced and battle hardened, quietly moving up hardly even taking any notice of any men going the other way.

CHAPTER 17

After two or three days of relatively quiet relaxation George Smith spent a lot of time with Eddie Wilson. The latter returned to something like his old self as they chattered away about football and what life had been like before all of this and even what it might be like when it was all over. They had even had time to go back even further from the rear trenches to one of the local villages where a surprising large number of local people had remained behind. They had set up a small bakery, two or three estaminets and other places where the soldiers could rest up if they had a couple of days leave. The men were able to indulge themselves in some foul tasting local red wine and even had the company of some local girls of uncertain reputation, who were not backward in offering certain services, which many of the soldiers were only too keen to take full advantage of.

Smith and Wilson, together with three others, just kept to the wine, which after the umpteenth bottle began to taste much better. As time went on the songs became more bawdy and the French girls, having finished their business elsewhere, came and joined in. The revelry went on long into the night.

Of course, the next morning their heads were sore and the stomachs churning - not many of those who had been together the night before were able to face breakfast.

Their mood picked up during the day, made better by the fact that mail had arrived from home. Nearly everyone had a good pile as it had been sometime since the mail had been able to get through or they had been around to receive it.

Wilson had received his quota and spent well over an hour catching up with news from home. The letters were from his mother and his sister, Mary. She had lost her boyfriend when he was killed somewhere in the Dardenelles and was now dating a PT Instructor from Bolton who was in the Lancashire Fusiliers and had been on Bolton Wanderers books at the start of the War. Mary thought it unlikely that he would be posted abroad so at least he might survive the War and she hoped that when it was all over they might wed. She had news of several old friends and schoolmates of Wilson who had been killed or had returned home badly injured. She also said that the local paper had reported that none of the pre War Burnley players had yet been killed and it had a list of them in the paper and she confirmed that Eddie's name was there.

There was even a parcel from Mum, which had some thick knitted socks that Wilson kissed and whooped with joy. Although the rain and wet conditions had returned, the early days of his punishment had given his feet time to recover with the blisters healing completely. This new supply of socks would be a godsend as long as he could keep them dry.

Cheered by all this the soldiers settled down to write back home with their news. Wilson in particular had come right out of his depressed state, helped by the evening out drinking. He felt so much better that he decided not to seek out a Doctor despite Smith and Renton pleading for him to do so.

As November arrived so did the cold weather and the rain still fell most days with the occasional snow showers. The land still remained sodden and ice covered at times. The men had much better protection from the elements in that they could keep dry but the cold nights and frosty, early mornings made them shiver in their temporary billets. Wilson more than once blessed his Mum for the extra socks as wearing two pairs helped keep his feet warmer. The trench foot had seemed to make his circulation worse than it had been and hence his feet got cold very quickly and it was more difficult to get them warm. Many men had put their feet really close to the fires to try to get some warmth but it had really only left them with chilblains which had made it extremely difficult for them to get their boots on and was absolute agony when they did manage it.

After a few more days it was clear their relatively relaxed time was coming to an end. Even more Canadians had arrived and there were now thousands within a short distance from the front line. The rumour had persisted that the Field Marshall's grand plan, whilst apparently having stalled in the mud, was about to restart with this major effort to secure this Passchendaele ridge, being the higher ground held by the Germans for so long. It was said that the Germans had suffered greatly during the October battle and far more than the Allies. So it had been decided at the highest level that the Canadians, with strong British support, would test their depleted numbers and waning morale. Hopefully, the offensive would at last put an end to the current stalemate and force the Germans back so as to free up the Belgian ports.

The cynical soldiers had, of course, heard all this before and took it with a pinch of salt but whilst they often laughed and joked a lot of the time, in quieter moments they ruefully considered what lay ahead for them. For Wilson, he retreated more into himself once more and was something that George Smith was quick to pick up on. He tried to rally his friend by arranging for Wilson to receive some concentrated training on how to support the machine gunner when in action and, if necessary, to take over if the circumstances dictated. Smith had, through Renton, reminded the Officers in charge that Wilson had not been part of their machine gun unit previously but had been seconded to them following the wiping out of his previous infantry squad.

Wilson had proved an enthusiastic learner and had been quick on the uptake and was more than proficient in supporting the gunner, his mood also visibly changed for the better.

Eventually Captain Morrison, who had led the men down the line, was to brief the group and then lead them on their return. As before they would move up under the cover of darkness and be ready to move off with the Canadians at first light. There would be the usual artillery barrage on the German line for a considerable period and as soon as this ceased they would move out of the trenches. Unlike at the Somme the previous year they would be supported by a creeping barrage, which would provide some sort of cover in front of them as they advanced, by ensuring the Germans kept their heads down.

The concentrated fire from a strategically placed German pillbox on the higher ground had hindered the previous attack in October. It was now deemed that this was a priority target but was unlikely to be too affected by the artillery so it needed a direct attack. Wilson's squad were to support the Canadians' frontal assault by concentrating their machine gun fire on the pillbox whilst the Canadians got close enough to hopefully destroy it with grenades.

The journey up to the Front was difficult as usual but on this occasion the weather was really cold and there was a frost in the late evening, which became harder as the night wore on. This had the benefit of hardening the mud but the previously wet duckboards and the ground itself were frozen solid and keeping balance was difficult. There were several casualties as men slipped through the thin ice on the old shell holes and the usual rush to help them ensued. There had been no orders on this occasion to just leave any that fell in the holes to fend for themselves. Dozens were saved in Wilson's company alone.

Unfortunately, of those that fell through the ice, several would be so cold it was difficult for them to go on as their clothes were soaked through and the material had frozen. Many of them had to be told to drop out and make their own way back down the line. Some were never to be seen again and it was generally thought that they had succumbed to the cold, collapsed and perhaps fell into another hole and just disappeared. Even many of the fitter ones who got back were later to succumb to pneumonia and to die from the complications this brought on.

Smith and Wilson not surprisingly had been paired together with Wilson the support man. They had taken turns to lug the gun up to the front line. When they arrived there they were quite exhausted and for a couple of hours got some sleep but the cold was so intense it actually woke them up. As zero hour approached the Officers and NCOs moved up and down the trench barking out their last orders, encouraging their men to do their best for King and Country and this time to finally knock the Hun out of his trenches and move everyone a step closer to victory. The men had heard it all before and they all stood quietly at the ready. Many smoked a last cigarette. An Officer came round with a tot of some awful French spirit, which he said might warm their insides and help them calm down. Most of the men spat it out. Some muttered prayers and, somewhat surprisingly, a Chaplain moved amongst them – he was a Catholic but he offered a word and a prayer to each man in turn.

Wilson remained quiet and George Smith continually glanced at his friend but they said nothing. Wilson felt his body shaking but then so was everyone else's in view of the intense cold – he did feel less nervous than in the past but beneath it all he felt that this would be the end for him – he had been lucky in the past seemingly to escape when his mates had bought it whilst he was in the latrine – he had also survived the shelling in No Man's Land and also possible capture. He had survived the shelling tied to his wheel but now, out there somewhere, he was convinced there was a bullet, a piece of shrapnel, a bayonet or whatever with his name on it.

The Canadian Officer shouted for all to be ready; the NCOs checked that the bayonets had been fixed and that the gunners and their support men were ready. He stood there looking at his watch with the artillery shells hurtling over their heads and noisily exploding hopefully on the German trenches. The Germans would know they would be coming and as soon as the artillery ceased they would normally run from their holes and man the front of the trench with a mass of machine guns at the ready. Word had already got to their Officers that the enemy were now using the creeping fire tactic so they could not afford to remain protected in their well made holes for too long and would have to have some of the guns trained on the enemy and ready to fire as soon as the attack started.

The pillbox was a little to the left and Wilson and Smith's squad were to keep together as far as possible and take a more measured approach towards it. The German gunners in the pillbox and those left to deal with the initial wave would have more of an eye on the other attackers as they advanced towards the German trenches, trying to pick them off with the crossfire. It was hoped that the pillbox assault squad would gain a few valuable seconds to get away from their trench and get some cover behind the rises in the land in front of the pillbox whilst the gunners were distracted.

The Captain had a whistle poised and Wilson and the other men crouched looking directly at the Captain. Despite the tension and reality that they may be shot to pieces in the next few moments, there was an air of excitement. Some of the men crossed themselves whether they were Catholic or not, as they just followed what the next man did. Smith slapped Wilson on the back and wished him good luck – Wilson offered his hand and took Smith's in a firm handshake. The whistle blew and with a shout they left the trench and moved off towards the pillbox.

CHAPTER 18

For a short while the swarm of men made good ground – the Germans had been slower than usual getting back to their defensive shooting positions and, in particular, their machine guns. The attackers found the hard ground far easier to cross than the deep mud they had experienced before and, in fact, such was the hardness of the frost that they were able to run across the icy tops of the watery shell holes. Some of the sliding was comical and the odd soldier crashed through the ice and had to be helped out where possible, although more often than not they were left to their own devices. Most of the men did not want to stop thus becoming a possible sitting target themselves for the German snipers.

The frontal fire coming from the German side was therefore far less than expected but the pillbox gunners to the left were much quicker in their response and their withering crossfire whistled past or thudded into the Canadians' bodies. Men were falling dead and injured all in front of Wilson's squad who, as planned, had actually moved more slowly than those to their right whose task had been to reach the trenches as quickly as possible. The fallen bodies provided some cover as Wilson's group dropped to the ground using the bodies as a shield whenever they could. The machine gun bullets continued to thud into the already lifeless bodies and Wilson moved forward on his stomach dragging his part of the Lewis gun. Mortars exploded all around, the noise was ear splitting not just from the bullets and shells but the shouts of the men as they fell and as they lay there injured calling out for help.

For Wilson there was too much to think about at that moment to worry about himself. Part excitement and part adrenalin drove him forward – the squad were all following Captain Morrison and a young Lieutenant he had not met until they had arrived at the setting off point the night before. These two had their handguns at the ready but Smith, like Wilson, had the rest of the Lewis and the ammunition. At times they dragged the gun, only to be admonished by the Lieutenant, who told them to carry it so it did not get damaged. It was a struggle and in the end they both took a chance and moved forward in a crouched position, looking to get out of the pillbox's line of fire as soon as they could.

To their right a whole stream of Canadians were moving forward now at no more than a walk because the artillery support from behind them had started up again and they did not wish to get so far ahead that they were fired on by their own side! The withering gunfire from the German trenches picked off a few but the firing was less intense than in the past suggesting that the artillery bombardment had achieved some of its purpose at least. The

Canadians, peculiarly, walked side-on and leant forward as they moved ahead as if the bullets were like driving rain coming at them on the wind.

Wilson's squad were at last told to crouch and get into somewhere that afforded some cover. There were plenty of holes and smaller depressions in this area. Smith was told to set up his gun within the best cover possible and concentrate fire on the pillbox so the rest of them could move forward and hopefully take it.

Wilson helped Smith put the gun together and with his shovel tried to dig more into the mud but it was difficult with the frost. However, in the end, they were able to set up with good protection and a clear line of fire on the pillbox, which was quiet for the first time as the British artillery fire landed close to it. Smith hurriedly worked to get the gun ready issuing shouted instructions to Wilson. He signalled to the Captain that he was ready – two other similar guns were set up to the left and on the Officer's signal they started firing and two seconds later the rest of the squad were up and running the hundred yards or so to the pillbox. As instructed they weaved from side to side largely around the shell holes and not across their frozen tops. As soon as they had moved off, the fire from the pillbox started up again.

Wilson and Smith's fire and that of the other two guns did have the effect of reducing the level of fire from the pillbox and an artillery shell landed just behind it. The explosion would have temporarily stunned and deafened the Germans inside and for a crucial few seconds the Canadians were able to run forward under no fire at all. Just when it appeared they would easily take their target there were two explosions almost simultaneously right in amongst them. It seemed like artillery shells and there was no way they had come from the German side.

They were decimated and all except two fell with some of the bodies and parts of bodies thrown into the air, even above the noise all around Wilson could hear the screams.

"Bloody hell," shouted Smith, "what are we gonna do now?"

"Come on," said Wilson, "leave the bloody gun and let's take these grenades and get rid of the sodding pillbox, if we stay here our own bloody artillery could get us." He bent down and picked up as many grenades as he could carry from the small store they had laid out earlier and then he and Smith were off.

The other two gun groups saw what they were doing and followed, running a few yards behind. The artillery shells were still coming over their heads from their own side but were still far too short of where they should be. Smith turned round and shouted in the general direction from where the firing was coming from, "Stop shooting you stupid bastards and give us a bloody chance!"

For a moment the pillbox was quiet again.

As the gunners got to the fallen Canadians, they picked up as many additional grenades as they could carry – stuffing them into their pockets and even down their trouser fronts!

One or two soldiers were still alive and appealed for help usually wanting water; the other bodies were hideously mangled up. Apart from the usual pieces of bone and flesh scattered around there were awful sights. One body had no arms or legs but the rest of the body had not a scratch upon it. Another had only the stomach downwards. Others had simply been killed by one piece of shrapnel hitting a vital part of the body. One man was still alive and he was stuffing his intestines back into the gaping wound in his stomach – it was the young Lieutenant – he appealed to them to shoot him and the six of them looked at each other. "Please," he shouted.

As Wilson and Smith decided to move off one of their colleagues fired a rifle shot straight into the Lieutenant's chest – he died instantly. A Corporal came up behind them and said to the group, "We didn't see that men, understand, now move off?"

Just at that moment the pillbox's guns started up yet again and the young man who had shot the Lieutenant, the rifle still in his hand, took three shots right across his chest and they threw him back right across the body of the Officer – he too was dead. He had been with another man who also took a hit – just one bullet – but it took off the top of his head and blood spouted four feet into the air.

Just as this happened, the remaining four hit the ground and Renton joined them – "Let's crawl the rest of the way," said Smith. They inched forward but the gunners in the pillbox saw them and the machine gun bullets spat up the ground all around them. The two lads with them and the Corporal had all come across on the boat with Wilson and he recalled they were from Rawtenstall. As this thought went through his mind the two Privates suddenly stood up and ran forward ten yards towards the pillbox. They were about twenty yards away from it when they were taken down by rifle fire, which appeared to come from the German line behind the pillbox. The Corporal also took a hit to his leg and he collapsed in a heap clutching his left thigh.

Wilson and Smith checked on him and he told them to go on and that he would be fine and not to worry about him. They stayed pinned to the ground and started to inch forward but stopped as the machine gunners in the pillbox strafed the ground in front of them. "What's the plan now then?" shouted Smith. "Get the hell out of here!" responded Wilson, "if only we could!"

Whilst they considered what to do for the best yet another shell from their side landed almost on top of the pillbox and as the soil and other debris started to come down on them Smith said, "Come on let's go and get 'em!"

They ran to the front wall now that the Germans had stopped firing. The pillbox was largely undamaged but once again its occupants were apparently stunned and, no doubt, concussed and disorientated by the shell that had landed to its right hand side.

The two men primed the grenades and dropped them through the slits and put their hands over their heads and dived to the ground. The loud explosion shook the ground beneath them and parts of the pillbox roof flew up into the air together with parts of the German soldiers who had been inside.

Wilson lifted his head and saw the damage. He pulled Smith to his feet, "Come on Smithy let's get the hell out of here!"

With that they moved beyond the remains of the pillbox and into the open land. Now that they were on higher ground they could see to their right that generally the Canadians had made good ground and in some places were in the German trenches.

Smith called out for Wilson to stop saying, "Eddie wait a minute, where are we going. We are on our own with no support don't you think we should wait here or at least move over and join that lot over there?"

Wilson thought for a moment and said, "Let's join them over there but first find a rifle, preferably with a bayonet on the end!"

Just as they moved to their right a group of Canadians rose out of an unusually dry shell hole, probably a new one, and charged towards them stopping abruptly when they saw the colour of their uniforms.

The Canadian Sergeant said, "How the hell did you get here?"

"We attacked the pillbox and put it out of action and thought we'd better join up with another group," said Smith.

"Are you all that's left – how many of you were there?" asked the Sergeant.

"Well, we were six machine gunners to start with. The other four got killed and the squad we were following and supported got blown up by our own artillery – so we carried on and threw some grenades in and that was that," answered Smith.

"Really? Christ! Well done! You'd better come with us."

With that they moved off – there was about eight of them. Suddenly there was a loud whooshing noise and then quiet.

Wilson was completely disorientated and as he got to his feet his head was spinning. The injured Corporal limped towards him, his trousers soaked red, "Get down you idiot, you'll get shot." He yanked at Wilson's arm and pulled him back to the ground.

It seemed to the Corporal that Wilson had absolutely no idea where he was. Wilson looked at the other man vaguely. Next to him was a lifeless body with the lower part of the face a mass of mangled teeth and bone with pieces

119

of wood sticking up out of the mouth - it was George Smith – he appeared to have been hit by a flying piece of branch from a nearby tree. The tree itself had snapped in half and now formed a perfect triangle with the top half of the trunk having toppled and embedded itself into the ground.

Wilson suddenly felt a pain on the back of his head. He touched it with his hand and felt a large area of soreness and the warm stickiness of quickly congealing blood.

To the Corporal it seemed like Wilson had also been hit by the same flying wood as Smith but in a place where there was more protection, the injury being just below the helmet.

The Corporal had taken over twenty minutes to get to them following some urgent emergency treatment that he could give to his leg, which had been sliced by a piece of shrapnel – a small wound but damned sore he thought.

He grabbed Wilson again by the shoulders and looked in him in the eye, "Do you know what happened to Smith?" he asked.

"Who?" said Wilson.

"Smith – look," he answered pointing to the gunner.

"Sorry?"

"Smith – you were with him – remember?"

"No," said Wilson curiously, as he peered around him almost as if he had no idea where he was. He was just about to put up his head even further when the Corporal grabbed him again, "For Christ's sake, keep down! Is your head alright?"

"Yeah, I think so," said Wilson touching the sore part gingerly.

Just as the Corporal suggested they moved on there was a sudden burst of shelling and machine gun fire concentrated on exactly where they were.

Suddenly, Wilson lay down and curled up as before and he brought his knees up to his chest and wrapped his arms around them. He started rocking back and forward and tears began to fall down his face. The Corporal looked on, "Come on Eddie let's go," he said trying to drag Wilson to his feet. The young Private refused to move and the Corporal tried again.

"No, No, No, No, No!" Wilson screamed at Renton "No!"

The Corporal was taken aback. The scream was hysterical and so loud it could be heard above the noise all around them. The Corporal tried again to pull him up but Wilson shrugged him off. Another shell landed nearby, mud was thrown up and landed all over them. With this Wilson screamed again and he pushed at the Corporal glaring at him with wide-eyed look. His eyes had a mix of anger and fear, yet tears still fell down the cheeks.

"Come on!" said the Corporal, "we must go - we'll die if we stay here, we'll have to go back and get some cover – let's use the rubble of the pillbox."

Wilson stood up as bullets whizzed overhead "I said "No" and I meant "No"" and with this he punched the Corporal with the back of his hand in a backhand motion right across his face. The Corporal was shocked to see the look of hate in this normally quiet man's face, which was now snarling and wild. Wilson hit him again and he reeled back, staggered and then fell onto his side. Before he could get to his feet, Wilson had gone – he had turned and ran. He kept running. The bullets still followed him, either spitting up the ground around him or passing close by in the air. He had no weapon and he careered onwards heading as fast as he could run with the watery sun to his left, guessing and hoping that this was North or even West. There were not many British or Canadian soldiers around but one or two he came across made token attempts to stop him. He just kept on going - his feet felt sore as his newly formed skin rubbed against his boots but he tried to ignore it.

His fitness was still such that he was able to keep going for over an hour by which time he was well away from the frontline and the noise of battle was very muffled to him. This was partly due to the distance he had covered but mainly due to his ears still suffering from the blasts from earlier on.

Eventually he stopped when he came to a small road. He felt breathless now and sat out of view in what had been a cornfield during the summer and despite the horrific warfare that had waged in this area for three years, a local farmer had stayed and actually been able to produce a harvest. The coldness of the early morning had turned into a warm day and Wilson felt comfortable as he stretched out on the grass; oblivious to the wet, he went to sleep almost immediately.

After about six hours he awoke and it was now night time. For a moment he wondered where on earth he was, as his head cleared it came back to him. He looked around but it was so dark it was difficult to see more than about twenty yards. He blinked hard and opened his eyes wide to try and see more clearly. Gradually his eyes became more accustomed to the darkness and he was able to see a little more clearly.

He could see the wet grass and the remains of the corn in the field that stretched before him. He could hear little noise but his head thumped with pain particularly from the back. He had no helmet on and he touched the back of his head. "Jesus!" he said to himself as he touched his wound, "What the bloody hell ...?" looking at his bloodstained hand.

He concentrated hard to try and think where he was. In the far distance and about four miles away, he guessed, he could see the odd flash of an explosion and hear the persistent rat-a-tat-tat of a machine gun but it was all rather faint to him.

He had no idea how he had come to be here. He still felt a slight ringing in his ears and then recalled the blast and nothing since. He had been with Smith he suddenly recalled.

"Smithy?" he shouted almost apologetically, "Smithy, you there – Corp are you there?" Silence.

Now at last his eyes had adjusted to make out virtually the whole field, the grassy bank, the hedge and road behind that. He remained totally confused; when he was with Smith it had still been morning. He recalled the pillbox raid and then crouching down as some shelling went on and then … nothing.

He was now wide-awake, he felt his bottom and it was soaking from where he had been sitting and his back was also wet so he guessed he must have been sleeping. What time was it? He had no idea as his watch had long gone - lost somewhere in the trenches. It must be early evening he assumed but was not really sure. The coldness had returned and he shivered. Now he could feel the soreness in his feet and he sat down on the driest patch he could find and took his boots off. Whilst his feet were themselves dry they were red raw again on the toes and heels from his boots. He would have preferred to leave his boots off completely but it was too cold for that.

Again, he stood up and wandered round trying to assess his situation. He worked out that he must have moved away from the Front but how he did that and how he came to be here was a complete mystery.

He tried hard to concentrate and clear his thoughts. Should he go back and just merge in with the men there and carry on as if nothing had happened? What had become of Smithy and the Corporal? He vaguely recalled that he had left the action before, so it was not likely to look that good for him if he's accused of doing it again.

He shook his head trying to help him think more clearly. He weighed up the options in his mind. He knew that if he went back he might be asked some awkward questions and might be accused of running away. On the other hand he could just say he had been stunned and injured during the attack and had only now recovered sufficiently to make his way back to the new line.

However, the more he thought about it the more he was sure he did not really want to go back and face death yet again. He knew he had been lucky so far.

What if he could get to a Channel port and get a ship back home – what would happen when he got there, if he got there? Would the Army be in such a state that they would think he had been blown up, buried in the trenches or even drowned in a shell hole? If the Army reports him missing to his family and he turns up no one need know, surely? The family would need to keep quiet but they and he might have to move away. This would mean no more football, no more Burnley, no more Eddie Wilson. All these notions rapidly passed through his mind. He stood up and walked around. He was now getting annoyed. He picked up a fallen branch and went up to a tree and hit the branch against it with all the force he could muster. The branch broke in half. He threw the half still in his hand as far as he could back towards the noise in the distance, letting out a shout as he did so. As he turned round, he kicked the broken piece of branch at his feet as hard as he could. He had completely forgotten he had taken his boots off and the pain of the wood against his bare foot made him swear. He hopped on his good foot back to where he had sat before and sat there again. He rubbed his toes where they had come into contact with the branch.

He returned to his dilemma and considered his options. He decided he might as well try to get home. If he gets picked up he'll stand Court Martial and if he goes back now to the line the same thing will probably happen anyway. That's it; he would not be going back. He would take his chances, try to get home and then perhaps start a new life.

He thought further about what to do and decided it would be too dangerous to travel by day so he would set off now – how far would it be to a French port? He really had no idea but knew that Belgium was quite a small country and the front line was not far from France so as long as he went towards the North West he would eventually arrive at the sea and could seek out any sort of boat. The trouble is, he thought to himself, where the hell is the North West!

He wished he'd listened more in Mr Newman's Geography class now because, on one occasion, they were told how they could find their directions if they were lost. He did however recall that this required a watch, which he no longer had!

Now, he thought to himself, the Front had definitely been to the East. This they had been told when they arrived. He turned in a complete circle and if that is over there, he worked out, pointing in the direction of the gunfire and that is East or perhaps South East then the North West would be that way, he said to himself, as he pointed his other arm in the opposite direction. That's it he would be on his way. Suddenly he had another thought, what if he had stumbled right through the German lines to the East and was now the other side? But then surely he would have run straight into the Germans, he reasoned. He had made the decision. He would travel away from the gunfire; that must be going towards the West, he thought to himself finally.

Having decided to trust his instincts he thought a little more about his situation. He needed to get some clothes from somewhere. He only had the uniform itself, which was all torn and mud-stained. It did not afford much protection from the cold and there was always the likelihood of rain at some stage.

He looked around him. The cornfield must have been cut within the past month and so the farmer must still live round here somewhere. If there was a farmhouse nearby he could maybe steal some clothes and ditch his uniform. He would need to find some food as he had suddenly become aware of how hungry he was – he could not remember when he had last eaten but it was probably more than a day ago.

It was unlikely the farmhouse would be lit up what with the artillery batteries and thousands of troops not that far away, so trying to find it in this darkness was going to be difficult, he thought to himself.

He moved off down the road in the direction he had decided on. He had travelled for about an hour. Occasionally he moved onto another road but trying to keep as far as possible in a straight line. He knew that when dawn came he would know exactly where the East was and hopefully confirm his direction theory. He then spotted a house along an unmade road to his left, he thought he detected a small light moving around the house and as he drew nearer he could see a figure, with a lantern, walking round and shutting doors to the various outhouses – whoever it might be was locking up for the night he assumed.

He moved quickly towards the house as the light went to the furthest outhouse. He arrived at a large oak door that was slightly ajar. He looked inside and could see some remains of a meal and in particular some bread and there was even a bottle of wine on the kitchen table. He was just about to enter and take what he could when an inside door opened and an elderly, plump woman entered with a pile of washing which she dumped near the kitchen sink. Wilson ducked down and then heard footsteps, presumably those of the woman's husband, coming back to the house. Wilson moved away and hid behind a large water butt nearby.

The farmer went in and shut the door drawing a bolt across. "Bugger," thought Wilson, what should I do now? He crouched and looked at the house. There was still a light in the kitchen area and another in what was presumably the bedroom. Suddenly the light in the kitchen went out and after a few minutes the one in the other room as well. He guessed that the man and woman were now in bed.

After a few minutes he made up his mind what to do. He would create some very loud commotion and try to lure the man out into the yard to see what was happening. Whilst the man was outside he would dive into the house and take what food he could.

About thirty yards from the house was some old metal drums. So Wilson went to them and pushed them over. They made a really loud noise in the quiet night air. He leaned with his back close to the side of the water butt waiting for the old man. He thought he would never come but eventually he did and holding his lantern and with a cloak over his pyjamas he walked towards the old sheds and barns. Like a flash, Wilson was inside the kitchen and he scooped up the bread, the bottle of wine and a piece of cheese – he even started to eat it! There was a noise from behind the kitchen door and further into the house. It was probably the wife. He saw an old pair of overalls in the washing so he grabbed them and ran out and moved back down the track towards the road he had left earlier. It was still so dark that there was little chance the farmer would ever see him. In fact, the farmer had already returned to the kitchen moaning to his wife something about foxes. He ushered her off to bed. Neither noticed the missing items from the table and the floor.

CHAPTER 19

The sky had gradually become lighter from the direction Wilson had hoped and he knew that he was at least going in roughly the right direction. For the next two days he rested during the day and only moved at night. Progress was slow and the rather palatable wine, bread and cheese he had picked up at the farmhouse had gone during the first day. In his attempt to avoid any troops coming in his direction he had kept to the fields as much as possible but this meant a more haphazard route involving several detours. Many of the fields were saturated from the rain and the going was slow. Whilst there was plenty of water for him to drink the only food he could find were some berries growing in the hedgerows. He wasn't sure what they were and some were very bitter. On two occasions they had given him terrible stomach pains followed by a severe bout of diarrhoea. There were no more farmhouses around that he could raid as before and anyway he decided to avoid any contact with any locals and skirt the small villages he came across.

By the end of the two days he was beginning to get a little desperate. The diarrhoea had weakened him as well as the general lack of sleep. The days had been reasonably warm for the time of year but there had been intermittent showery rain that had further dampened his spirits. So, when he finally saw a small house in the distance about a mile away he decided he might take a chance and see if he could get some food. It was about five in the morning and he was into his third day. He had been on the move for about six hours but progress had been slow and he had at one time sat down by the side of a field and fallen asleep.

Moving towards the house he came through a gap in the hedgerow and dropped down onto a rough farm road. The rain had started to fall about an hour before and this was all he could hear as it fell on the hedgerows either side of him. The wind had picked up too and rustled the trees as well as the hedges.

Suddenly, as the road straightened out and he could see a few hundred yards along it towards the house, a column of soldiers came into view. He quickly saw a small gap in the hedge to his right and he shot through it and laid down in the long grass the other side of it.

The men, presumably on their way to the Front, appeared to be in good humour despite the early hour and the rain. He could hear their singing and loud voices as they marched towards him. He could see their cigarettes glowing in the darkness.

He couldn't make out their insignia but he did pick up strong southern accents as they talked with one another as they passed only a few yards from him. He tensed up keeping his fingers crossed that they did not stop near him. The column took a few minutes to pass and gradually their noisy singing and loud talking faded as they headed off away from him towards where he had come from.

He thought for a moment about what might lie ahead for them. How many of them would be alive in a week's time? Did they really know what awaited them up ahead at the Front? They were all very young men and maybe this was to be their first experience of fighting in the frontline. For many of them it would be the first and last.

He felt sorry for them all. He thought back to all those mates he had seen killed or had simply disappeared. These poor young souls could expect nothing different. He shook his head and got up out of the grass and went back into the track and headed towards the house but when he got there it was in fact empty. The windows were all missing and it was derelict.

He did, however, decide to lay low there for the remainder of the day and rest up. He moved off again when it was dark enough. The rain had stopped during the early part of that day but returned in the late afternoon just before he started off. How it rained! Within half an hour he was soaked to the skin, he was cold, even jogging along could not keep him warm. Not only was it raining but also the temperature had fallen to such an extent that it was actually turning to sleet. The wind had also picked up and the sleet was horizontal. Just like the Ribble Valley in November he thought to himself and he even managed a smile!

Within minutes it was driving snow. To make matters worse the partly made road he had kept to now moved into more open countryside with no hedges to protect him. The wind and snow continued to drive across the flat, featureless landscape. He had very little to keep him warm. He had decided to wear the overalls he had picked up from the farmhouse over the top of his uniform and was glad he did. His head was exposed and was absolutely numb and it felt really tight across the wound. He walked for hours and the snow gradually turned to sleet then rain and then stopped altogether. The sky cleared from the West and the moon shone brightly for the first time for days. The trouble was it made everything freeze, in no time at all the landscape was white from the frost. Wilson started to run and wave his arms just to keep warm. His stomach ached from the lack of food and at times he felt very light headed and nauseous.

He was now on a proper road and the visibility was much better, so much so that he could see a house about a half-mile away. He stopped and sat on a fallen branch by the side of the road, he felt utterly exhausted. He looked down the road at the house and thought that perhaps this time he could get some food. The next thing he knew he was laying on his back staring up at the moon. His head was spinning and he felt extremely cold yet he was sweating underneath. His overalls felt solid, as the icy wind had frozen the wet cloth. He thought to himself that he must have passed out. He felt dreadful. He got to his feet but he tottered around as everything around him was spinning. He sat down again on the branch and put his head between his knees but he could not stop his head from spinning. He felt faint and twice he had retched but nothing came up. His stomach suddenly went into a spasm and he gripped himself round the waist and rolled off the branch and curled up into a ball. The pain was awful and then just as suddenly as it had appeared it went away again. He struggled to get to his feet. He managed to find a length of wood and he used that as a stick to support himself with.

He staggered off along the road towards the house. He thought that he would have to rely on the mercy from whoever lived there – they might turn him over to the Army but, if he was lucky, they might take pity on him.

It seemed to take ages to get there and during that last quarter mile he could hardly put one foot in front of the other as he swayed along. His overalls were now almost white with the ice. He had to stop every ten steps or so as the stomach cramps had him almost doubled up with pain. Once he even fell to his knees and crawled along the road on all fours. His head wound had opened up again and he could feel blood running down his face. It was going into his eyes and he could even taste it on his lips. He must have hit it on the ground either when he fell off the branch or when he was writhing on the road with the cramps.

Without really knowing what he was doing he slumped by the door of the house. He could not make out if there was anyone there and before he could do anything else he lapsed into unconsciousness.

As he came round he could make out someone talking to him in what he guessed was French and as he lifted his head he could see a concerned look on the attractive face of a young woman.

PART FOUR –
CALAIS, NORTHERN FRANCE
AUTUMN 1918

CHAPTER 20

The door of the cell opened again and the Corporal entered carrying a pile of clothes, Private Andrews stood in the doorway with his rifle held down by his waist blocking the exit.

"Right, Wilson put this uniform and have a shave, here's some stuff you can use," he said as he put the clothes on the floor and took out some soap and a razor from his pocket. "I think this uniform'll fit you, we picked it up from the local hospital last night and it's a bit soiled but it'll have to do."

Wilson picked up the uniform and took the razor and soap and put them in his pocket for now. Shipley walked up to him and touched Wilson's nose, "Does that hurt?" he asked touching the bridge of the nose. Wilson recoiled "Jesus!" he cried out. He had completely forgotten about the bang to his nose when he had run into the old man in the gardens the day before.

"It looks broken to me," said Shipley, "There's not much we can do about it except clean it up for now as there's dried blood on it and on your left cheek."

"Get a move on with the shave, get dressed and we'll be off. Remember, you are now a Private in the British Army so you'd better get used to acting like one and showing respect for rank and the uniform. Alright?"

"Yes, Corporal!" said Wilson as he stood to attention. Shipley was not sure whether this was mocking him or not but he decided to let it go for now.

Wilson shaved and cleaned up his face as best he could without a mirror and put on the uniform which had the Royal Engineers insignia on the shoulders. The top was in good condition which is more than could be said about the trousers which had a gaping, burnt hole in the thigh with bloodstains all around and other stains down both legs where the blood must have spattered from a wound. For a moment he wondered what might have happened to its previous owner. He presumed Shipley had picked it up from some hospital nearby as an emergency measure or maybe it belonged to one of his own men.

In the mean time Shipley left him to it and went into the office area where the Frenchman busied himself over a pile of official looking documents. Shipley had maintained a diary since he had joined up and took this opportunity to catch up not having had time in the past few days. It was not much of a record normally but the recent events had meant a little more to note. He was not sure the Army approved of this, especially from a military policeman, but he made sure he never made the notes when others were around just in case an officer spotted him. Soon after he started writing a young Frenchwoman appeared at the door and went over to the Frenchman sitting with his papers at the desk in the corner. They had an animated conversation which Shipley largely ignored but he could not help but admire the attractive woman with her pretty blond hair tied into a bun and a very colourful dress - a sight not very common amongst the Frenchwoman he had seen who largely seemed to favour dark browns and blacks. He carried on writing but suddenly found the woman by his side.

He was momentarily dumbstruck when she spoke to him in almost perfect English.

"Corporal, would it be possible for me to speak with your Officer regarding the prisoner? The gendarme has said "no" but I would appreciate the chance of speaking to him, so can you help?"

Shipley stood up and almost found himself saluting for some funny reason but then felt himself blush. "I'm sorry madamoiselle but he has left and it is only me and the Private left behind."

"My name is Coutteau and I am a friend of Private Wilson."

"Are you the person he's been living with since he deserted?"

The young woman took a step back and a look of anger spread across her face.

"I have offered Eddie the use of my house and provided him with help to nurse him back from his illness, if that is what you mean," she added indignantly. She went on before the Corporal could reply, "he was in a terrible state when he arrived at my door and I can tell you right now that he had no idea how he came to be detached from the other men, even to this day he does not remember anything. He was so ill then and even now he still suffers attacks of nerves and so on, losing all control of himself. Deserter is not what he is, confused, ill, nerves shot to pieces and put under terrible strain by the Army is what his problem has been and still is."

She flushed as she realised that this was not how she had planned to put over Wilson's case but this had all been building up inside her for such a long time and it all just came pouring out.

The Corporal looked startled and then started to say something but she interrupted him, " I have come here to tell someone in authority what he was like a year ago and what he has been through since then. He still needs medical help now. I am so worried that the Army will just shoot him without properly hearing what sort of state he was in."

"I'm sorry," answered Shipley, "but, as I said, the Officer has left and we are taking Wilson back to Belgium for a Court Martial and there is nothing really I can do for him right now. I'm sure he will get a proper hearing and all the evidence will be considered."

132

"Would I be able to speak for him then?"

"I don't see why not and I'll pass the information onto the Officer in charge and I'm sure you'll be able to speak to the Court. It would be unusual but the Army is not just about killing one of their own for the sake of it, we do still want justice for the men and if you have something important to say, and I'm sure you have, the Court will want to hear about it."

"But, despite what you say, that still normally means guilty and the soldier ends up being shot?" Her voice faltered for a second as she gulped and her eyes filled up.

"Not necessarily, even if guilty the final decision goes to the highest authority before that decision is made – he may just get locked up for some time. Not that many of those found guilty are actually shot, you know."

The young woman seemed to pull herself together and stood up straighter and smiled a little at the Corporal before going on, "Could I speak to Eddie now before he leaves, then?"

"I'm sorry that's not at all possible. As I have said already I will speak to my Officer or someone to do with the Court and tell them that you wish to speak for him. As I said, I cannot see any problem with that but then I don't make the decision about the matter, so I can't promise anything right now. I tell you what, if you want to write a letter for Wilson you've got five minutes before we go and there's some paper and pen over there on the desk and you can do it now and I'll give it to him for you."

The woman nodded, smiled again and moved towards the desk. The Corporal followed her over and found the paper and she picked up the pen and inkwell. The gendarme looked up but took no notice and carried on sifting through his pile of papers.

The Corporal turned to walk away but gently held the young woman's arm. "There is one thing you can do right now to help him and that is to tell him to make sure he has someone to represent him because in my experience too many of the men don't take up that option and their case is never properly put. You must persuade him to get help from someone qualified in the law and King's regulations. There are plenty of Officers around who have the right qualifications."

She had already started writing but stopped, "I can't believe that. It's awful that they could be shot because they do not even bother to defend themselves properly or get someone to represent them."

"That has happened in the past, believe me."

The woman slumped into the chair vacated by the gendarme who had now left the room. She was trying to take all this in and was shaking her head. She looked up at the Corporal and said. "Even if they have an Officer to represent them what will he know about the case and the circumstances? If Eddie Wilson is anything to go by, then the men in the frontline are mentally and physically shattered. They have experienced things in their short time there that we could not even begin to understand and some Officer who's worked for the justice people, or whatever you call them, and never seen action is going to try and save a man's life, what sort of chance do people like Eddie have?"

Before Shipley could reply, the woman stood up and moved over to the door leading to the cells and looked through. Andrews appeared and made sure she went no further. She turned and looked at Shipley and went on: -

"When Eddie first arrived at my house he was confused, it seemed that half his brain was working and the other half was not – part of him wanted to return to the Front and the other half wanted him to stay away. Even now he drops into such a state that he cannot put one foot in front of another, he shakes uncontrollably and cries just as if he was laughing – is it what you call hysterical? I think that's it – hysterical – it's just like a scream. It sometimes lasts for up to an hour and at the end of it he cannot remember a thing but he is soaked with sweat and more than once he has wet himself just like a child! No one is going to understand or put that over at a Court Martial are they?"

"Well, I do see your point and I agree it's going to be difficult but I'm afraid the Army is not sympathetic when it comes to deserters and thinks most of them are lying and cheating and, worst of all, letting down their comrades."

"Look, my husband was killed at Verdun and I sometimes think that might have been a good thing when I see the terrible state of those who came back from there, and other places, with their missing limbs and missing other parts and other terrible injuries not to mention their damaged minds. There are those who are now broken men who have seen things we cannot possibly imagine and they have been so frightened that they have these nightmares and fits just like Eddie. Some are so bad they are locked up in a sanatorium and will never be released - they are completely mad and it is said it is all down to the shelling and the shock waves it sent to their brains coupled with the sights they saw and the conditions they had to live in, let alone the gas!"

"But…"

"Do you think some Officer, who probably hates the fact that Eddie has apparently deserted, will really put a up a good defence – you might just as well go to the cell and shoot him now – go on!" The woman's voice was raised to such a level that Wilson could hear it from the cells and called out her name. She turned to Shipley: -

"Can I see him?"

"No, I'm sorry I would get into real trouble if anyone found out – it's against regulations as I said before and I'd get into trouble if I let you. Just sit down and finish the letter, it's the best I can do for you, I'm sorry."

"Look, there is no one here except you and the Private so who's going to know? It could be the last time I see him and surely you can find it in your heart to give me five minutes?"

Shipley thought for a moment and looked at the young woman. Her eyes were moist and she looked straight at Shipley and so intently that he looked away for a moment. He then looked back at her and this time she smiled and raised her eyebrows as if to ask the question once more without actually saying anything. He smiled back at her then nodded his head; "Just five minutes and Private Andrews will stay with you at all times, right?"

"Thank you that's very kind," she said in a soft voice and got hold of his arm just above the elbow and squeezed it gently.

Shipley led her towards the cell and where Andrews was standing. "Keep an eye on them Andrews and don't take your eyes off them. Madame, I'm sorry but I shall have to search you before you go in."

For a moment she hesitated and opened her mouth to argue the point but accepted the situation by emptying her small bag showing that she had nothing of any consequence. She then invited a search of her body by raising her arms but Shipley declined any further search but just told Andrews to make sure nothing passed between her and Wilson.

Shipley left and returned to his diary whilst Wilson greeted Marie with a fairly formal French type kiss on each cheek. Andrews raised his eyebrows surprised at the lack of intimacy and added, "No touching, remember."

"Are you coping with this alright?" asked the Frenchwoman.

"Not bad, thanks," said Wilson, "they're taking me back to Belgium for a Court Martial"

"Yes I know the Corporal said earlier."

"A waste of time really they're bound to shoot me, they always do."

"That's not what I heard and you must get a good Officer to represent you, it might be your only chance – you must not just give in."

"What's the point they'll just say I ran away and deserted my post and that's that – I've no possible chance?"

Marie grabbed him by both arms and Andrews stepped forward, "Madame!" he warned and she let go.

"Don't be so stupid Eddie, you must defend yourself as you are ill in the head from the shelling and so on. If you tell them about the state you get in as I described to you before, I am sure they will be a little more understanding. You might even get someone to examine you as there must be specialist doctors for this type of thing, surely?"

"I hope you're right but I don't hold out much hope and the Army doesn't like those who turn their backs and run, you know."

"But you didn't, you just didn't know what you were doing. You were in a complete state of shock. You must ask for a doctor as he will have had some experience of this condition and he might get a specialist for you. You simply did not know where you were or what you were doing."

"Yes, I know, but I should have gone back rather than stay away – that's the problem, it's too late now."

"But you were in no fit state to go back to the fighting or really to do anything – it took you three months to remember anything at all about where you had come from or even what Company you were in. You must defend yourself as best you can and find someone to help."

"Well, I'll see."

Shipley appeared at the door. "Time's up, can you leave now Madame? You can kiss him goodbye if you wish?"

With this Marie put her arms around Wilson and they hugged for a few seconds but there was no kiss. "Good luck Eddie I shall try to find out where you are and what happens but do write if you can. Whether I get the letter or not will be another thing of course!"

"Thanks and thanks for all your help and support and perhaps one day we can meet again without the world being in such a horrible mess." He then broke away and picked up the chair and turned it round. He sat down facing away from her and put his hands to his face covering his eyes. His shoulders gently heaved as he sobbed.

Marie kissed him on the back of his head and left with Shipley and returned to the office.

"Thank you Corporal that was kind of you. Would it be possible for you to let me know what happens, do you recall my address?"

"Not really. You had better write it in the back of this book, on the back page there," he said pointing as he passed over his diary and gave her the pen she had put down earlier.

Having jotted down her address she gave the book and pen back to Shipley and again thanked him and left.

Andrews having relocked the cell came back into the room and Shipley was just staring at the address. "What is it, Corp?" he asked.

He looked up and smiled ruefully, "Oh nothing, just thinking what a stinking horrid world this is right now." He wrote something in the book next to her address and said to Andrews, "You go back in there and guard Wilson. I need the toilet and when I come back we'll get moving." With that he shut the diary and stuffed it in his tunic pocket and left the room just as the gendarme returned to continue with his paperwork.

136

CHAPTER 21

When Shipley came back to the room some five minutes later he told Andrews to undo the cell door and make sure Wilson was ready to go.

Andrews undid the lock and went in with his rifle in hand. Wilson was standing by the window and appeared ready to go. Andrews turned and shouted back to Shipley that they were ready. Shipley appeared at the door with a pair of handcuffs he had picked up from the store next to the toilet. The gendarme had unlocked the storeroom for him and together they had sifted through a selection of handcuffs and other restraints.

The ones chosen were unusual in that they had a longer chain than normal between the two cuffs.

Shipley joined the other two in the cell and got Andrews to attach the cuffs to the Corporal's left hand and the other to Wilson's right hand, which left about six feet of chain between them when fully extended.

Shipley told Andrews to leave his rifle with him and go and get the lorry which had been parked round the back of the police station. The Corporal took the rifle in his right hand and motioned Wilson to follow him out of the cell. The old gendarme was pottering around behind the desk again and looked up as they entered and quickly moved to one end of his desk where he picked up a large register type book and a pen and motioned to the Corporal and spoke animatedly in French. Although Shipley had no idea what he had said it was clear that the gendarme wanted the Corporal to sign his book before he left.

Having done that the Frenchman thanked them routinely and returned to whatever he had been doing behind the desk. Andrews came back in and said the lorry was ready and the two soldiers walked out into the bright light with Wilson in tow. They all blinked to adjust to the sudden brightness although really it was quite cloudy with a few spots of rain already falling. Andrews had left the lorry running and it was chugging away in front of them. The lorry did not look like it had ever been washed; its canvass back was torn and riddled with what were definitely bullet holes and it had one of the two front windows missing.

Shipley helped Wilson into the cab where Andrews sat behind the wheel. It was a tight squeeze and eventually after much shuffling around they were reasonably comfortable and the Corporal released his wrist from the cuff and then placed the cuff around the base of the seat with the other end still attached to Wilson, who sat in the middle with only one cheek on a seat and the other wedged between the two seats.

Reg Andrews had never really driven before and it showed as they bounced off down the street clearly in the wrong gear as the old lorry was finding it difficult to pull away. Eventually it picked up speed but they slowed down again as Andrews fought to change gear. This time he picked up a low gear by mistake and with a great roar the lorry shot off with all three hitting their heads on the front window frame. After a mile or so Andrews seemed to get the hang of it and they chugged out of the town with the Corporal giving instructions from the map across his lap. The lorry appeared to have a maximum speed of about fifteen miles per hour and was very drafty and cold inside the cab due to the wind whistling through the opening where one of the front windows had been.

For a few miles nothing was said by any of them. Andrews had quickly worked out the gears and seemed much more in control of the lorry and was the first to speak.

"That Frenchwoman was a tasty bit of stuff, no wonder you wanted to stay in her bed as opposed to fighting in some god forsaken trench and dying with your mates," he sneered.

"It wasn't like that." Wilson replied as he shuffled his now numb bottom between the seats.

"You mean to say you've been with this woman for nearly a year and you haven't tried it on with her? You can't be serious?" sneered Andrews.

"Look the poor woman has lost her husband. She has also lost countless other family members since '14 and looks after elderly relatives and she helped nurse me and that was all. Whilst we got on well there was no trying it on as you call it; I had too much respect for her than that but I can't expect some idiot like you to understand."

Andrews wasn't finished, "You must have been tempted though, I mean, bloody hell I would have done. You can't turn down such a chance as that; I mean it could have been on a plate if you'd tried a bit harder."

"That's enough Reg – shut up and leave it alone," interrupted Shipley.

"Come on Frank the bloke's got a screw loose or can't get it going anymore, perhaps his tool got damaged in the line and it doesn't work like it should!" he mocked.

"Why don't you shut your bloody mouth?" Wilson said as he grabbed Andrews under the chin with his spare hand, lifting him out of his seat. Andrews momentarily lost control of the lorry and it swerved across the road and tilted on the steep bank forcing them to lean to the left. Shipley was squashed up against the door, which flew open, and he held onto Wilson to stop himself from falling into the road. Andrews swung the steering wheel to the right and they all shot across to their right and the door next to Shipley slammed shut but not before it hit the Corporal's knee right on the side of the kneecap and he swore in pain.

Eventually Andrews righted the lorry and Shipley told him to pull over to the side of the road. Shipley and Andrews got out but left Wilson behind still attached to the seat.

"Did you see what that fool did – bloody grabbed me round the neck and nearly choked me," Andrews complained.

"I'd have done the same if you'd said that to me – just leave the bloke alone. Now get back in the cab and I'll sit between you."

They both got in the driver's side and Wilson shuffled across to the window but remained chained to the seat under where Shipley was sitting.

"Now Wilson behave yourself and sit there quietly, we've got a long way to go yet and I don't want any more trouble or arguing, right you two?"

"Whatever you say, Corp," replied Andrews with more than a sarcastic smirk but Wilson said nothing and stared out of the window.

Nothing was said for about thirty minutes before the Corporal asked Andrews to pull over, as he needed to relieve himself. He asked Wilson if he wanted to go but the prisoner smiled and said he was fine and just stared out of the window. Andrews duly pulled into the entrance to a field alongside a thick hedge and got out of the cab to allow the Corporal to get out and both stood up against the hedge and started. Shipley turned his head back and shouted at Wilson back in the cab "Are you sure you don't want to go, we've still got a bit of travelling you know?"

"No thanks but I'll drive off in the lorry next time if you leave me alone again!" he laughed.

"No chance," said Andrews, "You'd need the starting handle and to go round the front to turn the engine and you can't do that with the cuffs on!"

"Ah yes but I'm working on the chain and I'm nearly through!"

Both men shook their last drips and rushed back to the cab with their flies still gaping. Each went to either side of the cab and stood up on the running boards and both peered at the chain, doing up their trouser buttons at the same time.

Wilson laughed, "Only kidding chaps," as he held the perfectly formed chain up above his head. "Oh look Reg you've pissed all down your trousers, sorry about that," he mocked the Private.

"Bugger off Wilson – do something like that again and I'll smash your face in."

"Easy Reg," said the Corporal, "that'll do." He turned to Wilson. "Very funny, Wilson, but let's not do that again, shall we, there's a good fellow?"

"Yes Corporal!" he saluted back most rigorously and not a little contemptuously but with a broad smile on his face. The Corporal smiled back and Andrews went round to the driver's door to get the starting handle from under his seat.

Shipley climbed back in next to Wilson. Andrews cranked up the engine through the hole at the front of the lorry and the old lorry chugged into life.

"Right Reg let's get going," said Shipley, "it'll be dark before we get there at this rate and it's bad enough trying to find the right roads in daylight let alone in the dark. This bloody map's useless as it doesn't have half the roads on it."

They moved off just as the rain got heavier making it difficult to see out of the windows. Spray came through the open front window and began to soak onto their trouser legs.

More than once during the next hour they had to stop because of the heavy rain, as it was impossible to see anything out of the front window. They were now getting very wet as the rain came through the missing window and their tops as well as their trousers were wet through. The roads were nothing more than a sea of mud in places and the lorry's wheels occasionally got stuck but Andrews managed to slide out and away before they got completely bogged down. They had been on lower lying ground for a while but now the countryside was hillier with wooded dells. The lorry struggled up the hills and Andrews had to speed downhill in order to get enough revs to allow them to pull up the hill the other side. He managed it each time but only with his foot right on the floor with the accelerator. The lorry would slither from side to side as it coped with the slope but considering his lack of experience Andrews did well given that for the whole time the rain was lashing into his face as well as soaking him down his front.

Suddenly the skies began to lift and the rain eased to a drizzle and there was blue sky away to the right to the south.

"Looks like it's going to clear up," said Shipley as he leant forward and looked up at the sky, "there's blue sky over there – look." He pointed to the south.

"Not before time," piped up Wilson who had been dozing with his head against the window. "That horizontal rain reminded me of home on the moors above Burnley or more like the time I was in the trenches."

"Those that you ran away from you mean?" smirked Andrews.

"Give it a rest mate," said Wilson, "you know sod all about it living the bloody easy life away from the Front. You'd last about a day in the trenches. You're so thick you'd probably stick yer head up and get it blown off by a sniper! I've seen it countless times – all of them as thick as shit like you!"

"I've told you Wilson, one more word out of you and I'll do you in," shouted back Andrews.

"I'd like to see you try," mocked Wilson.

Andrews rose up as if to do something but Shipley grabbed his arm and pushed him back into his seat. "That's enough Reg – keep your bloody eyes on the road or you'll have us in the ditch – Wilson…. Shut up!"

Wilson waved his free hand dismissively and settled back with his head against the back of his seat and stretched out his legs and yawned.

Andrews was still fuming and his hands gripped the wheel tightly. He was roaring the engine as they approached the crest of yet another hill and dropped to first gear. As the crown of the hill came the lorry suddenly shot away down the hill as Andrews floored the accelerator. He soon got to top gear and the lorry was travelling at top speed increased by the considerable down slope.

"For God's sake man slow down," shouted Shipley.

"Well this is fun it's the fastest we've been all day, don't worry Corp all in hand!"

Wilson had sat up, "You're going far too fast you'll bloody kill us at this rate!"

"Frightened again are we – you can't run away this time!" he laughed.

The lorry careered down the hill sliding a little in the mud. This was one of the steepest slopes they'd been down and there was the usual wooded copse at the bottom of the hill. Whereas most of the roads to date had been pretty straight this one had a tight right bend at the bottom and too late it was dawning on Andrews that he needed to brake to make sure he could get round it. His inexperience showed as he hit the brakes hard and the lorry immediately turned broadside. He turned the wheel violently to his right but nothing happened. Shipley grabbed the handbrake next to his right knee in an attempt to slow the vehicle down.

Momentarily it corrected itself into a straight line with the handbrake applied and Andrews was frantically trying to keep it straight. Shipley leant over and grabbed the steering wheel to help out and Wilson grabbed the door handle as if trying to get out and then realised that was not an option what with his chain still attached. Instead he put his arms over his head and bent forward as if bracing himself for a crash.

"Look out there's a sharp bend down here and you're not going to make it at this rate - use the brakes more," shouted Shipley.

"I've got my foot right down and it's not stopping it," shouted back Andrews.

Shipley released the handbrake and then pulled it up again violently; the vehicle jerked and appeared to slow down and Andrews almost seemed to have some control.

"Turn it right man, turn it right!" shouted back Shipley.

Andrews and Shipley both swung the wheel to the right, as the bend was no more that ten yards away. Just as they did so a smaller lorry appeared round the corner coming the other way. As they headed towards each other Andrews quickly threw the wheel to the left. He could see the other driver clearly trying to do the same. They caught each other on the right hand sides a little more than a glancing blow. The other smaller lorry veered off to the left between two trees and up a bank and ended up on its side with the two right side wheels spinning round.

Andrews had no time to correct their lorry until it glanced off a tree, hit the bank on one side and actually completed a forward somersault and ended up on its roof. Steam flew out everywhere and the tree crashed down on top of the lorry.

Wilson's door had flown open in mid air but Shipley had grabbed him with his free hand and the chain had held them both in place but Wilson cut his head as the top of it hit the roof of the cab as they landed upside down.

Shipley had been thrown forward and had hit his head on the frame of the window and knocked himself out cold even before the lorry came to rest.

Andrews had fallen against the steering wheel as he lost control only to be pinned back against the seat as he was pushed back with the impact. He had felt a sudden blow to his head and pain in his chest before he too lost consciousness. The roof also dented inwards compressing his head into his shoulders trapping him completely. The right panel beyond the door and the door itself had crushed into his leg just below his knee snapping the bone. He came to briefly and screamed out before he passed out completely and slumped in the seat unable to move.

Wilson, having been momentarily dazed himself, pushed the remaining glass from the front window with his foot and slid forward as far as the chain would allow. Some nettles and grass flopped forward onto his face; the nettle leaves stinging his face. He recoiled and pushed them away with his hand. His face was right in the middle of this thick patch of greenery but from his upside down position the sky had a peculiar look to it. He rolled out beyond the nettles onto the grass and stood up still a little dazed. As he started to move away his chain yanked him back and he fell down into the grass, having forgotten he was still linked to the strut of the seat.

He could see the steam rising from under the bonnet of the lorry and there was a strong smell of petrol both in the air and on his clothes.

Looking across the road he could see the spinning wheels of the other lorry and heard two distinctively separate groans coming from inside it.

He ducked back inside his lorry and leaned over Shipley and rummaged in his right hand pocket for the key to the lock on the chain. It was awkward as Shipley was lying more on that side but eventfully he gripped the small key, took it out of the pocket and quickly undid the lock. He rubbed his, by now, sore wrist where the chain had cut in. Just for a moment he thought "Christ I could get away from here and run for it" but soon thought otherwise as he eased the still unconscious Shipley out through the door and well clear of the vehicle. The Corporal groaned but did not come to – Wilson checked him over quickly but could only see a bruise on the head and guessed the man had just been knocked out.

He moved round to the other side and to the door. He had to lay flat to the ground to see in and look closely at Andrews. He too was unconscious with blood all over his face and even more petrol on him than on Wilson himself. Wilson felt down the side of Andrews to see if he could move him from the extremely confined space. As he touched his leg he could feel the bone sticking out from the Private's trousers. Wilson recoiled away and looked down at his hand it was covered in blood from Andrews. A compound fracture he guessed similar to what he had seen in a match at Burnley a few years back.

It was going to be difficult to get the Private out and impossible to do it on his own. He went back round to Shipley but he was still out of it. He ran across to the other vehicle and saw two men in uniform pulling themselves groggily out of the door, which was pointing up towards the sky.

They had unusual uniforms and just for a second Wilson tensed himself as he thought they might be Germans but then suddenly one of them spoke in English, "Give us a hand here will you?" The middle-aged man looked up, still somewhat dazed, at Wilson and said, "Hell, are you a German?"

"No you're alright I'm British, what are you?"

"American. Here give us a hand and get my driver out."

Together they pulled at the younger man and eased him out of the vehicle just as he came round, shaking his head to clear the effects of the accident.

"Look," said Wilson to the older one, "I need your help here as our driver is out cold and trapped and he has a broken leg – if not worse. Also there is petrol everyone and the engine is steaming and I can smell burning and if we're not careful the whole lot could blow up with the driver in there!"

The Americans stumbled across the road with Wilson and knelt down next to the upturned vehicle and the side where Andrews lay trapped. The older one spotted the prone Shipley "Is he alright?"

"Yes just knocked out as far as I can see and we'd better move him back onto the road out of the way until he comes round." With this Wilson dragged Shipley away supporting him under his shoulders.

The two Americans began to check over Andrews and the older one said, "Arnie you'd better find our first aid kit - there might be something in there we could use." The younger man started to move off and the other shouted to him, "See if there are any tools and bring the starting handle."

Wilson on hearing this found their starting handle and guessed the idea was to use it as a jemmy. He thrust it between the door and the front panel and with some effort prised off first one hinge and then the other with the help of the American driver.

The other American peered into the upturned cab and especially at the damaged leg, "You're right about the break – it looks nasty but I don't think his leg's trapped so if we can lever up the floor of the car we might be able to release him."

At that moment Shipley arrived at their side and they briefed him quickly and agreed that two of them would use the starting handles from the two vehicles to prise the floor away from the legs with the other two easing Andrews out.

Just as they started a small flame appeared from the back of the vehicle. It was small but it made them look at each other with a degree of concern. "We'd better hurry," said Shipley, "as we could get burnt or blown up."

They all worked furiously on the floor and it moved slightly. This allowed them to ease Andrews back and out slightly so at least his head was clear out of the doorway. He started to come round and the pain from his leg suddenly hit him and he started screaming out. They stopped what they were doing for a moment but then Arnie pushed them out of the way, moved Andrews's head out of the way of the door frame and hit him with a huge haymaker right hook knocking the injured man out cold again.

The two Englishman looked at Arnie, who was rubbing his bruised knuckles, and then to the older American. He smiled, "I was brought up in Boston, we do a lot of fighting there!"

For what seemed ages they all worked hard on trying to release Andrews but it seemed the ankle of his left foot was somehow trapped between the seat and the floor and just would not budge. The flames had almost subsided towards the back as time went on then suddenly there was a burst again and they went much higher than before.

"This is going up in a bang in a minute," said Arnie," we going to have to leave him or else we'll get killed."

"Come on then we must just pull him out – it'll do more damage to him but it might save his life and ours – he'll stand no chance covered in petrol the way he is," shouted Shipley.

"Try once more to prise him out or we'll have to do that, "said the older American.

"I'm sure he's coming round again," said Wilson as two pulled whilst the others held up the floor away from his left foot.

Suddenly they were all thrown back away from the lorry as the back end exploded as the part of the petrol went up but the front was still intact. Wilson and Shipley had both discarded their petrol soaked tops and started to move back in. The Americans weren't quite so sure and hung back.

Just as Wilson and Shipley moved forward there was another explosion just behind the cab and they were flung back once more. This time the flames had caught Andrews and his uniform was alight. Shipley moved forward and Arnie grabbed him back, "You've got to leave it," he said as Shipley moved against him.

The older American was holding back Wilson but he wrenched himself clear and got hold of the trapped man's shoulders and with one strong pull he pulled him free. There was a sickening crack as the leg broke just above the ankle.

Both men's uniforms were ablaze and the other three rolled them onto the grass and almost fell on them to douse the flames. With this done they pulled them right back into the road and the lorry exploded for the last time. Parts flew everywhere and the three men had to drop down covering their heads protecting themselves from the pieces of metal that fell all around them. Wilson was prone on top of Andrews to protect him further.

They all laid there motionless for about ten seconds but it seemed that time was standing still for Wilson until he realised that the badly injured Andrews was beneath him. He stood up and looked at the stricken Private – he was still unconscious and his tunic and trousers were blackened from the flames but whilst his face was clearly burned the damage did not seem too bad.

Arnie the driver was next to stir and crawled on his knees to where Wilson stood and lifted the injured man's head and placed his jacket under it and eased Andrews back onto the grass.

The older American and Shipley were dusting themselves down and the old man spoke first, "Look our camp is about five miles back over there," he said pointing to the North East, "our lorry looks like it's alright as long as we can get it upright – we can put this man on it and get him back there as fast as we can."

"Right, we'll help with the lorry – Wilson come with me and help get this thing upright," said Shipley as he moved off.

Arnie left Andrews and indicated to the other man to take over dabbing the burns with the water from his drinking bottle using a crisp, clean handkerchief. Andrews stirred but was still out of it.

The three younger men found the task of righting the vehicle more difficult than they thought it would be and eventually had to find a piece of branch to lever it up. The other American eventually joined them and with all four putting their weight into it the lorry became upright as the two wheels slammed back onto the ground. Arnie jumped inside and checked it over while Shipley cranked the engine with the starting handle. The engine fired into life and Arnie backed it out between the two trees and back onto the road. The other American checked all round and removed some of the pieces of twig, branch and foliage clogged around the wheels.

"Right load him up," he said to Shipley and Wilson. Shipley had found some rope in the back of the lorry and used this to tie Andrews's left leg to his right to give him some support. Wilson suggested that they could use a narrow branch as a sort of splint so Shipley removed the rope and Wilson added the support and the rope was wrapped around the thin branch and both legs.

The Americans had cleared the back of the lorry but there was barely room for the stricken Private in the small space.

"Look," said Arnie, "there's not going to be room for all of us."

The older American spoke to Shipley, "Corporal, I am Major Levinson, just so you know, and I reckon we, that's Arnie and me, take your man here back to our camp. Where were you going anyway?"

"Andrews," he said pointing to the injured man "and me are Military Policemen escorting Wilson here back to Poperinghe camp for his Court Martial."

"What's he done then?"

"He deserted the trenches about a year ago and we caught him a couple of days ago near Calais."

"Well from what I've just seen, the man's a damn hero – saving this here man's life, that's for sure."

"You can say that again, I hope Andrews recovers and what Wilson did here might just save his life – you never know – the British Army does some bloody odd things at times and don't always give much leeway to deserters!"

The Major thought for a moment and went on, "Look we can't take you both back with us – you'd better continue on foot. No promises but I'll try to send a truck back to take you to your camp but I'm afraid you might have to walk because my Company were due to move out shortly and when you hit us I was on my way to a briefing. When we get back we'll have all the necessary medical staff and equipment to patch up your mate. I'll try and send a letter to the Commanding Officer at Poperinghe giving my version of what's gone on – that should help – now what are your names?"

Having duly noted these he helped secure the back of the lorry with Andrews inside. He and his driver shook hands with the two British men and took off back down the road.

Wilson was wiping the mud and bloodstains from his trousers and top with pieces of grass but not with a great deal of success, "How much further to Poperinghe then?"

"Dunno to be sure but I would reckon about twenty miles, give or take – trouble is the map went up with the lorry and I've no definite idea of the way there but as long as we head a little south of east that should be fine. We're bound to come across someone that will tell us where to go. Look there's no point relying on these Americans to come back for us – from what the Major

146

said he could be sent off in the opposite direction for all he knew, so we'd better start walking. It's going to take us about a day, if we're lucky, to get there and we'll have to find somewhere warm and dry to sleep tonight and then get there in the morning. I'd better see if I can find the handcuffs as they might have survived the blast. Did you keep the key?"

Wilson reached in his pocket and held up the key and passed it to Shipley who was already looking round for the chain. After a couple of minutes he gave up, "It must have been blown clean away especially if it was still fixed to the seat."

"Well, I did leave it fixed so looks like you're going to have to trust me not to run off!" Wilson said and smiled.

CHAPTER 22

The sky had brightened a lot after the accident and a bright autumn sun provided some welcome warmth following the dismal morning weather. There was hardly anything they could salvage from the wreck of the lorry that smouldered as a pile of twisted metal. Odd parts were spread over a wide area with one of the wheels hanging from one of the trees no doubt blown there as a result of the explosion.

The Americans had left a full water bottle and some dry biscuits, which is all they had with them. Arnie had given Wilson his jacket to replace that burnt by the fire.

For nearly an hour Shipley and Wilson trudged along the same road. It ran almost in a straight line for a couple of miles. There were no houses along it but there was the occasional farmhouse down long tracks. They decided not to visit any of these for some food and decided to walk on until evening and then look for somewhere they could use for their overnight stop.

Shipley suggested that they rest for ten minutes because he needed to go to the toilet for a "sit down job", as he called it. He again warned Wilson what would happen if he ran off. Shipley went into the field through a wide opening and pushed through the long grass behind the hedgerow to do his business. Wilson could see Shipley's head just above the grass, which was about three feet high. He laughed to himself at the comical sight of Shipley's head bobbing up and down keeping one eye on Wilson and the other on what he was doing. Wilson heard the tearing of the grass as Shipley was obviously using this to wipe his bottom.

Eventually Shipley stood up doing up his trousers, "That's better!"

"I bet the grass was a bit wet and coarse, did it stain your arse?" Both men laughed.

"A little!" added Shipley "I hate having to do that, it's about the first time I have in my adult life!"

Wilson laughed, "Good job you weren't in the trenches then, some of the men had to go in their trousers because they were unable to move from their positions. They had no choice but to clean themselves up the next day and sometimes they had to stay like it until their time in the advanced trenches or taking part in attacks came to an end. Even at the front the latrine wasn't the sort of place you would want to spend much time in as they made going in your trousers a better option at times!"

"Mmm not very pleasant, by the sounds of it."

"I'll say – still, one visit to the latrine saved my life."

"What do you mean?"

"I was caught short and had to dive into the trench's bog but the Boche started shelling when I was in there and before I could get out a shell had landed right in our trench, by the time I came to and stumbled out of the bog all me mates had gone."

"What over the top?" enquired Shipley

"No – blown up! Gone! There was a few bits and pieces of them and that was all – whether some had run off I dunno but I was left on my own."

"Bloody hell – what did you do then?"

"Well, I waited for my head to clear then a load of Canadians turned up – what the hell they were doing there I can't remember – some sort of recce I think. Anyway this Officer told me to go back down the line and link up with some of our blokes further back."

"Did you find any of your mates who'd left the trench?"

"Nope – they were all posted missing and as far as I know that's how they remained and still do, probably – unless they're on the run!" he added dryly as he looked knowingly at Shipley, who smiled back.

Shipley thought for a minute and then went on, "Must have been bloody awful at the Front – the stories you hear about it..." he tailed off shaking his head.

"You don't know the half of it Corp – hell would have been a better place, believe me mate. If it wasn't for a call of nature I'd be dead and if it wasn't for trench foot I'd be dead as well. I was taken down from the line once to get it treated as we'd stood so long sometimes up to our chests in water that me foot went rotten. Whilst I was out of the line and during the next day my mates got blown up just like the other lot - never to be seen again!"

With that Wilson stood up and marched purposefully off down the road. He had to do it as he felt himself about to break down in front of the Corporal and he also felt his hands and arms beginning to shake and his legs were going weak as well – the same old feeling he had had for more than a year, on and off.

For well over an hour Wilson walked alone. Shipley made no attempt to catch up with him and remained ten or so paces behind. The sun had long since gone behind the ever thickening cloud and it was now quite dark as the early autumn evening drew on.

Eventually Shipley ran up to Wilson and told him that they must seek somewhere to stop. There had been several isolated farmhouses and cottages in the distance but none on the road that seemed to be inhabited. A mile or so ahead there were flickering lights of a small village not much more than a hamlet really, just a few cottages and what seemed like a barn or large outhouse.

Shipley told Wilson that they would seek shelter there and perhaps get some food from a local family. He thought that it might be a bit of a struggle with the language with his French being very basic but having shared this with his charge he felt better about it as Wilson said he had picked up a fair amount of French, living with the young woman and her family.

A further ten minutes on and they were outside the first cottage but despite several knocks on an old wooden front door no one answered. They walked further down the street and on their right was a large, somewhat dilapidated, old barn. It had two huge front doors that clearly did not close on properly but the roof was intact and hopefully they would be able to rest there with some protection from the cold night and at least be out of any rain should it start up again.

The dirty old white cottage beyond it showed a light, which shone brightly now that the early evening dimness had turned to darkness in what had seemed such a short period of time.

Shipley had to knock twice on the door before anyone came and as the door opened slightly all that showed at first was the front end of a blunderbuss through the narrow gap. The gun looked like it was at least fifty years old and unlikely to have fired a shot for some time and it did not look like it was capable of firing one now either.

Shipley moved out of the way so Wilson could speak into the small gap.

He explained that they were British soldiers returning to the line and that they had lost their truck and were having to walk. He was not sure he got all the words right but thought the person holding the old gun would at least get the gist. To his surprise they replied in a different language but it seemed to have a smattering of French then it dawned on him that some of the Belgians had their own language in this western area and that must be what it was.

Despite this small problem, the door opened and a small woman, less than five feet tall, stood with the gun pointing at them both. She ushered them into the room and told them to sit on the old settee in the corner. Wilson put his hands out in front as if to placate the lady and discourage her from firing. Although he suspected the gun would never work, he was not taking any chances.

With a combination of French, slowly spoken English and a considerable degree of sign language with much pointing at their uniforms the woman lowered the gun and propped it up against the wall.

She rattled off a whole stream of the local language. She then left them and went into what looked like a scullery.

Shipley spoke, "Well we seemed to get the message over and she at least understands we are not going to harm her!"

"She must be Belgian because they do have a language of their own and I heard it when we passed through some village on the way to the Front last year," said Wilson as he took off his jacket and stood next to the small fire on the large wall straight ahead from the front door. He warmed his hands and then turned to warm the backs of his legs and bottom. He was unable to stand to his full height, as the ceiling was well less than six feet high and the beams even lower.

"We'd better ask about sleeping in the barn, any ideas how we do that?"

Wilson moved away and held open the scullery door, as he had seen the woman coming his way with a tray. On it were large chunks of bread and cheese together with some brown steaming broth and two tumblers full of what appeared to be some red wine.

Shipley stood and took the tray from the woman and placed it on the table. There was only one dining chair and he offered this to her and she sat down. She smiled revealing her toothless gums and nodded her thanks. She took her bowl and broke off some bread and indicated for Shipley to take the tray away and sit down with Wilson on the settee and eat the rest.

The two men had not realised how hungry they were and soon cleared everything. With this the woman returned to the scullery and came back with a half eaten pie filled with apples and she poured some milk over the top.

The men had two helpings and the woman smiled all the way through often speaking animatedly and laughing but the two soldiers could not understand a word but nevertheless joined in with the laughter.

Eventually there was a lull and a silence when they all looked at each other smiling and nodding but saying nothing. Shipley then proceeded to ask, mainly with sign language, if they could sleep somewhere. He opened the front door and pointed at the barn and put his hands together on the right side of his head and leant his head over to indicate sleep. She got the meaning straightaway, nodding furiously. She disappeared into the only other room and after a few minutes came out with two blankets and two small pillows. She passed them to Wilson who had stood there with his arms outstretched. She then took Shipley by the arm and led him through the scullery and out of the back door. There was an outhouse with two doors. She opened one of the doors and showed Shipley what was inside. It was a neat, clean toilet with old newspapers pushed between the pipe leading from the tank and the wall. She nodded vigorously and pointed to the little room and then to Shipley clearly showing him it was his to use.

Coming back into the house she picked up a pail and went outside and filled it up from the water butt. She then threw an old flannel into it and then draped a small towel on the rim and gave it to Shipley and ushered him back into the living room.

She opened the front door to let the men out and walked across the small courtyard to the barn and fully opened the doors. A single cow turned and stared with its doleful eyes and then turned back to munch its hay. The woman took the men to the right hand corner furthest from the cow and pointed at the newer straw and indicated the sleep position with her hands to her head just as Shipley had done earlier. Offering their profuse thanks the men sat down and the woman left with a parting wave accompanied by much nodding and smiling.

"Well that's a bit of a good result for us," said Shipley as he stretched out on the straw, "it's amazing how you can talk to a foreigner, or at least make your point and be understood, without a word of each other's language!"

Wilson remained standing, "I'm just going to use the toilet, is that alright, and do you trust me to go on my own?"

"Go on … I trust you," he said with a laugh. However, when Wilson went outside he stood by the door and kept an eye on the outside toilet with his rifle by his side.

After five minutes, Wilson returned and collapsed onto the pile of straw pushed up against a boarded screen that had been used to separate the animals from one another in days gone by. The old cow continued to munch away near the doors and took no notice of them.

Shipley also stretched out a yard or so from Wilson and both were on their backs looking at the ceiling. Nothing was said and each thought the other was asleep but Shipley eventually spoke: -

"What a day, I can't believe what's happened in such a short space of time; let's hope Andrews is alright but those were two bad breaks by the looks of them. Still, the Americans should have everything possible to help him back at their camp. I forgot to tell them where Andrews would have to go back to, so I hope he remembers!"

Wilson said nothing at first and then went on, "Do you know, this place reminds me of my first night over here after our bloody horrendous boat crossing – God, I felt so ill and was sick so many times on that bloody boat. We slept that night in a place just like this. It was infested with rats and we had our first experience with the lice. We all knew being called up to the Army was never going to mean a pleasant life but it was a bit of a shock to go through that day what with the crossing, then the march in bad weather and ending up sleeping rough in a place like this. Little did we know that was like paradise compared with the front line!"

"Where did you go to complete your training then?"

"We didn't – such was the demand at the Front we were sent straight up the line; all we'd had was the basic training and a bit of time practising combat work but not a lot more than that. It was a mess really."

Shipley blew out his cheeks, "Blimey, I didn't know it was that bad – I heard something similar happened last year in France but I thought we'd learnt from that."

"Apparently not!" added Wilson sarcastically.

"A bit of a change to all our lives when you think about it. Take you, for example, at the Cup Final with your team and hoping for great things in your future life and then you end up in this shit! You didn't play in the Cup Final did you?"

Wilson laughed out loud, "If I had a shilling for every time someone asked me if I was playing in it I'd be living in a swanky house on the Lancashire Moors away from all this, bribing someone to keep me out of the Army! No, I wasn't anywhere near getting into the team but I went down to London with them. The game wasn't good but we deserved to win – and the celebrations – well you wouldn't believe it; both after the game and back in Burnley parading the Cup and the parties! They thought enough of me to allow me to stay at the hotel and then go round in the charabanc and I reckon I might have got some games the next season but all that's gone now. I'd be surprised if I ever saw Burnley again."

"You never know, if that American and me put in a good word about how you saved Andrews that's surely got to help you."

"Come on Corp – you know the British Army better than that, when was the last time they showed any sort of common sense?"

"Look, you don't have to call me Corporal, my name's Frank and whilst we're here together call me that, Eddie."

They both smiled at each other and Frank went on," I had some trials at Bristol Rovers, you know – not quite the same as Burnley but I thought I had a chance."

"What happened then?"

Shipley thought for a moment, "It was my Mum and Dad really – they had a business to run and needed me to be there, so getting to Bristol and devoting time to it was impossible."

"Where did you live then?"

"A small village called Wedmore in Somerset not far from Wells – you might have heard of Wells at least – it's got a well known Cathedral?"

"No I haven't, sorry, but it must be well way from any football clubs of any size?"

"Yeah, that's right, it just wouldn't work – a bit different than you when you've got all those clubs in Lancashire and, I suppose, Yorkshire to choose from?"

Wilson seemed to be reflecting back to what seemed an age ago and said nothing and Frank went on, "I wonder if any of your team have died in this War, most of them would have ended up out here or in the Dardenelles?"

"The last time I heard from home no one had been lost up to that point as far as my family knew but who knows now that the East Lancs boys and the Lancs Fusiliers have been involved out here in France and Belgium for well over a year? Nearly all the players joined up and most would have joined the local regiments so they're bound to be out here. I hope most of them come through it all because we'll have a hell of a team if they do!"

Shipley stood up and stretched his arms up and rubbed his sore head where he had hit it in the crash. He walked over to the cow and tapped it on the backside. The cow was unmoved and continued to eat away at the hay.

Shipley turned round and said to Wilson, "This can't go on much longer, did you hear that there is talk of the Boche looking for a peace treaty and it could be over by Christmas?"

"Yep, I'd heard that but didn't some people say in 1914 that it'd be over before Christmas?"

Shipley smiled, "You're dead right there, but if peace is that close it might help you at the Court Martial."

"Don't deserters get shot then?" Wilson added sardonically.

"Not always, apparently – it might depend on the circumstances. That Frenchwoman you lived with said that you'd been ill when you turned up on her doorstep and remained so for months. What was up with you then?"

Wilson said nothing as he took off his boots, taking an age to undo the laces, when both had been removed and he'd rubbed his feet, he stood up next to Shipley," Well I've still got it really – from time to time I start shaking and go all cold but I'm sweating, I'm shaking and can't control it and because of that I can't walk – I just cannot put one foot in front of the other."

"How long does that go on for then?"

Wilson went on, " Anything up to three days but provided I sit quietly or lie down it more often than not goes off sooner."

"I've heard of other people suffering from that, it's to do with the shelling and the effect it has on your brain, apparently, but the Generals think it's just a ruse to get out of the fighting."

Wilson laughed, "They're bound to say that – they're not affected by all the shelling sitting a couple of miles behind the line, if not more! When I was last in the trenches, I saw a lot of blokes suffering from these types of things like deafened or not knowing where they were or wandering off and many of them being picked off by snipers because they stuck their heads up without thinking. I can't remember anything from being there in the line and then waking up in a bed and Marie giving me a drink. That's the honest truth. I still can't remember exactly what happened but I must have run away but how that came about I'm not sure and I must have wandered for ages without realising where I was and what I was doing, I was in a right state."

Both men sat back down into the straw with their legs crossed and Frank started to take off his boots as well but went on, " Your record shows that you'd disobeyed an order in the past and got a field punishment, so what was that all about then?"

Wilson thought back for a moment, "I was out on a night patrol; I was so scared and things got so hot I admit I wandered off – well ran away really from the job I was doing but it was not like desertion I was not going anywhere and I'd seen loads of men do that in the past; it was just so bloody awful that anyone would do the same. I had every intention of going back to our lines. Our Sergeant knew that and only put me on the charge of disobeying an order when he could have said desertion – so I was lucky that time, I suppose. Christ, I shouldn't have told you that because only me and the Sergeant knew that and now you can use it against me if you wanted to."

"Don't worry I won't, there'd be no point now, but disobeying an order is going to be a problem for you as it will be taken into account, you know. Hopefully, saving Andrews might help you a bit but these blokes on these CMs are not very sympathetic, or so I've heard."

"He's not the only one I've saved, you know," Wilson said quietly.

"What do you mean?"

"Well there was this lad in our company, I forget his name, but on the way up to the front line he lost it and went to shoot himself through the head. I dived at him and deflected the shot and it still caught him but didn't kill him. He was in bad way and got carted off and we never saw or heard about him after that."

Shipley sat up, "Well that's something more in your favour, Eddie, what was the bloke's name, we could find out more about him."

Wilson said that he couldn't remember. "You've got to," said Shipley, "It could save your bloody life."

Wilson slumped back into the straw, "Christ, I just can't remember but it'll come to me, I'm sure."

"Look we'd better get some sleep – I'm gonna have to tie you to something or I'll never sleep because I'll be wondering if you've run away!"

The Corporal found some long lengths of rope at the back of the barn and tied Wilson's right hand with the rope and fastened it to one of the roof supports. It would do for now he thought.

The two settled down and remained quiet, each with their own thoughts about the day just gone and the day to come. Wilson could not get out of his mind the time he was with the young man who wanted to end it all. He tried to recall the man's face as he recalled how he dived on top of him to save his life. But he was not sure of the face, so many flashed through his mind – those he had known but had gone. He started to count up how many had died close to him in such a short space of time but in the end they merged into one – a young bright, smiling face and it was as if they all took on the same persona – they just all looked the same.

Shipley's breathing slowed but became louder and Wilson looked over at him – the Corporal was lying on his back with his mouth open. Gradually the heavy breathing turned more into a snore. Wilson turned his back and pulled his tunic over his head to block out the noise and he started to go through the alphabet each letter at a time and as he did so ran through a whole series of christian names for each letter. His concentration wavered after a while when he got up to H and he found his eyes drooping. Shipley's snoring had stopped and his breathing was constant but shallow.

Despite the autumn cold outside, the barn surprisingly offered warmth perhaps from the straw, some of which was in the loft above their heads and so provided a form of insulation. It must have warmed up a little outside as light rain began to fall and this soon became heavier.

Some time later Wilson woke up with a start with the noise of the rain on the wooden roof of the barn. Confused he jumped up and moved away only to be wrenched back as the rope yanked at his wrist. He swore at his forgetfulness but it woke him up and, realising where he was, he sat back down on the straw.

He looked at the Corporal who was now on his side but no longer asleep – he was staring up at Wilson, "You alright, can't sleep?"

"Not really, I was dropping off but the rain woke me up and I didn't know where I was for a minute and nearly broke my wrist when I tried to walk to the door!"

"Sorry about that and I would like to take that off your wrist but I'm sorry I can't – you'll just have to try and remember it's there!"

They both laughed. Wilson liked this young man. He was sure he could be a right bastard as all MPs were, or so he had heard, but there was a warmth about him and they did appear to have a lot in common. Wilson had always found it difficult to get too close to those in his unit especially after they had arrived in Belgium as they were likely to be dead the next day and it was difficult to cope with all of that sort of thing on a regular basis.

Wilson started to speak and turned to Shipley but the Corporal had already gone back to sleep so Wilson laid back onto the straw and listened to the rain which had by now become even heavier. The wind had also got up and was driving the rain against the side of the barn and the wind howled round the eaves. He shut his eyes and, whilst it was comfortable on the straw, the noise outside made it feel like he was back in the trenches with the constant wind and rain lashing down for what seemed like hours on end. The images of that time flashed across his mind and he thought of the fear that went with it in that death was all around and he might only live for maybe just a few minutes, such was the constant danger. Here in the relative warmth and comfort it was strange because he feared that his certain death, this time from a firing squad, might just be a few days away.

As he slipped towards sleep, those awful memories made him shudder and he tried desperately to think of something else. He thought back to the day at Crystal Palace and the Cup Final. He tried to recall Freeman's goal but even that was hard. It seemed that it was a lifetime ago and it was almost as if he had not really been there at all. When he tried to visualise the joyous scenes at the end of the match and the players and fans hugging themselves and jumping up and down, the scene was played out in silence in his mind but gradually all he could hear was the whiz of the shells and the trench mortars, the loud cacophony of explosions and shouts and screams. Eventually they were gone.

CHAPTER 23

Shipley stirred and wondered what the noise was. He looked across the barn, which was in total darkness. It took him seconds to work out what was happening. He suddenly jumped up and turning round and saw Wilson, screaming so loudly that it was almost unreal. He grabbed the Private's arm and as he did so Wilson's hand grasped his throat and pushed him backwards and Shipley rolled over with Wilson on top of him.

The hand was squeezing the life out of him and he fought back trying to grab Wilson's hair. He got hold of his shirt instead and it was wringing wet, sweat dropped onto his face from Wilson's head. He managed to roll away to his right but Wilson came with him and landed a thumping blow on Shipley's cheek, but at least it caused Wilson to loosen his grip and Shipley was able to completely roll away far enough so that Wilson's rope restraint stopped him from following. Throughout all this Wilson was screaming at the top of his voice and his whole body was shaking with rage, it was as if he was in a trance and had become a different person.

Shipley had stood up as he had staggered away and was coughing and spluttering. He had to sit down again to gather his breath. He gasped in the air holding his neck at the same time. The neck felt red-raw and extremely painful.

As his eyes became more accustomed to the darkness, he could see Wilson flat out on his back and quiet now but his body was twitching and jerking out of control and he appeared to be chuntering away to himself incoherently. The young Private's hair was wet as if he had been outside into the rain. Likewise his shirt and trousers were saturated.

Despite almost ten minutes of Shipley shaking Wilson's shoulders and lightly slapping his face, he could not get him out of this trance like state but gradually the body movements slowed down and became less frequent. Suddenly the barn door opened and the old woman appeared with a lantern and shone it towards the young men. She was gabbling away in her own language but clearly wanted to know what on earth was going on. Almost certainly she would have been woken up by the screams. She saw Wilson and shone the lantern in his face, there was not a flicker and he just stared ahead with the occasional jerk of his whole body; the sweat was still running down his face.

She looked at Shipley and spread her arms wide as if to ask what was the matter with the other man. Shipley also spread his arms and shrugged his shoulders as if to say he did not know and then he put his finger to the side of his head and rotating it to indicate that the young Private was off his head.

The woman also shrugged and looked again at Wilson, staring right into his eyes but there was still nothing, not a flicker and they remained fixed on a point a yard or so in front of him. The woman turned towards Shipley and did the same motion with her finger as he had done and turned and walked away to the door, talking away to herself as she did so.

Shipley knelt down in front of Wilson and shook him again, trying to get him to look at him but to no avail.

He just sat there looking at the young man as he now rocked rhythmically with the jerking and twitching having stopped. He wiped some of the sweat off Wilson's face.

Gradually the rocking slowed right down but Wilson still did not come to, as such, but it allowed Shipley to gently ease him over onto his side in the straw. Wilson brought up his knees so he almost curled up into a ball and he hugged himself as if trying to keep warm. He was shivering yet still sweated profusely. Shipley lay down beside him and watched as Wilson gradually relaxed and then went off to sleep. Shipley then nodded off himself.

Shipley came to with a bright light shining straight into his eyes and a shadowy figure looming right above him, he rolled over and grabbed his rifle but as he did so he realised the light was the low sun coming through the open barn door and the figure was the old woman standing there with a large wooden tray in her hands.

She spoke this time in French and whilst he found that difficult to understand he did at least recognise some of the words and got the gist of what she was saying. She was clearly worried about Wilson who had been in such a state when she was there just those few hours earlier. She moved towards Wilson who was still asleep. She looked at him as if she was really concerned about him and she put the palm of her hand on his forehead to feel his temperature. Shipley knelt beside the Private and gently nudged his shoulder. He was keen not to get the same reaction as the night before when Wilson had gone for his throat!

Wilson stirred and his eyes flickered for a moment but that was all. His face was deathly pale. His previously sodden clothes had largely dried out but there were still some sweat stains mixed with the dried blood and other stains from their previous owner! Wilson remained still and actually screwed his eyes shut as if to say "go away".

Shipley stood up and took the tray from the old woman telling her that the young man was going to be alright. " Bon, bon – Merci, merci," he told her.

Then he had another thought, "Madame, Poperinghe, Poperinghe, how far?" he spread his hands to illustrate distance "how far" he repeated. He mouthed the words more precisely than normal and with a slow deliberate voice.

The woman seemed bemused but was nodding just as Shipley was nodding. "Poperinghe?" he repeated. "Poperinghe?" he mouthed more slowly and spread his hands again.

The woman suddenly smiled and then laughed out loud. "Ah Poperinghe," she said pronouncing it quite differently from Shipley's version, "dix kilometres," and she pointed to the South East directly towards the sun.

"Merci Madame, merci." He sat down and put the tray on the straw. The woman looked at Shipley then down at Wilson and slowly shook her head. She bent down and kissed her hand and used it to gently touch the top of Wilson's head and she smiled at Shipley as she did so. She said something that Shipley did not understand but it was definitely with a note of concern. With that she went out of the door and back into the sunshine.

Shipley looked at what she had brought. There was some milk, two hot drinks, meat, cheese, some bread and even the half empty bottle of red wine from the night before. There was more than plenty for the two of them but Shipley smiled. He thought back to the times his Mum similarly used to bring him his early morning breakfast before he went off to school. There had always been so much there and it was so filling that it would have lasted him all day, yet his Mum still insisted he took his sandwiches for his lunch!

He now sat staring into nothingness for a moment as he thought back to those schoolboy days, which seemed like a lifetime ago and almost like they had been part of some sort of dream.

He turned and looked at Wilson who was now half sitting up resting on his elbows. Shipley was taken back by how white the younger man's face was. It was tinged with a greyness that Shipley had only seen previously on the faces of the dead.

"How do you feel now, Eddie?" he asked as he poured out the steaming hot drink, which he took to be coffee.

"Like shit," said Wilson who eased himself up off his elbows and stood up and stretched his arms above his head and moved forward towards the sunlight only to be yanked back again as he again forgot about the rope around his wrist.

Shipley quickly undid it. He was sure Wilson would not run away but did not really want to take that chance especially with a rifle near at hand and bearing in mind Wilson's antics during the night. So, he decided to tie the rope around Wilson's ankles allowing him to walk but not that well. This would stop any swift movement towards the rifle or any attempt to attack him or run away.

"God, you frightened me last night and damn well near killed me!" Shipley went on angrily.

"Really? Look, I'm sorry Frank but I honestly can't remember anything much about it. What happened then?"

Shipley spent some time telling him what had gone on earlier.

Wilson was upset by what he had tried to do to Shipley.

"I really don't know what to say, Frank, I'm so sorry. Apparently I've been having these nightmares ever since the trenches and Marie has told me that I have attacked her and her father on more than one occasion. All I can recall is a sort of dream where this huge German with one of those spiky hat things they wear is attacking me in a trench. This bloke's got a huge nose, flaring eyes and pointed ears and looks like the devil and he has me round the throat and I am passing out and just about to die. Apparently, I then come out of the dream and all I then do is sweat and feel sort of numb and then curl up shaking."

"Well, as I said, that's exactly what happened and you say you can't remember a thing?"

"No – not a thing, really I can't."

"Bloody hell – how do you feel now because, you're right, you do look like shit?"

"I feel so weak and trembly and a bit light headed. I don't feel like eating anything but if I do it'll make me feel better.

Wilson sat quietly and ate slowly – the food moving round his mouth as he chewed far more than normal. His concern was that, if he swallowed, it might come straight back up. He knew though that if he got it down him it would do him a lot of good. And so, after about twenty minutes, he had finished his share of the food, gulped down the last glass of wine and smiled looking at the empty glass, thinking to himself that perhaps he should always have some wine for his breakfast, as he now felt so much better.

The two men picked up their belongings, such as they were, and went over to the house to thank, and say goodbye to, the Frenchwoman. Shipley gave her all the local money he had on him but she refused to take anything, instead she led them to the gate near the road and pointed to the South East – "Poperinghe," she said and smiled and nodded. She stayed there and waved until the road turned a corner and the men were out of sight.

Shipley had removed Wilson's rope before they left and attached it to his own left wrist and Wilson's right one – but once out of view from the woman Shipley removed the rope completely and tucked it back into his rucksack.

Neither said much for a while as they trudged along the road with its thick hedges on either side. Shipley noticed that Wilson's colour had returned and he appeared much better but his eyes were dark and sunken. To Shipley the young man looked thinner and much more gaunt than when they had first met in the garden a few days before.

"What's that?" he said turning to Wilson.

"What?"

"That noise."

They stopped. There was a sound coming from the wood about five hundred yards ahead.

"It's whistling," said Wilson.

"You're right. What on earth…?"

"It's German," said Wilson.

"How do you know that?"

"I've heard it at the Front – it's one of their songs."

Suddenly it stopped. Then singing started but softly almost like a quiet, low hum.

"That is German, "observed Wilson, "it's the same song. What the bloody hell's going on – there can't be any Germans here – the Front must be much further away from here?"

"We'd better get out of here and hide the other side of this hedge," said Shipley as he started to move off but Wilson grabbed his arm.

"Wait! Look!"

From the protection of the wood a small group of British Tommies appeared, most of them smoking, rifles hooked over their shoulders and helmets at more than a jaunty angle than would normally be expected.

They were also moving slowly. No purposeful march. Behind them was a straggly line. The blue-grey uniforms a giveaway that these were Germans. They were indeed singing or at least most of them were.

"Quick," said Shipley, "you'd better wrap this round your wrist and I'll do the same." He took the rope from his rucksack and passed it to Wilson, who hurriedly tied it to Shipley's right wrist and his left.

The Tommies slowed as they saw two of their kind coming towards them. They quickly took their rifles from their shoulders and held them at the ready. They came to a complete halt but Shipley and Wilson moved forward towards them. One of the men, a Sergeant, called over his shoulder and a young Officer appeared from the ranks behind. He moved forward towards the two men.

"Corporal?"

"Yes sir – Corporal Shipley escorting prisoner, Private Wilson, to Poperinghe for Court Martial, sir."

"What are you doing walking and without anyone else?"

Shipley explained as quickly as he could all that had happened. The Captain was more than a little taken aback and seemed a little sceptical but finally appeared to accept all that Shipley had said.

"Look, I'm Captain Milne. We have just come from our camp near this Poperinghe place and are escorting these Germans to Calais so they can be deported, probably to the United States as prisoners of war. Then our orders are to take leave at home."

"How far is it to Poperinghe then?" asked Shipley.

"About five miles – it would take you about two hours on foot but you can do me a favour. We have lost one of the Germans."

Shipley and Wilson seemed surprised.

"No, not lost so we need to find him, but lost as in dead!" continued the Captain, "it would be better if you took him back with you as I don't want a rotting body with us for a couple of days."

"What happened to him then?"

"We don't know, Corporal, apparently he just collapsed near the back and when I got to him he was dead. There was nothing we could do. It looks like a heart attack or something similar, there had been nothing wrong with him before that. Anyway he's on a cart at the back and you can have the cart and the two horses and take him with you, so at least you will not have to walk the last part to the camp. I'll give you a note confirming what has happened as you might find it difficult to explain how you came by him if I don't!"

Having taken a good five minutes to find a pencil and some paper he duly wrote out a summary of events and signed the paper and passed it to Shipley.

In the mean time the two horses and cart had been brought up. The Private with the reins seemed somewhat aggrieved that he was now going to have to walk and was muttering under his breath.

"Thanks for your help then, Corporal, we'll get going – good luck!" He saluted and Shipley went to salute back with his right hand but forgot he was tied to Wilson so his hand only got halfway. He then saluted with his left hand and apologised. The Captain laughed out loud and his men all smiled.

Slowly the column shuffled off as Shipley and Wilson climbed onto the seat at the front of the cart both throwing a cursory glance to the dead German prostrate in the back. The face was covered with his tunic.

The two men and their horses had to wait for the long line of prisoners to pass by. Almost all glanced up as they passed, their singing and whistling having stopped as soon as the Captain had called a halt earlier.

Shipley commented to Wilson how bedraggled and downcast the Germans were. The hollow cheeks suggested they had not eaten much recently and seemed to show that the rumours about starving troops on the other side was in fact true. As they went by, their dark, lifeless eyes were typical of the defeated. It was interesting that they were either all extremely young, almost like schoolchildren, or very middle aged. This, the two men agreed, gave more support to another rumour that the Kaiser was really down to his last options. Curiously, thought Shipley to himself, whilst they all looked a rather sad and beaten group of men, they were mostly all smiling. The singing he had heard as they approached suggested that maybe they were content now with their lot. They all probably wondered how long it might be before they ever see their homeland and their families again but at least they had survived, they had come through the hell of it all and now perhaps there would be a life in the future for them, whatever and wherever that might be.

Just as the last of the German filed by one of their number broke ranks and came over to the cart. Shipley awkwardly grabbed his gun and the two guards at the back of the column also ran over pointing their guns and shouting. The German was only a young boy and he was pointing at the body and shouting at Shipley and Wilson. It was clear he was trying to tell them something about the dead German. All four of the British men relaxed and lowered their guns. The boy seemed to be very upset about something and equally frustrated that no one could understand him.

One of the guards spoke, "Wait here a minute, I'll go and get Captain Milne, he speaks German which is why our unit got the job of escorting this lot in the first place, so he could speak to the prisoners as and when."

With that he was off and in a couple of minutes he was back announcing that the Captain was on his way. Shipley, still tied to Wilson, jumped down from the cart and knelt down beside the boy who was now sitting down on the grass verge with tears trickling down each cheek. He patted the boy on the shoulder and the boy looked up and more quietly now spoke softly in German. He could only be about sixteen, Shipley thought, as he tried to get the boy to stand but he pulled his arm away when lifted by Shipley under the armpit.

The Captain arrived and this time the two guards lifted the boy up so the Officer could speak with him.

For several minutes the two conversed, the Captain seemingly more sympathetic by the second. He seemed to agree something with the boy who passed him a folded sheet of paper, the Officer found the pencil he had earlier in the top pocket of his tunic and passed it to the boy.

The German went across to the cart and whilst the paper was pushed against its side he wrote furiously almost filling a complete page. He neatly folded the sheet and then wrote a name and address on the front.

All the other soldiers had kept silent as this went on until Shipley spoke, "So, sir, what was that all about?"

The Captain spoke with the boy again and the boy turned and went down the road followed by the two guards. The boy appeared to thank the Captain who smiled and appeared to offer good wishes in return.

"Sorry, Corporal, what did you say?"

"Sir, I asked what was that about?"

"Well, it turns out that the dead man is the boy's uncle. The boy has already lost his father and two older brothers since '14 and now he's lost another member of his family. The letter is to the man's wife explaining what has happened here, in case they want to know roughly where his body will be buried. The boy thinks it was a heart attack but the man had been very ill with pneumonia and his body just might have given up. The boy also says that there is some stuff on the body that he would like sent home to his aunt with the letter. I gave my word that I would do all I could to make sure everything gets sent home so I'm passing the responsibility to you Corporal. Can I have your word as well?"

Shipley was more than happy to agree and took the letter and put it in his trouser pocket. "I'll check the body later for the other stuff."

With that the Officer was off, jogging down the road to catch up with the column

CHAPTER 24

The two horses had quietly edged to the side of the road and were eating some of the many apples that had fallen onto the road and the verge from a tree overhanging the ditch from the adjacent field.

Shipley took up the reins and guided them round to face the right direction and with a sharp crack with the reins the two trotted off. Behind them the singing from the column was caught on the wind and drifted past them. Wilson looked at Shipley and smiled and shrugged, "Looks like you've done this driving lark before."

"Yes we had a horse and cart at home which my dad used for his work so I've been driving these things since I was about four!"

They said nothing more for about twenty minutes but then Shipley said, "Do you know those are the first Germans I've seen and this bloke is obviously the first dead one."

"Well, I've seen a few dead ones and quite a few bits and pieces of them as well, I can tell you!"

"Have you actually killed one?"

"Not as far as I know but when you're shooting blindly you just don't know, I might well have done."

Shipley was more curious, "When you say bits of Germans, was that as a result of our artillery into their trenches?"

Wilson was quiet for a moment and he just stared out along the road ahead without focussing on anything in particular. He then fidgeted uncomfortably and went on.

"We were sent over the top one night for a quick raid on their trenches to try and capture some of them for information and get some guns or food or anything we could use. Normally at night we did not see much artillery action but unbeknown to our Officers, it seemed, there was a lot more activity and some shelling took place on Fritz's positions ahead of us just where we were headed. After about twenty-five minutes it stopped and we waited another ten just in case they decided to start up again. They didn't so we moved off. As normal it was wet and slippery and we had to avoid the shell holes and old slit trenches filled with water. We scurried along like the rats around us, stopping every so often to check there was no one coming the other way. It was often the case that you might bump into Fritz doing the same thing as us!"

"We had an idea from previous scouting missions that the right end of their trench was less populated than the other part and we might nab a few of them unawares and take 'em back. One of us was sent ahead to have a look and when he came back he said that where their latest trench had been there was nothing but smoke coming out of large hole. We crawled along towards this hole and what remained of the trench. The trench line here was quite wavy and it was always easy at night to drop into it without being heard even by the enemy who could be just a few yards away."

"Anyway, after we dropped into the hole, the sight was unbelievable, the whole trench was smouldering as our bloke had reported and all that was there was a heap of human remains. We counted about four heads not on bodies, about another five heads attached to top halves, some without heads at all and a lot of innards and limbs scattered everywhere. The smell of burnt flesh was awful, like burnt sweet lamb, and then there was this horrible smell where the stomach and bottom contents had been splattered on everything. Several of our blokes were ill, which didn't help the stink either!"

"On top of this lot of freshly cut and burnt flesh was an army of rats. In fact, having gorged on dead Tommy and Fritz for a few months, they were so fat they waddled everywhere and I've seen dogs smaller than them!"

"Our Sergeant wasn't sure what to do. There were no prisoners for us to take back but should we hold the trench? Yours truly was sent back to speak to an Officer for orders. On my way back our shelling started again, passing over my head and landing where I'd left my mates. Shit! I thought, do I go forward or back. I was pretty sure the Officers in our trenches would have got onto the artillery and told them to stop shelling our blokes and perhaps I should go back to them to see if they're alright."

"I turned and scrambled back to the German trench and when I got there the sight was even worse than before. The remaining German bodies had been further churned up along with the rats. There must have been a thousand bits of German and rat lying there on fire. Two of our blokes had been hit and were dead – one, a Scot, had no legs left but the rest of the men just seemed dazed and only slightly injured and I went round them checking they were alright but I couldn't find the Sarge. I asked the others if they knew where he was or where he had been standing when the shell landed. They all pointed towards the hole that stretched across the trench and into its wall beyond the burning bodies. He'd gone, blown up. We looked for some sort of sign but there was nothing."

"As we looked around this new shell hole we could also see loads of old bones. We thought it might be a horse that had died and been buried but it wasn't it was nearly all of human origin and we found a skull, some leg bones and one complete skeleton.

There was no way of telling whether these were German or British. We searched around for some sort of evidence, like pictures or letters but everything must have rotted in the mud. These bones were from bodies buried there some time back."

"Our Officers definitely must have got through to the artillery as the shelling soon stopped. We were later told the artillery blokes were from the Essex but no one knew for sure but when we met some later we moaned at them for killing our blokes but they denied it and were quite upset that we thought badly of them. There was a bit of a set to with them in this bar but some of your blokes turned up and sorted it out."

"Anyway we scarpered from the trench taking our two dead blokes with us for at least a proper burial. They were just another two dead to add to the list. Two more bloody telegrams and more sadness to follow for another couple of families."

"Did you know that this sort of thing went on night after night after bloody night? We never really found out much on these sorties and I always wondered if they were just a waste of time and also a waste of the lives of the men who were killed out there."

Shipley had remained quiet throughout Wilson's story. All the time though he was visualising what the whole thing must have been like, not just what Wilson had just described but also the conditions in their own trenches and the sort of life these men had to put up. Death never far away. The wetness, the rats, the lice, the appalling food and lack of sleep due the shelling or just the fear that you might go to sleep and not wake up or just the dread of what might happen the next day or on those that were to follow.

"Do you know something Eddie? I must say that I would've done the same as you."

"What's that?"

"Run away from it if it got that bad – it must have been sheer bloody hell and I'd never have coped."

"Nah! You would have been alright it was bit like an adventure really but the trouble is I didn't run away. Well…. I did I suppose, but I didn't realise I was doing it."

"So you've said!" said Shipley with more than a hint of sarcasm.

"Look, if I was going to run away don't you think I would have done that long before it was supposed to have happened? I could have done so after the incident I've just told you about when I was on my own for a while and there were countless other times too when a similar thing happened. Like I've said before, the time I did leave the line I didn't know what I was doing, I had some sort of breakdown and by the time I felt a little better, which was months afterwards, it was too late to go back."

"You're wrong, if you'd gone back and told them what had happened and got the Frenchwoman to tell her story you would have been alright especially if the medics had checked you over. You might have got a bit of a sentence but I bet you would not have got the firing squad. By leaving it so long you've burnt some bridges, you know."

"It would have made no difference, the only chance I've got with this thing is the War coming to an end and they haven't got to make an example of me."

Shipley thought for a minute and added, "Well I don't think you were that wrong and I believe your story about your illness, as the Frenchwoman told me what you'd been like. Whilst you've been living with this woman and her family there's been a lot of important people also suffering from the effects of being in the trenches. I mean trouble with their heads. There's this poet bloke, whose name escapes me, but he's had it and there's been a right argument about it, apparently.

Also, in Australia they shot a bloke for desertion, I think it was, and then they found he was ill or something and they pardoned him. Not a lot of good to him now though but the upshot of it has been that the Australians won't shoot anyone now unless it's a capital offence like murder. Now there's been talk that we might be doing the same. Not many of our men get shot, you know, as there's only been about three hundred. When you compare this number with the number of our troops out here and the number of actual offences that have been tried at Court Martial that's not that many!"

"Still three hundred though!"

CHAPTER 25

For about thirty minutes neither man spoke, the horses gently trotted along the narrow road with the thick hedgerows either side sheltering them from the wind, which was now beginning to blow quite hard. Dark clouds scurried across the sky and some coming towards the two men clearly carried some rain. Within a few minutes the heavens opened and it began to pour. Shipley steered the horses to an entrance to an open field that had two large trees either side. They offered good cover with the leaves just turning to their autumn brown and yet to drop. He suggested they stop for a while to let the heavy shower pass.

The two men got under the cart to shelter. The German's body was covered with a greatcoat and stretched across the back of the cart. Gradually the rain eased and the two men came out from under the cart and, still bound together, moved behind the cart and Shipley checked the body was still covered and started to move away but then could not resist the temptation to lift that part of the coat covering the German's face. As he did so he recoiled and fell backwards onto the wet grass pulling Wilson with him.

"Bloody hell, he's still alive!" shouted Shipley. They both stood up and Shipley pulled the coat off completely.

"Don't be stupid, man – he's just been left with his eyes open – look I'll shut them." He lent over and placed his fingers into the eye sockets and closed the lids.

"Christ, that gave me a fright, I've never been that close to a dead body before and I didn't realise that could happen!"

Wilson laughed, "When you've seen dead bodies like I have you'd have known, believe me! Do you know when I couldn't get to sleep last night I tried to count the number of dead bodies of mates I've seen and tried to name them all. I got to over forty but, of course, there's a load more. Then there's all those others whose names I didn't know then there's all the Germans…" His voice tailed off and he looked blankly into space

Both men stared at the German's face. It was devoid of all life and looked parched just as if the blood had drained out of it completely. The mouth was still open as if it was trying to breathe in air.

"This bloke's no youngster is he?" added Shipley, " what would you say, mid-forties?"

"At least that, remember it was his nephew we saw in the column back there. The old Kaiser must be getting a bit desperate sending kids and old men out here. I wonder who he really is and where he came from?" asked Wilson.

Shipley moved closer to the body, "He must have some papers or something on him and I'll have a look and try and send these to his family, as I promised."

He rummaged in the coat pocket and then into the top pocket of the tunic. He pulled out two photographs and a little book.

He showed the photos to Wilson who took them from him to look more closely. The first was of the man's family. It was easy to see the German standing erect behind his wife seated in front with two teenage children, a boy and a girl, seated either side. As was the vogue of the time they were all unsmiling and looking almost frightened. The German was in his dress uniform and the teenage boy was also in uniform although he only looked about fourteen. The older woman wore a hat with a neat skirt and blouse under a short jacket and had her ankles crossed. The young girl had a bonnet, a lacy blouse, long dark skirt and short laced-up black boots. It was a picture so common of that time and was not much different from thousands carried around the world by soldiers of all sides.

Wilson held the picture for some time and was lost in his thoughts but then went on, "It's really sad to think that this poor woman and her children have no doubt got word from the Germans that the man has been captured. They probably feel so pleased that their man has been spared. Whilst they don't know when they might see him, they at least they think he's safe and will eventually return to them in one piece. Little do they know that he's lying here in the middle of nowhere in Belgium with a couple of Tommies and he's as dead as can be and they won't know about it for ages?"

"Yes and look at this." Shipley passed the little book to Wilson who opened it up. Inside was what was almost certainly the soldier's pay record. There was a signature against a series of figures and was probably the amount of pay, countersigned by an Officer clerk or something similar. The book was wringing wet and some of the ink had run but there was a name at the top of the page and Shipley checked that it had the same name as that on the note given to him by the young nephew earlier.

"Wolfgang Muller and a date which looks like twenty second of February 1874 – so that makes him what? Forty-four," Wilson said as he passed the book back to Shipley.

"Hang on what's this tucked inside the back pages?" He pulled out a postcard and they both studied it. It was a picture of a village and turning it over they could see it was addressed to the man. Despite their limited German it was clearly a Christmas message and appeared to be from his wife – the lady in the photograph presumably.

The other photograph was of the same woman as before but many years earlier and the two men guessed it was probably a wedding photo as the woman had a veil and was even smiling this time.

Shipley found a watch in one of the trouser pockets together with a battered lighter. "I'll send these back with the nephew's letter and write about what has happened and how we came by them."

"I wouldn't send the lighter if I was you"

"Why not?"

"Because it's British!"

"Christ, you're right – bloody hell," and with this Shipley threw it away across the field. "He must have nicked this off a dead Tommy, the bastard."

"Sorry, but we all do things like that in the trenches. Life's like that there, I'm afraid."

Shipley covered the man's face and walked back to the front of the cart dragging Wilson with him and shaking his head.

As they got back into the seat Wilson asked, " Do you think my family know what's happened to me, what does the army tell them?"

"I'm not exactly sure but I do know the family will be told you've gone missing in the sense that you are absent without leave and they'll be warned of the dire consequences if they know where you are and don't tell, or even hide you should you turn up at home."

"If, for argument's sake, I get shot by a firing squad what do they get told then and do I get thrown into some unmarked grave?"

"As far as I know they'll be told exactly what's happened but I don't know about the body. Anyway that won't happen to you – if you explain your illness and we get the Frenchwoman to back up your story I'm sure you'll just get a sentence with hard labour. Even I could speak up for you."

"Would you be allowed to do that, being a policeman and all?"

"I don't see why not."

"Could you represent me at the Court Martial then?"

Shipley thought for a moment, "No. I'm sure that wouldn't be allowed. You get allotted an Officer normally from your regiment or you can choose not to have one at all. Trouble is your pals from the East Lancs are all over the place now and it might be difficult to find an Officer from them to do it."

"That and the fact that most of them are dead anyway," added Wilson ruefully.

"That's as maybe but you must have someone represent you or it will be more difficult for you – take my word on that."

"I'll ask for you to do it – I don't want some bloody Officer doing it who doesn't give jack shit!"

"Believe me, you'll be wasting your time, mate."

With this Shipley shook the reins and the horses trotted off. The sky had begun to clear and the veil of cloud and rain had lifted. In the distance two columns of smoke rose from a group of buildings and there were tents and vehicles visible around the large stone buildings. He guessed it was the camp at Poperinghe.

As the road twisted down towards the camp Shipley halted the cart as they passed through a small copse and, out of sight of anyone who may be looking out from the camp, released himself from the restraint and secured Wilson to the support strut behind the driver's bench.

"I'd better make it look like you've been tied up away from me so I can cover you with my rifle. You'd better take the reins and I'll get into the back with the German and cover you. Understand?"

"Whatever you say, sir!" added Wilson with a grin and a smart salute.

"Look Eddie," Shipley went on, "the next few days are not going to be easy for you. I can't really believe you are taking all this so well, I really can't. With me being from the disciplinary side of the army I can't support what you've done in one way but from what you've said and from what I've heard from elsewhere, you have gone through an ordeal along with thousands of others that no one, and I mean no one, should have to put up with. As I've said before, it would have sent me off my head if I'd been out there like you and I'd might have done exactly what you've done given what you've seen and what has happened. I'll do my best to help you that I promise you. To start with I've decided to really push to have them allow me to speak for you because, if I don't, you'll probably get some idiot just out of university who knows nothing about anything. If I can't speak in the Court for you, I shall at least give as much information to the Officer as I can or even write to the Court if they won't hear me. Are you alright with that?"

Wilson had gone very quiet and was looking down at his feet and with his free hand wiped his running nose. His eyes had filled up as Shipley had been speaking. Choked up he managed to thank Shipley but for a moment that was all he could say and he just stared ahead blinking to hold back the tears.

Shipley was embarrassed for the man and he even felt himself welling up inside and to cover any embarrassment to himself he jumped down from the cart and busied himself with the horses, making out he was checking their harnesses.

For more than five minutes nothing was said between them and eventually Shipley hopped onto the back of the cart, further adjusted the coat covering the German, picked up his rifle and sat directly behind Wilson with his rifle in a readied position.

"Better move off," he said to Wilson, who cracked the reins so that the horses moved slowly away.

"Frank, it's very kind what you have said and "yes" I would like you to do anything you can. You're right and I very much doubt they would ever let you, just a Corporal, speak up for me even though you're in the Police. Look, I just want this whole thing to come to an end – I'm not frightened of being shot; I lived in the front line, don't forget, and the threat of death was there all the time and in fact death was more of a promise than a threat and I've had a year more than any of my mates but … there we are."

Shipley interrupted, "They can't possible have you shot – this whole thing out here is going to be over in a matter of weeks so what's the point of shooting anyone now to set an example? Yes, if you'd killed an Officer or something like that then maybe that would be different but I would be very surprised if they'd shoot you now but you must put all the facts before the Court so you make sure this happens."

"Yes I know, Frank, and you've said all that before but I'm not counting my chickens about this and whilst you might be able to help I don't think these senior Officers on the Court Martial are going to take much notice of a bloody Private from Burnley, or with due respect to you, a sodding Corporal."

"We'll see but all I can say is I'll do everything I can for you. We might be able to get the Frenchwoman to say something about you and what about the soldier whose life you saved perhaps we could get something from him or even his family – it's all got to help, surely?"

Wilson shrugged "maybe" was all he could manage.

The cart was now in full view of the camp guards who readied themselves as the horses approached. They relaxed a little as they could see the British Army uniforms and one of them slung his arm through his rifle strap so it was over his shoulder and he held the horse nearest to him so that the cart came to a complete standstill.

Shipley put down his rifle next to the covered German and jumped down. He spoke to the other Private who covered them loosely with his rifle.

"I'm Corporal Shipley from the Police and I have a prisoner for Court Martial, he's Private Edward Wilson, you'd better get an Officer."

The Private with the rifle let go of the horse and with an "I'll go" disappeared into the large wooden hut to the left of the gate and inside the perimeter fence. After about twenty seconds during which time no one spoke back at the cart, the Private emerged from the hut followed by an Officer adjusting his clothing and putting on his peaked cap after smoothing his hair.

He moved towards Shipley who saluted and the Officer just managed an abbreviated, swift response.

"I'm Major Burnside and I take it you're Corporal Shipley; we've been expecting you for a couple of days, where the hell have you been, has Wilson caused you a problem?"

"No sir, nothing like that, we ran into some Americans and they wrote off our lorry and nearly wrote off the Private helping me with the prisoner, sir." He went on to elaborate, explaining what had happened.

"Good, well done anyway, Shipley – so this is Wilson then, has he tried to escape at all?"

"No sir, in fact he could have done so when we had the accident in the lorry but he pulled my Private out of the wreckage and might have saved his life, sir!"

"Really? Interesting. Well, you'd better undo him and get him over to one of the cells."

"There is one other thing, Major, we've got a German with us in the back of the cart."

The two guards immediately readied their rifles but Shipley stretched out his arms suggesting they put them down.

"It's alright, he's dead."

He explained to Major Burnside how the poor German had apparently just keeled over and died. He gave him the note the Officer in charge of the prisoner column had written out. Burnside took the piece of paper and quickly read it through.

"Umm?" queried the Officer, "I'm not sure what we do with him now, I suppose I'd better have a doctor look at him or do I just record all this and send the body off to the German burial area up the road there?" He pointed to the East and all the other four men turned and looked that way. The Major went on: -

"Do we know who he is?"

"Yes sir," replied Shipley. He got the documents out of his breast pocket and showed them to the Major who said, "We 'd better take these inside and I'll get one of the clerks to record all this. Shipley you'd better give me a brief note of what happened with him. I'll get the Doc to confirm the cause of death as best he can, at least to confirm no one has put a knife in him or something like that."

"Sir?" said Shipley, "The German had a nephew in the column and he asked the Officer in charge if we could write to the dead German's family explaining what happened because they think he's alright and on his way to a prisoner of war camp. I have a note here in German from the young lad and the column Officer who spoke German confirmed it was just a simple message and not telling them where our big guns are, or anything like that, Sir!"

Everyone smiled. "I'm sure you're right, Corporal," added Burnside, "Right, let's get Wilson to the cells and the German off to the medical room. Shipley you'd better go and clean up and grab something to eat and then get yourself a clean uniform from the stores, they do have one for you. Oh, and by the way, you can also pick up a third stripe as I had a note through to say you've been promoted to Sergeant, well done! At the stores they'll have some clothes for Wilson and perhaps you could pick them up as well and take them to him." He turned round, "Private?" he said to the guard, "take the prisoner away and organise something for him to eat and drink. Take those clothes off him once he's in the cells and throw them away, Shipley will bring over the clean ones later. Right everyone, let's move."

The Private motioned Wilson to move on with his rifle. There were a series of buildings to the left and Wilson looked along them – there was the general office and then the stores – he saw Shipley pass through the door and close it behind him. Beyond this building was the Officer's Mess and next to this a makeshift chapel of a sort – it was like a large shed but someone had nailed a cross to the wooden door. The courtyard then swept round to the left and there were what appeared to be the ordinary quarters extending along a small track. The Private nudged him in the back saying "To your right."

There was a single building on this side of the courtyard with two doors. The first had a red cross on it and was some sort of treatment area but not big enough for a hospital as such, perhaps it was where a doctor worked from. The other door had two barred windows either side and it was to this one that Wilson was directed.

He opened the door and went in followed by the Private. The room was dark and dingy with only a paraffin lamp on a table at which a Sergeant sat busily writing in a large ledger. There were two other chairs opposite him across the table and two wooden bureaux in the corner on the right. To the left was a thick oak door and this presumably led to the cells thought Wilson.

The Sergeant looked up as the Private closed the door. "Ah, the infamous Mr Wilson I presume – we've been expecting you – sit down a minute." Wilson pulled the chair out from under the table and sat opposite the Sergeant.

"Right, I have all your details down here," he said pointing at the left hand page of the ledger, "so I'm going to put you in the cells behind me here and you can get out of your clothes whilst the Private here will organise your replacement kit. You'll have two lots, one for sitting around in and the other for your Court Martial. This will take place in three days time. We have got an old East Lancs uniform so that will be appropriate. You will eat in your cell and pee into the bucket in there and you'll be able to empty that when you are allowed exercise in the small yard at the back for half an hour a day. At that time you'll be allowed to have a crap – if you have to go at any other time you'll have to use the bucket. Is that understood?"

"Yes, Sergeant."

"You'll need a shave so the Private will bring you a razor and some soap plus a bowl of water – he'll have to stay with you whilst you shave – we don't want you cutting your throat, now do we? Any questions?"

Wilson thought for a few seconds, "Would it be possible for Shipley to come and see me some time later? He was the one that brought me here from Calais."

"I don't see why not."

He then spoke to the Private, "Can you have a word with him when you get Wilson's stuff? Thanks."

The Private told the Sergeant that, in fact, the other Sergeant had already been told to bring over one set of clothes but he would make sure the two needed would be brought over.

The Sergeant then spoke to Wilson again, "Have you any other questions?"

"Er, will I have an Officer to represent me?"

"Oh yes, sorry, I meant to say, Major Burnside will drop in later and go through this with you – it might be him to do it but I don't really know. Right follow me, Wilson."

He got up and picked up a set of keys from the top of one of the bureaux and moved towards the oak door. They moved through to the next room, which was just a small hallway with two further doors in front of them. The Sergeant opened the one on the right and ushered Wilson in. "I'll arrange for someone to bring you something to eat and drink in about half an hour."

With that he went out and shut and locked the door behind Wilson. The cell was lighter than the outer office as the barred window was rather large for the room and he guessed that originally there had been just the one room and it had been partitioned to create the two cells.

There was a small table under the window on which was an empty glass and a large ceramic water jug. On closer inspection this was three quarters full of water. There was a small towel next to it. The room itself was about eight feet by twelve with a bed along the longer wall on the left, the door and window being at the narrower ends. There appeared to be no means of heating the room and it felt quite cold but the window faced what Wilson guessed was the south so when the sun was out it should warm up during the day, at least.

He lay on the bed that had the one pillow, a bare mattress, one sheet and a really thick blanket. He stretched out and realised how tired he was and he soon felt his eyes heavy and he was on the point of dozing off when he woke with a start.

Someone was calling his name. Slightly bemused he was not sure whether it was real or if he had been dreaming. Then it came again.

"Wilson, Eddie Wilson, are you there?"

It was actually coming from the adjoining cell. "Hello?"

"Yes, what is it?" said Wilson.

"Oh you are there then, you are Wilson, aren't you?"

"I am but who are you?"

"I'm Lance Corporal Blackburn from the Artillery. Call me Arthur. I heard you were on your way; you're a bit famous round here playing in the cup final and that. Is it right you deserted and you've been on the run for over a year? Bloody amazing that is!"

The Artilleryman was a typical chirpy Londoner. Wilson had always thought it made them all sound like wide boys and thick with it.

"Yes I am here because I've been recaptured but I'm not owning up to being a deserter but then that's a long story and I won't bore you with it because you won't be that interested I'm sure."

"Oh I don't know. But you have been on the run for a year then?"

"That's true but I was ill for a lot of the time."

"You seem alright to me, mate, so when is the Court Martial, then?"

"I've been told it's in three days time. Oh and by the way I didn't actually play in the cup final in 1914 although I was with Burnley at that time. It's true I was at the match and got to parade the cup with them and get my hands on it but that's it. I was hoping to play for them when this is all over but that all depends now."

"Bugger me, how disappointing and then there was me expecting to see your winner's medal, something to tell the children about!" Arthur laughed at his own joke, "I'm a Woolwich Arsenal man myself, we'll be challenging your lot after the War, and don't you worry about that, mate." He laughed again.

"What are you doing in here, then?" asked Wilson.

"Oh, I knifed another Lance Corporal when I was drunk and got involved in a fight in one of them bar places where the French tarts keep filling you up with the local shit they call wine so they can fleece you out of your money. I slapped one of these women who was trying to nick my wallet and this bloody idiot starts laying into me and to protect myself I picked up the nearest thing I could and unfortunately for me it was a rather sharp knife and I dug it in his side and he collapsed. He didn't die or nothing but he lost a kidney but that was alright as he's got a spare!" He roared with laughter at this.

"So, are you waiting for a Court Martial, as well?"

"No, mate, had mine yesterday. I got three year's hard labour and I'm waiting to be transferred to somewhere back in good old Blighty to do it. The powers that be did think it might be over here but the rumour is the fighting could stop at anytime so there was little point me being kept over here, so I'm being taken back tomorrow along with a lot of the injured from the hospital."

"So," went on Wilson, "what's the Court Martial like then?"

"Bloody nonsense because they don't want to know your story and they think you're guilty before you start. The bloody Officer I had, who was supposed to put my case, was a complete, chinless, waste of time. He seemed to be about twelve, never seen any sort of action, probably had a flunky at home to wipe his arse and comb his hair. Take it from me don't bother with an Officer, either do it yourself or just let them make a decision – they've probably made their decision before the whole thing gets started if the truth be known, you know what I mean?"

Wilson said nothing for a moment. This was definitely not what he wanted to hear.

"Who was this Officer then?" he eventually asked.

"Oh Mulligan-Sprake or some such name, complete tosser if you ask me, if you get him tell him to take a walk and do it yourself, mate."

"Do you think they'd let me be represented by an NCO? The bloke who brought me in is in the Military Police but he's offered to represent me if it was at all possible."

"Not a chance mate, this is the British Army we're talking about and King's Regulations, not a bloody chance!" he added.

"That's alright for you to say, Arthur, but I'm looking at the possibility of a firing squad here and you weren't, that's quite a difference!"

"Yeah, you're right, you'd better do what you think's best but it ain't going to be very easy. Even though the War might be over tomorrow for all we know, you won't be treated any differently than those poor sods were in the early years!"

Thanks, thought Wilson, thanks for cheering me up no end!

CHAPTER 26

Shipley had first taken the cart with the German in it over to the medical hut with a red cross on the door. A Private had been called over by Burnside to help Shipley with the body. Whilst Shipley went inside, the Private waited at the back of the cart.

There were two orderlies in the small office and their two desks were covered with stacks of paper. Shipley explained about the German and produced all the pieces of paper he had.

He explained that he wanted to write a letter to the German's family and to send the papers with it. The orderlies agreed that there was no reason why he shouldn't do this although they had never come across this type of thing before and looked at him as if he was mad. As far as they knew the details of the German's death would find their way back to the German authorities eventually but exactly when that would be, no one quite knew. However, the orderlies were sure that the War was coming to an end and these things would eventually be sorted out. What they would do for now is to record the man's details after the doctor had seen him and then they would pass over the body for burial at the German cemetery nearby. If Shipley wishes to inform the family what has happened then fine but they would have to pass his letter and the documents to General HQ. Someone there would have to work out how everything would get back to the Germans. They were sure the family will get everything but quite when that would be another matter.

Shipley felt he had done all he could for the German and told the orderlies that he would write the letter and bring it over to them later. They offered the use of their office if he preferred and he could also use their paper and ink for the letter. He then went outside and with the Private's help carried the lifeless body into the room where the orderlies were and they opened the inner door where there was a clear desk. The orderlies told the men to leave the body on there and they would fetch the doctor from the Officer's Mess. The body once examined would then probably be moved to the mortuary section of the hospital further into the camp.

Shipley and the Private then took the two horses and the cart and left them with a Lance Corporal at the stables.

The Private took Shipley to the mess hut for NCOs. There were no soldiers in at that time but only two of the dozen or so beds were not being used, it seemed, so Shipley took off his jacket and fell onto one of them. It felt good to have something comfortable at last to stretch out on after the night in the barn. Within minutes he was dozing and only came to when a group of fellow NCOs returned to the hut and woke him up. Having explained who he was and what he was doing there, he went to the washbasin in the ablutions block next door and cleaned himself up.

He picked up his jacket and went over to the stores to pick up his replacement uniform resplendent with its three stripes. Leaving there he went over to the medical office and spent the next hour or so having several attempts at writing to Muller's family. He must have thrown about ten sheets of paper onto the floor, as he just could not put the right words together. Finally he was happy with what he had done and left the letter with the orderlies. The Private who had helped him with the body earlier had come in just as he was about to leave telling him that the Sergeant was to go to the cell block as Wilson wanted to see him and Major Burnside had given his permission.

Shipley returned to his mess hut and got out of the old uniform and put on the new one he had picked up but not before he had had a quick shave having borrowed one of his fellow NCOs' razor and soap.

When he collected his new uniform he had picked up one for Wilson but had to return to pick up the second one following the message from Burnside via one of the Privates. He walked across the yard towards the cells and on his way there Major Burnside joined him. "Ah, Sergeant, I have been asked to tell you that you are to rejoin your unit on Monday at the police station in Calais. You can stay here until that morning so that gives you Thursday to Sunday as leave. Although you won't be able to get out and go very far, there are a couple of lively bars in the town here – you'll need to speak with Corporal Arkwright or one of the others, they know all the places where you can let your hair down!"

"Thank you, sir, when will Wilson's Court Martial be then, will it be before I leave?"

"It's planned for Friday."

"Will I be required to attend to give evidence?"

"Why would you think that, Sergeant?"

"I don't know, sir, but having spent the past few days with Wilson I have talked to him a lot and found out about much of what he's been through and these things should perhaps be brought out but I'm not sure Wilson's going to do anything about bringing this to everyone's attention and I think he should. He was talking about not even having anyone represent him and I think that would sign his own death warrant if he doesn't."

Burnside stopped. "That's his problem Sergeant, we've assigned Captain Milligan-Sprake to represent him but he does have the choice of representing himself."

"I see," Shipley frowned and followed the Major as he moved off again.

"Sir, would it be at all possible for me to represent him? Assuming Wilson wanted it, I mean."

Burnside stopped in his tracks and thought for a moment.

"That's an extraordinary request, Shipley," he walked on and Shipley followed a yard behind and the Major stopped again and turned to face the Shipley, "No, I'm sorry, that would really be out of the question."

"Why not, sir – out of all the people there could be, I feel I know him better than anyone and I am here for the next few days. Is it King's Regulations or something like that?"

"Probably but I'm not totally sure, however I will check for you but, anyway, I would have to refer this to a higher level so I wouldn't hold your breath!"

"I hope you will do what you can, sir. I know Wilson has done wrong and should be punished for leaving the line and all that but I do feel he was in such a state of shock and was really ill in his mind that he didn't know what he was doing."

"Sergeant, the Army does not accept that as an excuse for a man deserting his post and you should know that just as well as me. If I had a pound for every time we have heard that excuse trotted out then I'd be a very rich man indeed!"

"But sir we have the Frenchwoman he lived with, she would be able to tell the court how ill he was and how she nursed him back. He still is ill in my opinion, I have seen him have this sort of fit where he goes wide-eyed and as if he's mad for five minutes and I think he's still in some sort of shock."

Burnside was now at the door of the cellblock. "All I can say, Sergeant, is that I'll give it some thought and have a word, that's the best I can do and I'll let you know tomorrow but I would not hold out much hope. But what I would say is that, as you seem to be friendly with the prisoner, you should persuade him to co-operate with his advocate in every way he can. Too often these men just don't bother and leave themselves at the mercy of the Court, which, between you and me, is not the best thing to do. I have heard that the better the case put up the more likely the deserter will get a jail sentence or hard labour or something like that rather than the firing squad if he's found guilty. You know the Army has to maintain discipline and make an example of these people. You must think of the poor soles still in the trenches – they do not have a lot of time for their mates who run off into the soft comfort of a Frenchwoman's arms, or similar."

"I don't think it was quite like that, sir, but I would appreciate your help."

With that Burnside opened the door and went in leaving Shipley to close it once he had also passed through. As he entered the Private picked up the cell keys and opened the oak door again.

Inside the cell, Wilson stood to attention as the Major came in followed by Shipley.

"Right, Wilson, I'm here to brief you about the proceedings coming up. The Court Martial has been arranged for Friday. It will be held in the Poperinghe Town Hall and you'll be moved to the cells over there later today. Captain Milligan-Sprake has been appointed to represent you and I would urge you to make sure you use him properly. He has completed his Law Degree and had almost completed his training to become a Barrister when he joined up and he has represented others at Courts Martial and is very experienced. I have asked Sergeant Shipley here to advise you further after I leave – I understand you wanted to speak with him anyway."

"There will be three Officers presiding over the Court and they normally do not delay making a decision so you should know your fate on Friday. I have to tell you that if found guilty the ultimate punishment is execution by firing squad, you do appreciate that don't you, Wilson?"

Wilson nodded and looked at Shipley who smiled and offered an apologetic shrug.

"If the worst comes to the worst, any sentence will have to be ratified right down the line as far as the Commander-in-Chief and this might take ten days or so. There is no appeal as such but everyone will see details of your defence and an explanation of what happened to you so it is imperative that you make sure you make as good a defence as you can, I can't emphasise this enough."

He turned to Shipley and went on, "You will make sure he understands this and perhaps you'll talk him through the whole thing. Won't you?"

"Yes sir, I'll do what I can."

Burnside turned back to Wilson, "Have you got any questions?"

"No, sir, thank you, sir."

"Right then, Wilson, I'll leave you and the Sergeant to talk it through. Right, Sergeant, he's all yours."

With that he turned and left pulling the door on as he did so. Shipley put Wilson's two new uniforms on the bed and the two men sat down on it and for almost a minute said nothing until Shipley spoke: -

"Look Eddie, I've been thinking about this. If the Court Martial goes ahead on Friday that doesn't give us much time because I think we must get the Frenchwoman to come along. She will at least be able to provide first hand evidence of the state you were in when you turned up on her doorstep. What do you think?"

Wilson put his head into his hands and then propped his chin with both hands and rested his elbows on his knees. He then rubbed his eyes with both hands, "I don't know that getting Marie here is really going to help bearing in mind what you've just said and she has been through so much herself, what with her husband and all, and she's pretty fragile and I don't want her to be upset in any way."

"Yes but it's your life we're talking about here, man, it's not like you're going to get off this, it's just a question of how severe the punishment might be and, with the War likely to end soon, it's got to be important that you get a jail sentence as it's bound to be reduced or you'll get released early when we all go home!"

He looked at Wilson expectantly but Wilson just lowered his head and stared at the floor.

Eventually with somewhat of a weary sigh he lifted his head and stretched his arms up. "I suppose you're right but how are we going to get her here by Friday?"

"Eddie, you'll have to leave that to me, I'll get it postponed, if I can. I'll speak with Burnside right away and then I'll go back to Calais and speak with the woman. I know where she lives and she's bound to be there, if she's teaching."

He got up and started to move to the door, "Oh, what was it you wanted to speak to me about?"

"God, yes, I've remembered the name of that soldier, you know the one who tried to do himself in and I dived on him to stop him pulling the trigger? Well he was Private Jimmy, Jim presumably James perhaps, Simpson and he was from Nelson, near Burnley from what I remember. For all I now he might be dead, he was in quite a bad way when he left us."

"Well that's good that we know his name, we might be able to trace him or his family – if you've saved his life, like you say you have, it's got to help your defence, hasn't it?"

Shipley continued, "That's all the more reason we get this Court Martial put back so we might get in contact with his family and see if they could write a letter or something but right now I'll see if I can find out something about him. The East Lancs are still around somewhere and they might be able to help – even if we can't get anything before the Court Martial we could get something to reduce the sentence or something like that even after the Court has made a decision, because the Major said these sentences have to be approved right down the line of command."

"You know, Frank, I'm really grateful for your help here but you've got to think of yourself. A Military Policeman helping a deserter in court and you've just got to Sergeant so you don't want to cause a stink somewhere and get yourself into trouble with your own Officers, just to help me."

"Don't be stupid, Eddie, I wouldn't do it if I didn't feel sorry for you! As far as I'm concerned I want to do this for you. Look, I'll just get something to write with and some paper and you can send a letter to this Simpson's family."

With this he went outside and spoke with the clerk and returned with two small sheets of paper, a pen and an old mug with some ink in it.

For the next half an hour or so they put together a letter to Jimmy Simpson's family as best they could asking that if the young man was alright and would they mind writing to Major Burnside confirming, if they could, what had happened to their Jimmy and how, as it seemed at the time it all happened, Eddie Wilson had saved the boy's life. They did not explain exactly what Wilson's situation now was but they did mention it was matter of life and death.

"Right," said Shipley when they were happy with the wording, "I'd better go and see Burnside and get him to give me permission to send this and I'll see you later."

Shipley returned the ink, paper and pen to the clerk telling he'd be back shortly but perhaps he should lock Wilson's cell door for now.

Shipley headed across to the Officer's Mess where he found the Major enjoying a mug of tea and a biscuit. Shipley explained what he had done and Burnside asked to see the letter. "I'm not totally happy about some of the wording and I'll change some of it but generally it's alright. It will have to go to the East Lancs back over the water and I believe they are based in Preston but, as I said earlier, there are some of their chaps around here so I'll check with them. Anyhow I'll find out and get it off but it's unlikely anything will come back before everything is done and dusted, you and Wilson do appreciate that, don't you?"

"Yes, sir, I had thought of that. Wilson would like to call the Frenchwoman he lived with as a witness as she would be able to tell the Court exactly what Wilson's state of mind was and so on. She used to teach in England and speaks English very well, you know, so that's not going to be a problem. I've got to go back to Calais, as you are aware, so I can go and see her and get a message back to you. However it would be helpful if the Court Martial could be delayed for at least a week and this would help with a possible response from Simpson's folks. Is that possible?"

Burnside blew out his cheeks and thought for a moment and then smiled, "Alright, Sergeant, I'll do what I can, Colonel Bishop is a reasonable chap and he is in charge of setting up the Court Martial and I think the extra days would give him a chance to get some East Lancs people over as possible witnesses. Between you and me there are already two who will give evidence against him but he might want to call his own witnesses as well as the woman."

"Also, sir, bearing in mind what I said earlier on, could you ask the Colonel if I could represent Wilson, as the accused's friend, instead of the Captain or at least give evidence?"

The Major stood up, "You're not giving this up very easily, are you Sergeant, just be careful how far you go with it – if I were you I'd let the Captain use his experience to represent Wilson and you give evidence for him. Now, wait here and I'll go and see the Colonel. He's around as he was in here about ten minutes ago."

With that he smartened himself up and was gone. Fifteen minutes later he was back.

"Right, Sergeant, it's alright to send the letter and it's on its way to Preston as we speak because one of the Colonel's aides was East Lancs and he confirmed Preston was the place to send it and they would have this Simpson's address. The Colonel will not let you represent Wilson and the Captain will continue with the job. You can approach the Frenchwoman but she'll have to agree to it, there is no way we can force her to come, as we have no jurisdiction over her, do I make myself clear?"

"Yes sir, thank you sir, is it alright with you if I tell Wilson what's happened?"

"Yes, Sergeant, off you go – oh, the Court Martial will be at 1100 hours next Friday – you can tell him that as well but we'll move him to a cell in the Town Hall in the morning. Go!"

With a smart salute, Shipley left and went back to Wilson to give him what he hoped was good news for the young Private. He was a bit disappointed with Wilson's attitude, which had suddenly become worryingly negative to say the least in such a short space of time. Shipley promised him that he would leave for Calais in the morning, as he was more likely to get a lift then rather than try to get there today especially now it was dark. As an alternative, he had already thought that he could use the horses and cart again, as they were still at the camp, rather than rely on army transport.

CHAPTER 27

Wilson sat quietly in his cell for a few moments. The night was beginning to draw in and the movements of men and tractors, carts, horses and such like began to ease off. There was the distant sound of artillery drifting in on the wind with the occasional burst of distant machine gun fire.

Arthur Blackburn in the next cell tried to engage him in trivial conversation but gave up when it became very clear that Wilson was just not interested. The guards brought in some late supper which was a welcome cup of tea, some bread and a opened tin of Scotch Mutton and a piece of tasty fruit cake. By the time he had finished eating this Wilson was done in – he briefly spoke with Blackburn having become a little embarrassed by his rudeness earlier on. It had not bothered Blackburn, it seemed, and he remained as chirpy as he had been when they first met.

In the early hours of the morning some banging on the wall from Wilson's cell next-door woke up Blackburn and he could also hear the man gasping for breath.

"Wilson, you alright, what's the matter?" There was no reply. "Wilson, is that you, what's going on?"

The banging on the wall continued and the gasping was now interspersed with sobs.

Blackburn went to the cell door and banged on it and shouted for the guard. The young Private with his rifle held out in front of him burst through the outer door.

"What is it, Blackburn, what's all this racket?"

"It's Wilson it sounds like he's going mad or something!"

The guard peered through the small grilled opening towards the top of the door. His jaw dropped as he could make out the Wilson's figure sitting on the bed slowly banging his head against the cell wall and there were also convulsive jolting of the upper body and he seemed to be gasping for breath.

"Is he alright?" asked Blackburn from his cell.

"No, he's not," shouted the guard as he ran back into the outer office. His mate there had already stirred from his doze having heard all the commotion. The guard told him to fetch the Major and the MO, at the double.

He grabbed the keys from the hook on the wall and first unlocked Blackburn's door.

"I need your help, run away and I'll shoot you, right?"

"Come on get the door open," was Blackburn's only reply.

Once inside Wilson's cell the guard placed the lamp he had brought with him on the small table next to the bed and grabbed Wilson by the shoulders. He could feel the soaking wet shirt of the prisoner as he pulled the head away from the wall. He could pick out the blood pouring out of the head wound on Wilson's forehead above his right eye. He had been rocking forward towards the wall and simply head butting it; there was already a smear of blood on the wall. The guard beckoned for Blackburn to get hold of one arm and lower Wilson onto the bed. It was difficult as his body was convulsing with him gasping for air. Blackburn stared into the young Private's eyes and they were rolling around and not focussing at all. Sweat was pouring off Wilson and his clothes were soaked. The blood from the head wound had covered most of his face and had dripped onto his shirt.

"I think he's having a fit or something," said Blackburn, "what should we do?"

"Get that jug of water off the shelf there and throw it over him that might bring him round a bit," said the guard as he fought to pin Wilson down onto the bed. He stood back as Blackburn threw the water over Wilson's head. Some of it went into his mouth and he almost choked on it but, as he coughed up the water and it shot across the bed, this did seem to regulate his gasping and it appeared he could now get his breath properly.

At this moment the MO arrived followed by Major Burnside but by now Wilson was calming down – the guard and Blackburn had him pinned on his back on the bed each holding an arm and shoulder. The man's staring eyes had got more focus but he was still breathing very quickly just as if he had finished a long race.

The MO knelt down on the floor beside the bed and lightly slapped Wilson's face at first and called his name. At first there was no response and the slapping got a bit harder but less frequent.

"Wilson," said the MO, "Look at me, try to breathe deeply and slowly, no, look at me, Wilson, please look at me and breathe slowly – in, out, in, out." This went on for over a minute but the MO stopped the face slapping and gradually, with their eyes focussed on each other, Wilson's breathing got more regular and his body relaxed to the point where Blackburn and the guard slowly let go of the shoulders.

Wilson seemed completely back with them and sat up. Burnside spoke, "Take Blackburn back to his cell for the night, then come back and help the MO clear up Wilson's face but first you'd better get him a dry shirt as this one's soaked with water and blood. You'd better get the blood off the cell wall too. Now I'm off to my bed we'll talk about this in the morning, you'd better do a report about what happened," he said to the guard and to the MO he said, "We'd better have a complete medical assessment and report on this. You would have to do a medical report on Wilson for his Court Martial so you'd better include all of this."

With that he turned and left together with the guard and Blackburn at his side. The guard locked the prisoner back in his cell and went to fetch the items as instructed by the Major.

The guard returned to rejoin the MO and Wilson bringing with him a bucket of water, a cloth and the replacement shirt. He cleared up the blood from the wall and the floor and left leaving the MO alone with Wilson. Wilson still seemed a little dazed and not quite with it. He looked like a prizefighter that had been knocked out and was still coming round. The cuts and grazes above the eye added even more to this look.

"You had better get some sleep, Wilson," said the MO, "I'll come and see you in the morning and carry out the assessment and so on, has this happened before as far as you know?"

Wilson nodded, "I've been told it has but I can't ever remember much. This is the first time I've injured myself though," he said pointing to his forehead, "sometimes I've got violent, apparently, when I was with Sergeant Shipley I tried to attack him during the night when he was asleep but I can't honestly remember anything about it."

"I see, well we can talk more about this tomorrow." With that he left and the guard shut and locked the door. Wilson changed into his dry clothes and turned the mattress so he could sleep on the drier side. Within ten minutes he was asleep.

CHAPTER 28

Just after eight Shipley had spoken with the transport office and found that there was a truck on its way to Calais later that morning and he was told he could go with it, if he wanted to. Shipley said he would leave the decision for a while and let them know as soon as possible. He left the office and went to the stables and checked the horses that had brought him and his prisoner into the camp. He was told in no uncertain terms by the Sergeant Major in charge there that the team were fit enough to go back from whence they came and he did not want them left there.

Shipley started to argue that he had no idea where these horses had come from or how they had come into the possession of the German prisoner column but then suddenly had a thought. He knew a perfect home for them so agreed to take them, his idea being that he would drop them off with the old woman whose barn he and Wilson had slept in on their way from Calais.

Having got the word that all was well with the animals, he arranged for the horses to be hitched back onto the cart and he agreed with the transport officer that he would be picked up by the truck at a point near to where the old lady lived so he could deliver the horses and cart.

With this he prepared to leave but just as he was walking across the parade ground area to go back and pick up his things he saw Major Burnside hurrying towards him.

"Ah, Shipley, I'm glad I've caught up with you, the Court Martial has been re-arranged for a week today, Thursday, and not the Friday. There'd been a problem getting the right people to sit on the bench as it were, so hence the initial delay but now it's been brought forward a day. The Colonel has taken the trouble to speak with even higher authority about the requests you made and has had it confirmed that there is no possible way you can represent Wilson, it's totally against King's Regulations, apparently, and so he will have to rely on Mr Milligan-Sprake. All I can say to you is that if you want to help then do it quietly and don't get on the wrong side of people over this. I can only reiterate that you would be better spending your time gathering as much information as you can give to Mr Milligan-Sprake especially from this Frenchwoman. Alright Shipley, you'd better be off, you will be able to come back to give evidence, I'm sure, but I'll drop a note to your unit and tell them what's happened and that they will have to let you come back for next Thursday."

"Thank you, sir, that's kind of you. Any news yet of the end coming?"

"Well there's still talk of what's called an armistice happening well before Christmas, it might even be in November. That's the rumour anyway but who knows we've had so many promises before and then, of course, the whole thing was expected to be over by Christmas 1914 in the first place. However it's got to end soon as everyone's fought themselves to a standstill and the Boche have got little left in them to carry on so they'll have to negotiate some sort of deal. Anyway we'll see and I'll see you next week. Good luck!"

Shipley thought for a moment then decided he'd better see Milligan-Sprake before he leaves for Calais to let him know what he intended doing regarding Marie and the evidence she could give plus his intention to provide evidence himself. He also wondered if the Officer was aware of the letter sent back to England in an attempt to get information on Private Simpson and hopefully some sort of testimonial from him or his family.

He detoured to the Officer's Mess to look for Milligan-Sprake and he found him reading and smoking his pipe at the back of the Mess. The Officer was very young looking and seemed a little odd smoking a pipe at his age. He looked up as Shipley approached "Sergeant.... what can I do for you?"

Shipley was invited to sit in the armchair opposite and he sat down taking off his cap.

He soon found out that Major Burnside had briefed Milligan-Sprake about the matter quite fully and he seemed well acquainted with the facts. He said he had already sent a second letter to the East Lancashire Regiment HQ in Preston just in case the first one went adrift.

He had already been given details of Wilson's army record and was more than a little concerned about the fact that Wilson had already served a field punishment for disobeying an order and feared that this might count against the man in court. There was also some evidence that he had been seen furtively leaving the frontline as if to desert at the time of the alleged offence. As this was now over a year ago, there was no certainty that those who saw him can be traced and questioned in view of the time that has elapsed but the Prosecutor was trying to track them down.

Shipley confirmed he would arrange for Madame Coutteau to be in Poperinghe the night before the Court Material and he would return then as well provided he could get permission from his unit, which he told the Officer he was confident of obtaining.

The young Officer, to his credit, did seem keener than Shipley thought he might have been in preparing the defence for Wilson despite his apparent laid back style.

"What do you think Wilson's chances are, sir?"

The young Officer thought for a moment and poked the contents of the pipe with a match to stimulate some action and then drew on the pipe exhaling a cloud of smoke before answering: -

"Well, the fact is that he left the line, that cannot be disputed, he might have been dazed, shocked, had a breakdown or anything like that but the fact still remains that he made no attempt to return once he had recovered, however long that might have been. This was some months from what I have been told. The Frenchwoman will be able to confirm what he was like – does she speak English or do we need an interpreter, by the way?"

"She speaks excellent English as she used to live and teach in Kent before the War."

"Good, that will help then – what exactly will you be able to say – is it right you are willing to support Wilson?"

"Yes sir, only in that he has related to me what he had to go through which I accept was no different from almost every other soldier at that time but I am convinced he was shell shocked and this caused him to have these awful fits or whatever you would want to call them – he's not putting them on, that would be impossible."

"Yes so I've heard and he had another one during last night and damaged himself by repeatedly banging his head against the cell wall."

"Is he alright?" Shipley asked.

"Yes – he'll be fine, apparently, but the MO will be in to see him this morning and assess his condition and provide a report for the Court Martial. However, I agree that Wilson will find it difficult to convince the Court that he is innocent of deserting because he made no attempt to return and even I feel he should suffer the consequences for this. However, hopefully, the testimonies and in particular anything from this Simpson's family should get the sentence commuted to a term in prison instead of the firing squad. However, the MO's report and assessment could prove very crucial. Anyway, when you get back from Calais come and see me with the Frenchwoman so I can have a longer chat with you both – by then we might have the MO's report. If we can't get anything from Simpson's people we shall have to rely even more on the mercy of the Court."

"Thank you, sir, you seem to be well organised already, so I'll be off – thank you."

With that he stood up, saluted and returned to the parade ground, went and picked up what gear he had and returned to the stables where he found the horses and cart being tended to by the Lance Corporal who was clearly annoyed that the Sergeant had delayed his start.

By lunchtime he had returned the horse and cart to a very pleased Belgian lady and had picked up his lift to Calais.

CHAPTER 29

Having reported back to his unit the following day, Shipley found that Andrews had been patched up by the Americans and then dropped off by them at Etaples from where he was being shipped back home for further treatment. He was expected to make a full recovery from his injuries but was not expected back in France, especially not with peace just around the corner.

Permission was granted to allow Shipley to return to Poperinghe for the Court Martial and to visit Madame Coutteau to arrange for her to give evidence on the next Thursday. His Colonel had already received a note that morning from Major Burnside requesting his presence at the Court.

Shipley was allowed the rest of the day off to enable him to visit the Frenchwoman and he arrived at her home around lunchtime only to find her out and just her father there. It was difficult to make the old man understand the reason for the visit from a British soldier bearing in mind his complete lack of English and Shipley struggling with a more complex explanation than his moderate French would allow!

So rather than frighten the old man too much, he decided to wait outside in the street for the woman to return. He had got enough information from the old man to establish that she was due back for her lunch.

After about twenty minutes she appeared and genuinely seemed pleased to see him. She asked after Wilson and Shipley explained the apparent fit the man had had the previous night and the injuries sustained. He told her of the arrangements for Thursday and she readily confirmed she would attend; however, she would have to get permission from the school but did not see that as a problem, given the circumstances.

Shipley told her he would be staying at the Poperinghe camp but would arrange a room for her for the night before at a nearby boarding house that he knew of. He wrote down the address and provided a little map showing where it was in relation to the main road into the town.

She prepared a light lunch of bread and cheese with a glass of wine and they sat in the front room in the two armchairs. Her father had retired to his bedroom for his afternoon nap leaving the two of them to talk through how they should approach the Court Martial.

The young woman was the first to speak, "Tell me Frank why are you making all this effort to support Eddie when I would have thought your rank and Military Police position would make that virtually impossible."

"It is a bit difficult, I know, but having got to know Eddie pretty well during our journey back from here earlier in the week, I am convinced he is, and was, ill. As I keep telling everyone including Eddie, I cannot condone what he did in leaving the trenches and most importantly making no attempt to return once you had helped nurse him back to something like good health. However, he should not be shot for what he did because off his state of mind and by giving evidence I hope we can show that and at least get him a prison sentence, it would be monstrously unfair if he had to be shot."

"Well, I hope you're right about that. Has he been assessed by the Army yet, you know by a doctor or a specialist?"

"He's being assessed by the Poperinghe MO today, apparently, at least that's what I've been told."

"Does this man have any specialist training for understanding this shell-shock as people are calling it?"

"I doubt it," said Shipley and went on, "I was not impressed from what I heard about him, he deals with all sorts of cases, as you'd expect, and was a village doctor before the War apparently – so no definitive training. I would imagine he must have seen a lot of shocked men over the years, so you never know!"

They remained quiet for a few moments and Shipley looked at the young Frenchwoman and her beautiful eyes, which set off the rest of her face. She had her hair tied back and this accentuated the dark brown eyes. Her high cheek bones were set off by her slender nose and she definitely had that look of Mary Pickford or one of those beauties seen on the screens at the camps. She was about five feet six, which was tall compared with most of the women Shipley had seen over here and she had nice strong, shapely, legs and a firm bosom. Despite the seriousness of the situation and the fact that she had lost her husband at such a young age and, as he had found out, five cousins in the first two years of the War, she had a certain brightness about her that he found really attractive!

He wondered if, in fact, she had had any sort of relationship with Wilson although the prisoner had told him he had not.

"I tell you what, Marie, is it alright if I call you that?"

"Of course"

"Why don't I pick you up on Wednesday after you've finished at school and them we can go to Poperinghe together, it might be easier for you and I can get some transport for us too?"

"Yes, that'll be good, thank you," she smiled broadly at him and he felt himself blushing for some reason.

"Right, that's it then I'll pick you up at about four and we should get there before it's too dark"

He got up and proffered his hand, which she took in her left hand and pulled him towards her slightly and she kissed him on both cheeks holding his hand tightly. He blushed again. As he walked back down the street she waved both times he looked back. He jogged back to his quarters; the War seemed a million miles away at that moment.

CHAPTER 30

The guard opened the cell door and Wilson sat up somewhat bleary eyed. He recognised the MO behind the Private. The guard ordered Wilson to stand to attention in the presence of the Officer. The MO thanked the Private and told him to leave. He told Wilson to sit on the bed and he drew up the wooden chair, which had been pushed under the table in the corner.

"Private Wilson, I am Captain Thorogood and I am here to assess your state of health and more importantly your state of mind both now and at the time you left the trenches. My assessment will be used at your Court Martial as evidence one way or another. I shall try to keep an open mind on the whole thing. Do you understand?"

He spent the next hour asking a series of prepared questions on a whole manner of things even going back to Wilson's childhood. Whilst he was sympathetic one moment and a little hostile the next, Wilson was impressed by the time being taken but beneath it all he had the sneaking feeling that the Captain was not impressed by the fact that Wilson had left the trenches in the first place and even less impressed that he had made no attempt to return. Wilson tried to explain that he could not cope with the thought of returning. He tried to explain that he made every effort to return on many occasions but each time became a gibbering wreck just before it came to it, as Madame Coutteau would confirm.

The Captain, disappointingly, dismissed this almost out of hand and told him that there was not a frontline soldier who did not feel exactly the same as this every time he returned from leave or went back into the line and he saw this as little excuse for Wilson's actions, or lack of them.

As time went on Wilson became more exasperated to the point where he became truculent and uncommunicative as it seemed to him the MO had made up his mind about the whole thing and this was really just a waste of time.

The Captain had made pencil notes on the sheets of white paper he had brought with him in his folder. Finally he picked up the sheets and stuffed them back into the folder.

Before he left he checked Wilson's damaged head following the earlier wall-banging episode.

He also touched Wilson's swollen nose and the Private winced. "How did that happen then?" asked the Captain. Wilson explained how he had run into the neighbour, Du Feu. "It looks as if it's broken but there's nothing I can do except give you some arnica to put on it, it'll bring out the bruise and reduce the swelling. Still this nose is probably the least of your problems at the moment though."

With this the Officer knocked on the cell door and left when the guard opened it. Wilson lay back on the bed. He felt pretty miserable and tears welled up into his eyes; he didn't think that it had gone very well at all. The guard reappeared with some breakfast that Wilson barely touched.

During the next few days Major Burnside had spent a considerable amount of time with Colonel Bishop putting together the Court Martial arrangements. One problem they encountered was the make up of the three Officers who would judge Wilson's case. This would normally be a representative from the accused's regiment but the East Lancs had been decimated by their involvement in the various campaigns. Some of their battalions had been reduced to cadre strength and others moved into other battalions. Whilst there were East Lancs people around Poperinghe there was no one of suitable rank for the Court Martial. However, still in Belgium were the East Anglian and it was into them that the remains of Wilson's own battalion had merged. So Burnside found three appropriate Officers and this had been approved by Colonel Bishop and by the Corps Commander's office.

The MO's report had been passed to the Colonel and he and Burnside read through it together. They both concluded that this was pretty damning evidence against Wilson with the MO not supporting the point that Wilson had had a possible breakdown and thus would have been unfit to return to the line in any case.

They passed this to a disappointed Captain Milligan-Sprake so he was now left to hastily prepare a modified defence for Wilson.

Burnside had arranged for a Captain Selkirk supported by a Lieutenant Hughes to handle the prosecution side. Selkirk had just been called to the Bar when War broke out and Hughes was a trainee Solicitor in a large City Law Firm when called up in 1917. Selkirk had been involved in several cases previously, especially following the Gallipoli campaign.

Burnside and Bishop had given much thought to Shipley actively supporting Milligan-Sprake's defence of Wilson but decided that this was impracticable given that Shipley would be giving evidence. Confirmation of their decision was sent to Shipley at his unit in Calais but it confirmed he and Madame Coutteau were to be called by Milligan-Sprake as witnesses for the defence.

PART FIVE -
THE COURT MARTIAL,
POPERINGHE, BELGIUM
OCTOBER 1918

CHAPTER 31

Wilson had been up since just after six in the morning and it was still dark when the guard arrived with a hot drink of coffee and some bread and jam for breakfast. Since earlier in the week, Wilson had been in one of the two rooms in the Town Hall that were now being used as temporary cells. The other one had been in use for the first day Wilson was transferred there. He had been told its occupant was a senior German Officer but he had been taken away to GHQ during that night.

The food and accommodation were much better than in the camp with the room retaining an old armchair, a table and chair plus pen, ink and writing paper. Bars had been fixed to the wall either side of the large window that made the room very bright during the daytime and there was even a view out across to some fields heading towards the West.

With the Court Martial taking place in the Town Hall it was general practice to move prisoners to these cells a day or so before a Court Martial began.

After he had served the breakfast the guard also brought in a shaving kit, which he carried on a pile of clothing brought from the clothing store. There was a shirt, a pair of trousers and a jacket together with a pair of brightly cleaned boots, to this had been added a clean khaki vest, some pants and a pair of socks, this set was to be worn at the Court Martial. Later he supplied a cap for Wilson. The uniform carried the East Lancs insignia and quite remarkably everything seemed to fit well including the boots. Wilson was told that he could keep the original uniform set aside for the Court Martial given to him when he first arrived but he should now wear this new one today.

The guard remained whilst Wilson shaved at the sink in the corner of the room. There not being any warm water and no facility to heat the cold, Wilson refreshed himself by drenching his head and upper body and wiped himself off with the towel but not before he had washed his hair with the hand soap provided. It had a strange carbolic smell but it felt good to have his hair clean for once. His hair had been lank and thinned for a long while after he had arrived at the Frenchwoman's house and it took some time for her to get rid of the lice that had got into his scalp and a lot of his body. He had infested her house without thinking and it had taken over a month to get rid of the lice. He still gagged at the memory of the handful of lice he had picked up from his armpit when the Frenchwoman had helped him off with his clothes the day he turned up at her house.

Just after seven the guard left with the shaving kit and the empty plate and mug. By now it was getting light and Wilson stood on the chair and looked out of the window. He could see an aircraft flying close to the ground across the field some half mile away – it must be where the airfield is he thought as he had heard the droning planes at various times whilst he had been here. To the left and right the view was of the back of various buildings; some private houses mixing with the back areas of the shops along the main street of Poperinghe.

He stood watching the sky clearing from its greyness of night to the bright blue autumn sky of the morning. There was the occasional rumble of artillery fire drifting from the North East on the strong breeze and was a reminder that the War was still not that far away. To Wilson it seemed such a long time ago that he was part of it but he grimaced as he reminded himself that the reality of it all was about to be brought harshly back to him. He had tried to put the time in the trenches and the mud and slime and death and that awful smell of death out of his mind but he still had vivid flashbacks and even during the night just passed had woken up in a cold sweat and it had taken almost an hour before his shaking stopped.

As he was far away in his thoughts the door to the room opened and the guard let in Captain Milligan-Sprake who proffered a bright and breezy "good morning" as if they were about to leave for a picnic on this bright sunny day.

Wilson had grown to like the Captain who, despite his initial apparent indifference, had genuinely listened to all that Wilson had to say and had been greatly affected by Wilson's account of the frontline experiences he had had to endure. They had spoken at length in the earlier part of the week whilst Wilson was still at the camp as the Captain went through the story so he could piece together a reasonable defence.

He had not been that pleased to have been given this task by Major Burnside in the first place but following his meetings with the prisoner he had really got into the case and, with this, his attitude to it had changed completely.

He had told Wilson all along that it would be very difficult to deny the charge of desertion but the Frenchwoman's evidence of the state he was in when he got to her house would be critical. If only they could get something from the Simpson family this might help show Wilson in a better light.

The Captain had asked Wilson if there was anything else that could be used to help show that Wilson was actually a brave soldier just like anyone else but had been affected by the awfulness of the frontline.

Wilson had forgotten all about the saving of the life of Andrews in the lorry accident with the Americans and how he had pulled Andrews and Shipley away from the burning vehicle that did actually explode soon after he had got them to safety. Milligan-Sprake admitted that he knew about this as he had received a note about it from Shipley the previous day. Shipley had also been able to find out that the American Major involved in the crash had, indeed, written to Shipley's CO telling them what had happened and how the young Private Wilson had heroically probably saved the lives of his fellow soldiers.

It was now so important to get some sort of verification of exactly what happened with Simpson but despite every effort this had so far proved impossible. Milligan-Sprake had even tried to get in contact with the men who had been with Wilson at that time but despite Wilson giving him a list of all those he could remember every single one of them was dead, missing or, it seemed, captured.

The Prosecuting Officer had received the written report about what had been behind Wilson's field punishment and had passed this to Milligan-Sprake. It had disappointed the Captain and he had explained to Wilson that was not likely to help his case but the Captain promised he would do his best and had carefully explained to Wilson that the best they could hope for was probably a guilty verdict but with a prison sentence. The Captain was very hopeful that he could persuade the Court not to ultimately decide that execution for desertion was merited.

After they had talked through all this, the Captain asked," How are you feeling Wilson?"

"Not too bad, thanks, I had a bad night. I woke up in a terrible sweat but I wasn't as bad as the last time and didn't need any treatment this time."

"Good, now look, the Court will sit from eleven this morning and there are a few things I would like to go through with you. When you get into the Court be polite at all times as we must try to get sympathy from the Presiding Officers and the Prosecutor. However, he will try to intimidate you and say things that might get you riled but you must keep quiet and calm. Do you understand?"

Wilson nodded.

"The report on the field punishment will work against us and so will the MO's report. I cannot believe he does not accept that you have had severe shock and still suffer from the effects of the shells and the general experiences of the front line. What I do know is that he considers that, if every soldier was like you, we'd all be at home and speaking German!"

Wilson smiled and shrugged.

"I have spoken with Sergeant Shipley and he will put in a good word and provide details of your mental state as he saw it during your journey back here to Pop. Then there is the evidence from Madame Coutteau and that could be crucial, even more so if we hear nothing from England on the Simpson matter. Then we've got the accident evidence."

Wilson nodded again and looked down at the floor and nothing was said for all of half a minute when the Officer said, "Are you alright, do you have any questions?"

When Wilson raised his head there were tears in his eyes and he wiped them away with his hand and he shook his head. The Captain stood over him and put his hand on his shoulder, "Come on, Wilson, I am sure we can get some sort of result. Remember when your team went to the Final, they were not expected to win but they did, let's have the same sort of spirit your chaps showed that day!"

Wilson looked up again and smiled but he still had to wipe away another tear. The Captain tapped him on the shoulder again and left explaining that he would be back at about ten-thirty.

By the time the Captain returned Wilson had put on his uniform and dusted the familiar cap badge of the East Lancs. He sat in the armchair holding the cap in his hands between his knees and twiddled it nervously round and round. He looked up at the Captain and smiled,

"I guess this is it then?"

The Captain said nothing but moved back to the door and held it open. He nodded and spread out his right arm as if to say "after you" and Wilson went through. Outside there was a bristling Sergeant Major confronting him. His cap almost covered his eyes and the jet-black moustache twitched before any words came out but he barked at Wilson to come to attention and to put on his cap. Then with instructions to march at the double he walked alongside the Private shouting out "left right, left right" in the double time. Their boots echoed around the tall room, which was a sort of foyer with a desk at which sat a Lieutenant with a bundle of papers. Just inside the front doors stood Marie Coutteau and Frank Shipley. Wilson glanced across and even in an instant saw how lovely Marie was, dressed in a red coat and blue beret-style cap. He felt his cheeks go red but it was barely a second before he passed into the next room yet he could see they both smiled and nodded at him.

The Sergeant Major pulled open the double doors and a bright shaft of sunlight hit him and Wilson. They both squinted and the Sergeant Major shielded his eyes momentarily and then realised that perhaps he shouldn't be doing that. He came to an exaggerated attention calling out for Wilson to halt. Wilson was a yard behind and the Sergeant Major turned to face him.

Wilson, using just his eyes, glanced round the room, which had such an incredibly high ceiling. The sunlight streamed from the two windows directly in front of him – they stretched almost from the ceiling to the floor and had equally long curtains down their sides. Between them was a large fireplace that glistened with its polished wood and brass ornate fixtures. Above its mantelpiece was a large painting of a battle scene from what looked like the Napoleonic times with almost exclusively red and black colours.

In front of the fireplace and across the room was a long narrow table with three chairs on the fireplace side. At the table end there was a single chair and the Lieutenant who had been outside at the desk was now taking up his position and it appeared that he was likely to be the person recording the proceedings to follow. Just to Wilson's right were Captain Milligan-Sprake and Lieutenant Bellamy acting as his assistant. They had been sitting at a desk but stood up as Wilson came in.

Further along the right side of the room and at right angles to Milligan-Sprake was another desk at which stood the Prosecutor, Captain Selkirk, and his assistant, Lieutenant Hughes.

To the left side and also at right angles was about half a dozen chairs. Major Burnside sat on one and the MO on another; the other four were empty.

There was a door in the left hand corner and after about a minute's silence this opened and the three Officers who were to preside over the Court Martial and decide Wilson's fate came in one behind the other. They stood behind a chair and the one in the middle nodded at the Sergeant Major who called for a salute. The Officer in the middle thanked him and asked for all to be seated. A Private standing behind Wilson quickly placed a chair at the back of Wilson's leg and pulled him down onto the seat. The Private went to the back right hand corner and stood at ease whilst the Sergeant Major closed the double doors and initially stood to attention and then made an exaggerated and noisy clatter with his boots as he also stood at ease.

The presiding Officers took their seats and the one in the middle introduced himself as Colonel Graham and he then proceeded to introduce his fellow Officers. To his right was Captain Westerham and to his left was Major Ryan. He explained that all three were from the East Anglian and went on to explain why they had been called upon instead of anyone from the East Lancs. The Colonel then invited Major Burnside to confirm to everyone, but mainly for Wilson's benefit, how matters would proceed. Wilson had already heard most of this once and the Major finished by saying that it was hoped the verdict would be given today and, at the latest, by this time tomorrow. He told Wilson that if the ultimate verdict were made it would have to be ratified all the way up the line to the Commander in Chief. He also explained that the witnesses would be allowed to stay in the room if they wished after they had given evidence and been cross-examined. He also explained that the MO would be here from the start as he would not give evidence and only his report would be read out.

The Major started to sit down as he thought he had covered all the points but Milligan-Sprake jumped to his feet and asked if he could raise a point of order. The Colonel allowed him to proceed.

The Captain explained that he felt that, on behalf of Private Wilson, he had the right to question the MO on his report and that some points he would make could have a significant bearing on Wilson's eventual fate.

At first the Colonel was reluctant but the Officer to his right tugged his sleeve and he whispered something to the Colonel and then all three spent a good two minutes in animated, yet whispered conversation. In the end the Colonel announced that he would allow the cross-examination and he asked a distinctly unhappy looking MO to leave the room and wait outside with the others until he was called.

The Sergeant Major came noisily to attention and opened the doors to let him out.

The Colonel asked the Lieutenant with the pile of papers to read out the charge. He stood up a little nervously, put his hand to his mouth and coughed:

"On the 23rd October 1917, 263087 Private Edward Arthur Wilson of 63rd Battalion of the East Lancashire Regiment did desert his post during an attack on German held positions in the Passchendaele area in Belgium. Whilst fellow members of his Company fought under the most trying conditions and suffered numerous casualties, Private Wilson was seen to leave the trenches and head in a westerly direction away from the front line. It was recorded in the Battalion Diary by Sergeant Cecil Owen Beardsmore that he saw this action and as a result of this report, the Military Police were alerted to the desertion. They finally arrested him in Calais on the 29th September 1918.

I have been asked to point out that Sergeant Beardsmore will not be able to give evidence to the Court as he was reported missing in action on the 12th November 1917. It is believed he was killed."

The Colonel thanked the Lieutenant. He addressed Milligan-Sprake, "Is it correct Captain that you are acting as "prisoner's friend" before the Court?"

The Captain stood up. "Yes sir, I am and I am assisted by Lieutenant Bellamy."

"Thank you Captain and how does your client plead in answer to the charge before the Court?"

"Sir, I have discussed the matter with Private Wilson and he admits that he left the line and headed away from the action. However, he was in a confused state and says that he can recall nothing of that time and considers he was suffering from shock from the shelling with even the possibility of brain damage. He wandered for some time; he does not know for how long or even where he actually went. His first recollection is more than a week later when he regained some memory whilst being nursed by Madame Coutteau, who is here to give evidence. She will be able to provide details of Private Wilson's mental sate at the time and how long his recovery took. Sergeant Shipley from

206

the Military Police will be able to confirm the arrest and give details of what he perceives as Private Wilson's mental state by what he observed during their journey from Calais back to here.

It was hoped that we could also provide evidence that he actually saved the life of one of his fellow soldiers in his Company who was about to shoot himself. I still hope that corroboration can be received either during this Court Martial or during sentence. I say "sentence" because whilst Private Wilson admits deserting his post it was under the most extreme conditions of shock and we would therefore ask the Court to bear this in mind and be relatively lenient in deciding on a prison sentence rather than execution. There will also be placed in front of the Court details of an accident involving two vehicles, one an American and the other a British lorry. Such was the severity of the accident that two British soldiers who were transporting Private Wilson back here were pulled by Wilson from the burning wreck just before it exploded and certainly the life of one and possibly the other was saved by Private Wilson. Thank you sir."

With that he sat down. As he did so the Colonel sighed and slumped back in his chair. Milligan-Sprake looked disappointed as he saw this as an indication that at least one person on the panel did not have much time for the defence. The young Captain looked at Wilson who raised his eyebrows having, it would appear, also seen this disappointing reaction from the Colonel.

The Colonel went on, "Captain Selkirk as you are in charge of the prosecution case could you outline to us who you will be calling and in what general area their evidence will concentrate on?"

"Yes, thank you, Colonel," as he got to his feet. "I have the report from Sergeant Beardsmore from the Battalion diary which I will read to you in full. I also have details of previous disciplinary action taken against Private Wilson and this will be included in my synopsis of his rather brief army service. I shall also provide the MO's report following his assessment of Private Wilson and now that Captain Milligan-Sprake wishes to cross examine I shall probably ask the MO to report his findings himself and then provide any clarification you and your colleagues might like, sir."

He stopped for a moment and looked at the Colonel who nodded as if giving him the go ahead to continue.

"I would also ask Sergeant Shipley from the Military Police to provide details of their search for the prisoner and the capture. Therefore, sir, I would like to proceed and firstly read from the Battalion diary."

For the next ten minutes he slowly read through the detailed account from the Diary about the circumstances of the apparent desertion. The three Officers on the panel made certain notes but did not need any further clarification or had any questions. Captain Milligan-Sprake had no questions he wished to raise at this time but would address some of the points made when Private Wilson gives his evidence.

Captain Selkirk then asked for the MO to be called to read his report. The Sergeant Major, glad to have something to do, provided an exaggerated exhibition of leaving the room and returning with the MO. A seat was offered to him just to the left of the head table a few paces inside the door and facing away from the windows.

Captain Selkirk remained standing and asked the MO if he would be kind enough to read out his report. The MO got to his feet and started to read. There was a considerable amount of preliminary information including details of what it was he was really looking for during his assessment. He then got to the main body:

"When I asked Private Wilson of his experiences in and around the action near the Front he was clear in his recollections of the normal soldier experience in those trying conditions. He, like all his comrades, had experienced problems with lice from the time they landed from England and once in the trenches he had suffered with trench foot but, whilst this would have been painful and with some discomfort, it was something that our men had to put up with and carry out the job they had been sent here to do. I checked over the current state of Wilson's feet and they were in a better condition than many of those of the survivors from the trenches at that time, in my opinion that is. I checked him thoroughly for any other illness of the body and found no evidence that there was anything wrong and as one would expect from a sportsman he was in good shape. I had to make the important assessment of his mental state and following a series of pre-prepared questions I was able to establish that there seemed no problem with his mental state. I was aware of these alleged nervous and anxious attacks from which Wilson has reportedly suffered. This did include an examination after one episode when he appeared to be having some sort of fit. It is my view that this is a calculated ruse to fool us and the so-called fits were just an act of deception to help in his defence to this charge of desertion."

At this point Wilson started to say something but saw Milligan-Sprake wave him down, so he said nothing.

Instead the Colonel spoke, "Thank you Captain Selkirk, now Captain Milligan-Sprake," he said somewhat disdainfully, "now is the chance to carry out the cross examination that you asked for!"

The Captain gave him a sideways glance and stood up. He fidgeted with his tie and smoothed his hands down his chest somewhat nervously. He spoke to the MO, "Sir, is it true that before this War started you were in fact a General Practitioner in Lincolnshire?"

"That's correct, Captain."

"During this time in General Practice and during your qualification period to be a Doctor, did you receive specific training on mental health issues and the treatment of mental and nervous breakdowns?"

The MO looked at the Colonel who sat up from his relaxed position and nodded at him as if telling him to proceed.

"Not as such, " he answered.

The Captain went on," Since 1914, when you joined up have you received any specific training on dealing with the stress experienced by frontline soldiers, by the conditions they lived in, the constant danger, the effects of the shelling and the general experiences of seeing your best friends blown apart by a shell?"

"Not as such, Captain."

"What do you mean by "Not as such" has there or has there not been specialist medical training given to you so you could professionally and competently assess the mental state of any man? For example are you aware of the contents of a lengthy article in the British Medical Journal from March 25th 1916 written by Major R.G. Rows M.D.?" With this the Captain held up a copy of the Journal and its supplement.

Clearly agitated the MO bristled and shuffled from one foot to another and twice glanced at the panel that all sat forward intently; the two Officers either side of the Colonel resting their heads on their folded hands and elbows on the table. The Lieutenant, writing his notes, lifted his pen and it hovered in mid-air whilst he waited for the MO's answer. Captain Selkirk rose to say something and got as far as "Sir" as he looked at the Colonel but was waved down.

The MO carried on, "I am sorry Captain but I do not think you have the right to question my integrity in this way. Whilst I might not have pieces of paper that say I have been trained or have studied in this particular area, I have had nearly four years of practical experience seeing all sorts of these so-called problems like this at first hand. Yes, I have seen and acknowledged that some of the men have been mentally shot to bits and have recommended that they are sent home or assigned to less stressful duties."

"But," interjected the Captain, "you have not had any specific training, have you?"

"No," said the MO emphatically, as he looked round the Court for some support. Everyone, though, remained quiet and impassive.

"Have you read this article which gives specific information on the shell shock phenomena and has prompted lengthy investigation and debate since?"

Again the MO looked for support from the panel but again they ignored him.

"Well?" asked the Captain again.

"No, I have not."

The Captain was now warming to the situation, "Also, sir, it is true that you met with the prisoner only recently at the camp and carried out your assessment of his mental condition then, isn't it?"

The MO nodded.

"Therefore, sir, there was over a year for Private Wilson to convalesce from the dramatic effects of trench warfare and all that that entails. So, would you not surmise that, certainly with the help of the Frenchwoman, as we shall hear, that the obvious effects of the traumatic time in the frontline of battle would have sufficiently worn off so as not to be in evidence routinely? Do you agree?"

Again, he nodded.

"Do you recognise that the phenomena that is shell shock can re-appear at any time with, for example, hallucinatory interludes, as outlined in the British Medical Journal in 1916?"

"I understand that this has been reported as happening but have never seen it myself."

"However, sir, do you not agree that there is very little comparison between his state of mind when you assessed him recently compared with what it was that day last year in the trenches under continuous fire?"

"In my experience, Captain, it would not be possible for Wilson to have recovered that well if he really was that affected a year ago. It is true that there are some repatriated soldiers who are in a terrible state and will probably have to be kept locked inside an institution for many years, perhaps for the rest of their lives. Yes, Wilson might have nightmares and we probably all will at some time and none more so than those who have fought and still fight in the trenches. However, it is my considered opinion that Wilson is not seriously affected and, with the four years of experience I have gained first hand as I said, these current problems are normal and temporary."

The room went quiet and still. The Sergeant Major took a handkerchief from his pocket and noisily blew his nose and everyone looked at him. "Excuse me," he said clearly embarrassed. "Sorry" he quietly said again as he nodded towards the Colonel.

Finally the Captain spoke, "Thank you sir, but I would like you to confirm that there was no medical evidence available in this assessment based on reports from Wilson's time in the trenches and you have formed your opinion on that one meeting a few days ago?"

"Yes sir."

"Also, can you confirm that you do not hold any professional qualifications in this particular area of medical practice and by this I mean mental health?"

The MO eyed the room again and lingered on Wilson for a second or so more. "Yes sir" he answered quietly.

The Colonel sat up erect. "Captain, have you finished with your questioning?"

Having sat down, Captain Milligan-Sprake stood up and said, "Yes sir" before sitting down again.

"Captain Selkirk?" the Colonel asked inquisitively.

Selkirk stood up and said, "No sir," and sat down again

"Thank you," the Colonel said to the MO, "you can stay in the room now if you wish for the rest of the Court Martial but for now I suggest we adjourn for some lunch. Sergeant Major please take the prisoner back to his cell and feed and water him."

With that the Colonel stood up and everyone in the room followed his lead and filed out. Wilson and the Sergeant Major followed at the rear to be joined by the Private who had acted as the guard earlier. All three returned to the cell. The Sergeant Major locked Wilson and the Private inside and went off to organise some food and drink for himself.

"How's it going then, Wilson?" asked the Private when they got back to the cell. Before waiting for the answer he busied himself pouring out some tea from a pot on the table where there were two mugs, some biscuits and a bowl of really thick broth.

"Not too bad," Wilson replied as he sat at the table, picked up a spoon and ladled the piping hot soup. He recoiled a little as it burnt his lips and he coughed as it hit the back of his throat. "The MO is adamant I was not ill but I really cannot remember anything from when I was in the trenches until a few days later when I suddenly found myself at the house of these French people. He doesn't believe me and I'm not sure the Colonel does either. If the other two feel the same I'm done for because I can't deny I left the line, can I?"

The Private didn't say anything but he sat down opposite the prisoner and started drinking his tea before moving onto the soup. They sat there for about ten minutes finishing off the soup.

"Anyway," the Private eventually said, "you still have the Frenchie to speak for you and the MP, he seems a decent bloke and the woman will be able to say what you were like when you turned up. Do your family know what's going on?"

Wilson had forgotten all about them recently. He had been told that they were initially informed he was missing and then were officially told he had absconded. He had also been told that they had frequently had visits from the MPs back in Lancashire. When he was captured they were told he would be sent for Court Martial. Wilson had been given the chance to write to his family but thought he would wait until he knew the sentence and then do it.

The Private seemed surprised when he told him saying he would have written before now. That was the end of the conversation and the Private took away the bowls and mugs, stuffed a couple of biscuits in his pocket and left, locking the door behind him.

CHAPTER 32

As he left the courtroom Milligan-Sprake headed towards the kitchen to collect his lunch but before he got there Major Burnside approached him.

"Captain, the Colonel would like a word with you in the room over there," he pointed to the door to the right. He ushered the Captain towards it, knocked and opened it all in one movement.

It was like a study with books almost covering the four walls. The Colonel and his two colleagues were sitting in three of the four armchairs. The Colonel was smoking his pipe and the other two both had cigarettes in their hands. The whole room was acrid with the freshly lit tobacco. The Colonel stood up as Milligan-Sprake was let in and Burnside went back outside the door.

"Ah, Captain," said the senior Officer, "I would just like to remind you of your responsibilities in the Court. This is not the Courts of London, it is a Court Martial in which the prisoner has admitted he deserted, you said so yourself at the beginning. You are "prisoner's friend" and nothing else. Haranguing the MO was beyond your brief and I would ask that you just put the case for leniency and we leave it at that. Our role (he swept his arm as if to include his two colleagues in what he was saying) is to determine the guilt of desertion. That is already established and that really is the job finished and if we take the MO's report into account then I can see no other option than a recommendation of the firing squad for this Wilson. There have been countless similar cases since 1914 of such men claiming they can't remember anything and how they cannot cope and how they are in shock. They have been shown no sympathy and this Wilson chap is going to receive nothing more than the rest of them. Do you understand that?"

He went on not expecting answer, "We are almost of the opinion that we can call a halt now, you have given your plea for clemency already. The rest is a waste of our time and yours."

At this there was a knock at the door and it opened and Burnside appeared with Captain Selkirk. As before, Burnside let the other Officer in and left.

"Ah there you are Selkirk, I was just telling Sprake here of what we are all thinking."

Milligan-Sprake opened his mouth to correct the Colonel on his name but thought better of it.

The Colonel went on, "There is no doubt the man's guilty and even Sprake agrees and I suggest we move on swiftly to bring matters to a close. The guilty verdict will be passed up the chain of command for additional consideration. We believe the MO's report will damn the prisoner and I'm not sure any pleading will help but you have the right and we will allow you, Sprake, to give a brief overview of the apparent mitigating circumstances by hearing from the woman and the MP but we want this short and to the point, do you understand?" Again his tone suggested that this was an order and not a question.

Milligan-Sprake stood for a moment with his mouth wide open; he looked at Selkirk who immediately turned away and took a book off the adjacent bookshelf so as to avoid eye contact.

"But sir," he eventually managed, "this is a man's life we are dealing with here and he has every right to …"

Before he could go further the Colonel interjected, "Captain, let me remind you of where you are, who you are and what you are doing. If you wish to get on in this Army it is not a good idea to upset senior Officers and it is important that you know your place. We will allow you to, briefly, have the two witnesses tell us what happened and what they saw. No opinions, nothing. Do I make myself clear?"

The Captain started to argue but thought better of it. "Yes, sir." He turned to Selkirk again but he was looking down at his book and carefully turned a page as if he was reading.

The Colonel opened the door and let the two men out. Selkirk hurried out of the building as if to avoid any contact with Milligan-Sprake, who had a look of thunder on his face. He spotted Major Burnside. He went over and started to complain but the Major showed him into the toilets saying, "We'd be better off in here, what was that all about then?" He looked round as he spoke to check there was no one in the two cubicles there.

The Captain told him all that had gone on in the other room.

The Major thought for a moment and then said," I'm sorry but that's the Army for you and in a way the Colonel is right, they can only decide on guilt, which has been admitted anyway and pass on the evidence. You will just have to make the best you can with the time the Colonel will allow you with the witnesses; so try and keep it brief but relevant. Then I suggest you go away at the end of this day and do all you can to get some sort of details of the circumstances where Wilson saved one of his mates, you're right to say how important this is to Wilson. I normally have no sympathy with deserters and I feel they should be shot ordinarily but I have some for Wilson. I have to tell you that the Colonel is having a word with Sergeant Shipley as we speak and it's not about the cessation of the War, that's for sure!"

The Captain seemed shocked. "What do you think it's about then?"

The Major was a little embarrassed. "It's probably to remind him that he is a Military Policeman and of his duty to his King and Country and, I guess, to point out that maybe it was not his place to have got so involved!"

"But that's outrageous, he can't do that surely?"

"I'm sorry this is the frontline not the Old Bailey and the rules of procedure get changed, believe me!"

The Captain was absolutely fuming as he left Burnside who went into one of the cubicles as Milligan-Sprake stormed out slamming the main toilet door behind him.

He went straight to the kitchens and asked the cook there for a mug of tea. It was pointed out there was food left for him in the Orderly Room next door yet Milligan-Sprake said nothing but instead sat down in the corner of the kitchen on the steps that descended into the basement. He cupped the mug in his hands and sipped the sweet, warm tea.

CHAPTER 33

The cell door was unlocked and the Private came in, "Time to go, mate, the Sergeant Major's outside waiting."

Wilson tidied himself up having taken his tie off earlier and undone his top button. The Private led him outside and the Sergeant Major bawled at him to come to attention, which he did. The NCO walked round him inspecting his turn out. He then ordered a quick-march and they quickly arrived in the Courtroom where all but the top table were present. Again he caught a glimpse of Marie and Frank who both broke off from their conversation and smiled at him and Marie gave a little, almost apologetic wave barely raising her arm as if she did not want anyone to see.

The Sergeant Major barked out his orders to Wilson; his boots again making an almighty noise on the floor, which made most of the others present frown with annoyance.

Wilson and the Sergeant Major remained at attention for almost five minutes until the side door opened and the three Presiding Officers entered. Everyone else came to attention but only the NCO saluted, as all the others were not wearing their caps or hats.

The Colonel spoke first, "Captain Milligan-Sprake could you confirm how you are to proceed from here; what witnesses do you have and will the prisoner be giving evidence?"

"Sir, I have two witnesses who will be able to vouch for the fragile mental state of the prisoner and in the case of Madame Coutteau will be able to confirm exactly the state of Private Wilson when he arrived at her home a few days after he left his unit. Sergeant Shipley from the Military Police observed whilst the prisoner was in his custody certain unconscious actions by the prisoner, which suggest that Private Wilson is still not mentally well even after a year out of any action in the line. I shall be calling on the prisoner to explain his actions."

"I would just like to remind the Court and you," continued the Colonel," we are here to establish guilt as to desertion and this has been admitted so we are now only concerned about mitigating circumstances. My two colleagues here will review the prisoner's military record, although it is a very short one. Nonetheless it will be relevant to our decision in view of the apparent ill discipline he has already shown, resulting in a serious field punishment. Right, proceed Mr Sprake."

The Captain again started to correct the Colonel but instead changed his mind and asked the Sergeant Major to bring in Madame Coutteau.

Apart from the Captain all were seated as she came in. She had removed her beret a little earlier in the foyer and her hair had been ruffled by it, yet she still looked stunningly attractive as she moved towards the chair provided by the Private in the corner.

"Please sit down in the chair Madame Coutteau, there is no need for you to remain standing," said the Colonel, "I understand you speak very good English but if there should be anything you do not understand then do please ask us to stop. Major Ryan here speaks your language fluently and will be able to help."

Marie smiled at the Officer that the Colonel pointed to. Ryan blushed slightly and smiled back with a nod.

Wilson could not take his eyes off her and actually felt his hands shaking with nervousness for her and indeed himself. It was as if for the first time he appeared to realise just how important the next few minutes, and indeed what Shipley has to say later, will be towards the Court's decision. His mouth now felt a little dry and he had that queasy feeling in the pit of his stomach, something he had not had since waiting in the trenches for the order to advance.

The Colonel asked Milligan-Sprake to proceed and the Captain stood up from his chair.

"Madame Coutteau, thank you very much for coming today, I would like you to tell the Court what happened the night Private Wilson arrived at your house and would you detail how you nursed him after that?"

Marie looked round the Court and noticed how all those sitting were leaning forward awaiting her answer with probably more interest than at any time during the proceedings before lunch. Even the Sergeant Major by the main door shuffled his feet so he could get a slightly better view of the young woman.

"Eddie, sorry Private Wilson, arrived on this most dreadful, wet night in October last year. I was frightened when I found him at the door. He was wet through and in a collapsed state. He was shaking from what I thought at first was the cold but his eyes were staring really at nothing at all. I managed to stand him up but his legs would not work properly and it was as if he was drunk. I gave him a hot drink and some food and eventually he seemed to come back to the world. He clearly did not know where he was and when I asked he did not answer. I had asked in English but then had the thought that he might be German as his clothes were so covered in mud it was difficult to see what side he came from. He still did not reply so I cleaned off some of the mud from his shoulders and then saw the British Army markings. I managed to find some of my father's old clothes and he changed into these…."

At this point the Colonel interrupted, "Madame Coutteau, I'm sorry, but could we please just hear about Wilson's mental state then and during the year he was with you and the reasons he gave for not returning to his unit when he had recovered. Captain Sprake could you address your questions accordingly. Thank you. Please proceed Madame Coutteau."

"Thank you, sorry Colonel, I'll do my best. It was almost two weeks before he could even tell me his name. He was conscious but was not really there, if you understand what I mean. He barely ate and appeared thin and drawn and almost every day would get this shaking as if he was having some sort of fit. By the Spring he was better. We did talk about his circumstances and he could recall more about the past but said he could not remember anything of the last days he had in the frontline or how he came to be at my door.

Even right up until when the soldiers came, after we had moved to Calais, he still had this shaking and sweating and unsteadiness on his legs. I had also treated him the whole time for the problems with his feet that he had got from the wet and cold in the trenches."

"I'm sorry to interrupt," said Major Ryan, "but you just said that you had moved to Calais. Where were you then when Wilson appeared in October?"

"At a small village right on the Belgium borders just a few kilometres from the frontline."

"Oh – thank, Madame Coutteau." He wrote something down onto the sheet in front of him.

"Please carry on Madame Coutteau," said the Colonel.

"Well, that's about the story really –but you wanted to hear about what he said about returning? I'm sorry I nearly forgot. He did talk about it when he had got over the worst of his problems. In fact, he twice made an attempt to go back but each time he became so upset he could not even step outside the house. He thought he might try to get home at one time and I think this is because he would have given himself up back in England rather than here because, he said, he was less likely to be thrown back to the Front. He knew like us all that the end of the War was likely in the near future and he would then be able to report back either over here or in England."

She stopped and looked around the room. No one said anything for a few seconds until the Captain thanked her and looked at the Colonel who asked Captain Selkirk if he wanted to question the witness.

"Madame Coutteau, I'm very sorry to have to ask you this but your husband died in the early part of the War, is that correct?"

"Yes, sir, he died at Verdun."

"I'm very sorry – you lived with your father is that correct?"

"Yes."

"Again, I'm sorry to have to ask you this but how close were you to Private Wilson?"

"How do you mean?" She blushed a little.

"I'm sorry but were you lovers?"

All the men moved uncomfortably when Selkirk asked this question and Milligan-Sprake immediately jumped to his feet and addressed the Colonel, "Sir, this is an outrage!"

Before the Colonel could say anything Selkirk went on, "Sir, I'm sorry but I'm trying to establish the relationship between the two so you can judge how keen Wilson might have been to return to his unit if he was - eh – enjoying his life in Calais."

The Colonel was about to say something when Marie somewhat angrily said to him, "Colonel, all I can say is that we were like brother and sister – no more than that - I was and still am in mourning for my husband and Eddie has always respected that."

"Again, Madame Coutteau, I do apologise but felt I had to establish this relationship." With that Selkirk sat down.

The Colonel was a little embarrassed but smiled at Marie who was dabbing her eyes and she then blew her nose into a small handkerchief. "Madame Coutteau, thank you again for coming here. You have been able to provide us with an insight into the prisoner's situation for the past year, which will be helpful in our deliberations. You may stay in the room or leave if you wish."

Marie nodded and headed for the door. The Sergeant Major came to attention and opened the door; she thanked him and he smiled at her. Outside she burst into uncontrolled sobbing and was immediately comforted by Shipley who led her over to one of the chairs by the desk. The Private at the desk brought over a glass of water for her.

Back in the Court, Wilson felt worse now than before. He had wiped a tear from his eye when Selkirk was questioning Marie. He was now just staring at his boots, head down, his legs bent and apart with his hands clasped between his knees.

It was as if the whole room was in a state of shock but then the Colonel invited Milligan-Sprake to continue. He asked the Sergeant Major to bring in Sergeant Shipley.

Shipley was in his full uniform with his Military Police insignia glistening in the sunshine that streamed through the large windows to his left. He chose to remain standing as Milligan-Sprake continued. He established Shipley's details and the circumstances in which he became involved with Wilson during their journey back from Calais.

Shipley confirmed that he absolutely supported that charge of desertion and that Wilson should be punished for it. He did however feel that there were a number of issues that should be taken into account by the Court.

Milligan-Sprake agreed with him that they would deal with each in turn.

"Sergeant," said the Captain, "could you explain to the Court the story related to you about how Private Wilson saved the life of a fellow solider who was about to shoot himself."

Shipley spent a long time detailing what he knew of the Simpson incident and how he had put in motion appropriate action to try to corroborate the story but how, to date, nothing had been forthcoming from England but he had not given up hope. He also detailed the incident when Wilson, apparently having some sort of fit, had attacked him before realising what he was doing, He also recounted the accident during which Wilson had come to the aid of Andrews and might even have saved his life as well.

After all of this Milligan-Sprake asked, "In your opinion Sergeant, as a member of an Army disciplinary unit, what should be the fate of Private Wilson?"

"Sir," he turned and looked at the panel, "I believe there are special circumstances and I feel that Wilson should be spared from death but serve an appropriately long prison sentence. Yes, he ran away; yes, he should have returned; yes, he has let down himself, his comrades and the Army but I do believe he was, and still is, suffering from the shock of the shelling and is quite ill in his head."

With something of a resigned air the Colonel asked, "Sergeant Shipley, it appears to me as though you have become too personally involved with the Private and this is clouding your judgement. I am right in saying that you have no medical qualifications to comment on Wilson's state of mind? Also, apart from the incident with this other Private in the lorry accident, you have no evidence at all about his mind and this saving of a young man's life yet you are taking Wilson's word for what might have happened. This was from someone who admits he deserted his comrades leaving them to their fate?"

"With due respect, sir, that is partly correct but I am confident that evidence will shortly arrive here that Private Wilson has acted more like a hero to save the life of one soldier and you already have evidence from the American Major of how he saved my driver. I would urge you to consider that these actions are not those of a coward."

"We shall consider what you have said, Sergeant," added the Colonel, sniffily. He looked towards Wilson who was still sitting as before and then turned to Milligan-Sprake, "Sprake, are you going to call the prisoner?"

"Actually, sir, it's Milligan-Sprake, sir." The Colonel put both hands up to acknowledge but said nothing as he leant back in his chair.

Continuing, the Captain said, "Sir, could I have a few moments to discuss something with Private Wilson?"

"Oh if you must," said the Colonel, "you and Wilson stay hear and the rest of us will take a five minute break."

When they had all gone the Captain pulled his chair over to Wilson who had still not moved his position from before. "Look, Wilson, the Colonel, and possibly the two Officers as well, do not seem too happy at present. The evidence so far has covered all the points and I do not consider that there is anything that you could possibly add. I don't want to have Captain Selkirk pull you apart. You saw what he did to the young Frenchwoman and he could be worse with you. I will be able to summarise the whole thing before the panel adjourn to consider the verdict and I would hope they would show some leniency. As I said before, a prison sentence is the best you can hope for but with an end to hostilities in sight it might get cut short if we all go home. Are you happy with not having to give evidence?"

Wilson thought for a moment and then looked up. He was crying. He nodded and looked down again. The Captain stood up and squeezed the young man's shoulder. He went back to the door and told the Sergeant Major that they were ready to resume.

In another five minutes Milligan-Sprake was on his feet putting together his plea and he thought that the panel seemed a lot more positive than before the break.

Before he spoke, Selkirk had also provided a brief summary and asked that the Court confirm the ultimate sentence by virtue of the fact that Private Wilson had left at the height of one of the fiercest battles of the War to date and left his comrades to their fate in a wanton act of cowardice leading to his desertion. Selkirk had added that Wilson was a disgrace to the uniform and whilst he might have carried out acts of bravery to save the two men, if that was true, there are thousands at the Front who have done the same, and probably more. However, they had not deserted their posts. He also brought further attention to Wilson's poor disciplinary record.

Finally, the Colonel and Ryan and Westerham stood, bowed and left the room. The Private on cell guard duty came in and under the watchful eye of the Sergeant Major took Wilson back to the cells.

Selkirk and his assistant went outside to have a smoke. Milligan-Sprake spoke with his assistant who left as if he had been sent to find something. The Captain joined Shipley and Marie who now looked more composed, if a little red eyed.

The Captain shrugged, "Well we did the best we could, thank you for what you said and as you were so thorough I did not call Eddie. He looked bloody shattered by it all and I did not want Selkirk to make mincemeat of him."

Shipley thought for a moment, "Colonel Graham has a bit of a reputation for being a hard man according to the Private who has just gone off with Eddie."

"Yes I noticed that too, the other two did not say much which is a little worrying because I doubt Graham is on our side in this, although he did seem moved by what Madame Coutteau had to say. Come on let's get a cup of tea and something to eat."

With that he led them towards the kitchen.

CHAPTER 34

Colonel Graham flopped into the armchair and lifted his pipe from his pocket and picked up the pouch from the table where he had left it during the recess and filled the bowl with tobacco and lit up sending a plume of smoke right across the room. It went straight into the face of Major Ryan and he coughed as he inhaled the acrid cloud as it drifted past him. Captain Westerham stood looking out of the window and he lit a cigarette.

The Major having cleared his throat asked if anyone fancied a whisky. Graham answered yes but Westerham declined and instead poured himself a glass of water from the jug and he then sat down next to Graham. Ryan topped up each glass of whisky with some water from the jug and sat down opposite the other two. He sipped the drink before asking, "Well, Colonel how do we proceed from now?"

The Colonel took a long draw on his pipe. "As far as I am concerned the man should be shot, there's no point discussing the question of guilt regarding the desertion as he and the Captain have admitted that. Yes, we've heard all about how ill he was but Thorogood the MO could find nothing wrong and any man who has been over here and either fought in those trenches or, like us, took the decision to put them there and with that putting their lives on the line, would have nightmares, flashbacks and be in a nervous and anxious state. We, the Senior Officers, might not have stood in the mud and water but we've got to live with the consequences of our orders for the rest of our lives and that, gentlemen, is not going to be easy."

He stood up and went over to the whisky and poured himself another measure before adding, "Wilson experienced exactly what all the other men did but did they run away and stay away? No – they fought on and they are not going to think much of us if we let these deserters off with some prison sentence that will be commuted when we get home. Even though we are near the end, there are still men fighting out there for King and Country and we must set an example for them."

He took another draw on his pipe before continuing, "Yes, we heard about these fits and other problems from the woman and the MP, who I thought was a disgrace in supporting a prisoner that he helped to catch and bring to justice – the new breed seem ignorant of what the Army is all about. If we had all taken this attitude the Germans would have trampled all over us years ago."

He reached over to the pile of papers on the table next to him and sifted through them before pulling out one sheet. He glanced at it and then waved it at the other two. This is Wilson's record and although not being much, as he has only served for such a short time, he still racked up one disciplinary offence and the NCO who wrote this seems a little lenient in my opinion. Instead of the charge of disobeying an order it looks to me like Wilson could have been trying to run away. I would have liked to hear from this NCO but he's no longer with us, of course. What are your views then Westerham?"

"Oh I agree with you sir, we need to maintain discipline right to the end and we cannot have the men just choosing to walk away and what clinches it for me is that he stayed away. If he was ill then he should have come back. The medical people would then have seen him at his worst and perhaps agreed he was in such a bad way that he should be sent home to recuperate. For me we have no option but to pass sentence recommending the firing squad. It might be that up the line the Commanders might take a different view especially as this Armistice is just round the corner, apparently."

"Ryan?" asked the Colonel.

"I'm sorry sir but I disagree. Yes, he is guilty of desertion and, yes, he has a bit of disciplinary history but I thought the Frenchwoman's evidence was compelling and even the MP's was important because why would he put his army career in jeopardy by coming out in support of a prisoner? Milligan-Sprake was right to question the MO's expertise and knowledge, or rather lack of it, when dealing with such cases. Wilson should be looked at back home by an expert before he goes before a firing squad; he surely deserves that."

The Colonel was clearly irritated by this but said nothing and got out of his armchair and poured out yet another very large whisky and downed it in one, spluttering at the end of it.

He sat back down having poured himself a glass of water from the jug.

"Westerham, are you still with me on this?"

"Yes, sir"

The Colonel thought for a moment, "Clearly Ryan, you are not going to change your mind on this so all we can do is return the verdict of guilty and recommend that he face death by firing squad but also record that this was a majority decision. When we send the written verdict and the notes up the chain of command we can let others make the final decision. We, to my mind at least, have done our job as best we can and others who might support your view, Ryan, can finally decide Wilson's fate. I know you are not going to be totally happy with this but it really is the only way forward."

Ryan shrugged and stood up, "If you say so, sir," was all he could manage.

The Colonel went over to the door and called in the Lieutenant who had taken notes during the Court proceedings. "Now, Lieutenant I want you to arrange for the summary evidence to be typed out and each witness must sign at the bottom of the section relevant to them. The MO has already completed his part and you must include the prisoner's Army Record and Conduct Record so that the whole lot can be passed on. I have already completed the sheet you gave me yesterday. I have filled in the section regarding the Plea as "Guilty but with extenuating circumstances of battle shock and disorientation" and the next section put "Guilty. To suffer death by being shot" and then signed the last column. Make sure you make everything neat and tidy as this will go right up to the very top and we don't want it to look shabby, do we?"

The Lieutenant thought for a moment and then said, "What about Wilson, as he didn't give evidence does he get the chance to make a statement or something like that?"

"Absolutely not, he and his representative had the chance for him to give evidence but they chose not to do so."

"What about this search for the fellow that Wilson is supposed to have saved, should you perhaps mention this?"

"What do you two think?" He asked Ryan and Westerham. They both nodded at each other.

"Definitely, sir," said Westerham and the Colonel looked at Ryan who nodded again.

"Right," the Colonel went on, "In the past we would defer an announcement for a day or so but in the past year the Presiding Officer has been encouraged to announce the verdict straight away. This is more important at present as the War could be over any day and we should get the papers on their way. From what I know they go to the Corps Commander and then to the Adjutant-General's department at GHQ, where the Court Martial proceedings are checked by the judge advocate-general in order to ensure that what we have done is within the regulations and guidance. If that is passed then it will go as far as the Commander-in Chief. Is that right Lieutenant?"

"Yes sir that is how I understand it."

"Good, can you ask the Sergeant Major to reconvene the Court and we'll be there shortly."

Within ten minutes it was all over. Wilson seemed unmoved by the verdict. It was as if he was in a trance. Milligan-Sprake and his assistant looked aghast. Marie was the most upset and had to be comforted and led away by Shipley but not before she looked back at Wilson as she went out of the door. Wilson did not look up but just stared at the floor. After everyone else had left the room, the Sergeant Major and the guard took Wilson back to the cell. Even the Sergeant Major was less intense with his authoritarian attitude than before and when he was alone with the prisoner after they got to the cell whispered:

"Don't worry, son, someone at GHQ will see sense." With that he left and turned the lock.

Wilson slumped down on the bed and stretched out staring at the ceiling. All he could really see was his house in Padiham and the small garden which looked out towards Burnley itself where for the whole time the town looked like a steamer with the large, tall chimneys at the mills belching out their smoke. He could see his Mother busying herself in the kitchen; however, it was not her face but Marie's. He, though, was just a little boy and was looking up at his Mother but Marie smiled back as she washed the potatoes. He then shut his eyes and now he was at the Cup Final with the crowds and the King. Then he was back in Burnley with the team and parading through the streets. He screwed up his eyes and a tear ran down the side of his face and dropped onto the bed. Now all he could see was a group of soldiers pointing their rifles at him. The faces of the men were smiling back at him. They were the men he had known so briefly but were no more – there was Smith and Penrose and the young Simpson and all the rest.

Outside the courtroom, Milligan-Sprake had shaken hands with Selkirk, who left straightaway with Lieutenant Hughes, and then gone over to Major Burnside who was saying goodbye to the three Presiding Officers who, with the Clerk, were returning to the camp office to complete all the paperwork.

Major Burnside put his hand on the young Captain's shoulder, "You did well and you certainly did your best," he looked round to make sure no one was listening and moved his arm round the Captain's shoulders and whispered, "I have been told it was a majority verdict so I suggest you make sure this gets known at GHQ just in case the Colonel forgets to put some sort of note on the report form he has to complete."

"Thank you, sir," With this the Major smiled at him and left, giving the younger man a pat on the back. As Burnside went through the door, Milligan-Sprake's assistant Bellamy came back through.

"Any news, John," he asked informally.

"Well, I have some news at last, a letter has come through from Preston. This Private Simpson is alive but not in good shape. He was apparently in some sort of Institution and is in such a bad physical way that he is in a wheelchair and it could be that his brain's been affected, too, so he might not be of any use. However, his Mother is still around but the problem is she's moved and there's a rumour the lad is with her now. The Institution, you would have thought, would have her new address but apparently they haven't, they only have the old one. She must have just moved but the Padre from the regiment has been round to her old house and asked the neighbours but they say Mrs Simpson just upped and left one night about a month ago and no one knows where she is. The Padre has written to her sister in Carlisle to try and find out."

"Well done, John, you must keep on this trail, it's likely to be Wilson's only hope and we've got to find her. How come this Padre is doing this?"

"Apparently, he worked at the Burnley Football Club and knows Wilson from his days there as one of their promising youth players and wants to help."

"We need some luck to go our way, you'd think that if it goes up to the C-in-C even the great man himself will show some pity now that the disciplinary clamp down might be less than in the early years of the War, what with peace just around the corner."

"You would hope so," replied Bellamy. They both then left by the main entrance and walked back to the camp.

PART SIX -
CARLISLE, ENGLAND
OCTOBER 1918

CHAPTER 35

The Padre had spent most of the morning on three different trains trying to get from Preston to Carlisle a trip that normally took very little time at all. For some reason he was diverted off the normal straight-through line and two of the trains had to be replaced due to some mechanical malfunction.

The resplendent station at Carlisle was teeming with soldiers, all neat and tidy and clearly on the move. They were gathered at Platform One in an orderly line that stretched out into the street and round the corner out of sight. The noise was deafening with their chatter and general good humour. The Padre grimaced as he wondered how long that would last for them. As he passed along the line towards the exit, they dutifully saluted as they recognised his Officer insignia and respected his religious collar. He smiled and saluted back.

Close to a large "For Hire" sign he found a line of smart looking carts with their horses feeding from their nosebags. The drivers were all gathered in a group chatting away and as he walked towards them, the tallest of them stepped forward in greeting. He was smoking a brown pipe and had a crutch under his right armpit supporting his one leg, the right one was missing.

"Good afternoon, Padre, can I be of assistance?"

"Yes, thanks, I need to go to Putney Street, is it far from here?"

"Just about a mile or so."

"Right then, I'll take a lift with you, if I may."

With some agility the driver clambered on to his seat making light of the fact that he had just the one leg. The Padre sat beside him rather than in the more comfortable rear seats in the cart.

The Padre asked about the action that the driver had presumably seen and the man explained that he had had his leg blown off by a shell at Ypres in the first battle there and been invalided out. He told the Padre that he had found it hard to make ends meet but thank goodness he was alive is what he always told people. He said that he did this job as well as that of a caretaker at the local primary school, something he always did in the mornings.

He asked the Padre what brought him to Carlisle and the Padre explained his mission to find the family.

"I know of them, down Putney Street, I used to go to school with one of the boys."

He wanted to ask the Padre exactly why he wanted to find them but thought better of it.

"Here we are then Padre, Putney Street, what number is it?"

The Padre had forgotten and fumbled in his pocket for the piece of paper with the details on it.

"Number 22, thanks."

The cart pulled up and the driver nimbly jumped down to give the Padre a hand. "Do you want me to wait, Padre, or shall I come back later?"

"Oh thanks – sorry I didn't catch your name."

"Fenwick, sir."

"Well thank you – just in case we miss one another here's something for the fare and some extra."

The Padre gave the man a pound note, "Enough for a good night out, Mr Fenwick!"

Fenwick at first would not accept it but the Padre refused to take it back.

"Keep it but come back in about an hour and pick me up, please."

With that the man saluted with his left hand, which made the Padre smile realising that if he had saluted normally with his right hand he might have keeled over!

The Padre walked to the door of number 22. The typical terraced row was neat and tidy with polished steps and smartly painted doors at every house.

There was no doorknocker on 22 so he rapped firmly on the wood. He had to knock three times before a small middle-aged woman in a pinafore over a flowery dress opened it. Her hair was in a net covering some curlers. She had a grim weather beaten face but smiled when she saw the caller's collar.

"Mrs Adamthwaite? Mrs May Adamthwaite?"

"Yes that's right – how can I help."

"I'm looking for Mrs Dorothy Simpson, I understand that she is your sister and that she might be living here with you?"

"That's correct, sir, she's here with her son, why do you want her then?"

"It is to do with her son and the injuries he received. Can I speak with her please?"

"Of course, sorry, do come in. Can I get you a cup of tea?"

"Yes, that will be very nice, thank you very much."

The woman ushered him to a settee in the front room and she moved towards the parlour and kitchen at the back. "My sister's in the garden, I'll get her to come through whilst I get the tea."

A minute or so later an almost identical looking woman but in a different dress came into the room. The Padre stood up and the woman laughed as she saw the look on his face.

Pre-empting his question she said, "Yes, we are identical twins, we used to wear the same clothes when we lived together as children but not now! My sister said you've come about my son."

The Padre explained his mission to help the beleaguered Wilson and the woman listened intently and shook her head more than once as she heard of

232

the young man's plight. When the Padre had finished they both sat there for a few moments in silence.

"Padre, I know Eddie Wilson, my husband used to be a trainer for Burnley Football team when Eddie was in the Boys team. I don't think they knew each other but my husband always thought he would do well as a professional but of course the War has put a stop to that and, by the sounds of it, it could be forever."

"Do you know what happened to my son?"

The Padre started to talk about the incident that resulted in his injuries but was interrupted.

"No, I mean after he got back here?"

"No," said the Padre, "I'm sorry I don't."

"Well, the bullet from the rifle had passed through his head and damaged part of his brain. He can still just about talk and has all his marbles but can't move his arms and legs so he has to be in a wheel chair. He thinks Eddie's a hero, and so do I. He might not be able to do much but at least I've got him. I know so many wives, mothers, sisters, daughters and so on that've lost their loved ones. I shall be forever grateful to Eddie – he risked his own life to save my son and he's given him back to me. I'll do anything to help him, what do you suggest, is it too late?"

"Hopefully it's not too late. I propose to ask you to write a letter to the Commander-in-Chief himself and explain what has happened to your son and how you feel and that you would like leniency for Private Wilson."

"I'd be pleased to do so but I'm not so good with the writing so could you do it for me?"

"That'll be fine but I'll need you to sign it, is that alright with you?"

"Yes, fine, thanks."

They found some writing paper and some old ink and an even older pen but the Padre was quickly able to set out the letter from Mrs Simpson asking for clemency, explaining the effect of Wilson's actions and what it has meant to the family. The padre promised to let Mrs Simpson know what happens.

Her sister had brought in the tea and some biscuits and had stayed sitting quietly in the corner. She comforted Dorothy at times as she became emotional as the Padre wrote out what she wanted to say. Mrs Adamthwaite suggested that the Padre might like to meet her nephew who was out in the garden and she led the Padre through the kitchen and into the small garden. The young man was sitting in the only area not in shadow beyond the small outhouse, which contained a coal shed, and toilet. For about five minutes the Padre chatted with the chair bound young man who was surprisingly bright and cheerful despite his obvious disabilities.

The Padre eventually looked at his pocket watch and realised that Fenwick, his driver, would be waiting. With the letter tucked into his attaché case he bid farewell and returned with his driver to the station. A much quicker journey got him back into Preston before dinner but it was still too late to send the letter off that night and he would have to wait for the morning. Also, he felt that he must write out a copy of the letter to keep with him at the Preston Barracks whilst the original was whisked off to GHQ in Belgium.

After a light supper in the Officer's Mess, the Padre returned to his room and copied out what Mrs Simpson had signed and wrote a further letter to go with it marked for the attention of Captain Milligan-Sprake. He placed one in an envelope addressed to the C-in-C using the special address he had been given and the other to the Captain in Belgium. Hopefully it would be in time and be helpful to Wilson's cause, the Padre thought to himself.

The letters went first thing the next morning and marked with high priority and the original one was expected to arrive at GHQ by the end of the following day.

PART SEVEN -
NEWHAVEN, ENGLAND
OCTOBER 1918

CHAPTER 36

The wind had risen strongly in the last hour and this was whipping up the waves and the white tops could be seen right out towards France. The Captain looked at his watch and then to the sky; the dark clouds were getting ever lower and threatening rain at any moment. He went into the small office and the Harbourmaster was sitting at the tall upright desk pouring over a map, drawing on his pipe. The Captain lit his cigarette and poured some tea from the urn in the corner and added some milk from the jug on the small table in the middle of the room.

"It's looking like a bad storm, the forecast is for a Force Eight for the next few hours, are you sure you want to go, you could always leave it until the morning," the Harbourmaster growled, with his pipe firmly fixed in the corner of his mouth.

The Captain sipped his hot tea and leant against the high windowsill. He wiped the back of his hand across the misted windowpane and peered out into the gathering gloom. "I must be mad but I'm going to go over, apparently there are quite a lot of injured men to come back and some of them need specialist treatment so I feel duty bound to go. Anyway the crew's all here and they're just about finished loading up the postbags and supply boxes. It's amazing how much post there is but I suppose we've so many blokes out over there now so it's not surprising!"

"Well we hear they might be back home soon if the rumours are true. Not before time but the fighting's still going on as much as ever it seems. Anyway, good on you for going, mate, rather you than me, I have to say!"

The Captain finished his tea and checked the barometer in the Harbourmaster's room – it had moved right round to "Stormy" not uncommon, he thought, for late October. He put his hat on and turned up his collar and opened the door. A gust of wind nearly blew him over and the Harbourmaster had to hold down his maps as other pieces of paper flew across the room. "See you tomorrow then," he said to the Captain who went outside with a final wave. Even though he shut the door behind him the wind blew it open again and the Harbourmaster cursed and went over and shut it on this time pulling the bolt across. He went to the window and looked out. He could no longer see the sea, which was no more than a hundred yards away. The rain had started and was so heavy that a dark misty curtain enveloped the port. "Bloody mad!" he said under his breath and went back to his maps.

The Captain arrived at the boat and checked with the first mate just how things were going. They stood in the rain and watched as the men loaded the last lot of postbags into the hold and pulled the flat door across. Some of the loaders would be staying for the crossing but the rest were looking forward to their pint down at the Ship Inn, their work now finished for the day.

The Captain got the old vessel underway almost immediately. She had seen good service over the years running almost daily across the Channel before the War for the local Shipping Company and Captain "Pitch" Black had worked for them for over fifteen years. He could get to Calais blindfolded and in this early evening he would almost have to do so with the weather closing in. He thought again about not going and chatted with the Mate about it but felt he had to go on.

The old craft had been requisitioned in 1916 ahead of the push in Western France to carry anything but everything over to Continent, often bringing back the wounded and too often the dead. For the past six months it had really been solely used for shipping mail and bringing back sack loads of the same on the return journey and occasionally some human cargo both dead and alive.

All went fairly well for about half an hour as they moved out of the port but the full force of the gale hit them a few miles out. Even the Captain felt a little queasy as the swell pitched and tossed the boat all over the place. Suddenly the engines stopped and the boat slowed. The Captain went down to the engine room where the stokers were just standing there leaning on their shovels. The Chief came over mopping his hands with a dirty, oily cloth. "Captain, we're knackered, the bloody drive shaft's cracked – we'd better get a tow back to Newhaven – it's much nearer than Calais, I guess, and we'd be better off out of the storm as quick as possible."

"Are you sure we can't do anything, Chief?" The Chief shook his head.

"Right then," went on the Captain and he turned to the Mate, "get a message back to the Harbourmaster in Newhaven and ask for the Mirabelle to come out and tow us back in, there's no point going across tonight, especially as we can't transfer the cargo to another boat in this weather."

It took more than five hours to get the towline on and it was well past midnight before the Mirabelle got them back to the port. The weather had worsened if anything and had made the job mighty difficult for all concerned so the Captain sent his entire engine room crew home for the night and told them to report back at nine sharp in the morning.

The storm had not really abated as the rest of the men assembled in one of the sheds on the quay as the Captain came in. "I've spoken with the Chief and looked at the damage, we're not going anywhere I'm afraid and I've sent the engine room home, but I'm going to have to keep you here for a while and get you to unload the post and boxes and bring them all in here."

An hour later the postbags and the boxes were piled high again in the store shed. The bags and boxes were all sodden with the rain and difficult to carry in. The postbags in particular were wet through but fortunately had been strong and thick enough for the letters and so on to remain dry. Two youngsters struggled with one heavy bag and, as they lifted it onto the tall stack they had already made, the top of the bag tied with string split open and the letters fell over their heads and onto the floor. One of them fetched another new spare, dry bag and they began to fill it up. The Captain came over and wrote GHQ on the bag the same as had been on the other bag that had broken. He helped pick up the envelopes and the last one left on the floor was addressed to the Commander in Chief, intrigued the Captain turned it over. It had come from the East Lancs Regiment HQ in Preston. He wondered for a moment what it could possibly be then tossed into the box as the Mate came over to speak to him.

With the weather so bad for two days and with no other boat available the post stood in the shed drying out. The Captain had to come to terms that his boat was indeed completely useless and may have to go to the knacker's yard as it was already thought impracticable to repair the problem.

Eventually and four days after his boat had first left in the Force Eight he was able to load up the post and set sail for France. His newer boat had come up from Southampton once the weather had improved.

PART EIGHT - BRITISH GENERAL HEADQUARTERS, WESTERN FRONT OCTOBER 1918

CHAPTER 37

The Commander-in-Chief held the soldier's file behind his back as he looked out of the window across the pretty garden at his Headquarters. He had read the contents of the file at least three times and was still undecided on what his final decision would be. A series of senior Officers right up to General level had seen the file and upheld the decision of Private Wilson's Court Martial but they did not have the final say, as he did. Nevertheless, he felt he would have to take their views into account.

However, a man's life was at stake and the Commander had been in this position many times before when being the final arbiter on a soldier's fate. It always lay heavily with him, as he knew a particular man's life was at stake. Over his years in the Army he had made decisions that had meant thousands of men had met their deaths, yet when you have the life of just one man it did seem more than just a life. He thought of the man's family and he thought of the man himself and it always seemed different from the others to decide whether this man, a man whose photograph he had just seen, should live or die.

The Commander moved from the window and sat at his desk. He opened the file again and sifted through the pages. Certain facts stood out. He was unhappy about the lack of training this man had experienced and he knew only to well what his men had had to put up with at Passchendaele but then again it was no different from the Somme and all the other previous battles. The other gnawing facts were what if this man had indeed saved the life of the young Private before they even got to the Front in 1917, should this not be a reason for him to show some clemency? He had also acted bravely on at least one other occasion, possibly saving another man's life. Yet even with the War drawing to a close, he felt deep down that an example still had to be made and the offence did happen at the height of the 1917 campaign. It would be an insult to those executed in the past if this man was not treated as the others had been. Then there was the man's record. The Commander had to take into consideration that the man had previously been disciplined. Even if he had been severely disabled, mentally, at the Front he had made no effort to return once the French family had nursed him back to health.

The Commander closed the file again and leant back in his chair but was suddenly shaken from his thoughts by a knock at the door. He got up from the chair and went over to the door and slid the catch he had put across earlier so he was not disturbed.

It was the General who had been the last Officer to sign Wilson's file approving of and supporting the original Court Martial decision.

The two spent the next half hour debating the issue of the man's sentence and at the end of it all the C-in-C added his signature to the list but not before he had called in his Adjutant to confirm that nothing further had been heard about possible evidence from back home that supported Wilson's claim, and that of his advocate, that he had saved a man's life at severe risk to his own. The answer had been "No" and both the C-in-C and the General were of the opinion that it may just have been a ruse all along.

The Adjutant was told to ensure the decision was conveyed to Poperinghe as soon as possible so that the execution could be arranged without further delay.

The C-in-C and the General immediately left for talks with their French counterparts and the liaison group who had contact with the Germans. There were now more important matters to attend to they had agreed.

The Adjutant wrote out a note to Major Burnside at Poperinghe and despatched the messenger.

PART NINE -
POPERINGHE CAMP, BELGIUM
OCTOBER 30TH 1918

CHAPTER 38

Burnside had been out when the document had arrived but it was passed to him late in the afternoon. He was disappointed with what he read and immediately sent for Milligan-Sprake. The Captain arrived no more than ten minutes or so later.

After reading the Adjutant's note and having seen the various signatures and odd comments made by all those up the chain of command who had seen the file, the Captain turned to the Major. Burnside sat glumly behind his desk drawing on his French cigarette. As Milligan-Sprake closed the file, Burnside stubbed out the half finished cigarette.

"This is a rum do and make no mistake, Captain. Any news from this Padre fellow back in Preston?"

"No, nothing sir, absolutely nothing."

"Well, I'm sorry Captain but I'll have to arrange the execution for the day after tomorrow or maybe the day after that but HQ never like these matters to hang in the air for too long. If anything turns up before, then you must let me know immediately. I have already sent a note back with the messenger to the Commander's Adjutant asking him to keep an eye out for anything from the Padre at their end. We'd better go and tell Wilson – not very pleasant is it?"

With that the two men left and headed for the cells.

PART TEN -
MILITARY POLICE HQ, CALAIS,
NORTHERN FRANCE
NOVEMBER 1ST 1918

CHAPTER 39

Frank Shipley had received the note in Calais from Major Burnside at Poperinghe when he arrived back at his HQ. He had spent the day in Court dealing with a group of soldiers who had damaged a local bar during a drunken fight whilst on a short spell of leave.

His heart sunk when he saw that the decision had gone against Wilson and that the execution was set for the 7th of November. He immediately went to see Captain Watkinson to ask for a couple of day's leave, which the Captain granted immediately.

Shipley went round to Madame Coutteau 's house straightaway to break the news as gently as he could. After he had told her the news, she had become very emotional and had flung her arms around him and sobbed into his shoulder. She held him for several minutes until he sat her down in a chair and went to the kitchen to get her a glass of water.

When he returned they chatted for nearly an hour about Eddie and how unjust the whole thing seemed. Marie kept breaking down in tears and Shipley had to comfort her several times. However, she was adamant that she wanted to travel to Poperinghe and at least be there when the execution took place. Shipley promised he would join her. He told her about his leave and said he would go on ahead there the next day and would fix up a room for her at the local place he knew. He wrote the address down onto a piece of paper for her and they agreed to meet the next evening at about seven.

PART ELEVEN -
POPERINGHE, BELGIUM
NOVEMBER 7th 1918

CHAPTER 40

"You awake Jim?"

"Yep, been awake all night," replied the little Mancunian, with the slightly high-pitched voice, sleeping in the next bed.

"I slept for about an hour but have been tossin' and turnin' ever since about midnight – this life's bloody shitty at the best of times but this is beyond me," whispered Wally Broadbent as he sat up next to his little friend, Jim Asprey.

"Well, spare a thought for poor bloody Wilson, what's he gotta be feeling like – do you sleep before this kinda thing, do you eat anything? If it was me I'd say, "what's the point of it?" you know what I mean?"

"You're right there, no bloody point of it all?" went on Wally, "from what I've heard this bloke's not right in the head, the War could be over any day, or so the talk goes, and he's just being used to show us discipline. I've spoken to other blokes who've been at the Front who were under so much shelling that they said they just walked around stupid-like and didn't know where they were or what they were doin' – I bet this bloke's just the same."

"Yeah it ain't gonna make any difference what they do to him now; you're right, at first it was all down to disciplinin' and making an example but it's all ruddy pointless now."

With this, Jim gesticulated with his right arm and knocked over the one candle on the table next to his bed, this being the only thing lighting up the small barrack room. "Shit!" he shouted as he scrambled to find the candle and a match from the box next to his bed to relight it.

His loud, high-pitched voice made the other four men in the room stir from their sleep.

"What the bloody hell are you doin'?" asked Lofty Watson from the far corner.

"Sorry mate," said Jim as he put the candle back in its holder and struck the match, which brightened up the room. Watson was sitting up but the other three men had turned over and gone back to sleep. Watson continued, "Was that you two talking just now?"

"Yes Lofty, we was talking about Wilson and what a bloody disgrace it was and that," piped up Broadbent.

"What bloody rubbish! He deserves all he's getting, bloody deserters they're not worth a fig if you ask me," shouted Watson angrily, "should 'ave shot him without wastin' time with a trial. Bloody put 'im up against a wall and shoot 'im - he's as guilty as bloody sin if you ask me!"

"Well, thank you Kaiser Bill for those few kind words!" said Broadbent sarcastically, "you can't say that without the facts of why he might 'ave run away what with his state of mind and all that."

"Look, nearly all the bloody soldiers out here have at some time put their lives on the line only to be let down by these bloody deserters. I say they deserve all they get. What if we'd all run away, we'd be speaking bloody German by now if we had, wouldn't we?"

Asprey stood up and went to the washbasin and sluiced his face with the cold water," You and we don't know the facts – I heard he'd had field punishment one and had been shelled at and shot at without proper cover, you've heard what that's like – bloody disgraceful putting someone through that – it would even make me go mad and run away!"

Broadbent joined in, shouting and waving his arms towards Watson, "And I'd heard he'd been put in the trenches without proper training and had lost all his mates last year and seen things that were awful; things like we've never seen. And anyway what War have you had? You've only ever been behind our own lines and spent half the time guarding Turkish prisoners in Egypt before you got here and now you know it all. I tell you these blokes are mental and need help, not bloody shooting. What's the point of that?"

Broadbent took a step nearer to Watson, who did the same so that they were no more than two inches apart and they glared into each other's eyes. Broadbent went on, "When you've seen what these others have seen and been shot at, blown up, picked up pieces of your mates, caught every bloody illness going, been gassed and faced death every day then you can give us your opinion and we might just listen!"

"Look you idiot you've got to have discipline and if we all ran away it would be a real problem. You gotta have discipline," replied Watson taking a step back and turning back to his bed and sitting down.

By now the other three were awake and sitting up supported by their elbows.

Watson went on, "I'm looking forward to shooting him because his sort are the scum of the earth and it's right that they should be punished in this way, the rest of what you have been saying has nothing to do with it – he ran away and stayed away and that's the end of it. Why should he be treated any different from some bloke who did the same in 1914 just because the War might end; he knew the score when he did it, if not right away then for sure after not very long?"

Two of the three men nodded silently in agreement but the other seemed not so sure and laid back down on the bed.

Asprey went on, "Sorry, but Wally an' me think the Chief should not 'ave signed this bloke's life away until we know if he was right in the head or not and what with some sort a peace coming it ain't gonna make much difference to discipline – not now anyway – yeah, I agree that four years ago it happened to others but things are different – we should understand more what it's like and what it does to us."

Broadbent added, "Quite right Jim and, whatever we think, I'd rather not be doing this."

"Well I'll be aiming straight between the eyes and you'd betta do the same – the Army don't take kindly if we all aim to miss. And another thing, he used to play for Burnley and I bloody hate them!"

"God! You don't half have a weird outlook on life if you want to kill someone for supporting one football team over another," chipped in Asprey. "Who do you support then Watson? Bloody Blackburn, I suppose!"

"I might but I'm going back to sleep so keep it quiet," and with that Watson rolled onto his right side and pulled the blanket completely over his head. The other three settled down under their blankets. Broadbent and Asprey put on their great coats, picked up their cigarettes and went outside the main door to the courtyard and lit up.

"Idiot that Watson. Knows all, knows nothing as my old Mum used to say," said Broadbent as he drew on the cigarette and blew out into the cold night air, the smoke mixing with the mist caused by his warm breath meeting the cold air.

"I think old Wilson should be disciplined and put in prison for a while, that's all. I think these blokes are ill and we should give the medical people the chance to make a better look at them when the peace comes, then we'll know for sure. I bet you anything you like that some time in the future everyone will agree that they were ill and say that these blokes should never have been shot and I bet someone gives 'em a pardon – you mark my words little man!"

Asprey jokingly punched his mate lightly in the stomach. "My sister told me that there's blokes back in Manchester who can't do anything – their legs are all wobbly, they can't go out, getta job or barely talk, it's like the brain's been damaged."

Broadbent drew again on his cigarette and narrowed his eyes as the smoke went into them, "I heard that too and some quite well known blokes have got it also – blokes who were or are Officers – some have been put in a sorta home – so the army's aware of it and you'd think they'd be more lenient until they can look into it proper."

"Well," went on Asprey, "I'm gonna shoot to miss and let Lofty do what he likes – at least I won't have nightmares about it as much as if I felt like my shot killed the poor bloke."

"Me too, but the only good thing about all this is that we've been brought here just because we are East Lancs and the Army still wants to make a point and so it gets the bloke's own regiment mates to shoot him. If we weren't here we'd have some bloody German trying to kill us and this with the end of the War maybe only a matter of days away."

"What happens Wally if we all miss – I mean Watson's never seen any proper action and he might miss given that he's never shot under any sorta pressure."

"I heard that one of the other three, you know the bloke from Todmorden, is a crack shot and I bet they've put him in the squad to make sure Wilson's hit and anyway the Officer has a handgun and finishes the bloke off if he ain't dead already, or at least that's what I've heard."

Asprey thought for a moment and then looked up at the sky, "I know they said dawn but what time's dawn in November I've not been awake at this time for a while?"

Broadbent dropped his butt end and trod on it with his sock covered foot and winced at the heat having forgotten he had no boots on, "Apparently whilst they say dawn they really mean six o'clock as zero hour for these things. I daresay we'll get a call at about a quarter two – so that gives us about another two hours or so to wait"

"I hope we're not expected to eat beforehand - I might manage something after but not before."

"Me too!"

"Bloody funny, Wally, to think that we've been out here for nearly three years never seen a German, never shot at a German and the only bloke we should shoot to kill is one of our own blokes, bloody ridiculous!"

"Yep – that's the British Army for you mate!"

CHAPTER 41

Frank Shipley woke when he heard the two voices outside in the dark. The Sergeant's mess was close to the hut being used by the men chosen to make up the firing squad. He guessed the men, like him, could not sleep. He was unable to hear what they were saying but recognised the squeaky voice of the likeable Private Asprey. He didn't envy them their job, a British soldier shouldn't have to kill one of his own unless it was for murder or rape or something like that but for running away when you are in such a state of shock, you have no idea what you are doing, never!

Before Shipley had eventually got to sleep he had lain there staring at the ceiling for about an hour ever since the other Sergeant and the Corporal had put the two candles out. They were a couple of Yorkshiremen who had brought in a young Private who had shot and killed his Corporal during an argument about a Belgian girl during a drunken night in a town up near the coast.

This Private was due to be shot the day after, once confirmation had come through from General Headquarters and this was expected that coming morning.

They, like Shipley, did not agree with what was happening to Wilson and they had all discussed the morality of the matter at length before they had put the lights out and turned in. They all agreed that after more than four years of fighting there was hardly a soldier out here who would agree with this punishment anymore and instead of trying to show the discipline of the Army, morale was being shot to pieces by such things.

Shipley could still hear the faint chatter from the two Privates and he guessed that the other one would be Asprey's mate Broadbent. He wondered how Wilson was feeling. What can it be like to know that after all he'd been through his comrades would send him to his God – doing something the enemy had failed to do!

How would Marie be feeling at the inn a mile or so down the road, he thought to himself? He knew she had nursed Wilson through a lot and had put herself out to help him. It was brave for her to come to the Court Martial but disappointing that she had been dismissed pretty well out of hand by the Army. It seemed to him that the Court saw it purely a matter for the Army and its code of discipline and regulations and nothing more.

Shipley thought of Wilson's family back in Padiham who knew very little yet of what was going on – he guessed that all they would have had in the past month was a heavily censored letter from Wilson that just probably said he was alright and not a lot more. They would have been pleased to hear that he had now turned up but then they might well have had something from him when he had been at Marie's.

They would be more relaxed now about his future, what with the papers talking of peace. Like most families, they had dreaded a telegram arriving, once their young man had gone abroad. They would had seen the old telegram man delivering the messages of death in all the streets around for nearly four years and, in the aftermath, the misery that came with them. Each day they would have waited for the man to pass by on his bicycle at about eleven each morning and were just so pleased when he did ride on by. In their road he was never the normal postman with his bag of letters, it was just this old man with little envelopes tucked into his pockets.

Well, in a few days' time he won't ride by and they will get that dreaded message. Shipley thought it highly unlikely that it will tell them much of what had really happened but he had no idea what could possibly be put in them. Killed in action? Died of wounds or some disease? Who knows? Did an Officer send a letter in explanation as with other deaths in the field? He also wondered what happened to the body - he doubted if it got much more that a cursory burial. He hoped someone kept a record so perhaps one day it will get some sort of proper recognition once someone decides a wrong has taken place.

He knew he would get no further sleep and the other two were quietly snoring in the room so he put his coat on and went outside where he came across Broadbent and Asprey. They were just on their way back to the hut and Asprey had his hand on the door handle but released it when he saw the Sergeant.

"Couldn't sleep either then?" Shipley asked.

"No Sarge – bit of a rum do really – I bet you think the same?" replied Broadbent, "you must have been through a lot trying to help him from what we hear?"

"You could say that – I did my best but still feel I've let him down somehow and I'll never forget this, you know?"

"Is it right that you've kept a diary about all of this?" asked Asprey.

Shipley looked surprised that they knew of this. He blushed a little. "Yes, I started it properly on my way back here with Wilson from Calais. It's mainly in notes but I might write it up when we get back home – you never know I might write a book about it once I've left the Army!" he smiled and turned away, "I hope you cope with what you're being asked to do and that it doesn't haunt you too much in the future."

"Quite frankly Sarge we're going to aim to miss him because we know Watson and at least one of the other blokes are shooting straight and the Officer will finish him off anyway," said Broadbent with a shrug.

"Well, be careful, don't get into trouble – maybe aim for his legs then you'll know that your shot won't have killed him, I'm off now." With that, Shipley opened his hut door and returned to his bed.

CHAPTER 42

To Marie the bed at the inn had felt damp and so she had spent the last few hours shivering in the cold sitting in a very old armchair. She had to keep getting up to try to keep herself warm and to ease the stiffness in her back as a result of trying to curl up in the old chair. The inn had no fuel, not even wood for the fire. At least that is what the Belgian owner had told her. He had shown a distinct lack of interest in the young woman, which she found odd given that most men invariably seemed to show eagerness in her company.

She had told him why she had come there and why she had this interest in just this one soldier. He told her that, being an old soldier himself, he had no time for deserters and had little sympathy for either her or her man.

As she moved about the room, she now felt so tired and her eyes also felt heavy partly due to the lack of sleep and partly due to the amount of crying that seemed to overtake her almost all the time she was awake.

However hard she tried she just could not settle. Her mind was full of so many emotions. She felt she had tried so hard to get the Army to listen to her and, despite all Frank Shipley's efforts as well; it now all seemed like a waste of time. The School had given her three days off when she explained what she wanted to do but she would have to return in the morning once Frank had confirmed that Eddie had indeed been shot.

Her thoughts turned to Wilson and what he might be feeling right now. He looked so young and helpless when she last saw him. So thin and pale and all she now wanted to do was to hold him close in a hug and take him home and make him strong again and show him some love, more than she had felt able to do from that time he turned up on her doorstep all that time ago. She had never really shown him her true feelings. The grieving she had for her poor dead husband and her sense of honour to him had held her back from letting her emotions fully come out. She had just not feel it right to get involved with someone else so soon. Now she felt strangely so much different about it.

Not only was there Eddie but also she had been taken with Frank Shipley as soon as she had met him. He had done so much for Eddie and for her. She felt very comfortable in his presence and felt this warmth towards him almost as much as she now had for Eddie.

Now that Eddie was about to be finally taken from her she wished she had made something more of their relationship. She felt deeply about him and it now so seemed to her so sad that she would not see him again. If they had met under different circumstances, or if the Court Martial had turned out differently, they could perhaps have settled down together either in France or England at some future date.

She felt even more tearful and started to cry once more, wiping the tears away from her cheeks with her handkerchief. She returned to the chair and tried to make herself comfortable. She curled up, hugging her knees into her chest, shivering more than before. After about ten minutes she finally drifted off to sleep.

CHAPTER 43

Wilson sat on the hard wooden chair with his elbows on his knees and his head cupped into his upturned palms. He felt really weird. The bed, such as it was, remained unused on the floor. The plate of food next to it was untouched but he had drank half the cup of water which had some brandy in it, slipped into it by Shipley when he had called late the previous evening to offer some comfort. Wilson knew though that the visit was just to say goodbye.

He had no idea of the time except that there was no sign of dawn on this dark November night but guessed that there would be about two hours to go.

Shipley had tried to encourage him by saying that maybe the Commander-in-Chief would change his mind after Shipley had sent his last plea for mercy. Wilson knew there was no hope but had thanked his friend for all his kindness and help in the past two weeks, knowing that Shipley had put his career in the Army on the line for him.

He thought of Marie. He had been so stupid with her in the time he was in her life. He saw love in her eyes when they parted so dramatically what seemed ages ago but was, in fact, a little more than those two weeks. He had always thought she needed her space to get over the loss of her husband – she had been soft and kind but more sisterly than like any girlfriend he had had in the past. However, he felt her eyes betrayed her when he had to leave that day the soldiers had arrived.

When Shipley had asked during his visit the previous evening what more he could do for Wilson he had been asked to look after Marie – to make sure she picked up her life. Perhaps a fresh start in England would give her a new challenge and be something to take her mind off what had happened during the War. Shipley had promised Wilson he would do everything he could for her.

Wilson walked across to the window and saw the very faint lightness in the East. Not as long to go as I thought then, he said to himself. He sat back down on the edge of the bed and cupped his hands again under his chin and rested his elbows on his thighs. He gazed into nothingness, his mind taken back to his Mum and Dad and younger sister and wondered how they would cope. He thought of the lads at the club, how many of them would return and play? How many were dead already? The team was on the brink of greatness but what will it be like after all this? Will there be any football at all afterwards, there's hardly going to be a lot of fit players and how long will they have to stay in the Forces?

His mind went further back to those boys from school. There had been thirty-four boys in his class when he was twelve but he knew of at least ten that were now dead and three maimed for life. What a waste and he was about to join them.

He thought to himself what could it be like to be shot by more than one bullet at once? Would he feel anything? What if he was still alive after the squad had fired? Would it really hurt or would his body just be in shock and would the Officer shoot him in the head at the end to finish it all? Would he watch him do that? What happens then? Would there be a marked grave? Would his Mother and Father ever know what had really happened? He was comforted by the fact that at least Frank knew and he had their address and promised to visit them as soon as the war was over.

He was disappointed that he was not allowed to write to them right now to let them know exactly how he felt about them and the rest of his family and to apologise for what he had done.

All this and more passed through his mind. He stood up from the bed and returned to his chair and resumed the same pensive position.

He was amazed at how calm he felt now. When he had been in the trenches, he had been so nervous and anxious when an attack was about to be launched by either side. He knew then that death might be just around the next corner but now it's a certainty. He felt different. Odd this, he thought to himself.

After a while he felt so tired and he moved from the chair to the bed pulling the blanket over him. It took more than an hour for him to drop into a disturbed sleep. Suddenly, he felt his body jump and, opening his eyes, saw the room much lighter than before.

It must be time he thought.

CHAPTER 44

The door of the hut burst open and Asprey jumped a mile dropping the rifle he had been aimlessly cleaning just for something to do to kill the time. Broadbent was sitting close to the candle writing a letter home and stood up as Corporal Arkwright came in, creating a small shaft of light across the room. Watson was still dozing along with the other three and none of them stirred at first.

"Right," said Arkwright, "get dressed and shaved I want you ready in fifteen minutes then you should have some breakfast in the cookhouse tent, then I want you ready to go."

"But I don't want any breakfast and I'm sure most of the others feel like me, we don't really fancy anything really," said Broadbent.

"Well, it's up to you but I would have thought it better to have something inside you. Anyway you can wait 'til we get back if you like but you might not feel like it then either. Why don't you have a quick cuppa at least? Now get going!"

All six busied themselves having a quick shave and getting their uniforms on and guns ready. No one said a word for almost ten minutes.

Suddenly Asprey's squeaky voice broke the silence "God, I wonder what Wilson feels like now?"

"Who bloody cares?" said Watson.

"Well, most of the bloody soldiers out here for a start!" said Broadbent angrily.

"As I said before, he's only getting what he deserves."

Broadbent dismissed Watson's comment with a wave of his arm and went outside followed by Asprey.

They could hear Watson carrying on about how right he was about Wilson and it seemed the other three appeared to be agreeing with him.

Broadbent and Asprey tried to eat the broth served up as breakfast but could only manage a mug of tea. The other four arrived together and sat at a table away from the others.

"Don't forget, Jim, just go for the legs, probably just above the knee, I reckon," Broadbent pointed out to Asprey, "we'll probably miss anyway!"

"Do you think he'll be blindfolded, I don't really want him looking at me – what happens?"

"Don't know for sure but he must be blindfolded, surely?"

The Corporal routinely inspected the men but he had made sure the night before that their uniforms, belts, boots and so on were clean. He made Asprey do up his top button and put his helmet on at a less jaunty angle. He made them fall-in with two ranks of three, without his normal loud and aggressive voice. He told them that Captain Fontaine would be here shortly to brief them and then they would go to the back courtyard and Wilson would be brought out. In the mean time they should sit and wait here in the mess tent and try to relax.

CHAPTER 45

Shipley had spent the last hour or so writing in his diary all about the past two weeks, finishing off about the journey back here, the Court Martial and now the imminent execution of his friend. He felt that putting everything into words on the paper helped in getting his feelings off his chest, easing the anger and disappointment he felt inside. He was still upset as he felt the Army had got it all wrong about these people and Eddie in particular. The Army should not be dispensing their battlefield justice in this way. He even vowed to himself that after this damned War was over he would do all he could to get the Army to change the way they dealt with these things in the future.

He knew that he would also always ask himself if he could have helped Wilson more – he felt frustrated that, as a mere Sergeant, his words at the Court Martial did not appear to carry as much weight as those of an Officer might have done. What had been disappointing was that in the end Wilson had not seemed bothered whether he spoke up for him or not. Wilson had just seemed resigned to his fate and, if he had not persisted, would not have put up any sort of defence. Not that in the end it would have done any good anyway, he felt.

He carried on writing but must have looked at his old pocket watch a hundred times before the slowly brightening of the light outside told him the time was getting nearer.

He knew he would not be allowed to observe the shooting but he had decided to get as close as possible. Perversely he thought, what if the War ended right now, this minute, would the execution be halted? It would have to be, surely, maybe not though - he did just not know. Too late now though he thought as again he looked at his watch – ten minutes to seven, not long now if it's going to be at seven.

He placed the diary and pencil into his rucksack and went to the toilet at the back of the room. The other two slept on, their breathing shallow and relaxed. He wondered what they would feel like tomorrow when it's the turn of their charge to meet his end?

He went outside and saw the group of six men smart and erect standing with their Corporal at attention – their Sergeant and Captain Fontaine were clearly addressing them and walking up and down in front of them. I don't envy those Privates their job – how must they feel right now, he thought to himself?

He stood and lent against the door to his quarters and looked beyond the squad to the small brick outbuilding, which served as a makeshift series of cells. The Sergeant and the Captain left the squad and went towards this building. As they did so, Major Burnside emerged from the Officer's mess and joined them.

CHAPTER 46

Unable to sleep for more than about an hour and a half, Marie had left the inn quietly not wishing to disturb anyone, the last thing she needed was another encounter with the old innkeeper, who had annoyed her with his indifference and rudeness when they met before. It was over a mile to the camp gates but it only took her a short while to get there. To the East there was lightness in the sky and she guessed the time was about six-thirty.

When she arrived at the gates she recognised the young Military Policeman who stood there with an even younger Private who was just an ordinary soldier. In turn the Policeman recognised her.

"Hello Madame Coutteau, I'm sorry but I can't let you in today. I know why you're here but you will have to stay outside."

"Yes I know that but could you get hold of Sergeant Shipley and tell him I'm here as I want to see him? Is it still going ahead at seven?"

"As far as I know it is and I saw a squad falling in about ten minutes ago and I've heard nothing different. I'll send Private Ferguson here to find the Sergeant for you. Off you go George."

With this the young Private disappeared off in the direction of Shipley's mess.

"I'm sorry I can't let you in but there is an old ammunition box over here, empty of course, and I'll get it for you and you can sit on it out there." He pulled the box towards the fenced gate, opened it and pushed it out to Marie."

"Thanks," she said with a small smile and sat down pulling her coat around her as she shivered, although it was not really that cold.

CHAPTER 47

Wilson had tidied himself up a bit in front of the two Officers and the Sergeant.

Major Burnside cleared his throat and took a piece of paper from his pocket.

He read out, " Private Edward Wilson number 263087 of the East Lancashire Regiment you have been found guilty by Field General Court Martial on the 5th November 1918 of desertion. The sentence is that on November 7th 1918 you be shot at seven a.m. at Poperinghe by firing squad by order of the Commander-in-Chief – may God have mercy on your soul."

"Right, Sergeant," he continued, "take him to the rear courtyard."

The squad had fallen in and had marched to the courtyard at the rear of the small chapel and the Officer's mess. They passed a stake in front of the wall, which formed the perimeter of the courtyard opposite the chapel's west wall. All six men and the Corporal turned their heads to look at the stake which itself had what looked like bullet holes in it and beyond was the wall with even more bullet holes in it. Asprey tripped on the cobbles as he faltered to look to his left. The Corporal halted the men under the bare apple tree and told them to stand at ease.

Meanwhile, Shipley heard the footsteps of Private Ferguson who somewhat breathlessly told him that the Madame was asking for him at the main gate and could he come now.

Shipley grabbed his greatcoat and followed the Private. He could see Marie sitting on a box beyond the fence; she was hunched with her head bowed.

As he approached the gates the MP opened them and let out his Sergeant and closed them behind him.

Marie stood up and Shipley hugged her to him. "What are you doing here, you shouldn't really be here you know."

"Yes, I know Frank but I wanted to be as near as possible. No last minute reprieve I suppose?"

"'Fraid not, I think they're bringing Eddie out now. Are you sure you want to be here for this?"

"Not really but I just couldn't stay away. Poor Eddie, it's really a disgrace – all of this."

"Yes I know and they are still saying that the War could be over at any time now the Germans have caved in, apparently."

He pulled Marie a bit closer and she wiped her eyes. They said nothing more and waited.

CHAPTER 48

The Sergeant held Wilson's arm and led him through to the courtyard followed by the Officers. As they came through the gap in the wall, Wilson saw the stake, the wall and the squad under the tree who were brought to attention as he arrived. Wilson strained to see if he recognised anyone in the squad as they were all supposed to be East Lancs but there was no one he had seen before.

"I hope they do bloody blindfold him," whispered Asprey.

"Bound to," said Broadbent, quietly out the corner of his mouth.

"Be something to aim at!" smirked Watson and the other three laughed.

Ignoring this Broadbent whispered to Asprey, "Now don't forget what we said let's not try to kill him!"

"Quiet in the ranks," shouted the Corporal, "Squad, squad 'shun!"

They all came together. The Corporal walked out in front of them and got them to present and shoulder arms and then marched them until they were opposite the stake in front of the wall. He stopped and kept them at attention. After a brief wait the squad under command then completed a left turn and remained at attention.

The Captain was blindfolding Wilson.

Wilson at first refused the blindfold but the Sergeant tied his hands to the stake and the Captain finished tying the white material over his eyes and round the back of his head.

The squad despite being to attention shuffled their feet and some swayed and even Watson looked grim and pale. Asprey looked to Broadbent to his left and frowned and shook his head. Broadbent responded by mouthing "Legs!"

To all present Wilson seemed so calm and, apart from the reaction to the blindfold, seemed almost compliant and accepting of his fate.

The Captain moved away and looked at the Major, "Ready, sir!"

"Proceed, Sergeant," Burnside ordered.

The Sergeant moved across to the squad and the Corporal joined the ranks. The Sergeant spoke quietly, "Men you are not to fire to miss and should aim above the waist." Broadbent and Asprey looked at each other and both raised their eyebrows. Watson whispered, "Blindfold lads, go for the blindfold or the chest if you have to!"

The Sergeant continued, "Assume the firing position and load."

The men readied their rifles and brought the guns to their eye level.

"Ready? Aim!"

"I love you M…" shouted out Wilson, just as the Sergeant finished with "Fire!"

The volley echoed around the walls and was ear splitting. Birds shot out of their trees startled by the noise. It took an age for the echoing to die away.

Wilson had slumped forward. Blood was seeping through the blindfold, the arm of his shirt and his trousers. The wall behind had been hit either by the bullets missing him or passing straight through. There were two bullet holes in his trouser leg between his knee and his groin.

The Captain moved over with his revolver drawn. He lifted Wilson's drooped head. He felt for a pulse. "He's dead sir," he reported to the Major.

With this the squad were marched away and the Sergeant, Captain and Major returned towards the chapel. Burnside crossed himself as he went.

A couple of Privates moved in with a wheelbarrow and started to untie Wilson; they had already dug out the grave the day before and next to all the others in the old kitchen garden just beyond the courtyard.

The squad marched almost at a quicker rate than the Sergeant's barked "left/right" almost as if they could not wait to get away. As they neared their quarters Watson peeled away towards a small clump of bushes and stumbled forward almost bent double as his hearty breakfast splattered all over the paving and partly over the bush. He sunk to his knees and groaned and was sick again – this time entirely into the bush. Two of the squad at the front had stopped but the rest behind kept going and as a result they all ended up falling over each other just past where Watson was still on his knees retching but with nothing now coming up. Broadbent looked towards Asprey and sneered his nose up at the awful smell from the partly digested breakfast but Asprey smiled back saying:

"Not so bloody cocky now is he?"

"Too right, mate," Asprey laughed back and tapped the stricken Watson on his back. "There, there, old boy we'll save you some bacon and egg!" With that the two friends headed towards the mess hall. Watson's friends were helping him to his feet with the Sergeant, hands on his hips, watching and he shouted at them, "Get him inside and clean him up and get a bucket and a broom and clear up this mess on the path before anyone else comes along." Watson stumbled towards the door to their quarters looking as white as a sheet with the two friends, equally ashen-faced, supporting him under his shoulders.

Asprey took a small helping from the Mess Orderly and sat down at the long wooden table in the Mess tent and Broadbent joined him with just a cup of tea. "Still don't fancy much, I'll get something later."

"Yeah you're right, I can't eat this," said Asprey pushing the plate away and picking up his mug of tea, placing his hands around each side and sipping the hot milky tea.

"Did you aim at his knees?" asked Broadbent eventually. "I definitely did."

"Yep, just above the left knee and it looked like two shots hit him in his legs as there seemed to be two bullet holes."

"But the others hit his chest and it looked like one in the head and the Officer didn't have to finish him off so he must have been dead straightaway."

Asprey put down his cup as Watson's friends entered without their mate, "Oh here they are - murderers all!"

"What do you mean?" said the one in front.

"Well, you know, we only shot at his legs so we didn't kill one of our own like you did!" smirked Broadbent.

"Just following orders, mate, like you should've done," said one of the others and they all helped themselves to a mug from the Orderly and went and sat at another table.

"Is old Watson alright?" enquired Broadbent with more than a hint of sarcasm.

"He'll be fine in a minute."

Asprey and Broadbent turned away and looked at each other and laughed.

Asprey continued in a whisper, "Bloody horrible thing that though, I feel bloody rotten inside and for as long as I live I'll forever see Wilson in my nightmares to go along with all the other bloody awful things we've seen. Shooting one of your own is about as bad as it gets."

Broadbent nodded and remained quiet for about a minute as they both stared into space reliving the past ten minutes or so. Then Broadbent spoke:

"Do you think anyone will record who formed the firing squad so our names might come out at some time, what do you reckon?"

"Nah, if they did record it they wouldn't tell his family or anything like that."

"Yes but others know, like Frank Shipley, and I heard he promised Wilson he would visit his family back in Burnley and tell them what happened and how it all came about."

Asprey thought for a minute and added, "Nah the army won't record it I'm sure but I see your point about Shipley – perhaps we should have a word with him later and get his word or something. But I can't see any point in telling his family the names of the firing squad – it's not like they can do anything really and they ain't gonna track us down, are they, not really?"

Broadbent shrugged, "Yeah, I suppose you're right but let's see Shipley anyway – he's bound to want to know what happened and we might as well tell him and at least we can say how we're upset by all this and where we aimed and all that. I'm sure he'll be sympathetic."

Asprey thought for a moment, "Let's be careful though, we don't want to be put on a charge for that if Shipley grasses on us!"

"I'm sure he won't – he did represent Wilson at the CM after all. He's bloody livid about all this and he got really matey with Wilson, you know."

They pushed their mugs into the middle of their table, lifted their legs over the bench and left the Mess passing the still ashen-faced Watson at the door. He held it open for them and as they passed muttered "Arseholes" as they smiled at him.

CHAPTER 49

Back at the gates both Shipley and Marie tensed as they heard the commands being shouted out. They both thought they heard Wilson's voice just before the shots rang out but were not sure. They jumped at the reverberation of the shots and looked skyward as the birds flew in every direction.

The two Privates on the gates looked at each other and then at the couple. Marie was inconsolable and screaming out in a complete state of shock. She had become hysterical and was staggering round with Shipley trying to get hold of her. He grabbed her arm but she pulled away. The Privates went to help Shipley and together they managed to get hold of her and support her. The Privates put her arms across their shoulders and brought her through the gates. Shipley followed having picked up her handbag that she had dropped when she was reeling backwards after the shots rang out. They sat her on the chair in the guard box but she had passed out.

Ferguson looked at Shipley to see that he had tears streaming down his face and the young Private had to look away.

It took some minutes before Marie fully came round. Ferguson had given her a sip of his somewhat tepid tea but she had spat it out. Shipley had resorted to lightly slapping her face and gradually some colour came back and she opened her eyes and looked round at the three men, it looked for a moment that she had no idea where she was. Shipley had reached inside his pocket and pulled out a small flask that he himself had already drunk from. He put it to her lips softly saying, "Here, take some of this it's better than the tea."

The young woman sipped and swallowed and coughed at the burning sensation in her throat and her chest but then took another sip. "Where did you get brandy from?" she spluttered.

"Probably best you don't know," Shipley smiled back; pleased to see she seemed to be recovering with the colour slowly returning to her cheeks.

Marie lent into him and brushed her head against his thigh as he stood above her and in return he squeezed her hand and she smiled at him.

Outside the guard box Asprey and Broadbent had arrived and were talking to Ferguson, who peeled away and returned to the box where he spoke with Shipley. He turned away from Marie as the Private spoke:

"Sarge, Asprey and Broadbent would like a quiet word if it's convenient for you?"

"Tell them I'll be there in a minute."

With this Shipley turned to Marie and crouched in front of her:

"Are you alright now?"

She nodded.

"I won't be long I just need to speak to these two men and I'll be back."

Having given a quick squeeze of her hand he went outside and beckoned Asprey and Broadbent well away from where Marie, Ferguson and the other Private were.

"Well, what do you want – how did it go?"

Asprey spoke first, "Well, he died instantly and the Officer didn't need to finish him off and his body's been taken away presumably to be buried somewhere."

Shipley carried on, "We heard a shout just before the shots but couldn't make out what it was but it sounded like Wilson's voice, what did you hear?"

Broadbent looked across to his mate and frowned. "I'm not sure," he hesitated and again looked at Asprey with an enquiring lift of his eyebrows.

Asprey looked down and thought for a few seconds, "Well I did hear him shout but it was cut off but it sounded a bit like "I love you Mum" but the last bit got drowned out so it could have been Mum, Ma or Mother or something like that but I'm sure. He never finished what he wanted to say, I guess."

Broadbent nodded in agreement as Shipley looked at him for confirmation. Shipley then asked him, "What did you want from me anyway? I've Madame Coutteau to look after as she's not too good. She's due back in Calais today but fainted and has just come round. I've got to get her well enough to travel back."

The two Privates looked towards the guard box but could not see her as the MP and the Private were in front of her.

"I see," went on Broadbent, "but we actually wanted a word because we heard you promised Wilson that you would visit his folks to tell them what happened and we were a bit concerned that you'd tell them that it was us that shot him. We just wanted to say that we both aimed at his legs and it was the others what killed him but we hoped you wouldn't tell them we were there even if they asked."

"I wouldn't tell them but I would very much doubt if they'd ask anyway. It's not like they know you, is it?"

"Well no," piped up Asprey, "but we feel bad enough about the whole thing and we've got to live with the fact that through all this bloody War the only person we've killed is one of our own blokes!"

Shipley reassured them again that he would never pass on any information and also was able to confirm that the Army never kept a record of the members of the firing squad as far as he knew.

He was intrigued by what Wilson had shouted out and pressed the two Privates, "Could he have said Marie instead of Mum or Ma. What do you think?"

Broadbent and Asprey looked at each other enquiringly. The latter spoke hesitatingly, "Well, it could have been but I'm sure he never got any further than M…"

"Perhaps the Officers or the Sergeant heard something because all we heard were the shots," chipped in Broadbent. He looked at Asprey and they both turned to Shipley and nodded.

Shipley thought for a moment before adding, "Perhaps, but I doubt they'll tell me because since I spoke up for Wilson I seem a bit "persona non grata" with everyone around here!"

"Well for what's it worth Sarge we're both with you on this," Asprey spoke for them both. "It's a bloody shambles – he should never have been shot when you look at everything, I'm sure."

"Thanks lads, I must see to Madame Coutteau so you'd better return to your duties and I'll see you later."

With this Shipley returned to the box and was pleased to see that Marie was now standing up and doing up the buttons on her coat and she picked up her handbag, which had been left on the table in the middle of the small room.

"I'd better get off now," she said, "what did they want?"

"Oh nothing much – they were upset about being in the firing squad and wanted some assurance that their names would not get out especially to Eddie's family – not that it ever would anyway. They are not very bright and things like this play on their minds unnecessarily".

"Did he die straightaway?" she enquired.

"Yes and his body's been taken away to be buried – no ceremony is allowed but I'll find out where the grave is and perhaps we can return when this War's over and sort out something decent for his body."

She hesitated for a minute and Shipley shuffled his feet. Marie spotted his nervousness, "Was there something else?" she asked.

"Apparently it was his voice we heard and he said something like I love you M.. But the last word was drowned out but it could have been Mum, Ma or Mother… or even Marie!"

Marie stopped fiddling with her bag and looked at him and her face flushed. She coughed nervously, "I'm not so sure he would say that – anyway I'm off – I must get on my way to Calais, the man at the inn said he could get me some transport to the French border but what happens after that I'm not sure. I know some people there from when I lived in that area and I'm sure they will help me."

It had clearly seemed to Shipley that she was more than a little embarrassed and flustered after he had mentioned that Wilson might have called out her name.

"Well, I wish I could come with you but I can't, so be careful and look after yourself, I'll come and see you when this is over or I get some decent leave. Whatever happens, I'll try and get a letter to you soon."

With this the young Frenchwoman was off down the road and headed back the way she had come earlier. Shipley watched her all the way until she went round a bend and disappeared from sight. She turned round a couple of times but did not return his wave either time.

CHAPTER 50

The men detailed to bury Wilson's body lifted the lifeless frame and put it into the wheelbarrow and wheeled it back across the courtyard and round the back of the cells to the small cemetery in the kitchen garden.

In two neat lines were makeshift crosses and a mound of earth in front of each. The crosses bore nothing more than an army number, a date and a surname.

There had already been numerous discussions at the highest level on how these deaths were to be recorded and where the bodies might be moved to, if at all, when the hostilities eventually came to an end. No firm decision had been made but it was felt that the bodies could not be taken to some special cemetery to lie forever alongside those who had died in action or from their injuries sustained in battle. It seemed they were to be kept separate for all time.

Major Burnside never liked these executions and it was about the fifth he had overseen in his time at the camp. He returned to the Officer's Mess and slumped into the old leather armchair taking off his cap and belt as he did so. He thought he would relax for about ten minutes or so then get himself some breakfast. As he stretched out the senior orderly brought him a mug of coffee and left it on the small table to his right.

"Thanks very much, I'll have my breakfast in a short while if you wouldn't mind telling the cook."

"Yes sir, I'll tell him, right away." The orderly left the room and just as he did so the mess door was flung open and a slightly out of breath Private, who was the senior clerk ran in.

"Sir, this note has just arrived from GHQ and it's from the C-in-C's office – they've been trying to contact us by telephone but the lines are down somewhere and this has turned up from a messenger, sir." He handed over the fawn coloured piece of paper and the Major unfolded it and read it quickly.

He suddenly jumped up out of the chair. "Shit! Have you read this?" he asked the clerk.

"No sir, I took it out of its envelope but bearing in mind where it came from, I thought it might not be something I should see."

"Quite, well done, can you get me Captain Milligan-Sprake? Do you know where he is?"

"I think so, sir, he was down by the courtyard having a cigarette when I came over here, I'll get him right away." He turned and got to the door but before he could open it the Major said, "On second thoughts tell him to meet me at the graveyard straightaway."

"Yes sir." With that he left and the Major slumped back in the chair and re-read the message. He put his belt back on and reached for his cap just as the orderly came back from the kitchen area.

"Tell the cook breakfast will have to wait, I am off to the graveyard and then going to see the Colonel. I'll be about an hour." He stuffed the note in his pocket and headed back towards the yard and found the two men lowering Wilson's body into the makeshift grave.

The Major called over just as they let go of the body, "Sorry, men, there's a change of plan, you'll have to lift it out again and take it to the mortuary."

The two Privates looked at each other and, with a slightly resigned shrug, climbed down into grave to pull out the body, one at the head end and the other with the feet. They had wrapped it in old pieces of cloth and tied two small pieces of rope round the ankle and neck so it resembled a mummy.

As the Major stood watching them he was joined by Milligan-Sprake.

"What's up, sir, you wanted me urgently?" He looked down at the body in the cloth held by the two men. "Is that?"

"Yes sir," one of them said.

The Major said nothing but reached into his pocket, pulled out the crumpled note and gave it to the Captain.

The Captain looked at the Major who shrugged. Milligan-Sprake read the note carefully and then he read it again. For a moment he just stood there staring down at the small piece of paper as if trying to take in what it said.

"Bloody hell, sir, why didn't we get this message earlier?"

"This came by messenger because there's been a problem with the telephone lines apparently. I'm moving the body to the mortuary for now; we'd better not leave it here with the others in view of the General's comments. I'll speak with the Colonel so we can decide what's to be done."

The Captain then went on, "What do you think they mean by "fresh evidence" we've sent nothing more than the original decision and associated papers and the General had seen it but said nothing at the time and passed it on to the C-in-C? I've never heard of the death penalty being changed like this at such a late stage."

"I'm not sure what's happened but whatever the reason it's come too late for Wilson. We'd better report to the Colonel and perhaps you'd better come with me after all, so we can discuss where we go from here. Why on earth didn't they get the message to us a bit quicker they must have known the execution would not be delayed for long? Bloody odd business, we'd best keep this to ourselves and I've not said anything to the two men here but they are going to wonder what on earth's going on and word will get around, it's bound to."

The Captain helped the two men lift the body onto the wheelbarrow and watched as the two men left for the mortuary, earnestly speculating with each other on the reasons for all this. He and the Major then left for the Colonel's office.

The Colonel was standing and looking out of the window at them as they approached. They entered and the Colonel turned and spoke to the two clerks. "Can you two go and get some tea or coffee and leave us for about fifteen minutes, thank you?"

After they had left the Colonel indicated to the two Officers to sit at the small table with four chairs round it in the far corner of the room.

"I hear you've received the same message as me, Major, bloody awful do this, would you believe that I've now managed to get through to GHQ on the field telephone and spoke to the C-in-C's office! Apparently he received a letter from home from the mother of some Private whose life Wilson was supposed to have saved. The letter had taken an age to get there due to some problem getting it across the Channel. On the strength of what was in the letter C-in-C has rescinded the execution order and suggested penal servitude instead to be decided by those who presided over the Court Martial. I have told his office what's happened here this morning and I'm waiting for the C-in-C to come back to me. He was out somewhere and would be back in about an hour or so then he'd need a bit of time to decide how we should proceed from here."

Nothing was said for a few moments until the Major went through what he had done with the body for now and the Colonel agreed with the action and suggested that it should perhaps be put into the military cemetery with the normal casualties and they'd have to decide what sort of record be kept of all this. He added, "This incident of Wilson preventing the Private shooting himself came up at the Court Martial and the MP, Shipley, said he had tried to contact the family of the Private but nothing had been forthcoming. Clearly something now has come along but it's all too late."

Milligan-Sprake was almost lost for words but added, "I know about this we'd contacted this Padre in the East Lancs and he was tracking down the poor Private's family to get them to plead for Wilson's life to be spared."

"Is Shipley still here?" asked the Colonel.

"Yes sir," said the Captain "He was down by the main gate a little while ago with the Frenchwoman that Wilson had lived with. Are we going to tell him what's happened then? Would that be wise as he's got into a right lather about this whole thing and it might not be the best thing for us to do. What do you think, sir?"

The Colonel thought for a moment and got up from his chair and walked to the window and stared out. He turned, "I feel we must tell him, we probably owe him that at least, he's an MP and a Sergeant, he'll be a bit upset but he'll know his responsibility is to the Army. Major, I'll leave you to brief him on what happens and tell him we'll let him know what we'll finally do with the body and how we record this. I'll have to consider what Wilson's family is told and I'll speak to GHQ but my first thoughts are to record "died of his wounds" but Shipley'll have to keep the matter to himself. Do you think he'll be alright with things?"

"As you said sir, it'll be an order and he'll have to follow it. There's not much we can do now anyway, it would be different if Wilson was still in the cells – this is just another casualty of the mess that is war, sir, I suppose?"

"Yes, I guess you're right about that - over to you then Major."

With that the Colonel returned to his desk and the other two saluted and left.

Burnside headed towards the main gate but before he got there he spotted Shipley chatting with the horse handler near the stables. He walked over and as he did so the handler made his excuses and left going back through the stable door, closing one of the two large wooden doors behind him.

Shipley stood to attention but as both were capless he did not salute, as was the custom. He gave just a sharp, traditional enquiring "Sir!?"

"Ah yes Shipley," he hesitatingly began and coughed. He looked around him to make sure there was not anyone close enough to hear what he was saying. Quietly he went on: -

"Sergeant, there is no need for me to tell you this but the Colonel and I believe that it is only right that we do so but first I must remind you of your responsibility as a soldier and NCO of the British Army and especially your position as a Military Policeman. In the theatres of war there are many unfortunate, even tragic, episodes in the general mayhem of this modern warfare and we have just witnessed one of those, I'm afraid."

Rather sheepishly he recounted the events of the past hour. Shipley's face turned from a look of stunned horror to one of utter devastation to the point where he nearly broke down. Spotting this Burnside again reminded him again of his responsibilities and urged the Sergeant to pull himself together.

For almost a minute after Burnside had finished Shipley just stared ahead occasionally looking round at the other man as if to speak but then closed his mouth and turned his head to look in front.

The Major was fighting to think of something sensible to say but the sight of the Colonel hurrying towards them saved him.

Slightly breathless he approached the Major. Shipley stiffened to attention and glanced at the Colonel who glanced sideways at him but looked back at the Major.

"Major Burnside.... Sergeant," he now looked at Shipley then looked away again just as quickly, "I've been called to a meeting about this at the C-in-C's HQ and it is to decide what we do about advising Wilson's family and how we record his death in Army records. I've also been asked to take all of Wilson's personal stuff with me when I go so, Major, could you let me have those, have you still got them?"

"Yes sir, they are with your orderly at the moment."

He turned to Shipley, "I'm sorry Shipley, has Major Burnside explained the situation and what we expect? I know how much you supported the man but you've got to move on and let it pass – if we dwelt on all the mishaps that happen in this type of warfare then we'd get nowhere."

"Sir!" he confirmed standing to attention.

"Fine, are you returning to your unit?"

"Yes sir, they are in Bethune and I'm leaving right away." He lied as he had no intention of going there today – instead he had, during those past few minutes, decided he was going to see Marie in Calais. He had not decided whether he could really tell her about the turn of events. He was torn between his duty to the British Army, whom he really felt had let Wilson down, and his blossoming feelings for the young woman.

CHAPTER 51

The vehicle carrying Colonel Bishop turned through the main gates and the two sentries saluted as the Colonel and his driver swept into the camp and pulled up outside the Officer's mess. Before his driver could get round to the back door to let him out the Colonel had leapt out and strode towards the door of the Mess. His face was like thunder.

He opened the door and went in slamming the door behind him. The six men inside instinctively stood up. The Colonel looked round the room and spotted Major Burnside, "A word with you, Major, in here if you please!"

The Senior Officer went through the toilet door at the back of the room and Burnside followed. The Colonel checked there was no one inside the one cubicle there and stood over the sink with his hands either side of it and looked into the mirror. Burnside stood just inside the door waiting for the Colonel to say something. "Sir?" he eventually said.

Bishop eventually moved away from the sink and kicked the cubicle door so that it banged against the wall and then sprang back towards him and the catch engaged. He swung round and looked at Burnside who took a step back wondering what the Colonel might do next.

"Major, this Army has done some things that we should be proud of but what I'm about to tell you is far from being one of them. I've just come from GHQ. You are not going to believe this but this Wilson situation is being totally swept under the carpet. There will be no record of what has happened here that will come to light in our lifetimes and that decision seems to have come from the very top. Also, only you and I will know the full story apart from the top brass. We have to put Wilson in an unmarked grave and record that he was posted missing and is presumed dead but I want you to take over the record keeping from the clerks. This whole thing disgusts me and I'm sure you will feel the same. Now come to my office and we'll discuss the finer points of what we need to do because someone will want to use this room shortly."

They both left the Mess and went to Colonel's office. The clerks were again sent away to the cookhouse and told to come back in about half an hour.

The Colonel sat behind the large desk and Burnside sat opposite, they had not spoken a word since they had left the toilet.

"Bloody rum do, sir," Burnside eventually said.

"Bloody disgrace, more like," answered the Colonel.

"Sir, how do we intend letting Wilson's family know what has happened, then?"

The Colonel thought for a moment and then said, "Well, as far as I've been told, we shall firstly have to put all the Court Martial records together and they'll be kept in secrecy for ever along with the confirmation that the execution was carried out. There will be no need to tell anyone involved with the case, such as the lawyers, that this is being done. They will know that the change of decision came through but they will also know that there is nothing we can do for Wilson now and that this is just another unfortunate incident of war. The second thing is we shall only tell Wilson's family the bare minimum and I want you to write to them and explain that Wilson had been returned to his unit and during an offensive had gone missing and not returned. It is to be assumed, therefore, that he has died but you'll have to say that no further details are available."

Burnside stood up and turned away towards the window, he could barely disguise his anger.

"I've seen and heard some things in my time out here but this really is appalling especially to lie to his family in that way and I'm not too happy to have to be the person that perpetrates the lie but if you insist, sir, then I'll reluctantly do it."

"I'm sorry, Major, but it would look odd if a Colonel wrote ordinarily to a man's family as you know all too well it's usually a Major or Captain or possibly a Lieutenant who would do it. I appreciate how you feel but we've been told to do it so we better had and draw a line under the whole sorry story. Can I leave it to you then?"

Without waiting for an answer the Colonel got up from the chair, went to the door and opened it so the Major could leave.

The Major stood and was about to say something more and looked at the Colonel but he was looking at his feet as if avoiding the Major's glance.

"Sorry Major," the Colonel managed as Burnside passed him.

PART TWELVE -
WELLS, SOMERSET, ENGLAND
1996

CHAPTER 52

The cottage door needed a little bit of forcing once the key had turned in the lock and George Shipley needed to put his shoulder firmly against it before it gave way.

"It must have warped since Dad left because, apart from Mrs Johnson next door, no one has been here for about 4 years and even then this door would not have been used as Mrs J probably came in the back anyway."

His daughter Maggie who ran her hand over the hall table followed him in, "Well I must say Mrs J has kept it really clean even since Granddad Frank died!"

"And, she's never wanted any money for it but we must get something for her because once we have emptied some of granddad's stuff and put the cottage up for sale, she won't be coming here any more but maybe she'll keep it tidy until we get a buyer," added her father. He went on: "Now all I want to do today is collect together all granddad's personal papers because anything of value must stay so the Valuer can assess it all and pass the information to John Stanford from Astling's Solicitors so Probate can be sorted out."

"OK – I'll start in the study with his old bureau, it's just old books and papers in there," said Maggie as she moved into the small dark room off the hall. The room smelt very musty and she needed the table lamp, which surprisingly worked even though the bulb was blackened and dusty and probably had not been used for years. Her father took a large case from the cupboard under the stairs, "I'll look through all these photos and see what we want to keep."

"Oh by the way, Dad, keep some of the really old ones to help with my family tree investigations it will be nice to have the pictures to go with the names – some of them must be about a hundred year's old!"

It was a week after Frank Shipley's funeral. After 102 years he had finally passed away in the Coniston Nursing Home where he had been for the past four years having lived in the cottage on his own for over twenty years after his second wife Joan had died. Right up until the last he had been very sprightly but the chest infection and finally the pneumonia had hastened the end but still, as everyone had said at his funeral, not a bad knock to get to 102. The Queen's telegram was his last treasured possession in his room at Coniston along with the countless photos of the whole family including one of himself from his army days of eighty years ago down to the latest great grandchild.

Maggie had been very close to her granddad and she thought, as she approached her mid-fifties, what great memories he had and how he liked to talk about his experiences. In her quest for information to help with her family search to put together the Shipley tree, Frank's recollection of old aunts and uncles and, of course, his parents were a great help. He liked to talk about his days in the police force and how it had changed from the 1920s until he retired in the late 1950s and he liked to show his disapproval of what the force had become in the 1980s and 90s.

Before joining the police force after the "Awful War", as he called it, Maggie discovered that her granddad had been in the Military Police in France during the fighting but he would never talk about it, however hard she tried to get him to change his mind. She knew he had some medals from that time and they would probably be somewhere in his study and she thought they might shed some light on what he had done and she was sure he had kept some other items from that time. She also knew that he had been married to her grandmother shortly after the War had ended but she had died in childbirth. The child was her Father.

For over twenty minutes Maggie sorted through the cupboard under the pull down top of the bureau. Indeed, she came across three medals from 1914-18 but they seemed to be simply campaign type medals so not that interesting. She put them back so the Valuer would not miss them, as they would no doubt be valuable to some people so they might fetch a decent price at an auction.

There were wads of old papers held together by ancient elastic bands ranging from payslips dated as long ago as 1951 to christening certificates and all sorts of family paraphernalia. Right at the back and loose on its own was a slightly curled up black book with a bookmark sticking out of it. It was pretty dusty and some of the pages seemed stuck together. As Maggie stood up to take it over to the light the small bookmark fell on the floor. Picking it up she saw that it was an old cigarette card with pen pictures of a sports team. She reached into her handbag for her reading glasses and then opened the book and flicked through it. It was, it seemed, a scribbled diary mainly written in pencil but in places some form of crayon had been used. She had opened it at the pages noted at the top as "1918 France" – it certainly looked like her granddad's somewhat spidery handwriting. Now she could see more clearly she looked at the cigarette card – it had "Player's cigarettes" across the top and she counted eleven faces in sepia. At the bottom of the card it said "Association Cup Winners Burnley, 1914".

Turning it over she read the very small print under the number 39 and the heading "Burnley, 1914" – it also said it was from a set of 50 issued by John Player and Sons.

The text told of a goal by Freeman that gave Burnley a win over Liverpool in the FA Cup Final in the presence of King George, this being the first time the Monarch had attended a Final. He had presented the cup in front of 72,000 people with both teams having shown, during the match, "grim earnestness and intense determination".

Maggie wondered why on earth Granddad Frank, a staunch Bristol Rovers fan all his life with also a fondness for Aston Villa, would want to keep a picture card of Burnley. Of course, it might have been part of a set that he had collected by why had he kept this one tucked into his old diary?

She kept the book open at the page where the card had been and she strained to read the scribble but noticed references to Burnley and what looked like an old player called Wilson. She then wondered if he was one of the players in the picture on the front of the card. She read certain parts of the following pages and was amazed to see that the notes all appeared to be about a soldier called Wilson who as it turns out was granddad's prisoner in 1918 and who, it appeared, had been shot as a deserter.

"Hey Dad come in here and look at this."

George put his head round the door, "What's up?"

"I've found this old diary of granddad's and it's from the First World War and all about a prisoner of his when he was in the Military Police. This prisoner seems to have been a Burnley footballer and I also found this card marking a page." She handed the cigarette card to her Dad.

"Bloody hell! It's a few years since I saw one of these." He looked at the front and then read what was on the back. He continued, "Do you think that the man mentioned is on the photo?"

"I don't know, Dad, but it would be nice to find out. If it's OK with you I'll take the diary and read it in a better light but I'll have to pass it to the Valuer eventually because I bet it's worth a few bob!"

She put the book and card into her handbag and carried on with the clearing up in the study.

PART THIRTEEN -
BBC TELEVISION STUDIOS, LONDON
AUGUST 2006

CHAPTER 53

The young assistant producer introduced herself as Abi Warren as she ushered Maggie and her son Richard through the double doors in the large reception hall towards the eight lifts. Maggie thought the girl looked about sixteen but on reflection she must be in her early twenties to hold a job like this. Richard as typical of a young man was taken with her immediately and engaged her in small talk to which she responded in a flirty way. Eventually the young girl broke away and turned to Maggie.

"Now Mrs Southey, or is it OK if we call you Maggie?" she continued but without bothering to wait for the confirmation went on, "Simon Read will carry out the interview but it's not going to be live so there's no need to worry because we can stop and start again or edit out any bits that go wrong. We hope the piece will be shown tonight when there will be a studio debate about these pardons and we will insert your piece as an intro to get it started."

She stopped talking as the lift came to a halt on the third floor and the doors opened. "Please follow me this way," said the young girl. Richard whispered to his mother, "Come on Maggie, keep up!" and smiled broadly and his mother gave him a playful punch on his arm and push him forward after the girl.

Abi held the door open leading into a darkened room and reached round the corner and switched on the lights. "We can wait in here for a moment and I'll give Simon a call and he'll be straight down."

"What programme will this be shown on?" enquired Richard.

"Oh sorry, I should have said – it's Newsnight so it'll go out at ten-thirtyish but depends on what happens around the world during the day which is why I said we hope to go tonight but it could be held over, it all depends, but we are committed to doing the feature in view of the amount of public interest."

She sat down and invited Maggie and Richard to do the same and selected a button on her mobile. Whilst she waited for the person she was calling to respond she told her two guests to help themselves to a drink from the array on a trolley in the corner and she then broke away to speak.

"Hi Simon – Mrs Southey and her son are here in the Green Room – can you come down?" She paused then nodded and said, "Oh good – see you in a minute then," and hung up.

Richard had assumed BBC Green Rooms were much grandiose affairs than this was, the drinks were all non-alcoholic and some of them had been opened such as the tonic water and bitter lemon.

"What would you like Mum?"

"Oh a tonic will be fine dear, thanks"

"Abi would you like something?"

"Just a coke please – sorry we have nothing stronger by the way. Someone has helped himself or herself to the gin!" she laughed.

He poured the two drinks and helped himself to a diet coke and sat back in the chair opposite his mother. Abi busied herself with her notes sipping the drink. The door opened and a young man in his early thirties came through. Maggie recognised him as Simon Read one of the leading BBC reporters and he introduced himself with a firm handshake and referred to them as Mr and Mrs Southey. He had an open necked shirt on and suit trousers and carried his jacket and tie over his arm. Richard identified the powerful Yves St Laurent scent but was impressed by the genuineness and politeness of the welcome.

"Has Abigail briefed you yet on what we are doing Mrs Southey?"

"She has mentioned that the interview will be recorded for Newsnight for either tonight or tomorrow," replied Maggie.

"Yes that's fine – I'll ask you some questions which I have had typed up and perhaps you and your son would like to read through them so you are not too surprised by what I say and so can formulate some of your answers. I only intend interviewing you Mrs Southey, is that OK?"

"Oh yes fine Richard's only here for a bit of moral support for me and you can call us Maggie and Richard, by the way if you prefer!"

"Good – thanks, here are the questions let me know if you are not happy with anything or if you want to add in anything or if I have got something wrong. We may stray away from the text depending on the answers but I'm sure you'll cope with that OK. Don't worry if we mess up we can edit mistakes out, and "No" that they won't appear on a bloopers show!" They all laughed. "I'll be back in ten – let Abigail know if you need anything."

Abi pulled up a chair opposite them as Richard moved closer so he could read the text over his mother's shoulder. Abi had her own copy and read through them as well.

Richard turned to his mother, "Looks good to me Mum, OK with you?"

"Yes, fine."

Abi folded the notes, "We shall probably tape about ten minutes but we have a five minute slot for this interview so it will need to be edited or perhaps the order changed or something like that."

Simon returned and this time was resplendent in his suit and tie and he had clearly had a dramatic makeover on his hair and make-up put on his face.

"Maggie we'll pop you down to make-up so the girls can give you the once over but you look fine to me. However, the studio lights are strong and we may need to tone your colour down a bit – so follow me. Richard you stay with Abi and she'll take you to the control booth in the studio and you can watch from there – see you later."

Fifteen minutes later following a visit to the make-up room and the toilet, Maggie was ready. Simon took her into the small interview room where there were three cameras, two chairs, a table, a decanter full of water and two glasses. The lights were very bright and made the studio seem very warm. They had been followed by one of the make-up girls who fussed over them as they took their seats. The soundman came over and attached the mikes to their fronts and asked them both to speak in turn. Following some small adjustments he was ready to go. The rest of the room was in darkness and a man's voice spoke pleasantly from behind the screen in the booth, "Hello Mrs Southey please relax – nothing to worry about – any time you like Simon"

Simon spoke directly into camera number one, "I have Mrs Maggie Southey with me and she has campaigned for over ten years for a pardon for Private Edward Wilson who was shot for desertion in the latter stages of World War One – in fact only a few days before the Armistice came into force. As a result of her campaigning and that of others, the Government has promoted the Armed Forces Act of 2006 to include a pardon for all 306 British soldiers shot for cowardice, desertion or other offences from the First World War. While this has to be welcomed for most cases there has been criticism that this might be a vote catching, symbolic act, not adequately thought through."

He paused before moving on, "The reason this has been said is because the Act says that the pardon, and I quote, "does not affect any conviction or sentence" - it is felt that modern standards are being applied retroactively and, in fact, many of those shot did have a history of cowardice and desertion and some had been guilty of other capital offences, it is alleged. However, there are many different stories to tell about these men. One campaigner, Maggie Southey, has unearthed much information about this Edward Wilson through a diary found ten years ago that had belonged to her grandfather. He had known Private Wilson very well. She has led something of a personal crusade for a pardon for Private Wilson. Because of this diary and her additional research, she can provide us with an insight into what really went on during those awful times and, in particular, not only the state of mind of the so-called culprits but also the mindset of the senior officers during that dreadful war. She has been able to show how harsh this particular penalty now seems and how little time was taken to medically assess the state of mind of some of the men who were sentenced, in many cases, without a proper trial. Sometimes these men were not even represented at their Court Martial. To add insult to the ultimate injury it appears that the Army tried to keep the full details of what really happened in the Wilson case as secret as possible."

He paused for a moment and looked up towards the gallery where the production team were, "Was that alright?"

A male voice answered from the darkness above them, "Yes, fine, Simon. Put your questions now to Mrs Southey."

Simon turned to Maggie, "Now Mrs Southey you are not related to Private Wilson so what made you take up his cause and how did you become involved?"

"Well, Simon, after my grandfather died in 1996 I was sorting through his things and came across a diary from 1918 when granddad was serving in France and Belgium as a Military Policeman. The main part of his work was to track down deserters. He captured Edward "Eddie" Wilson in the autumn of 1918 somewhere near Calais and he had to escort him back to Belgium for a Court Martial. The journey took longer than expected and during it my granddad wrote down copious notes about what had happened to Eddie and recorded what the man had been through, how poorly trained and ill-equipped he was and how badly he had been treated at the Front. Eddie lost all his mates it seems in one attack and was very lucky to have survived only because he decided to take a call of nature; he had to endure a field punishment in the trenches and that meant he was exposed to enemy fire tied to a wheel from a cart, with little protection from the shelling."

Simon interrupted, "That sounds awful but what did your grandfather think about it given that he was a Military Policeman and there to uphold King's Regulations and other military law and so on?"

"At first he was hostile to Eddie and this is reflected in his notes but gradually as more came out about what had happened he became more sympathetic and in the end considered that Eddie had run away from the trenches while his mind was scrambled by what became known as shell shock but what we now call, I guess, post traumatic stress."

Simon asked, "So when you looked into the case what did you find out about Eddie?"

"Eddie was in the East Lancs Regiment having been brought up near Burnley and in fact had joined the local football club as a sort of junior and was rumoured to have played in the 1914 Cup Final but he didn't. Because of the shortage of men and need for bodies on the front line he had none of the normal training and was really only a kid who had completed the most basic of training before being shipped to the Continent. We have all seen pictures of what it was like at Passchendaele and from what he told granddad it was ten times worse than what it looked like! He had countless escapades under intense fire; he lost friends in the most appalling circumstances and saw sights that would test the tolerance of anyone. In addition, there was the persistent shelling that inevitably had a devastating effect on their nerves as we now know. We talk today about our soldiers in Iraq and their lack of equipment and protection but what of those poor so-and-sos in the First World War – all they did have was a helmet and a rifle but that was about it, I'm afraid!" She started to carry on but Simon raised his hand to stop her so he could ask another question. She smiled and sat back in her chair.

"Did you or your grandfather ever trace any living relatives of this chap?" asked Simon.

"Well, I do know granddad visited an army friend's family after the war as he once mentioned how sad this was because the friend had been killed right at the very end of the war. I did manage to trace some of this family once I could access the 1901 Census but they appeared to have died off by the time the Second World War started. I had rather assumed this to be the situation which is why I really took up the case in the first place."

Simon held his hand up again off camera so she knew he wanted to speak, "So what did take place after he was captured – there was a trial or something similar, I imagine."

Maggie shuffled forward in her seat keen to take up the story.

"The Court Martial for Eddie was appallingly bad according to granddad, especially as everyone knew the War would end at anytime. My granddad, although by then a Sergeant but not an Officer of course, wanted to represent Eddie but perhaps because of this lowly status he was given short thrift but did give evidence in what seemed a very short trial. It seemed the defence case was largely dismissed out of hand although Eddie had saved the life of another soldier in dramatic services when the young chap tried to commit suicide. Then little account was taken of Eddie's mind and the state he was in at the time of his so-called offence."

She stopped for a moment as she felt she was about to cough and took a sip of the water she had poured into the glass earlier.

"The young Frenchwoman whose house Eddie eventually turned up at and who shielded him for about a year was prepared to give evidence of Eddie's mental and physical state when he arrived and how she nursed him through what was clearly a very bad case of shell shock. She was not really taken that seriously. No proper medical assessment was ever made of Eddie. The sentence was that he was to be shot at dawn like most of them. Of course, all this had to be ratified by Generals right up to the Commander in Chief. My granddad was adamant that these Generals were never made aware of the full facts."

Simon again raised his hand, "So what were the feelings of your grandfather about all of this and how did this make you take up the case with, clearly, so much passion?"

Maggie was so flushed with excitement that she was almost standing up. Suddenly from above her came a voice asking that Simon put the question again and would she sit back in her chair as her sudden movement had meant the camera on her had lost the focus. She apologised into the darkness assuming the voice was the director from the control room.

Simon waited for her to settle back down and on the command from above put the question again.

More relaxed Maggie spoke a little less animatedly, "There is no doubt that Eddie did run away and this was, it seems, all the Army was concerned about and found him guilty without taking into account much else. We all appreciate that the Army had in those days a much stricter code of discipline than it has had since but to actually have him found guilty without hearing all appropriate evidence and then have him shot by his fellow British soldiers was appalling. In many ways it rebounded on the Army because morale, and in some areas discipline itself, became even more of a problem. In particular, having the sentences often carried out by men from your own regiment, had a profound effect on them and their comrades, even well after the Armistice was signed. To make matters worse it seems that the death sentence should not have been carried out on Eddie. Apparently, right at the last minute, some evidence came to light that forced the Commander of the British Forces to change his mind and he always had the final say. However, by the time this decision reached the place where the execution was taking place Eddie Wilson was already dead. Then the Army tried to cover this up and I would not have known about it and nor would anyone else but granddad had received a letter from some Major who had been told to instigate the cover-up in 1918 and had eventually, shortly before he died, confessed this to my granddad and gave full details of what had gone on."

Maggie thought she had better shut up as she found her voice rising, her face blushing and that she was again edging right on the front of her chair.

Simon carried on, "I can see that you are passionate about the injustice but what was this cover-up, then?"

"Well, Simon, apparently Eddie's death was put down as "shot at dawn" in Army records but reported to his family that he was "missing in action presumed killed". His name appears on a memorial in Belgium with all the rest of those with no known graves and I have been told that his name also appears on a memorial in his hometown in Lancashire. We assume that his family were not aware he was actually shot as a deserter and I'm sure my granddad would not have said anything to them when he visited. So at least one good thing came out of it all!"

Simon put his next question, "Now that the pardon has happened how do you feel?"

Maggie sighed a little and relaxed back in her chair, "Simon, for a case such as Eddie's it is the right thing to do. I do appreciate that he might have done wrong but such were the extenuating circumstances that more sympathy should have been given and the death sentence should not have been carried out in his particular case, never mind that the Commander did eventually change his mind. I am not so sure about those now being pardoned who committed rape or murder. I have only campaigned for Eddie Wilson based on the granddad's diary and what he felt."

Simon leant forward and spoke earnestly, "Maggie you have certainly achieved what you set out to do and well done on your efforts which not only perhaps could be dedicated to the memory of Eddie Wilson but also to your grandfather, Frank Shipley. There is one other fact that also perhaps prompted your enthusiasm in taking up this case!" added Simon with a smile on his face.

Maggie smiled back "That's very true, the Frenchwoman that looked after Eddie when he ran away and nursed him back to health but was denied the chance to adequately speak for him at the Court Martial was my Grandmother!"

About the Author

Steve Little was born in 1949 and was educated at King Edward VI Grammar School in Chelmsford. After a working lifetime in the financial services industry he felt semi-retirement was now the time to write about the experiences his grandfathers and their brothers had faced in World War One. His great uncle, aged only 18, had disappeared in one of the many battles in Belgium in 1918. It was presumed he was killed but there is no known grave but just his name on a memorial near Ypres. This book was lovingly put together in memory of these relatives. It draws on the many stories told by them over the years before their deaths.

Steve lives in Leatherhead, Surrey and has been married for almost 40 years and has two grown up children and two grandchildren. He is an avid student of military history and in particular the two World Wars. What spare time he has is spent enjoying gardening, golf and watching football and cricket.